# Satvinder's Story

Colin Hodgson

Published by C E Hodgson
Colchester,
United Kingdom

Second edition January 2015


ISBN: 978-0-9569498-7-5

## Acknowledgements, Reference and Inspiration

- Wikipedia
- "Indigenous early warning indicators of cyclones: potential application in coastal Bangladesh" *Philippa Howell, Benfield Hazard Research Centre. July 2003*
- *"Massacre"* [1972], p. 50 and 102 *Robert Payne*
- BanglaCenter.
- http://www.hinduhumanrights.info/hindu-genocide-in-east-bengal-71/ Reference to visit by Edward Kennedy
- "Blood and Tears" *Qutubuddin Aziz First Edition, 1974*
- Pres. Yahya's Views on Mujibur, Bhuto, and Pakistani Politics. *Source: The American Papers- Secret and Confidential India.Pakistan.Bangladesh Documents 1965-1973, The University Press Limited, p.481-483*
- "The Englishman Who Went Up a Hill But Came Down a Mountain" *Ivor Monger*
- "Dead Reckoning: Memories of the 1971 Bangladesh War" *Sarmila Bose.*
- SOS-arsenic.net
- "Arsenic Free Clean Water and Sustainable Local Technology" *Abul Hussam and Abul K. M. Munira*
- www.pakistanweatherportal.com/2011/07/05/the-bhola-cyclone-not-so-bhola-at-all/
- "India - Pakistan War, 1971; Introduction" *Tom Cooper, with Khan Syed Shaiz Ali Oct 29, 2003, 04:46*
- "Chuknagar: The largest genocide during the Bangladesh Liberation War in 1971" *Source: Muntassir Mamun, The Archive of Liberation War, Bangabandhu and Bangladesh Research Institute*
- "Foreign Evacuees froom East Pakistan Tell of Grim Fight (Sydney H. Schanderg, in New York Times-

April 7, 1971)" *Source: Bangladesh Documents, vol – I, p.393-395*

- "Indo-Pakistani War 1971 and Bangladesh Liberation War Timeline"
  http://paginas.tol.itesm.mx/Alumnos/A01184083/Apuntes/Indo-Pakistani%20War%20Timeline%20(1971).docx
- "Eyewitness accounts" Source: Muntassir Mamun, The Archive of Liberation War, Bangabandhu and Bangladesh Research Institute
- "Introducing Maulana Bhashani, Representative of an Emancipatory Islam" *Dr.Peter Custers November 1, 1999*
- "Proclamation of Independance Oorder, dated April 10, 1971 Text of Proclamation" *Press report on April 18, 1971 Source: Bangla Desh Documents vol 1, Page no: 281 -282*
- "Evaluation of Adaptation Capacity of the Coastal Dwellers to take Shelters in Infrastructures during Tsunami & Storm Surges – Draft Report January 2009." *Institute of Water Modelling. In association with House of Consultants Limited and Bangladesh Institute of Social Research*
- "The Translation of the speech of BangoBondhu at 7th March 1971 in the race coarse."
  http://stoppressonline.wordpress.com/2011/07/03/the-translation-of-the-speech-of-bangobondhu-at-7th-march-1971-in-the-race-coarse/
- "R-564-AID September 1970. Analysis of Demographic Change in East Pakistan: A Study of Retrospective Survey Data." *T. Paul Schultz and Julie Davanzo. Published by the RAND Corporation.*
- Many other inspirational sites, photographs and documents, too many to list.

# BACKGROUND 1970

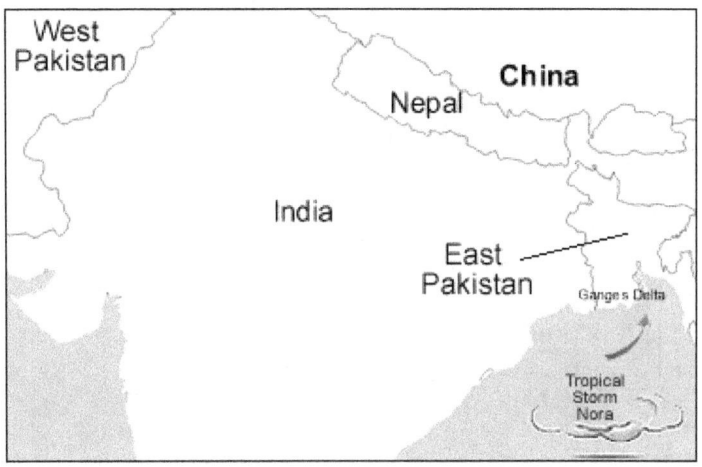

In nineteen-seventy Pakistan was the largest Muslim state in the World, but was deeply divided by political, economical and social conflicts, and the two wings of the country, East Pakistan and West Pakistan, were separated by eleven hundred miles.

The many differences between the two wings had resulted in the country becoming a dictatorship, led by the military forces of General Yahya Kahn, and essentially meant that the West ruled the East.

However, when President Yahya Khan promised democratic elections in nineteen-seventy, everything looked rosy for the East Pakistanis as they strove to rid themselves of the military yoke from the West and achieve equality and regional autonomy. But before the elections could take place the country was thrown into turmoil by the Tropical Storm Nora which hit the Ganges Delta. She caused more destruction than any other storm in the twentieth century.

It is in that desperate, unstable environment that Satvinder's Story begins and, in many ways, ends.

# IMPORTANT NOTE

All reference to the following individuals has been based on written history:

Yahya Khan (General/President);
General Tikka Kahn;
Zulfikar Ali Bhutto;
Sheikh Mujibur Rahman;
Major Ziaur Rahman;
Maulana Bhashani;
Moulana Noorani;
Moulana Mufti;
Zhou Enlai;
Colonel M. A. G. Osmani;
Mr Tajuddin Ahmed; and
Indira Ghandi.

All other characters are fictitious and any resemblance to any real person is purely accidental and coincidental.

# OTHER 'QEERVY' STORIES

Satvinder's Story
## Contents

Colin Hodgson

# PRE-AMBLE
# WHO STARTED THE WAR -- NORA?

November 1970, The Bay of Bengal

Tropical Storm Nora was on the move and having completed her duties in the Western Pacific she crept across Vietnam and Cambodia, weakening as she lashed the lands. The remnants of her anger spilled out into the Bay of Bengal and there she waited, feeding on the warm, moist air.

By the eighth of November her low mood had turned into intense depression, becoming angry, wildly so, and preparing for her most ferocious attack. But she waited. Her accomplice, the high spring tide, was not due to join her until November the twelfth, and her ally, India, watched with intrepid interest without saying a word.

As the cyclone spun around her eye, wielding gales as strong as one hundred and fifteen miles per hour, Nora decided to make her move. The tide was finally in position and the people waited. There was no defence for the unfortunate farmers and fishermen, just winds of one hundred and thirty miles per hour, tidal surges of over thirty feet high, and total ruin. The assault was perfectly planned and relentlessly executed.

The thirty-foot waves surged across the low-lying Bhola Island, Monpura and the other Chars of the Ganges Delta, the storm raging through the night and into the following day, leaving East Pakistan a broken soul. Nora's foot soldiers eventually dispersed into the hills.

The cyclone which ravaged the lowlands of East Pakistan on November 12th, 1970, is considered to be one of the worst natural disasters of the twentieth century, reportedly killing as many as half a million people. It has often been credited with the dubious title of 'Warmonger', accused of sparking the East Pakistan uprising. But hey, how does the act of God really compare with the act of man? It all seems quite tame by comparison.

When later questioned by God about her intent, Nora answered in her own defence, "I serve God without malice or greed, with openness, honesty and integrity. When my time is right, I go with the flow, sometimes with impunity, sometimes with the devil in my heart, but *never* with intent." And when God asked Nora if she had started the Bangladeshi war of independence, she replied with a huff, "Not guilty! I start winds and tidal surges and the rest is down to man. The five hundred thousand innocent fishermen, farmers and their families who died during my storm will be remembered, but soon forgotten. And, like myself, the fishermen will rebuild and regroup and continue the cycle of good and bad, and maybe next season our acquaintance will be renewed with varying consequence, but with the same old respect. That's *not* to be said for the war of independence."

God accepted Nora's plea and judged her to be not guilty of war mongering, but simply to have been in the wrong place at the wrong time. The court also noted that she had been the subject of malicious propaganda, one of man's many tools when stuck in a corner, and one which was used to capital effect by the poorly armed Awami League.

The Bhola cyclone certainly resulted in an unexpected gift for the Awami League, and maybe the kiss of hell for everybody else.

# CHAPTER 1 -- THE SIGNS

It was the eleventh of November 1970, in the Ganges Delta. Satvinder Nair had taken a tiny river taxi to Char Monpura, unaware of President Yahya Kahn's plans for the Islamisation of the masses. He was also blissfully unaware of tropical storm Nora's plans to weild the most ferocious cyclone ever to hit the lowlands of East Pakistan.

Satvinder studied the distant mangrove swamps as the two oarsmen worked the tiny boat. The river taxi was to deliver him to Char Monpura where his uncle had made arrangements for his stay, whilst writing his book about the struggle for life on the char.

The three-men-in-a-boat approached the char along the west side, between Monpura and Bhola, and it was a long journey for the tiny wooden country boat, and a long way out from the mainland. The flat-bottomed vessel looked like a top-heavy, open canoe with two sharply pointed ends, and with one oarsman at the front with his legs dangling each side of the bow, and another at the back. Satvinder only just managed to fit into the middle section and, despite being a mere speck in that most open expanse of the kingdom of heaven, he was feeling a little claustrophobic.

The sky was deep blue with wispy white clouds, the water still and green, and the visible land shone with the magnificence of an emerald. The far-away mangrove swamps were the highest points on any of the horizons, and the tiny boat's destiny was just visible, showing as a bright green line between the sea and the skies. They were on the edge,

11

between the waters from the mighty Ganges and the Brahmaputra rivers, and the tropical seas of the Bay of Bengal.

"Will we be much longer?" asked Satvinder.

The young oarsman at the front pulled his paddle out of the water and looked around. He grinned, his irregular teeth contrasting against his very dark complexion. He pointed towards the green line on the horizon. "That's where we're going. A little while to go." He turned back to his paddling.

Satvinder was about thirty years old, average height for an East Pakistani (which is not very tall) and clean-shaven. He dressed much like his taxi drivers: light-coloured shirts with checked pattern, and beige trousers, but he wore shoes. He was a city dweller, from Dhaka.

"Why you here?" asked the front, younger oarsman.

"I'm planning a book about the life on the chars. My uncle has got me a place to stay with his old friend." He paused. "You know, char means 'children of the land'. Some of this silt has come thousands of miles downriver to settle here, as islands. They're nomadic islands, on their way to somewhere else, forever looking for a home to call their own. A bit like some folk." Satvinder suddenly realised, "Course you know all this, you live here. Anyway, I'm Satvinder, from Dhaka University. I teach English normally."

The older oarsman, at the back, finally joined the repartee as he began to giggle. He was a lot older than both Satvinder and the front oarsman, grey hair, and maybe much wiser. "You've come at a good time to see the chars. You'll see them at their very best and their very worst." He stopped paddling. "We had crabs in our home for several days, and still this morning." He then carried on with his paddling, taking cursory glances at the seagulls, kurpals, which flew high above them, constantly crying. "And they know, they're crying out their warnings."

That strange statement left Satvinder wondering.

"Look!" the front oarsman expressed. "That's where we're going. The tide's low, so you'll have to take your fancy shoes off." He chuckled at Satvinder, and then frowned. "If Shafia's crabs are honest and the kurpal aren't mistaken, you might see some bad storm. If you can do another fare, you can come back with us in the morning."

Satvinder raised his eyebrows and looked hard at the approaching village with its decrepit, flimsy fishing boats. The ramshackle buildings, made from bamboo, corrugated metal and grasses, looked very delicate as they sat above the mud bank, but they were at least built on a man-made plateau, higher than the surrounding land; above the flood level.

"I think you might be over-reacting." He looked hard into the older man's, Shafia's, eyes, but they never flinched. "Do you think there's a big cyclone coming?"

The older man smiled. "I might be wrong but I've seen evidence. The crabs have been indoors for a few days now, and the foxes joined the wailing dogs last night. And the kurpals: they know. They all know. If Allah is to punish us, it'll be soon. Come back with us tomorrow."

Satvinder was a Hindu and Allah had never punished him. He just kept quiet.

Shafia sighed and continued, "I know that it's not really Allah who's punishing them, and that they should all make preparations for a storm if it's coming, but they can't. You know, Satvinder, the poorer you are, the more unlucky you are, and the more unlucky you are, the more Allah punishes you with his storms. It becomes a never decreasing cycle of torture, like Jehannam. Allah has punished the poor many times before, so they now cannot afford to run away. Even Allah is money orientated." He grinned. "Pay us another fare and come back with us tomorrow."

The younger oarsman looked down at the water.

"Are you ashamed of me Mia?" Shafia asked his friend.

"You shouldn't talk like that about Allah in front of a stranger."

"The stranger is a Hindu, who doesn't talk to Allah. He'll not tell on me."

Satvinder smiled at the Pakistani fisherman-philosopher and assured him, "I will *never* tell of your doubts. And I suppose saving my life would also make you a tidy profit from the return fare."

Shafia chuckled, and then, "We would *all three* be very happy, and alive. And we then could wait for another day before going to Jehannam. And I'm very concerned that if you're killed in the storm, we'll lose the work to take you home. Not good business for us."

The muddy landing-bay suddenly became alive with people as they approached, mostly children. Satvinder removed his shoes and walked the last bit, onto the hard.

A short man awaited, his grey hairs contrasting brilliantly with his dark skin. He was also dressed in the checked shirt and grey trousers, and the children milled around him with an insatiable curiosity. Who was the man with the brief case, being delivered by water taxi?

"Satvinder?" asked the man.

"Yes," he replied, and limply shook the man's hand. "You're Ali?"

One of the young boys took Satvinder's brief case.

"Yes. I'm an old friend of your uncle's. I'll look after you, if you'll allow me to."

Satvinder replied with a frown, "Of course I'll allow you."

"Then go home with the taxi-men." He looked to the two oarsmen. "Hey you! Can I speak to you? Come over here!" Mia and Shafia approached the man. "When're you going back?"

Shafia replied, "In the morning. We'd be grateful if you could direct us to some lodging."

"You can stay with me if you like: I've got no women in my house. But you must take my friend's son home with you tomorrow."

The sun was quickly going down, and there suddenly began a wailing from some dogs. Then more began, as the mournful crying spread across the char. Shafia bowed his head to Ali before turning to Satvinder. "The kurpals know, the dogs know. You can come back with us in the morning."

"No!" Satvinder looked into Ali's face and stressed, "I came to see the life on the chars. A storm'll be an unexpected bonus. You can't make me go back."

Ali looked sternly at him. "I'm a union parishad official. I can have you removed if I have to. I've promised my friend that I'll look after you. And I *will!*"

Satvinder was speechless. He was being sent home, back to Dhaka, with little information about the precarious life on the chars. He turned to Shafia. "Maybe we'll save Jehannam until another time."

Ali led the three men and his boy through the small village. The buildings had been put onto an artificially raised area, about two metres high, designed to stand proud of the flood waters. They were all very basic, constructed from bamboo and wood, some with tin roofs, others with grass thatch, and if they had been in a city they would have been considered slum dwellings. The brightly dressed women moved inside with their children as the strangers moved past their homes.

As they reached the edge of the village, the plateau dropped down, almost to sea level, and there were three large ponds from where the soil for the village platform was dug, and small mangrove trees lined the water's edge. The flies and mosquitoes were pestering the cattle which had been tied behind the mangrove trees.

Shafia spoke to Ali. "My friend, you're going to have a big storm. I hope we can get home before it hits. If we don't, well, you know where we'll be."

Ali nodded. "You know about these things?"

"I'm not telling my age, but I'm quite old, and still alive. Don't these folk know the signs?"

"They know the signs, but they have to hope that it's a small storm." He pointed back into the village, at a flag-pole flying a red flag. "We all know the signs. See that good, strong building over there. The one on high stilts." He pointed to a substantially built building, raised on two-metre high stilts. "That is the home of Kala Motabab Hang. He's the money lender, shafts these poor folk, and can afford to run away from the storm. He's already left. The rest of us pray to Allah, or whoever, and that's all we do." Pause. "Apart from burying our valuables."

Satvinder listened with intent.

As they walked slowly along the muddy path, which had been raised about one metre above the surrounding fields, the young boy pulled at Satvinder's shirt. "Look, sir. Over here." He left the path and approached a lonely sundari tree. There, amongst the fissured bark, was a line of ants. They were carrying eggs up the tree to safety. "They're taking their little ones to a safe height before the flood."

They continued on their route to Ali's home. He was a relatively rich man on the char, and his home was on two metre-high stilts, and protected by three large sundari trees to the south, and another three to the north.

Ali nervously suggested, "You can all stay in my house if you like until *after* the storm. Everything is pointing to a storm by tomorrow. It'd be irresponsible for you to go to sea tomorrow when you don't need to, and maybe, Satvinder, that's what you wanted." The old man raised his hands in the air, in defeat. "So, my old friend's nephew, I must *now* make you stay. *That's* an order."

The three men agreed to stay with Ali until the storm had passed.

In front of the house a pond. It had been excavated to create a raised area about a metre or so high, on top of which three cows were tethered, and they were agitated and wailing as the swarming insects were causing them great discomfort.

While they stood on Ali's balcony he went to the pond to test the temperature, and Satvinder noted that the closest neighbours did the same.

Ali reported, "Temperature still ok. Probably twenty four hours before the worst." He waved to the neighbour, a woman, who was about to go back into her house, a small homestead which was not on stilts. She ushered her daughters in ahead of her. "She's worried about you strangers. Purdah rules here."

Satvinder frowned. "They could come up here with us when the storm begins. They'll be flooded out."

Ali shook his head and then grinned. "Your city upbringing has clouded your memory of purdah. They can't associate with you, you're strangers. And they'll put on extra clothing in case they get put out by the storm, and will be dragged down by their excessive saris if it's bad. It's all about purdah. They can't go out improperly dressed, so they often die, instead."

The three men began to look the other way, as if not to embarrass the women by watching them.

The south-eastern skies, across the Bay of Bengal, were clouding over. "My two sons are out fishing and won't return for four days. I hope they'll move into Chittagong if they see the signs. Hopefully they'll get warning from the Indian met office."

Ali clambered down his bamboo steps, and moved to the pond. He checked the water edge for snakes, and again felt the water's temperature. "It's not warmed up yet. We're safe tonight."

Colin Hodgson

# CHAPTER 2 -- THE WRATH OF GOD

The next morning was overcast, but so, so humid. Some rain had fallen overnight, and the noise on the tin roof had been a pleasant distraction from the constant howl and wail of the dogs, foxes and cows. The four men and a boy, accompanied by a million mosquitoes, stood on the balcony and watched out towards the southern seas.

"This's a different place today, Satvinder." Ali chuckled to himself. "The winds are starting. And look over there." He pointed towards a distant sky which harboured some rolling black clouds. "The storm is coming. Shafia, you're lucky not to be going out to sea today."

Ali had some union parishad duties to carry out in the village, and he promised them a breakfast once he had done.

Satvinder began to think that he was in a different world from the beautiful char to which he had arrived the day before as the skies rolled over from the south, and the mosquitoes began to pester him. "I'll be glad when the bloody storm's come and gone!"

As Ali buried his papers and some rice and water in a water-tight box, the others waited on the hard, enjoying some of the shrimps which the young boys had caught

Ali's son suddenly held Satvinder's hand. He was keen to tell Satvinder about his home and his life, and maybe get a mention in the forthcoming bestseller, the 'Chars'. "I'll tell you lots. I haven't been conditioned like an adult, so I'll tell you what I see." Satvinder smiled down at him.

The tide was on its way out, and the idyllic calm of the previous day had turned into a choppy, stormy cauldron, slowly picking up momentum. Occasionally a larger wave developed and rolled on for a while until it dropped down to join the others. Shafia looked over to his tiny boat, and shook his head. "Mia, help me to pull the boat right up to the hard." The old sea-dog knew that they would have been in great trouble if they had left for home that morning.

"My work is done." Ali approached them. "I'll get us some food." He asked them to remain near the hard while he went off to order the food from an open-fronted shack which had smoke rising into the windy skies.

"We can have some hilsa today."

The four adult East Pakistanis, with the child, sat down on some benches which had been rescued from an old country boat, and waited for their food.

"Ali, why haven't you told us your son's name?"

"I forgot, sorry. This is James."

The three visitors looked a little surprised.

"I can see your surprise. We're a mixed bunch sitting here. Two Muslims, one Hindu and two Christians. I'm a Christian, and so when James was born, and at the time that his dear mother passed away, we called him James, because his grandfather's middle name was Zebedee. I don't expect you to understand the connection. It's a bible-thing." Ali just smiled at his son.

"Well, try us." suggested Shafia.

"James was the son of Zebedee and he was one of the twelve disciples. My youngest son is the grandson of Zebedee. See?"

Shafia just frowned.

"It's good to have guests. You know, this is the finest restaurant on the island." Ali seemed to be very proud of his char.

The grilled hilsa chad fish, yellowed with turmeric, looked and smelled delicious, and the men's appetites were sent into overload. And the small side dishes of rice and dal completed the course.

Once they had finished the delicious meal, Ali went inside to pay. He returned after several minutes. "I've been asking the proprietor, Kolala Nouka, if they were making any special preparations for the storm. They've done the same as everybody else, buried their valuables and some food, and emptied some coconuts to help them float, and they pray to Allah. Kolala said that the tide was very high last night."

Ali looked out to sea. The distant green of Bhola and the other chars was no longer visible. The murky skies were getting heavier, and the wind stronger, so all five agreed that they should go back to the house and entertain themselves. As they walked back home, James held his father's hand tightly, knowing how much he must have been worrying about his older sons who were fishing. He had to hope that they could get into Chittagong or Cox's Bazar. But all he could do was hope.

The five of them felt safe in one of the highest properties on the char. With two good rooms and some very basic furniture, Ali was certainly one of the richest men on the island.

As the wind strengthened Ali closed his shutters. He then climbed down to the pond and checked the water temperature. It had risen dramatically. He said to his guests, "I don't know who you're going to pray to, but James and I will pray to Mary." With that he took his son and they settled in the bedroom, leaving the guests to ponder. The winds were getting gradually stronger, soon drowning out the sound of the dogs and the cattle.

The three all looked towards the peep-hole in the shuttered window, and the darkening skies reflected their sombre moods. The whole island was closing down.

Night quickly fell and the winds rattled the shutters, and the men kept quiet. They all thought about their families, some out in the open seas, some at home in Dhaka, others on the mainland north of the Char Bhola.

Mia stood up and looked out of the spy-hole in one of the shutters and could see the shape of the trees beginning to bend in his direction. "They could fall on us!" He was frightened.

Shafia warned him. "Mia, don't look out for too long. The wind's coming from that direction, and it could pierce your eye with a stalk of straw." The old man stood up, and pulled Mia to him. "It's going to be a big one."

Satvinder, in all innocence, suggested, "I'll go and check the water temperature."

"No!" snapped Shafia. He settled, and had a massive sigh. "We don't need any more warning, so you don't have to get yourself bit by mister cobra. And it's dark outside. We must sit tight."

As the noise of the wind picked up, the building began to shake. It shuddered with every peak and dip of the wind, and the rain lashed harder against the tin roof. The noise became deafening, but slowly the shuddering reduced as the wind became stronger and more sustained: the building was bending instead of shaking!

Bang! The men almost screamed as something crashed against the face of the house. Things were beginning to break and fly off with the wind, so Shafia, shouting, reminded Satvinder, "We're safer in here for as long as the house stays up. We could be cut in half by flying debris and tin!" He very warily looked out of the spy-hole, and then shouted above the roar, "The trees are still standing, and they're giving us some protection! We'll be ok!"

As he sat down, James rushed into their room, followed by Ali who screeched, "If it goes, stay together!" He peered out of the spy-hole, and then reported, "Water! It's broken the flood barriers!" Through the hole he could see foaming water driving towards him, the white caps standing out in the darkness. It reached the sundari trees, and then rushed through the stilts and under the building. "Not too much!" He grinned at the others, who replied with relieved sighs. "Look, Shafia!"

Shafia moved to Ali and peered through the dark hole. He suddenly stood bolt upright and roughly grabbed Mia. "Pray to Allah! Now!"

Ali took another look into the dark night, and froze. All he could see, right across the char was a black wall, topped with white. A tidal surge which dwarfed the trees and buildings. "Shit! Hold tight!"

The men panicked and grabbed anything they could as a thirty-foot high tidal surge raced towards their little dwelling. It towered above them, and roared even above the sound of the wind. Satvinder hung onto a chair, and Ali to his son, while the two oarsmen cuddled, as if good-bye. The roar heightened, and then a crash! The roof was ripped away by the wind and water, and they were engulfed, suddenly struggling for air. Satvinder was forced against the back wall, which gave way under the immense power of the water, and he was taken! He just went with the flow, helpless, blinded by the dark, and lost. His lungs were almost bursting. He twisted in the dark water for a few seconds, but hit into something: the trees. He was tangled up, and then something caught around his neck, and he pulled at it. It was strangling him. But, as he pulled at it, his grip on the tree slipped and he was almost washed away by the water. He just clung on for his life, and held his breath.

"I can't last any longer," he thought. "I'm going." But then the force of the water on his head changed. It became the force of the wind! He breathed out, and in. But he struggled to breathe as the thing around his neck tightened. He screeched, "Get off!" It was a snake. He hit the snake with his fist. And again, but it hung on, so he grabbed hold of it with one hand and pulled. The water was still washing at his waist and legs, so he tried to swing his body to release the creature. The more he pulled, the more it pulled into his throat!

Then came a whimpering noise. He released the snake, and put his hand down behind his back.

It was James!

He could not believe it. James clung around his neck like a python, and began crying hysterically, so he twisted around and grabbed the boy's waist. He immediately let go of Satvinder's neck, and they pulled together into the tree which had saved them from certain death. They both cried. "I thought you were a snake," sniffed Satvinder.

The wind never gave up, but the tidal swell dropped, leaving them clear of the water, breathing, but stressed, wondering what they would see when daylight returned. The little boy continued to cry and sob as he held so tightly around Satvinder's shoulders. Eventually he sniffled, "Don't send me away. Don't." He pulled even tighter into Satvinder's hold.

The tree was bending and whipping in the wind, and so they moved to find a more secure footing in the sundari tree. The wind lashed hard at them, and Satvinder remembered what Shafia has said. He stressed to James, "We need to move around to the back of the tree. We could be hit by something." They both shuffled in the dark, around to the back of the trunk and immediately noticed the protection from the wind. "We're ok." He whispered into James's ear. "We're ok."

It seemed like many hours as they waited for the light to return, and the temptation to climb down lower was stifled by James. "No! It might come back." But it didn't, and they stuck it out in the very spot where the good Lord had placed them for their safety. But Satvinder thought a great deal during his wait for the light, and realised that it was not the good Lord who had planted the sundari trees, for their protection, it was Ali, the man who had promised to look after his old friend's nephew. He'd done a good job and his for-thought and preparation had saved them from the tidal surge. Had it saved his other friends?

"Ali! Shafia! Mia!" He shouted several times into the darkness and through the roaring winds, but they heard nothing back.

"All dead," whispered James. He would not let go of his adult friend. "Dad's gone. Hope he went to heaven."

He gently held the boy's head as he attempted to relax the sobbing boy. "Don't think like that. He may be safe." They both knew it unlikely, but hope can keep you alive. "It'll be light soon."

The feeling of total enclosure, in the darkness of the storm, began to lift. It became light very quickly and as they scanned around the wind-swept char, they realised that few people would have survived. They looked down. It was not apparent how deep the water was, which had covered all, but for the trees. Many of the buildings had been moved, and spread around the delta in pieces. So had most of the people.

James suggested, "I'll go down and see how deep it is."

"Why? Where can we go?" The entire char was under water. "We should wait for it to drop more."

They didn't have to wait for very long. The tide turned and suddenly they could see some roofs. There was nobody on them.

The lad whispered above the wind, through a distraught face which looked like it had experience fifty years of suffering in his mere eight years, "One of the trees has gone. There were three here, and I bet it was Dad's that went." He was convinced that his father had lost his life in the surge. "He will go to heaven. He's good." He suddenly pushed himself away from Satvinder. "We can go down now. The wind won't hurt us now, all the debris has already blown away." They were about twenty feet high in the tree and James slowly climbed down. His pal warily followed him. They lowered themselves into the water, which came up to James's chest. "Follow me." He moved slowly away from the tree, and found the raised area where the cattle had been tethered, but the cows were gone. The water above the raised area was shallow, allowing them both to relax a little and consider their lot. "You're cut." James carefully touched Satvinder's damaged head, which probably caught a branch as he hit the tree. "And my arm hurts bad." He held the arm which had been around Satvinder's throat and began chuckling. "You nearly got rid of me." They grabbed each other and had a welcome giggle at their pure good fortune, momentarily forgetting about the fate of the other islanders. "Don't send me away, please."

Satvinder held him and pulled his head into his chest. It was evident that the farm across the way, which they had watched while the family made their preparations, had suffered sever losses. The eight or nine people who had milled around the place the day before had been reduced to two little children sitting on the roof. Most of the roofs, those few which had been spared by the flood, had no survivors on them. The community of Char Monpura was totally decimated.

James clung onto Satvinder like a limpet. He was agitated. "What if it comes back?" he asked with a whimper. Another high tide was due at about midday. "It might come back."

They both looked at the empty, flooded spot where Ali's home once stood, and at the low-lying buildings which were still flooded up to the roof level. They knew that there was nowhere to go. They then looked in the opposite direction towards the village. Through the murk they could see that the two metre-high plateau was beginning to clear, at least for the time being, and some of the buildings were still standing.

"Could we walk to the village?" he asked James. "We might find some other people." They knew by then that Ali, Shafia and Mia were certainly lost, so they decided to chance walking the raised path, which was still submerged in about three feet of water. "You'll have to lead. You know this path very well, so I'm in your hands."

With the rain again thrashing against them they carefully felt their way along the path, pushing through the three foot deep water. James found his coordinates, and warily headed towards the sundari tree in which the ants had taken refuge, and then carefully to the left of the small trees by the ponds. His local knowledge delivered them through and they safely reached the edge of the village. James continued to lead Satvinder by the hand as they finally reached dry land. The buildings had been devastated. Most had been washed away, including the rich moneylender's, but some had become snagged against each other and were able to withstand being brushed away with the others. But most of the village was gone.

"Help!" shouted James. "Help! Where are you all?"

They stood and listened, looking towards the hard, and at the restaurant building which was badly damaged but standing. They walked closer to the hard.

"Help!" he shouted, and then a call came back. James's face lit up. "Where are you?"

The weak voice returned something, and James latched onto its direction. He sped over to the restaurant building and looked inside, through the gaping hole in the front. He could see that there was also a gaping hole at the back. But in the corner a little girl sat holding another girl in her arms, and her face was pitiful. They were both naked. She suddenly opened her mouth and gasped as she recognised James. She waited for James to enter the building before trying to help the other little girl up. But she couldn't pull her up. As much as she tried, the girl just slipped through her arms and back to the floor, so James tried to help her. But the girl just slipped away with every effort. She was already dead. "Mummy," sobbed the girl as she pointed towards the damaged back wall. Her mummy and other sisters had been washed away through the hole.

Satvinder looked inside, and as he did, the poor girl shrieked and hid behind James. With all that had happened she could not dare allow a stranger to see her naked body. She was a young teenager, and soon to be a woman, and the purdah culture ruled supreme on the chars sometimes with devastating consequences.

"I'll wait outside for you, James." Satvinder moved away, to protect her dignity, but as he did, he noticed some colour in one of the mangled piles of woodwork. He took a closer look, and it was a drowned woman. He reached through the timbers, grabbed the shoulder part of her sari and pulled. It slipped off quite easily, leaving the body partly exposed, but it was dead.

"James, I've got some clothes for her!"

The lad came out and took the garment. Moments later he led the girl out of the building, draped in a bright red sari, and he pushed her to approach Satvinder. She was nervous and frightened.

As the rain continued to thrash, he introduced her to the responsible adult. "This is our good friend Satvinder. He's not a stranger, as you met him yesterday when you served our fish. So you can trust him." He pushed the girl, her face a picture of absolute fear. He continued solemnly, "He's going to take us back to Dhaka with him, away from the floods. He loves us both."

Satvinder frowned, and began to respond, "Now, James, I........." but faltered. He spent a long few seconds thinking, and looking around at the devastated lands and homes. He couldn't possibly lead them into false hope and had to be honest and up front with both the children. A big grin crossed his face. "I'd love to take you home to Dhaka. Will you please be my son and daughter?"

The poor souls just stood there for a while. Their fear still predominant on their expressions, they stared into Satvinder's eyes, until he had to break it.

"What shall we do?" he asked the children. That seemed to break them out from their trance, and the little girl spoke.

"My mummy's gone." She looked behind her at their home. "And all my sisters have gone."

A silence hit the group. James, just eight years old, pulled them together by putting his arm around the thirteen year-old's waist and grabbing Satvinder by the hand. "We'll be ok."

They found somewhere dry-ish to sit down. "What's your name?" Satvinder cocked his head at the girl.

She at last smiled, her stunning white teeth standing out against her dark face and jet black, shoulder-length hair. She was a tiny beauty. "My name is Ablaa, Sir. I'm Ablaa Nouka." She had been appropriately named, as it meant 'perfectly formed', and she was.

"And I'm Satvinder."

The two children looked sternly at each other. The chars offered a fair living for the poor farmers and fishermen when times were good, but the floods and typhoons constantly took their toll, leaving orphans in their wake, and tradition was, when you find an orphan you take it on. It was the nearest thing to social care in those unforgiving environments. Satvinder had to be brave.

"Ok," he nervously stuttered, "I'm your father."

The children acknowledged their approval with two very weak smiles. But then they burst into life. The family unit must remain together and those two survivors were not going to lie down and lose the only little piece of hope that they were left with. Ablaa jumped up, and ran into their depleted home. "Come in!" she shouted.

The two boys followed her in, and they grudgingly helped her to move her younger, drowned sister out of the restaurant, laying her to rest behind the building. They had no means of making fire, so they left her beneath some wooden debris. And then the girl went over to the corner of the

29

building and found a piece of rope which came from the ground. "Food!" She chuckled with pride. "You can dine at my mummy's restaurant for one more time."

Part of the preparations for the storm was to bury food and water. So they dug away at the soft soil, and there it was, a wooden box holding rice and smoked fish, and two large bottles of water. They would at least survive starvation and cholera. And, as the tide turned, to maybe replenish the flood-water, the group settled into the shelter of the restaurant, some praying to Allah, others to God, and one with his fingers crossed. The wind continued to blow, and the rain fell, but the tide never reached the height of the village platform: they were feeling a warm sense of survival as night fell.

The dark hours dragged for Satvinder. The children went to sleep, but he could only cat-nap, worrying about the next day. But his mind was kept occupied, listening out for the roar of the tidal wave which he remembered so vividly from the night before. It never came, and the winds lessened, and by day-break, he knew that the storm was passed.

They stood in the rain, relieved that the wind had let up, and looked across to the other children on the roofs. They had been on there all night. Knowing that they would have no food or water, Satvinder began to worry. He had never been a charitable person, his society had taught him to look after number one and his family, supporting each other until death, but he had temporarily been thrown out from that society and he was in a different, Martian environment. He looked down at James, and then at Ablaa. He had allowed them into his life, giving them promise and hope, but he couldn't take the whole surviving infant world from Monpura back to Dhaka with him.

Ablaa whispered, "We can pray for them, or we can help them."

Poor Satvinder fell instantly in love with his new-found daughter. He had never met people who really cared for others and he began to remember the beauty of the chars before the storm, and suddenly he was seeing the beauty of the people. "What do you think we should do?"

She frowned. "Will you beat me if you don't like what I say? Daddy used to, but Mummy never."

There was a moment of silence, and then, "I'll never beat you, for any reason. I've never beaten any of my daughters."

Ablaa looked disappointed. She asked, "You have other daughters?" She looked into James's face, and then back to Satvinder. "You won't want us, then."

He was lost for an answer. He looked over to the roof-children and made a life-long promise. "I promise that I will take you as my daughter, and James as my son, and my daughters will love you both. If I let you down, I'll burn."

The girl almost looked happy as she smiled. "Then I'll tell you what I think you should do. My mummy never believed in Allah, she said that he always let them down. She never told anybody around here because she would have been ostracised and we would have lost our business and life, as we now have. So she kept quiet about her disbeliefs, and when the storm was coming she said to her daughters, us, 'I'm going to observe purdah, but none of you have to.' My older sisters chose to observe, but me and Chumi were encouraged by my other sisters to take all our clothes off. We did. So when the wave came into our house and the holes bashed through, me and Chumi hung onto the post, but Mummy and my sisters ballooned up with the water in their roles of clothing and were pulled by the flow, right out of the house. And out of our lives." She hesitated. "Chumi couldn't hold her breath for long enough."

There followed a few minutes of silence, maybe in respect, before she continued. "So, Daddy, what you should do, is the right thing, from your heart. And Allah won't help you." She did not realise at the time that Satvinder was Hindu. "It's down to you to do the right thing."

They looked hard at the roof-children. Satvinder realised that in the testing environment of the chars, people must help each other. He knew that they should find a way to rescue the children.

James reminded him, with a giggle, "Don't forget, Daddy, that there are other buried lots in this village. We can all eat."

They set about looking for something which could be used as a boat. There were parts of broken vessels, and a little way up the coast was a fairly large fishing boat which had been bashed and broken on the banks. But the water was still too high to risk taking a look. There was nothing suitable

"We can walk the paths, James."

But James replied, sadly, "Past our old house the paths are not raised, and it'll be deep." So they sat watching the roof-children watching them, and all quite helpless.

As the pressures and excitement wore away, the reality of their losses hit the two children. They cuddled tightly and cried.

The tide was rising towards late morning and the winds slowed yet further, but with the light winds from the south, came something else. A noise! Ablaa shot up. She could hear something on the winds. They all ran down to the hard and looked out into the murky seas. It was a sound, getting slightly louder.

"It's a boat! With an engine!" Ablaa was shouting. "It's coming close! Wave and jump!"

They stood high on the village platform and shouted and waved. They could not see anything, and it was threatening to pass unnoticed, so they shouted louder and waved pieces of wood. Then, a boat! It came out from the misty rains and slowed. It was a launch from the Pakistani navy, metal-blue, and pulled two tenders behind. It was the most beautiful boat that Satvinder and his new children had ever seen, like a gift from God. But most importantly, it was a boat!

The crew moved the vessel as close to the shore as they could, then a sailor and a soldier got into a tender and they rowed into the hard. The children ran to them and laughed as they waited for them to land.

"We've found some!" shouted the sailor in Urdu, whilst shaking the hand of his soldier pal. He stepped into the water, and then approached the children, who instantly froze at the sight of the tall, fair-faced sailor. As the soldier pulled the tender onto dry land, the sailor saluted the children and then went to Satvinder and spoke in broken Bengalese. "Good morning." He shook Satvinder's hand heartily. "How many are you?"

They explained their situation, and that of the roof-children.

The sailor explained, "You're well south on this island, and we've moved right up the coast from the tip, and you're the only ones we've found so far." The mood swung between jubilation and subdued respect for others. "We'll pull both the tenders over the bank and pick those children up." The Pakistani navy collected six other survivors, all children. They were saved.

The sailors and soldiers treated the survivors like kings, and after picking more up from villages further north, and dropping off rice and water for those able to stay, they took them into the safety of the naval base at Chittagong. Although the port had taken some serious punishment from the storm, the refugees were well looked after by the forces and by voluntary groups. A businessman had given over an office-block to temporarily house the refugees, and there were many. Satvinder never let go of the children for fear of losing them amongst the thousands of lost souls, and as they waited for instruction he watched the hundreds of children who had been left entirely alone in the World. "I can't take them all," he whispered.

For twelve days they were fed and sheltered, until some of the panic subdued, and they were able to find a vessel which was going to Dhaka.

# CHAPTER 3 -- THE POISONED CHALICE

The return to a multi-million person metropolis was a welcome relief for Satvinder, but for the children it was frightening. They never let go of their new father as they left the Sadarghat Boat Terminal. "Stick with me. We've about three miles to walk to the University."

Dhaka was still a mess. Although it was two hundred miles upstream from Char Monpura, the city had been flooded to several feet deep in some places. It had caused serious chaos in and around the city but the water had receded, leaving a drowned urban environment which would take a long time to get fully back to normal. Satvinder suddenly thought of the Char, as the constant wail of the kurpal was replaced by the constant blast of hooters and horns: the kurpals were a warning, and he began to wonder if the impatient, noisy drivers were making a similar warning. A chill ran up his spine.

As they moved away from the river, life was getting back to normal, sort of. Street sellers were again lined up along the pavements, and the throng of people, male and female, went about their routines. They were all arguing about the price of the food, which had multiplied several times since the flood. Over and above the noise, the mass of colour struck the children. The women were out in their numbers with their brightly coloured saris, but often with no head covering, and the men showed a little adventure with splashes of blue or pink in their lungis. But the rickshaws took the main prize for splendour, and it seemed that the owners had taken personal pride in making them up as colourful as was humanely possible.

"They're beautiful," whispered Ablaa. "I've never seen so much colour in one place."

The walk was uncomfortable. The streets were crowded, and the cars which were passing through constantly blew their horns at the rickshaws, probably taking them out if they were not quick enough to move aside. And the three and four storey colonial town houses, with their multiple bays and verandas, were unmaintained and drab. They were a complete contrast to the rickshaws.

As they passed by the Naya Bazar, they heard an incident. There was shouting and what looked like a violent assault on a man and woman, so they held each other very tightly by the hands and moved on. But Satvinder was frightened to the point of curiosity and he stopped to watch. He could sense something. The man and woman had just purchased some rice and fish from a street trader, but when a group of students realised that the man and woman were Hindu, they set about them and stole the food. They were shouting about them taking 'their' food, and how they should get out of 'their' land. The warnings were beginning to mount and his hands trembled.

They reached the University, relieved. The grand old red buildings took the children by surprise. They were majestic, with many arched windows and hundreds of finials and canopies adorning the roofs, and stately entrances which were fit for a palace.

"Are we going to live here?" asked James. "It's better than in the other streets."

Satvinder suddenly felt a fear of the worst. Were his wife and children ok? It had been more than two weeks since they spoke, and although he had sent a letter from Chittagong, he was certain that it would not have arrived. It was a nerve shattering time for him.

"We live in here. Just stick with me and don't say *anything.*"

They entered the building and went up to the first floor. Just a little way along the corridor he stopped, and slowly knocked on a door. Nobody answered. He knocked again. Sweat was running down his face as he knocked for the third time, and after a click, the door opened enough for the occupant to see who was calling. Then it opened fully.

"Vinny!" The lady, Satvinder's wife, flung herself at him and cried uncontrollably into his neck. After a while she pulled herself away. "Get inside, quick." They went in and the door was slammed. A woman of about thirty five with her hair tied back, and showing signs of stress, stood in front of them and wept. "We thought you were killed." She had not received the letter. "I'll get the girls." As she went into one of the bedrooms, James and Ablaa sat down on some wicker tub chairs.

The two daughters emerged from the bedroom, in pyjamas, and launched themselves at their father, and smothered him for several minutes. Their mother looked on with a massive grin across her fraught face, and James and Ablaa just looked on. It was a little while before the twelve and fourteen year old girls allowed their mother into the frolic.

Eventually they all settled down and they sat around the table.

"We thought you'd been drowned in the flood. The local reports said the islands had been washed away, and that the Pakistanis refused to help the people."

Satvinder frowned. "That's not how we found it. They saved our lives, and many others."

"But we've heard that Monpura was washed away, and nobody has helped. Everybody's saying it."

"It isn't true. We were picked up quickly, and the navy and army looked after us and the others, like kings. Isn't that true, James?"

Suddenly the subject was changed. Kaling, his wife, looked sternly at him. Who is James? She didn't even have to speak.

"This is James. He's kind of related to us, and has lost all his other family in the storm."

With a hint of a growl, "What sort of name is James? We *can't* have a James in our house. And how is he related to us?"

James kept quiet, as Satvinder stood his corner. "You know Ali, the man who my uncle sent me to stay with. Well, this's his son."

"*That* doesn't make him related. Why's he here?"

Satvinder was beginning to strain over her questions. He hadn't expected them, and as such, had made no such rehearsal. "I think you're over-reacting, darling."

"*No* chance! Do you know what's been going on? That fucking storm has caused almost uprising. *Everything* would be alright if we self ruled our own areas. The elections will all be about the storm. It wouldn't have happened if we had our autonomy."

He gaped in surprise, and then slowly and deliberately asked, "Do you really believe that? Who's telling you all this shit? Because it's just shit. We've just gone past the Naya Bazar, and we witnessed how us Bangles are helping each other. Ten times the price for any food. A kicking by some of our students if they don't approve of which Bangles are eating the food. Is that self rule?"

Kaling put her head in her hands and sniffed. Clearly there had been more going on in Dhaka than Satvinder could have guessed at. She whimpered, "Sorry. We need to talk. A lot of talk." She looked up. "But you first. Tell me what's been going on."

He managed a smile at James and Ablaa, who had sat impeccably still and respectful, as his two daughters had.

"Ok. Back to basics. As you know, I went off for six months, supported by the university, to write a book about the hard times on the Chars. I went almost to the far southernmost section of the island, and paid the price. It became the worst hit. I don't want to go into all the details, but I lost my friends Ali, Shafia and Mia to the storm, and the island lost almost everybody else. I believe that Ali saved my life, on two scores, so I owe his surviving son a life."

"How?"

"He first forbade us to come home on the morning of the storm. We were coming home, but he and Shafia changed their minds about when the storm would hit, so as a union parishad official he forbade us to leave Monpura. Yes, I'd been ordered to leave the island, to save me from the storm. But we were too late, and he made us stay." He was solemn as he talked about his friends. "And then, many years ago he planted six sundari trees, which are now big and strong, and three protected the front of the house from the storms, and three sat behind the house, to catch some of the debris. Me and James were caught in a tree, and were saved from the storm. Ali, Shafia and Mia were not so lucky."

His wife gave him an old fashioned look. "That's a pretty weak reason. But it'll do."

He looked at Ablaa. "This is Ablaa. I owe her a life because she taught me about basic charity, and non-religious humanity. She showed me that people can help each other, irrespective of religion or family. So, as her mum, Kolala Nouka, made the best hilsa chad dish on Monpura, I owe her a life."

"That stinks." Kaling grinned as she spoke. "So we've got two new children." She looked at her own two children and asked, "Well?" They both smiled and nodded. "James, tell us about yourself."

The boy was uncomfortable and looked to Satvinder for help.

"Tell them about the shrimping, and the snakes, and your brothers."

"I want to hear about *him*, not his old lifestyle. We've got the rest of our lives to talk about that."

James cleared his throat like a little old man. "Well, my name is James and I'm eight years old." He looked at Satvinder.

"What about the important bits? We already know your name."

He grinned, "I'm Christian. That's why I'm called James."

A deathly hush fell. Kaling frowned at her husband, and the stress began to return. She said very quietly, "We have a Christian in our house? With our girls here?"

"Darling, the girls can learn from a Christian."

"Not in fucking Dhaka, they can't."

"Curb your language. It's that club."

"The club was *burned down*! Along with about thirty members in it." She huffed. "You've missed the beginning of the war. The storm wouldn't have happened if we self ruled, and got rid of the Paks and the Hindus. That's what's fucking happening. Oh, and the Christians, we need to get rid of them as well, and even the Hindus are saying that. So you can get rid of him!"

Satvinder held his head in his hands and thought very hard. He was up against it, and she didn't even know at that point that Ablaa was a Muslim. That would be the cream on the eviction.

Kaling cooled a little. "Look, these elections are going to be decided on brainwashing. The storm wouldn't have happened if the Awami League were in power, they can control *Allah*, and the ones with a brain, that don't believe it, will be violently encouraged to vote their way. It's already started. They won't be voting for the Awami League, they'll be voting *against* the West Pakistani rule. Last week a group of Awami League supporters, students at this very University, seriously beat up another group of students who were supporters of the Pakistan Democratic Party. When the police did nothing, a group of reporters came to the campus to report on the political violence, but they also were beaten to a pulp. And the police did nothing. Law and order is breaking down. And the club? It's only because us Hindu women meet there that it was burned. It was a religious killing, nothing to do with politics. But what you already know of these problems has just gotten worse since you've been away. The girls are not going to school since Captain Hussain called here. His wife used to use the club, but was not there when it was burned, thankfully. But through the police station, Captain Hussain heard that the Hindus are being targeted in many areas, and what's worse, the Hindus are retaliating." She frowned into Ablaa's face. "This pretty little girl should not have been brought here. We're sitting in the middle of a hornet's nest, and I'm so frightened for all of us."

She was right. Maybe the two children would be better fending for themselves, fighting the elements on the Chars.

They put their children to bed, with James and Ablaa sharing the adult's quarters.

Satvinder sat beside Kaling. "I'm sorry. I have these funny coloured glasses which distort what I see. I sometimes forget about reality."

They cuddled and kissed, but Kaling would not allow any much awaited reunion. There were strangers in the house.

"They're strangers to me and the girls. Perhaps not to you. And the girl, I didn't get a chance to ask her about herself." She had a smug grin on her face.

"Well, she's Ablaa Nouka. A pretty name, don't you think? And she's thirteen, I think. They don't keep records of ages on Monpura."

Kaling kissed her man on the lips. "Was she married before the storm?" She could sense that Satvinder was not sure. She grinned. "But I do know something about her. She's a Muslim." A silence fell. She put her mouth to his ear, "The

41

way she wears her sari, and, a real giveaway, her very pretty Muslim name."

The family had suffered racist or religious abuse before, and the memories flowed back. They had not been seriously hurt on that occasion, but had been forced to move away from the hub of the trouble, to a lovely job in the Dhaka University. Right then the lovely job was looking more like a death sentence.

"Vinny, we're both scholars. We know what's going to happen with the elections, especially if the Awami League gets a landslide. Khan quite rightly won't allow transfer from one dictatorship to another dictatorship, from West to East, and we all know that neither Rahman nor Bhutto will work together to form the new constitution. And Khan will never give up control of the army to an unstable, one sided government. He would be wrong to do so. We've discussed this many times during our evenings. Personal ambition will rule, and what do you think will happen?"

He huffed, smiled and replied, "Death. Lots of death. The minions, the ones who are always overlooked will die cruelly and violently. And somebody will celebrate a victory. And the *real* cost of the victory will be forgotten amongst the politics and the religion."

They held each other closely.

She continued, "And whose side will we be on? It'll be a license to kill. The Pakistanis will want to kill all, especially us, the Bangles will want to kill everybody except themselves, and just think: your new-found daughter will be your enemy." She shivered in the cool evening air. "There's something I haven't told you. Your talks on religious equality have been noted. Captain Hussain has warned me not to answer the door to anybody I don't know. He's given me a spy glass." She pointed to the glass on the sideboard. "It goes in the door. I don't know how."

Satvinder began to appreciate the reality. He had been noted. His time would come, for teaching anything but the true Islamic ways, and how can a Hindu teach that, even if he wanted to? And his family would not be left alone, once he himself had been taught the ultimate lesson. They were all in a very dangerous life.

"I've got to go."

They both knew that it was the only way.

Kaling was philosophical about the situation. "The storm has given the Awami League a chance to further fan the flames of hatred towards the Pakistanis, and they haven't allowed the chance to slip. But it's given us an unexpected hand of help. You're dead." She smiled, almost sarcastically. "Dead, my darling, missing, presumed dead. So unless you were seen coming in here, that's a good way to remain. You need to go into hiding, with James and Ablaa, and see what happens over the course of the elections."

He meandered, "Do you know what, Sugar? I've never loved anybody else. That'll keep us together, wherever we are. And also, I never want to teach bullshit in this University again. If I can't teach the truth, I won't teach. And do you know what, I've learned as much in the last couple of weeks from so-called peasants, than I possibly could have learned from the elite. And, you know what, when I was sitting in Chittagong, hanging onto the two children in the chaos, desperate not to lose them, I was astounded at the help which everybody was offering. Irrespective of religion. And the orphaned children. There were hundreds, and I dreamed of bringing them all home. Back here to us, and as much as it got to me as I wondered what would become of them, I knew that I couldn't. I never once dreamed, though, that I would be bringing them to a cauldron of hatred, intolerance and personal ambition. I'm as stupid as you get." He swallowed awkwardly. "You know, I cried as I watched them come in. Nothing, not even a mummy or daddy."

Kaling soothed the dead man. "Go and find other work, away from here, even in India, or England, and come for us. We'll be waiting for you. We can live that life of tolerance that we've always spoken about, a family of Hindus, Muslims and Christians. Do you think there's anywhere in the World we can do that?"

They snuggled down on the settle for a couple of hours kip.

# CHAPTER 4 -- KALING'S EVICTION

Into December, 1970, and the fervour over the elections mounted. There was no surprise when the final counts were returned and Sheikh Mujibur Rahman's Awami League were able to celebrate an overwhelming landslide, winning one hundred and sixty seven seats in East Pakistan out of a possible one hundred and sixty nine. And, in West Pakistan, Zulfikar Ali Bhutto's Pakistan People's Party had won an overwhelming majority, but not enough seats to prevent the Awami League from claiming power and the prime minister-ship. Although President Yahya Khan announced, during his visit to Dhaka, that Sheikh Mujibur Rahman was to be prime minister, Bhutto would not accept it. It seemed that the constitution had already been agreed based on the Awami League's six points, and an impossible task was then set by Khan's administration that the constitution be framed within a mere 120 days. All talks eventually broke down, and even while the talks were still continuing, Yahya Khan was planning the assault on the people of East Pakistan, in particular the Awami League. Yahya Khan postponed, indefinitely, the session of National Council which was to have been held on March the third, nineteen seventy one. The dream of democracy was turning into a nightmare.

The mood of independence and cessation was boiling over in East Pakistan, and it was reported in February that President Yahya Khan had made his famous suggestion that they should "Kill three million of them, and the rest will eat out of our hands." He was, of course, talking about the people of East Pakistan.

The festering hatred against the West Pakistanis was further stoked up by Sheikh Mujibur's address to his people at the Dhaka Race Course ground. The jubilant crowd waved sticks, farm implements and other tools and weapons in defiance of the military dictatorship from West Pakistan, and the Sheikh wound them up to the point of explosion.

"The struggle this time is the struggle for our emancipation! The struggle this time is the struggle for independence!" The nightmare gathered momentum.

But Satvinder's Story is not about the all-embracing gallant acts of war, the politics, nor the perpetrators, it is about the consequences of war: the fear; the pain; the loss; the personal destruction; the loss of tradition; the dismemberment of society and bodies; the joy of victory; the satisfaction of re-unity; the cholera; the hepatitis; the broken spirit; and for some the ecstasy of infliction and the self-satisfaction of the eradication of infidels and malauns. While the politicians and dictators bravely discussed war and peace around their tables, and the World watched on in anticipation, each backing their favoured side, the real people of the World from East and West Pakistan continued to be exploited and condemned, often for no apparent rhyme nor reason, and often from within. So let's get back to Satvinder's story.

December 22nd 1970, Dhaka University

"I'm very sorry to hear that our good friend and scholar has been lost to the storm. But at least since the elections, and since we're to get regional autonomy, we'll be able to better help our fellow countrymen."

The university superintendant, an old man wearing heavy, black glasses, sat opposite Kaling at her dining table. Her two daughters had been sent to their bedroom.

"Sir, we don't know that he's dead. Just presumed. Where does that leave us?" Kaling was treading carefully.

"Kaling, we all pray that he will one day turn up, alive and well, but it's been more than a month since the storm, and nothing. So it leaves me the dreadful task of informing you that his position is now vacant, and that *you* must leave the quarters. I'm very sorry." He sighed heavily. "Once you've found another home, I'll arrange for two porters to help and accompany you during your move." He stood up, pushed his glasses up his nose and bowed his head. "You must, as we all must, be very wary of others. Hatred is running un-halted amongst the Bengali Muslims and Hindus, as well as the Biharis. The papers are calling it civil unrest. We privately call it civil war. So be careful, and try to find a home amongst fellow Hindus, where we can support and protect each other. And, just for the record, Joy Bangla!"

Poor Kaling and her daughters had been evicted. The seven days notice was short, and so her only recourse was to contact Satvinder's uncle for advice and possible financial help. In response, Uncle sent a note for her to join him whilst she looked for accommodation. He lived in Sakharibazar, which was a predominantly Hindu area within Old Dhaka, an area of tradition and pride, and home to several hundred sakharies. Those traditional craftsmen and women made musical instruments and jewellery from seashells, and their wares had featured in Hindu tradition for hundreds of years.

The streets were tight, and the buildings high, often as many as four floors, ensuring maximum use of the cramped city environment. And some were beautifully adorned with delicate carvings, and the colours were chosen for their splashing effects, and certainly not for their blend. The contrasting colours of the rickshaws and saris made the whole scene one of a kaleidoscope of living splendour.

Uncle had a small shop and workshop, with accommodation rooms on the upper two storeys. His shelves were full of stock, beautifully carved bangles, crafted from solid sea shell and mother of pearl. The girls were in heaven, studying the intricacies of the carvings, trying to discover as many new icons as they could.

"Kaling, you're welcome to stay with me. My children have left, and I'm on my own."

Kaling looked out of the front door, and smiled, although a tiny hint of a tear formed. "Thank you, Uncle. That's the only nice thing we've heard for some time. Thank you."

They looked around the rest of the house and established the sleeping arrangements, before sitting down, around the table, to catch up with life. Uncle was quite old, probably about late fifties, and very skinny, with silvery-grey hair and a surprisingly light-coloured face. His eyes were dark, almost sad, and poor Kaling was reminded of her younger husband every time she looked towards him.

He spoke quietly. "I've heard from Biwi Nezamul Islam, a parishad official who shared an office with Ali. You know, Ali, who Satvinder went to stay with. The news from Monpura is mixed. He's shocked that the whole of the East is blaming the Pakistanis for the disaster." He chuckled. "The Pakistanis should be revered if they truly do have such accord with Allah. Puts us Bengalis at a real disadvantage." He giggled at his own slight of tongue. "And he sadly reports that from Monpura, *every* single adult woman is believed to have been lost. That's an unbelievable disaster. Shocking beyond apprehension. I wonder how many thousands of women that must account for." He waited for some response from Kaling, but she just remained in thought. He continued, "And other news. Some children reported to the Red Cross in Chittagong that they were from the bottom end of Monpura and were few in survivors, but an adult, a stranger to them, and two children who they knew, were taken with them to the naval base. They were saved from the floods." He raised his eyebrows. "It wasn't my good friend Ali: the children would have known him. But it was one of his guests." He studied Kaling's facial language. "It could have been Satvinder."

"It couldn't. He's dead!" She crossed her arms in defiance, but had forgotten about the children.

"Mummy, we saw him, didn't we." The little girl grinned from ear-to-ear. "He's gone away for work!"

Mum was confused and annoyed, but knew that it was not Uncle that she needed to convince, it was her daughters. In their innocence, they would allow the activists access to Satvinder, and almost certainly put the girls themselves into a position of capital danger. She needed to think on the run.

"Now, listen." She spoke quietly, and pulled the girls to her to cuddle. "There's something that you need to know." Her face was sad. "That man from the university, the superintendant, who came to tell us that we must leave, well, he told me some bad news about Daddy." She hesitated as she created the story. "Daddy went down to Khulna to meet his friend, Doctor Hussain, but, on the way, there was a terrible accident. Daddy and James and Ablaa were killed as the ferry sank." She held the girls tightly. "So we must remember Daddy as the lovely man that he was, but he has now gone from our lives. We must pray for their souls." The two girls were wetting up at the terrible news. "Say some private prayers for Daddy and the children."

They pulled into their mother's sari and wept. Kaling also wept with them, tears of genuine regret at having to break the girls' hearts with a lie, but she did not know of any other option.

Once they had gone to their bedroom, Uncle quizzed Kaling.

"I saw no sign of mourning as you told the girls. But I saw a broken heart from the stress of breaking your daughters' hearts. You can tell me the truth. Please."

"Please don't tell. We might all be killed if they find out." She grinned at Uncle. "I think you'll really look after us, so I'll be honest with you. Well, he's not dead. Don't ever tell the girls, but he's gone into hiding, while the war rages."

He raised his eyebrows. "So you think it's begun? The war? You must talk to me Kaling."

She sat silent for several minutes, not knowing where to begin, nor how.

Uncle asked, "Why has he gone away?"

The question helped Kaling to establish a line of thought. She whispered, "He's gone away to save our lives. He'll come back for us when he's made a new life elsewhere."

Uncle slowly asked, as he held his hand on hers, "What has he done which is so bad?"

"He's been teaching equality to his students. Just equality. And for his good heart he's a marked man, waiting for the mob to mutilate and murder him." She had tears in her eyes. "Captain Hussain is from the Patuatuli police station, not far from here. I know his wife who attended the Race Course club with me, before it was burned down by the students. He has been told that Satvinder is on a list kept by some Biharis, and he is a 'known troublemaker'. His views about the democratic future of Pakistan, governed by politics, not by religion, have been reported to the Dhaka Cantonment, and he is likely to be arrested one day. Or worse." She took her hand from his, and held it to her head. "But I don't know what to do, Uncle."

His skinny old face had dropped. "You need to do what Satvinder is doing. We should all do the same."

The Bihari, Muslims who had mostly originated from Bihar in India, had long been persecuted in East Pakistan. During the elections the situation had worsened as the hatred towards the West Pakistani military dictatorship, and everything else West Pakistani, was fuelled by the warmongering politicians. The Biharis were seen as the gophers and runners for the Pakistani military, holding many of the civilian jobs within the ruling government, and were known to supply local information to the military. Despite earning some protection by the military, they often paid the price for being on the 'other' side. Only a few days earlier, immediately after the election results were known, a small community of Bihari families, living close to the river, were attacked. Their houses were invaded by a mob that tore the homes to pieces as they looted their possessions, and in the process the mob cut off all the Bihari male's genitals, old and young, and left them stuffed in the dying souls' mouths. The females were gang raped before being mutilated and killed. The mob set light to the homes as they left.

An attachment of soldiers were sent from the Dhaka Cantonment (the barracks) but the police, who arrived very late, were unable to help them in any way with the identification of the attackers. Suspicion lay on the heads of both Muslim and Hindu.

"I fear Kaling that the situation has begun to deteriorate. You were in the south in nineteen fifty, and you remember having to move." She acknowledged him. "But I was right here in nineteen fifty, and I remember my wife and two of my children dying. It was a terrible afternoon, so many butchered and raped, and the police simply watched. Some joined in." His head dropped. "If things go on, the Hindu massacre of nineteen fifty will happen again."

He got up and walked downstairs to his shop. He returned holding a bangle.

"This is all I have left of my wife. I made it for her before our wedding. Please look after it." He held out the pure white bangle, intricately carved with the shapes of fish and dolphins. "I stayed and rebuilt my shop, because I'm a Sakhari, like my family for hundreds of years, so I defiantly rebuilt and restarted the family business. But my two boys went to India, where they stayed, never to return to these killing streets. As we were able to get passports in nineteen fifty two I sent them away." He paused. "I'll send you away, I have some money stashed. Before we all get cut to death by the war, go. Take the girls."

"But, go where? We've nothing left."

"I've just said, I *have* money. Take the ferry tomorrow, and go to Khulna then onto Kolkata. Please. I know you have passports, so go, while the war is still smouldering. I don't need my money any more. So go."

Kaling agreed to the generous offer. She begged, "Will you please write to Satvinder and tell him that we're here, with you. He'll be worrying. And when I arrive at somewhere sensible and secure, I'll write to him at the Doctor's and let him know." She wrote Doctor Hussain's address down for Uncle. "Don't let anybody know about where we are. Satvinder will hear from us as soon as we're settled. And I'll write to you. I promise."

After a tearful, quiet moment, Kaling retired, knowing that her next day was to be an arduous and challenging adventure.

The streets were busy the next morning as she left Uncle's, with one daughter on each arm, and carrying very little baggage. Their matching red saris glistened in the morning sun, and the local men stared in desire. She hailed a beautifully decorated red and blue rickshaw.

"We're going to the ferry terminal."

The driver looked around. "Where's your man?"

"We're alone. Please take us."

"But where's your man? You shouldn't be travelling alone."

"He's dead. And we must go to Khulna."

The suspicious driver looked at the two young girls. "Ok, but no trouble." The girls squeezed into the seat as they set off through the bustle, and he constantly rang his bell at the shoppers in the road. Old Dhaka was a tightly crammed metropolis of housing, shops and slum dwellings, but in comparison, made Kolala Nouka's uptown restaurant on Monpura look quite decrepit, even before the storm.

They had been travelling, rather slowly, for about half an hour when there appeared some kind of hold-up ahead of them. They reached the people in front of them and the driver asked a group of young men what was happening. They waved their hands in the air and shouted 'Joy Bangla!' before wandering further into the cauldron. Suddenly an army truck pulled up behind them, and the six armed soldiers disembarked onto the street. One was on the radio.

Speaking with an accent the one with the radio shouted at the people, "Please move aside. Please move aside." It fell on deaf ears, so he shot his pistol in the air. The people took heed and moved aside, and the truck moved forward. Three more trucks arrived, larger and with several soldiers in each. Two went ahead into the crowd, and one stayed back, the soldiers climbing down and taking up positions with their rifles at the ready. They positioned themselves to prevent any more people going along the street to join the affray. Then shots were heard.

"I'm going back!" shouted the rickshaw driver. "What are you going to do?"

Kaling held tight onto the girls. "We'll wait here. We *must* get to the docks." She paid the driver, and they climbed out.

"What's happening, Mummy?"

More shots were heard, and much shouting and screaming, and some people began running out from the affray, towards Kaling. They moved aside into an alley to avoid being bashed, and the people of all ages ran past, the soldiers making no attempt to stop them. Several dozen left over the course of a minute or so, but then came more shooting. The soldiers were nervous, and made a decision to stop any more from leaving, pointing their guns into the on-comers' faces, but as the ones who approached the soldiers tried to stop, the ones behind pushed them forwards. A soldier shot one of the men through the face, the ricochet catching the lady behind him. The push stopped. But as the shooting from beyond the crowd restarted, the crowd rushed forward knocking the soldiers to the ground, and the soldiers took flight. As they did, two more army trucks arrived, and over twenty more soldiers joined the action, grouping with the soldiers who had been overwhelmed by the mob. They shot several rounds into the air, and the crowd stopped in their tracks.

"Go home. Now!" shouted one of the soldiers.

The crowd, shocked by the noise of the guns, slowly began to disburse, but some firing continued from the other end of the street.

Kaling clung onto her daughters as she moved out of the alley and waited. After quite a few minutes the police arrived, but stayed back behind the soldiers and just watched.

"What are you doing?" called the army corporal to Kaling. She could not understand his accent, so he asked again. "What are you doing? You can't stay there!"

Kaling gingerly crept away from the small alley, and approached the soldiers. She stood shaking, and asked, "Can we get through to the boat terminal?"

The corporal looked towards the police, who deliberately avoided eye-contact, and then smiled at her. "We can give you a lift. You can ride in our truck."

# CHAPTER 5 -- THE LEPERS

Four weeks earlier, late November 1970, Khulna.

Satvinder and his two new children had taken the ferry to Khulna, and thankfully had not been involved in any disastrous accidents. They had gone to visit his life-long friend Doctor Hussain. On their arrival his wife Baka and two young sons were alone, as the Doctor was out on field-work. So, after some serious consideration, the Doctor's wife sent one of the lads to collect her uncle. He sat in as her chaperone while Satvinder, Ablaa and James were fed.

"I'm a good friend of Doctor Hussain's, and we went to University together. He may have spoken of me."

"No, sorry but he has *never* mentioned you. What do you do as a living?"

"I'm......." He froze, and wondered. Then, "Yes, I'm a geologist. I study the grounds, and I believe from a recent letter that Akhtar is doing some work on farming and health. I'd like to give him some un-paid help while I consider my future."

The two boys were too young to be interested, and so they took Ablaa and James outside into the street to talk to their friends. Khulna was a busy industrial city and had the usual Asian mix of prosperity and poverty, and was crammed and busy. The Doctor lived with his family in a very pleasant part of the city with well maintained buildings and roads. But as usual, he backed onto the slums. They were never far away from poverty in such a poor country.

Baka looked hard into Satvinder's face, studying his outward thoughts. She finally asked, "Do you know who Akhtar is? Really?"

He grinned. "Yes, and I know of you. You're the Hindu who he changed his name for." He suddenly realised that her uncle was with them.

She assured him, "Uncle knows who Akhtar is. He *has* forgiven me."

Satvinder smiled at her uncle, and then back at Baka. He held back the laughter, and then, "It took me a long time to get used to not calling him Bulu. And do you remember how depressed he became when he found that he'd misspelled his new name, and put the 'H' in? I wonder what you must have all thought." He giggled, along with Baka and her uncle, "He fell madly in love with a Hindu girl, so changed his name from a Muslin name, to a Muslim name!"

Chuckling, Baka quietly replied sarcastically, "My family were suitably impressed. Not only was I wishing to marry a Muslim, I was also to marry a clown. I think he charmed his way into our Hindu family through his total innocence. So *stupidly* innocent."

After a bit of light laughter there was a moment of silence. Uncle suggested, "Akhtar is a man of the people. We all love him now."

"And," stated Baka, "he has kept us very well, and has always fed us, so what else would we need?" She frowned, "And, *what* exactly do you know about geology? You're a bloody lecturer in political history and English in Dhaka. Or something like that." She had clearly listened to Akhtar's tales. She asked abruptly, "So, what *are* you doing here?" Her mood had become aggressive and she was not going to take any bullshit.

"I'm sorry." He sat and pondered what he was doing at his friend's home, and what his own intentions really were. "I probably shouldn't be here. I took some lectures at the University about the involvement of religion in politics, and I believe I'm a marked man. I should leave. I'm sorry to have put you at risk."

"So, they're looking for you? Just for some speeches, or lectures? The Maulana Bhashsani makes speeches and is not looked for. Why you?"

"I don't know, but one of Kaling's friends is married to a police captain, and he suggested to Kaling about the Biharis' keeping of notes, and I could be on a list. I don't know why."

"So you've put my family at risk?"

"No! No, definitely not. I'm *dead*. Nobody is looking for me."

"Satvinder, it's all getting a little bloody confusing, so please un-confuse it."

He smiled at the woman who was trying to be a virtual dragon.

"Don't just smile: tell me what's happening, before I consider whether or not you are a danger to my children. Now!"

The smile went. "I had a small grant from the university to go to the outer chars. I was to write a book about the life on them, but the day after I arrived on Char Monpura, the storm hit. We were on a very southern part of the island, and I escaped drowning with those two children who play outside with *your* children. Very few people survived from that part, just us and a handful of *other* children. Those two are now my adopted children." He looked down into his lap. "A couple of weeks later I arrived back at the university, to a shocked Kaling, who, like the others, had presumed me dead. So when I found out about the potential threat, she suggested I go away, and stay dead. That's why I'm dead. Only Kaling and my girls know that I'm not."

Baka took a very deep sigh. "So you're dead. What about those children. They're not yours are they? And the girl, she's an adult, and what about marriage? Is she married?"

He smiled as he realised that the reports that all adult women from Monpura died in the storm were not quite true. "You know, I hadn't thought of her as any more than a child. She's a young lady of marrying age." He took a deep sigh. "But I prefer to think of her as a child. And no, you're quite right, they're nobody's children. I briefly knew *her* mother and *his* father. And these two children have taught me tolerance, as well as..." He paused for thought. "I've been converted, from a dreamer who thought that lecturing to the students could change everybody's lives, to one who can now see the ground, and all the little grains which make up our lives. The dirt as well as the precious stones." He thought about Ali and the oarsmen as he raised his arms and screamed. The children heard the scream and rushed into the house, only to find the adults laughing. "Now I should introduce you to my adopted children." He beckoned them over to him, and put an arm around each child's shoulder. "If you want me to leave the house after our intros, just say. Now, this is James." He watched their reactions, but none. "He's a Christian. His dad told me before he died why he's called James, but I can't quite remember." Still no noticeable reaction. He looked into Ablaa's beautiful eyes. "And this is Ablaa, and her name means 'perfectly formed', and she's a Muslim." He raised his eyebrows, and his forrid creased, as he received no hostility. "Well?"

Baka grinned, "What you expecting? I married a bloody Muslim, so two lost children won't faze me."

They were accepted. In Satvinder's eyes, a miracle had just been performed, and the three wanderers cuddled and giggled in celebration. But the purdah culture gets everywhere, and Uncle reminded the group, "I'm here as a chaperone, and *you*, Satvinder, cannot stay in this house unless Akhtar is here with you. The children *can*."

So Baka instructed the boys to show their young guests where they would be sleeping, while she made the final arrangements with Satvinder. "Akhtar has told me a lot about your discussions when you were young. A couple of dreamers, who could change the World, and could change people, and cultures. It never happened. But you're so much like Akhtar: I know he would have returned with those lost children, just as you did, so changing their World really is possible. But the rest of the World? Only in little tiny bits. Now, if you can help Akhtar change his little bit, we'll feed you and your children. You, the geologist from Jessore, the dead geologist, can go to Chak Sahasa and work with Akhtar. You'll have to stay with Uncle tonight, and get off in the morning." Uncle nodded his approval, and the deal was done.

The next morning was wet. Still dressed in the beige trousers and checked shirt which he donned before going to Monpura he felt a little dirty. But Baka's uncle assured him that there would be good facilities in Chak Sahasa, so he gave him a lungi and another pair of pyjama trousers and sent him packing. He did also lend him one of his many umbrellas to fend off the torrential rain.

He had to take a bus trip from Khulna towards Dumuria Bazar. The old bus was packed and a little smelly, and the trip slow, and with the rain thrashing against the windows, there was little to look at during the ride. He was the centre of attraction and well studied by the other curious travellers.

"You need to get off here for Chak Sahasa!" shouted the driver. "Allah be with you!"

It was in the middle of nowhere. He looked down the muddy, hedge-lined lane and could see some smoke rising through the rain, but little else across that flat, wet land. He quietly thanked Baka's uncle for the umbrella which kept his top-half dry, but his feet began to sink. Good job it was the dry season!

"What've I got myself into?" he asked himself. He stopped and looked around at the paddy fields, and he could make out the shape of workers in amongst the crops. "Hello!"

One of the workers came towards him. "Is Chak Sahasa very far up here?"

"No. About ten minutes. Who are you?"

"I've come to see Doctor Hussain."

"He's in the clinic, on the right as you get to the village." The farmer went back to his duties.

Satvinder soon arrived at the village. In the middle were three substantial buildings, (godowns or warehouses) made from concrete blocks with corrugated iron roofs and large, sliding doors, and to the right a smaller but equally substantial building. An area in front of the large buildings had been concreted. They all stood out from the other wood, grass and tin dwellings, resembling the village on the Char. He took a guess that the building on the right was the one which the farmer had mentioned. The rain had stopped, but water and mud was everywhere and women and children ventured out of their homes into the mud to watch the stranger moving through their village. It felt like a special event to Satvinder, with everybody taking such an interest in just one single stranger. But their attention was morbid, and lacked excitement as if they were afraid of something.

The smaller concrete building had a sign over the door: it was the clinic. He knocked and waited, but nobody answered, so he wandered over towards the larger buildings. The dozens of villagers watched with acute interest as he moved. None of them said anything. Then a forty-year old gentleman in a shirt and suit came out from the largest godown and met him head on.

He asked, "Can I be of help? I don't recognise you."

"No, I'm a stranger here. I'm looking for a friend, who I hope to help with his work. Doctor Hussain."

"Have you been engaged by the company?"

"No, I'm a volunteer. I'm a geologist."

The gentleman very limply shook Satvinder's hand and beckoned him to follow. They entered the large warehouse through the small side door. It was airy, dry and open, and had grain stored to one side and lots of agricultural equipment. A pair of internal offices was to the right.

"Do you drink tea?" Satvinder was placed in a chair in front of the office desk. "We like the tea, it's very English. It comes from our own plantations in the hill tracts."

Satvinder grinned, "But most of our tea is drunk in *West* Pakistan."

"And that's what the government enjoys, but we think that the country needs more foreign trade, and are beginning to export our tea to other parts of the World. Exports are essential for any thriving democracy."

"The democracy hasn't happened yet. About three weeks to go. If it ever happens."

The gentleman thought carefully. "Are you interested in politics? My company has an insatiable interest in politics. We're putting a lot of resources into Bengal, and so the politics are crucial for our future stake in this country. Democracy would be perfect, military dictatorship bearable, but democratic dictatorship, by way of a landslide for the Awami League, would be disastrous for us. We would most probably have to pull out."

Satvinder was suspicious of the man's intent, with his pro Pakistani views. He carefully asked, "Why do you want my opinion?"

"I'm an Indian in East Pakistan. We're here on business, but we need a stable environment in which to do business, whether the environment is forced or volunteered. But cessation will cause turmoil for years to come, and that's not to our benefit. What's to your benefit, sir?"

"Well, true democracy will make my life bearable, or even better, a new life elsewhere. Elsewhere is rapidly becoming the most desirable option for me and my family." He hesitated for thought. "I'll ask again. Why do you want my opinion?"

"Because I find you very defensive. Hiding something, perhaps? Maybe you're a Hindu?"

Satvinder stood up. "I've come to see my friend. The rest is none of your business."

"Don't get shirty, old pal. Just making conversation with a geologist. So don't get shirty."

The young lady from the other office came in with a tray of tea.

"Ah, we can relax now. A pot of cha. Now sit down and join me."

He sat down, and had a cup of tea with the gentleman. He was surprised when he was told, "I'm Muslim, but you're Hindu, and so are most of the people around here. But not all are Hindu, quite a few Muslim, and we all work happily together. Work is not about religion, it's about the need for life. We work, we earn, we eat. Why would anybody want to ruin all that just because of inherited prejudice? And besides, you must know from your good friend the Doctor that nobody really wants to interfere with our community: we have all that leprosy within."

Well, that was the last thing he was expecting. He sat contemplating his lot if he were to stay: a tolerant community who were tied together by their great misfortune, one of man's oldest nightmares, leprosy. And that misfortune would be passed on to all those who join. He knew little about modern leprosy, but he believed that it was highly contagious and was the cause of many people being ostracised by their own communities, even their families.

Satvinder was shocked by the presence of the leprosy but was equally uneasy about the gentleman, as his manner was alien although very friendly. It turned out that he was the farm manager, and he explained that a large part of that region had been purchased by his company to grow grain, and some jute, but also to look at what other crops could be rotated in with those already being grown. They were an international company, enormous and diverse, with their main headquarters in the Anglia region in India, close to Kolkata and only a couple of hundred miles from where they sat at the desk. The commercial group consisted of a great many diverse companies throughout the World, and Satvinder at that moment was talking to an agricultural section which specialised in the development of third world agricultural business instilling new policies and practices. They made a great deal of profit from the poor, but boasted that they improved lifestyles, health and education in the process. Colonialism in private!

He stated, "The leprosy is not highly contagious. Ask your mate." He smiled, "Well, you know all about us. Now, why are you really here? You haven't come to catch leprosy, have you?"

Satvinder was warming to the man. "I'm here to see my good friend Akhtar. That's Doctor Hussain. I want to work with him, if he can find me some work. His family has promised to feed my two children if I can be of help to the Doctor. That's why I'm here."

"Everybody is somewhere for something. We'll just have to see why you're really here. Anyway, the Doctor should be back from his rounds by now."

Satvinder walked across the yard with umbrella in hand, to the clinic and knocked. This time it opened and there stood a shocked Doctor Akhtar Hussain. They held each other's hands tightly, before entering the clinic. He was the same age as Satvinder: they had grown up together and spent time at university.

"It's a shock. But it's fantastic to see you again, here in my proud clinic." He held his hands out and swung around full circle. The clinic was all painted white inside, with cabinets and shelves, and two plinths, or inspection couches. It had three clinic rooms, as well as a small living section. "You can have the spare bedroom. That's if you're staying."

"I hope so. I want to work with you."

Akhtar frowned. "Why? You're a budding Uni' thing. This's the back of beyond."

"Please don't make me go through all this again. I'm hiding, presumed dead, so nobody's looking for me. But I'm desperate to be somewhere without constant threat. Please let me help you."

"Where are the girls and Kaling?"

"Back at the University. I had to leave them, but I've got two other children, and they're at yours. I met Baka, she's fantastic." He chuckled, "Bet she keeps you in touch."

Akhtar looked hard at his friend. He knew that he was not on holiday, and that he would never run from his family without good reason. "The job's yours. I'll not ask too many questions, but you *must* keep your opinionated mouth shut around here. We're a mixed community, so we follow our beliefs at home, and we do our work at work." He held his hand out to Satvinder, "And I do believe that that's all you've ever wanted. You may have at last found your heaven."

It seemed that things were kind of working out for Satvinder, and after a brief discussion, with reassurances about leprosy, he agreed to stay with Akhtar in Chak Sahasa while working, and go home with him at weekends. It suited them all, even the children who were making new friends, and Baka had managed to get a private tutor for Ablaa and James, to get them started on their previously non-existent education.

Late December 1970, Khulna

The elections came, and there were demonstrations and some minor rioting in Khulna, but the army put down any trouble as it occurred. Two people were shot dead just behind Akhtar's house, in the slum streets. The police simply put it down to bad luck on their part and so, just in case, the children were made to spend most of their time indoors while the voting went on.

As we already know, it was a landslide victory for the Awami League. There was constant reference to that horrible Norah and her Bhola Cyclone, which was apparently caused by the West Pakistani military government to subdue the people, and the talk was that with autonomy for East Pakistan, everything will now be hunky-dory. Life was about to change and everything was to be fantastic and just for all the people of East Pakistan. Well, that's how the fairytales went.

A little while after the elections Satvinder received a letter at Akhtar's and Baka's home. It was from his uncle, and he was disappointed by its utter caution. He sat at the dining table and read it to the family. He had a tear in his eye.

"Dear Vinny, I hope you're well, and that you've found a place to be, with Ablaa and James. My niece Kaling who I believe you know, and the girls, were asked to leave the university rooms because her husband was lost in the storms, and it is unfortunate that the daughters had then to be convinced that their daddy had actually drowned in a ferry accident. They're learning to live life without a father. I tell you this so that they are not allowed to be given false hope. Please understand. When Kaling contacted me for help, I offered her a home above my workshop in Sakharibazar, and she gracefully accepted. The position here is not good, and there are some mob riots against the minorities, and against the authorities, but the army presence seems to have increased, so hopefully law and order will not be handed over to the mobs. I'll let you know of any further news about our mutual friends, but presently they have a home here with me. Please look after what you have. Uncle."

Akhtar put his hand on Satvinder's shoulder. "He's telling you that Kaling is with him, but you must stay away. It's for the best."

Satvinder had nightmares that night and began shouting in his sleep. Baka's uncle threw some water over him to wake him out of it, and then the crying began. Since walking out on the girls and his wife, he had been strong and full of hope, but the letter wasn't telling him everything and hope was fading. He was convinced that he had lost his family forever, never to return, but James and Ablaa were his godsend. They had already lost their families, and were younger and more adaptable, and so took to Satvinder like the real father that they needed, and this boosted his defences against the imaginary losses and scenarios. He began to believe that his family were already dead, and that he must do what his daughters were doing: bearing the loss, and starting again.

"You know, you could bring the kids to work for a break this week. They can miss their tutor for one week, and you could do some of your own tutoring. Get some really quality time together." Akhtar worked hard to keep his mate's spirits up.

"And what about the leprosy? I couldn't expose them to that."

"Tell you what, my very best friend, take them to work *next* week. *This* week I'll show you some real secrets." He grinned. "And we can come home a day early this week, and have a secret celebration. It'll be Christmas day, so we can have a special meal for James." He whacked his mate on the arm and then picked up a heavy jute bag. "Let's get the bus."

They went off on the bus towards Dumuria Bazar, and were dropped off at the end of the lane. The day was sunny and not too hot, as the cooler winter months were setting in, and the lane was dry. Satvinder jumped as a snake writhed across the road ahead of them.

Akhtar was in a talkative mood as they moved around the creature. "There's a lot of life in these grounds, and as you know, what gives life often takes it away." He took a heavy sigh. "This is a productive part of the country, which is why the company has bought so much of this land. They came to a village which was a strong, happy community and the envy of some poorer areas, and they bought most of the land from the old landlord who had fallen ill, and they then continued to lease to each farmer. But the company went further, and set up a cooperative through which all the produce would be sold, and built new godowns and some new houses, which were still poor workers homes, but a good standard. And everybody loved the company. Then the company built a small school. With nearly a hundred families here, there are lots of children, and they would be educated. Farmers' children don't get education normally, so they loved them even more. And the daughters, who had always been sought after, became even more attractive and the boys from the other villages all wanted to marry them. Even educated suitors wanted them."

Satvinder began to laugh. "Where's this taking us?"

"We still have a little way to walk, so you've got nothing else to do but listen. And besides, it's a crucial story about life, and medicine, and natural disasters, and me." He looked sideways to his mate. "The storm's not been the only natural disaster around here."

"Ok, carry on. They all loved the company, and they all fancied the girls from the village. Carry on."

"Right, the village of Chak Sahasa was the envy of the villages, and many of those villages wanted to become part of the company's cooperative set-up. The company was ready to pounce and take on a great deal more of the land around here when the terrible thing struck, the leprosy. Suddenly the village of Chak Sahasa went from stardom rating to, quite literally, leper rating. They were outcasts from society. Nobody will take on a girl from here because her children will be born as lepers and cripples. They've been ostracised by the whole of the Khulna Division, and all beyond. From the top of the tree to the bottom of the tree in a couple of years. That's when they consulted with the pharmaceutical company in their group, Sensar Pharmaceuticals. And they offered me a contract to come in."

They looked across to the fields where a group of workers were sitting down in the rice.

"They're so tired. They struggle to work all day. It's one of the first signs of the illness. Anyway, I came here, to a brand new clinic, and I have a nurse. The company wanted to know why they got leprosy, as there's so little of it around here any more, and it's not highly contagious unless you breathe in their air." He looked again at the workers. "Come here. Look over there, at that broken down godown. That was the original farm centre, where the storage and processing was done. The people got leprosy, and many have now died, but in *this* part there was no leprosy, so they relocated to here. Only about a year later the signs began to show in the new village. They also had leprosy. And they did not even mix with the ones from the old village."

He sat down on a bank by the hedge. "They don't believe me, but *none* of them have leprosy. You, my best mate, must believe me, and help me. They don't have leprosy! And what they have is not even *contagious*." He waited for his mate to join him on the bank. "They are potentially healthy people who don't get the water-born illnesses which all the other villages have to suffer. You see, the company, in all good intent, drilled tube wells, first in that old part of the village which has almost died now, and then in the new village, which is in the process of dying. So I followed the route of the drilling of the wells, which go deep into the ground and come up with clean water. There's no organic disease in it, and it's a revelation, especially after the floods which contaminated all the surface water, but *not* our well water. Nearly all the villages around here have suffered badly from water-born diseases, particularly cholera, because they only have surface water to drink. The recent floods have again hit them. They have no choice, because they haven't got the deep-water wells that we have here. Now I've got to convince the people of Chak Sahasa that they *can't* drink the lovely clean, safe water from the wells."

"What's wrong with it?"

"I've found alarmingly high levels of arsenic in the water. And I believe that they're all dying from the effects of arsenic poisoning. Skin cancer, renal failure, numb feet and hands, keratosis, the warts, stroke, heart failure and the gangrene. And before that it's the diarrhoea, vomiting, conjunctivitis, bronchitis and black foot, and the severe fatigue. I believe it's all coming from the arsenic in the water. The company have a real problem in believing my findings, because it will affect their development here, and most of it's been good for the people. But they must stop drinking the arsenic contaminated water. It can still be used for irrigation, but not drunk straight from the wells."

Satvinder fiddled with his hands, and asked the obvious. "Have we been drinking it?"

Akhtar became excited. "No. I've created a filter which reduces the arsenic levels almost down to nil. And that's what I'm working on, refining it and making it more productive. If they can continue to draw the water from a hundred meters or so down, but then make sure that it's properly cleansed of the arsenic, the people here can eventually have their dream life, in a cooperative as it is now, but with their health. Just got to convince them about the arsenic."

"Why can't they just boil the surface water? That's all they did on Monpura."

"They must have got by with using very little water. And, how did you boil it whilst the floods were up? That's the real problem with the surface water: surrounded by water but not a drop to drink. If they do, they'll probably fall ill, even die."

Satvinder had not realised just how precious those bottles were that were buried before the storm. They would have been the difference between life and death if they'd had to stay much longer.

Akhtar stood up. "Come on, let's get to the village."

"You know what, old mate, you've found your place. You're so happy, doing what you've always wanted, saving others. I'm so jealous."

"You'll get your chance. You've already saved the two kids."

"But I left all the others behind. Even my own children." His thoughts were spiralling him into a low patch, niggled by the devil who threw visions at him which showed his wife and children. Were they ok? He was ready for a cup of tea.

# CHAPTER 6 -- THE GARLIC BREATH

The two friends woke early on that Monday morning, in the Chak Sahasa clinic. Akhtar listened to his radio while breakfast was being prepared: fish and rice, again.

"There must be hundreds of tons of grain in the godowns. Are they all full?" asked Satvinder.

"Pretty much, but there're not hundreds of tons, more like *thousands* of tons. It's due for export to the Philippines, but the company's in negotiations with the Pakistani government to deliver locally. The flood disaster appeal is under great strain in many parts of our country and we're one of the few producers who have flood-tight storage. But I think the talks are not going well." He sighed. "Reports this morning were more about hating the governing junta than about helping ourselves. We are lemmings."

"Sorry, but you've lost me."

"Vinny, you surprise me. As a scholar and a leader of students, you should be able to see what's happening with the elections. Rahman won't accept anything but everything. It's a personal lust for him to be sitting in Yahya Khan's seat. Sharing doesn't come into it, not when it comes to power. Bhutto has the majority in the West, and *must* be part of the government and his PPP must be active in the framing of the constitution. And it won't happen."

In reply, "I fully appreciate that the *constitution* must be developed for the benefit of the country, and not for the party. So all seat winners must be included in the constitutional reform. If they aren't, then it's what the farm manager calls 'democratic dictatorship'. I know all this. But what do you mean, lemmings?"

"I mean, we can see it, but the majority of the people in this country seem unable to. They are, in Dhaka, demonstrating against the military government. Quite a few people have been killed by the army, and some by the police and by the mob, but they don't even know what they're demonstrating about. They should now be demonstrating their views about creating a *democratic* government from the recent elections, to include all seat winners in the reforms, not about cessationalism. Khan will work with a democracy, but he won't hand over power to one single group, knowing that it will just be a transfer of dictatorship. He'll hang on to the army, and as a consequence he will hang on to power. That's what I think, anyway."

Satvinder spent a few moments thinking. "You know what, if the internal civil war develops into official civil war and Bangladesh is created, the recent elections will be null and void, and if there are not further elections, soon after cessation, then I for one will consider the government to be a dictatorship, and not properly elected. The recent results were a vote *against* West Pakistan, and once West Pakistan is not part of the issue, the people should be allowed to vote in a Bangladeshi government which is party influenced, not country influenced. Until then, there'll never be true democracy in this country. That's what I think, anyway."

Akhtar grinned as he agreed. "These are worrying times. But remember what I told you about keeping your opinionated mouth closed, outside of this building."

"Don't worry, I'm just a geologist helping my mate out. I'll keep my mouth shut." He frowned. "The storm was terrible. I was there. But what's happening now is pathetic. This terrible natural disaster, which was under the control of God alone, is still being used to fire up all these stupid people."

"Don't be so judgemental! We're all led astray, brainwashed and taught discrimination from an early age. We've lived it, so don't slag them off for their fervour. It's the people who lead them who are wrong." Akhtar spent a quiet few moments. Maybe he was in a huff over Satvinder's labelling of the people as stupid, or maybe there was something deeper. Eventually he came back home and, "You know, we should all run away. While we still can."

Satvinder looked at his friend, and then down at his feet. "I've already run away. It's a coward's thing."

The two ate their fish and rice.

"Akhtar, I've been wondering over these last couple of days. You know people in Dhaka. You've got medical connections." He sat pondering before clearing his throat. Then he cleared his throat again. "And you're Muslim. You could find out if Kaling's ok."

"I'm Muslim. I know what you're saying, but your uncle said she was ok."

"You heard the letter. It said to stay away. And I've been having terrible dreams the last few nights. I think something's happened to them." Tears were appearing in his eyes. "I think they're dead. I dream that they're torn in half, legs apart and from the crotch upwards. Not just Kaling. All three of them." He wiped his eyes. "They're dead."

Akhtar, almost whispering, suggested, "Let's get today's work out of the way, then talk tonight. You've some poor sights to see today. You can sit in with me in my clinic this morning, and afterwards I'll show you my arsenic filter. Commit yourself to the work, it'll make things clearer."

He had been in Chak Sahasa for about two weeks, but had never been involved with the patients, those with leprosy, or maybe arsenic poisoning. In fact he hadn't really done anything useful, so this was his chance to get involved, and earn the good will which he had contracted to earn from Baka. She had kept her part, the children were well fed and safe, so now it was his turn.

"Then let's get to work, Doc."

He found it hard walking to work. It was all of about twenty feet, and he was in the clinic. Just through the door from the lobby and he was there, with no time to prepare, and no time to stress. There he was, sitting beside Akhtar at the doctor's desk, with the nurse about to open the clinic doors. He was strangely nervous.

The patients all sat outside on wooden benches which had been pulled around from the side of the clinic. That job was the responsibility of the first two patients, the price for being seen first.

The nurse led in a woman with a young son of about six years old. They were sat down on the chairs in front of the desk, and the nurse then got the notes out for the doctor.

"How are your feet today?" asked the doctor.

The woman was bent over and decrepit, but not very old. Her body was well covered by her sari, but Satvinder could see her hands, which were very blotchy, and one of her palms had a massive, broken wart.

"Not good. I can't feel them, and the big lumps have got worse." As she breathed out a strong smell wafted over to Satvinder, which made him want to retch, but he controlled his stomach. He thought it was a mix of garlic and blue cheese.

She held her legs up, and Akhtar looked carefully at the feet which had become black and white, with many fissured warts covering the heels and insoles. He stood up and took a pointed medical instrument from the work surface behind him, and proceeded to prick the woman's feet. She could not feel the tool sticking into her. He pulled one foot up and pricked an area just above the heel, in the lower insole. He did it several times, but no blood appeared, before lowering her foot to the ground.

In a sympathetic voice, "You have developed gangrene. I'll have to think about what we can do about it."

He wrote some notes. "Your husband has died, I believe. How are you coping with your children?"

She began to cry and then the little boy was sick. Doctor Hussain stepped over to the child, and looked into his mouth. He was dehydrated through diarrhoea and sickness, and his eyes were red, puffy and very sore.

"Has he been tired?"

She nodded. The doctor moved back round to his seat, and the nurse got the bucket and mop out to clean the sick off the floor and then disinfected everything. Akhtar made some notes, before talking to the distraught mother.

"He has the disease, but it's early. Hasn't he been drinking the bottled water?"

She sniffed. "There's not always enough."

The nurse helped her out, and led the next patient in. All the way through the morning the story was the same, some with a slight twist, but all pointed to the same set of symptoms at different stages of development. Satvinder was feeling sick by the end, part by pity for the suffering patients and part by the smell of their breaths. And by the end of that single session, he was able to recognise the malady simply by the smell of garlic. In fact, almost the last patient came in with a broken or badly bruised forearm, and he knew that the man was clear of the disease because his breath smelled of fish. Not a pleasant smell, but much better than the arsenic breath.

The session was drawn to a close with Akhtar making notes and lists of names.

"Are you ok, my old friend?" he asked, "Or have I put you off my work?"

"You're amazing. So much patience, and caring."

"I think you can begin to see the size of my problem." He finalised his notes, and put the list of names aside. "All these people are suffering from poisoning. The trouble is the company will not believe me and they've set me a budget, which I can't meet. They're prepared to cover the cost of treatment for the leprosy, and have supplied the required stuff, but all other treatment should be paid for, or they should go untreated. Of all the people who are treated here, about ninety percent are suffering from the malady, whether it's bloody leprosy or arsenic. So when they come in with a normal problem, it's nearly always at *least* aggravated by the poisoning, and I feel that I can't then charge them. I gave the man with the damaged arm a note to come back when the swelling has gone down, and I'll treat him accordingly, and give him a bill. If he can't pay it, it'll go unpaid. Next time he comes in with illness or injury, I would then have to refuse him treatment, and watch him suffer. Do you, my dear friend, think I can do that?"

Satvinder smiled, but nothing else.

"Anyway, that's my problem. The people's problem is the water. I have a list of names, each of which we need to visit over the next couple of weeks and deliver good water for their children to drink. Washing can be done with untreated tube-well water, but consumption must be only the treated water, or well boiled surface water."

"When you said to that first patient that you needed to work out what to do with her feet, what did you mean?"

Akhtar grumbled under his breath. Then he grinned, "I have to play God. It's the worst part of this job. You see, she's lost her husband. Although she's not really old, she's decrepit and ill, and nobody else would take her on, so her children are totally dependent on her alone. So, I'm thinking to myself that she has gangrene and it'll slowly kill her if she doesn't have the feet cut off, but the feet and hands are totally susceptible to the poisoning, so, are her hands next to go? And even if her hands don't get gangrene, without feet she'll not be able to look after her children, who are four, six, seven and eight. The eight-year-old might be able to fend for the family all by herself, including working to obtain food, but I doubt it. And while the mother is still alive, the children are her problem. Now put yourself in my place. I know, better than anybody else, that these people die of strokes and heart and renal failure very commonly, often before the cancer or gangrene kills them, and it's a pitiful release from their earthly hell."

He looked into Satvinder's eyes.

"I often wonder if they should suffer heart failure, *rather* than go through months, or even years, of pain, depression and degradation." He raised his eyebrows in expectation of a response. "And their young families would then be free to make lives of their own, unburdened by a dependant, dying parent."

Satvinder was ready to respond. He slowly and quietly asked, "Kill them? That's blasphemous. Terrible!"

"When you've watched them suffering for as long as I have, you'll learn to read their future. Some can be helped, treated, and can look forward to some kind of satisfaction from life. Others will never be treated to the point of finding anything but suffering from life. They're the ones who would gladly die, if only they were allowed." Satvinder never spoke, so Akhtar continued. "Suicide is forbidden in all our cultures and religions. Killing is not, especially mercy killing. Thousands of people are killed every day for questionable reasons like punishment, accident, control of law and order, politics and even the killing of infidels and malauns." He chuckled and poked his mate on the shoulder. "That's you."

"Careful!" Satvinder slapped him around the head in fun.

"Anyway, without joking, I have to consider what's best for the lady, *and* her children. Death, or burden. And don't try to judge me. I've limited help that I can give, so what help I do have should go to cases which can merit from the help."

Satvinder put his hands in the air, but this time he did not scream. "It's a hell of a responsibility. How do you sleep at night?"

"Sometimes I don't. But I've never had anybody to talk to, until now, so I hope you won't pre-judge my situation.

And you must believe me: I've never killed a patient before because I'm such a coward. But with some help, I may be able to better serve these poor people."

"Akhtar, Bulu, whoever you are right now, I'll never pre-judge you. I never have, so you can talk openly, without fear."

Akhtar began to laugh. "That was all very formal. It's not like us, is it. Suppose it's because it's real, not like our old discussions about everything outside of our reach. This is right here with us both. And I've had some days to think about it. D'you want to hear about my thoughts?"

"Go for it. But if I tell you to shut the fuck up, respect me."

A big, wide smile donned the doctor's face. "Right, in a nutshell I'm a doctor working for a major international company, Sensar, and you're an unemployed lecturer working for me. We are traditionally men of visions and dreams, ever looking for that challenge of humanity which eludes us, but forever wishing it to come to us. We want to save the World. Now, old mate, with your looks and my bullshit, we *can*. We can save at least a little bit of the World. Still with me?"

"Get to the point!"

"Ok, calm down. Now you've sat in on one of my clinics. You must have recognised some lost causes out of those fifteen patients. Some which would be better off dead."

"Shut the fuck up. I know where this is going, so respect my request."

"Are you really not interested in where I'm coming from? I can't believe you. You walk away from Monpura, a *miraculous* escape, with two lovely orphaned children, and you tell us all about how you cried because you wanted to take *all* the orphans back to Dhaka, but couldn't. What was all that about?"

"You're talking shit. What're you getting at?"

"All the children that you'd love to save and give a life to! That's what!" He then turned his mode to sarcasm. "Or is it just char children?"

They both sat looking at each other. They waited for what seemed a long time before the hush was broken.

"No, it's not just the char children. I'd really love to save all children. But it's just a stupid dream."

That broke the ice, and an air of joy and celebration burst into the clinical surroundings. Akhtar bashed the desk hard with his fist and exclaimed, "Then let's save the children! As many as we can."

Satvinder was still a little bit in the dark, but was beginning to feel part of a team which was about to set out on a journey of exploration and discovery. He just needed to figure out exactly what the team's intent was.

"Which children?"

"Well, there are already children who are being looked after, as a temporary arrangement, by already-overloaded family units. And then there are the others. The ones who are just hanging on. They're the ones who I'm talking about, the ones whose parents are the walking dead. Like the first patient this morning."

"Back to that. The killing of the suffering mother."

"Just listen. She's not able to properly look after her children, even now, let alone with feet missing. The children, as a consequence, are falling into the same black hole that she's in. She said that there aren't always enough bottles of good water for them to consume, so they drink poisoned water. It's only because she's too ill and tired to get the good water, and the children are too young to understand. So as long as she's still there she's contributing towards their possible illness and deaths. And while she's there the children won't go anywhere else. I've been down that route. Even the boy who was in today can probably be saved, by ensuring that no more arsenic gets into his body. He may suffer later in life, but he may not."

Akhtar stood up and walked around the room. "And we can make sure that the orphans don't touch the poisoned water. One problem is that the locals don't entirely believe me about the water. So some of them, especially the ill ones, carry on poisoning their own children. If we can have some orphans who do not get ill at all, like a test case, then they might begin to believe me. What do you think?"

Satvinder frowned with thought.

Akhtar continued. "This isn't a whim. The company has already agreed to pay a minimal amount each month for each orphaned child, just enough to feed them. That'll run an orphanage. It could be *your* orphanage."

"I still haven't agreed to go along with all this. We're still looking at having to kill people, and that's not in my make-up."

Akhtar stood up and went to the window. The day was dry and warm, and the village was alive with people sitting outside doing their chores and preparing food. A white Ford Cortina was parked outside the main godown which was home to the offices.

"Let's take some good water round to the sick lady. We'll see what she thinks of our plan."

They left the building and wandered across to the warehouse to the right of the main one. They entered through the service door. The godown was relatively full of sacked rice grain but in the far corner was a heath-robinson contraption which looked like a stack of water melons, in the half-dark. It was actually a system of round, brown stone water bottles, each about fifteen inches across, standing three high and connected from top to bottom by a plastic hosepipe. Another hose was connected to a tube well, and then hung across a bar above the top bottles. A teenage boy, wearing just a lungi, was pouring water from the hose into one of the top bottles. Satvinder counted nine sets of three.

"Well, old mate, this is it. This is my filter system. The boy puts raw well-water into the top bottle where it filters through beds of iron turnings, and then into the second bottle where it is filtered through charcoal and peat. When it comes into the bottom bottle, it's drinking water, with only a few parts arsenic, well below the hazardous level. Not bad for a country doctor, hey?" He waved to the boy. "I send new samples off every month to Sensar, and one filter set-up seems to last for several months before the sample readings start to deteriorate. With just a load more cast-iron turnings, peat and more charcoal I could create enough water for all the village. The poisoning and illnesses would be gone. And the cholera and sicknesses from the surface water would also be gone. And that bag of iron turnings which I collected from Khulna this week was enough for another filter. It's like gold-dust for us. Well?"

Satvinder was quite impressed. "And it really works? How did you get the right filter materials?"

"Trial and error. I had all nine of these filters going, with different combinations of organic and non-organic materials and oxidants, and sent off many samples to Sensar, and one day the news came back that system number one hundred and forty one was clean, almost no arsenic. I replicated the set-up across all nine sets, and they all came back with good test results." A tear appeared in the corner of his eye. "One day, old chap, I'll have somebody to celebrate with." The loneliness of the doctor was beginning to vent itself. "One day me and you will celebrate. Let's do it when the people come to us and say, 'you're right, we'll not drink the well-water.' We can then celebrate."

It seemed like a real anti-climax: such an achievement, done all by himself, and it was depressing. It felt to Satvinder that his mate had reached his goal, scored, only to find that the final whistle had already been blown. So, he tried to cheer up the proceedings.

"I'll do it." Satvinder held out his right hand, and they shook on it, like a couple of school kids who had just become blood brothers. "I'll do it. I'll look after the children. All of them if I have to."

It worked. Akhtar was suddenly elated. His face had the look of a winner across it, his dark skin shining as his excitement sent him into a sweat. He shouted to the boy, "This is Satvinder. He's my partner!" The boy left the water running, and climbed off from the platform.

"Very pleased to meet you, Sir." He limply shook with his right hand, before getting back to his water duties.

They loaded three water bottles onto a hand cart, and set off. The Ford Cortina had left.

"We're going to see the patient. Leave the talking to the doctor, please."

The villagers looked and pointed at the two partners as they pushed the water across the open centre, and into an alley. The smiling faces of the doctor and his partner spread to the villagers, who smiled back, some saying greetings to them. Perhaps Satvinder was suddenly accepted by the wary sufferers.

The patient's home was not far away from centre.

"Your water bottles. My mate here, will put them over there, and put the empties on the cart. Make sure the children only drink the bottled water. Now, we need to talk."

He sat on the floor with her, the children sitting outside playing in the dust and watched by Satvinder.

"Your gangrene will kill you. My concern is that if we amputate your feet, you will still be ill and you will be house-bound, possibly bed-bound. Removing the gangrene will not make you better. I'm sorry. It'll just remove the gangrene."

She looked out of the shack at her children. The two boys were almost bare, and the two girls in their yellow saris, and the boy who had been sick in the clinic earlier, was smiling and playing. The mother asked, "What can I do? I've nobody to help. Poor Nia is only young and she can't do it all."

82

He sympathetically sighed. "There is something. We're to start an orphanage in the village, especially for children like your own, without anybody to care for them. They could join the orphanage."

She thought hard. "I haven't got money. We've hardly any food: only what our neighbours give as charity." She began to cry. "My poor children."

"There's something you could do. If they were orphans, they could join our orphanage. They would be looked after: fed and cleaned, and could do some work for their keep. Depending on their ages, they could all help to look after each other. And drink *no* poisoned water."

She wiped her eyes with her sari. "I know you're right. Nia gave some well-water to the children, and he was sick today. It wasn't her fault, don't punish her." She kept looking at the children. "I have a pain inside my leg, right in the bone. How long will it last?"

"It's a problem with circulation, and that's killing your feet. You're dying. You won't get better, and all I can do is to prolong it."

They sat quietly for a while. She couldn't stop herself from crying. She snivelled, "You said that we'd discuss my feet later. Now's later."

Akhtar took a deep breath. "I know that you won't give your children away. Your religion wouldn't allow it. But I can offer a way out. Heart failure is usually quite instant, and it's more dignified than a slow death from gangrene. I can induce heart failure, and nobody would know, especially your children. Then they can be taken into the orphanage with the blessing of your people."

She thought carefully, then the crying stopped and she began to smile. "Thank you, doctor. But please, please, never tell my children. They can never know, and if I'm sent to Jehannam for my actions, I'll accept the suffering, to release my poor children. They mustn't get like me. This is the *real* hell."

Akhtar took a small packet out from his pocket and handed it to her. "This will cause heart failure. Before you take it, let me know, and I'll make sure you're cared for and your *children* are quickly taken care of."

"We won't talk about this to *anybody*, will we?" She had an air of contentedness about her, as if she could see the end of the plague. She was to be cured, the only way they knew how. She was going home.

The partners walked back to the godown with the empty bottles, and the boy rushed down to spray the bottles with antiseptic, before putting them back in line to be refilled. Satvinder was becoming a believer.

Over the next few days they delivered many bottles and exchanged them for empties. Some families refused to drink the filtered water, claiming that if Allah wanted to punish them with sickness, then it was his prerogative. The doctor thought that it was because they thought he was a Hindu, and was trying to administer his own brand of poison to the Muslims. There was nothing he could do about their prejudices, apart perhaps from publicising his religion, but he feared then that the majority, the Hindus, would then lose their trust in him. So he had to avoid playing any sort of religious card, and just pray for the children who were being caught in the web of their intolerance.

The farm manager sent the required telexes to his company, and they responded with enthusiasm about the orphanage, and made available a budget which would increase with each child. They were excited that the 'leprosy' was becoming under control and that they could then push forward with the development of the cooperative farming model. They could see their investments returning to profit, and their workforce being once again able-bodied and productive. But, almost as satisfying as the budget, they also added a note at the end. "And the filters?" They were beginning to believe him.

As they returned home on the bus, late afternoon, Christmas Eve, Satvinder had a growing belief that he had turned the corner.

Colin Hodgson

# CHAPTER 7 -- THE FIRST ORPHANS

December 25th 1970, Khulna

A muffled scream floated around the hall like a vulture circling, waiting on its next feed. And naked Kaling looked down from her meat hooks, onto her daughters, her blood dripping from the open wounds across her chest into the faces of her beloved sibling. She whimpered as the soldiers tore the girls apart, ripping them in two from the crotch up to the shoulders, but as the soldiers offered up the wooden steak, the writhing torsos bit into their legs, drawing green blood and smoke.

"No!" Satvinder shot bolt upright, and screamed, "No! Kaling!"

Uncle rushed into the room, and threw water over his face, and he woke.

But his nightmare was not over. He jumped off his bed and hit the wall, then threw the chair out of the door, and suddenly he woke. He stood looking at Uncle who was by then cowering in the corner.

"What….?" He squeezed his eyes closed, then opened them. "I'm sorry."

Uncle got up, and put his hand onto his shoulder. "It was just a dream. We're all right."

Satvinder and Uncle went round to Baka's, puzzled and frightened by the ferocity of the nightmare, but Uncle suggested, "It's James's Christmas day. Let's not mention any dreams."

So the family had a lovely meal in celebration of James, their very own family Christian. Baka had found him a present, a very small but detailed silver cross on a chain, and Ablaa and the boys had made him a carved figure of an angel. The figure was crude, but striking, and almost scary, maybe after the children's vision of a Christian angel. But probably just from the crudity of their carving skills.

"Thank you, Auntie Baka, and everybody." The cheeky little boy had a smile from ear-to-ear. "I didn't think we'd have Christmas this year. Can we say a prayer for my daddy in heaven, and my brothers who might be in heaven? And for Ablaa's family who are in heaven."

They all looked into their laps and said a private prayer. And that was Christmas day, 1970.

On Saturday afternoon, Akhtar and Satvinder called the children into the house.

Akhtar spoke, "Right, we came home early for Christmas. I hope James has enjoyed the festival, but now we must go back to work early, back today, and to work tomorrow. And guess what. Since two of you are not at a school, you can come with us to Chak Sahasa, and do some work, and join the school there. James and Ablaa, what do you think? Back here for weekends."

They looked at each other, then at Akhtar and then both shot forward to cuddle their dad. They approved.

"You'd better be right, Bulu." Baka looked harshly at him. He was always Bulu when he was naughty. "You'd *better* be right." She was referring to the leprosy, of course.

The children nervously held tightly onto Satvinder all the way to the bus, and for all the time on it. They were still nervous country folk, but that day Satvinder also felt a nervous twinge. As the bus driver stopped for them to disembark, a new mood moved into the bus.

"Joy Bangla! Joy Bangla!" shouted several of the passengers. "Allah be with you!"

Nationalistic, cessationalistic, whatever, but the mood was spreading. They tried to forget about it as they walked through the sunny evening towards the village. The children quickly relaxed, finding some sticks, and poking around in the hedges searching for snakes.

"That frightened me a little," admitted Satvinder. "Was it aimed at me and James?"

His friend snapped, "Don't be daft. They don't even know your religion. It could've been aimed at me and Ablaa just as easy. Or just the excitement of the time."

It did not really help him, and even Akhtar was uneasy about it. Several of the villages in the Khulna division were home to Hindus, and Chak Sahasa was known to be. But the villages in the division had all heavily supported the Awami League in defiance of the Pakistani government, and particularly the Hindus had come out in force in favour of the League. They were worrying unnecessarily.

Suddenly a horn was blowing. The white Ford Cortina was throwing up dust as it approached them, driving towards the village and close behind were two army trucks. They all climbed through a gap in the hedge to let the vehicles pass.

As they arrived in the village the trucks were being loaded with sacks of rice. A chain of village folk passed the sacks along the line, supervised by four soldiers, and they soon filled both trucks which then drove off down the lane. Once they had gone, the villagers emerged from their homes to join the loaders, and they all discussed the intrusion. Our group went straight into the clinic. Ablaa sat with her little brother at the window, and wondered what all the excitement was about.

"What do you think's going on?" asked Satvinder.

In response Akhtar raised his eyebrows and said, "That should be going to the Philippines, or down the south to feed the flood victims. Don't know." He lowered his voice. "We've a stash put aside in the old village. You remember the broken down godown which I pointed out, in there. There's no road access to there. That's for the village, as part of the cooperative agreement."

The nurse had made a small meal for the weary travellers, and once they had eaten, the two men sat and chatted, while the children went out exploring their new surroundings. With a little daylight left, Akhtar decided to walk over to the godown to speak to the manager. He took Satvinder with him. The white Cortina was still parked outside, with the driver waiting.

"This is Akhtar, and his new assistant, Satvinder." The manager made the introductions. The fifty-year-old stranger, tall and distinguished with a bushy moustache and dressed in a dark western-style suit, shook both men's hands tightly and heartily. He clearly was not a Bangle. "And this is Field Marshall Gnuru, a distinguished leader, formerly of the Indian Army under British rule. He has a lot of influence."

They all sat down around the desk.

"I hope we're not interrupting. We just wondered what the army were doing with our grain." Akhtar nodded his head.

The Field Marshall answered. "Thank you for your concern, but it's *our* grain. The company's. And we're just looking after our own interests. The grain is going to the Jessore Cantonment, and it's an offer of friendship."

Satvinder woke up. "Protection money?"

"If that's what you wish to call it. But, as a geologist from Jessore, you should know that it's the *East* Pakistan Rifles who reside there, *not* the West Pakistanis." He thought. "There's a lot of troop and equipment movement into East Pakistan at present, from the West, and it's not looking good for our position here. We need to buy your Hindu village some protection, or at least some time."

"And in the process you're alienating us from the rest of the East Bengal people. Just like the Biharis have been by *their* support for the West."

Akhtar stood up. "He's right. You could be signing our death sentences. Why've you done this?"

90

The Field Marshall dropped his head. "I'm following orders from our inner court. I note your objections." He thought carefully. "Yahya Khan's generals are scheming to remove the Awami League. There's big trouble ahead, and already I've heard reports of Biharis being slaughtered in their dozens in the cities across East Pakistan. Some suggest that the Freedom Fighters have refused to protect them. And so have the police."

Akhtar slammed his fist on the desk. "And *now* you're grouping *us* with the Bihari! We're our own minority and are just as much at the mercy of the Bihari as we are the Pakistani military. You've stuck us right in the middle of the ruck!"

"Please calm down. Things are changing very quickly, and had we known yesterday what we know today, we may have handled it differently. But all that aside, the army would have taken the grain if we hadn't given it to them. And I'll stress again, it's the East Pakistan Rifles who took the grain, not the West. They're our own countrymen and when the shit hits the fan, they'll be on the same side as us. And, again, they would've taken it anyway, whatever our objections." He looked into Satvinder's face. "I think you'll soon understand that they're *our* army."

A deathly silence fell about the group. The Field Marshall was privy to information through his company headquarters. "I received a telex this morning from my court. I've been given leave to act in the best interests of the company in any which way I need to."

The manager piped up, held both hands upside-down and, "And?"

"The relief operations for the flood victims tell a tale of desperation and pending civil war. West Pakistan is stocking up their larder, before their food supplies are reduced, or cut off. The East feeds the West. It's the West's market garden. Now, they, and the Americans, know something which they're keeping from the rest of the World, because they're preparing for famine in the West. Our inner court believes the famine will be caused by civil war in the East. And it's not far away."

The manager asked, "Why, old chap, do they think civil war is coming, and what about the food in the West?"

"The Americans are pally with West Pakistan because they need their presence in Asia. With the Russians being so pally with the Indians, the Yanks need East and West Pakistan to remain under the control of Lahore, and Yahya Khan. Now, our own intelligence has informed us that a shipment of over one hundred thousand tons of grain was destined for Chittagong, as flood relief, and it's been redirected into *West* Pakistan. They've taken the flood relief from the mouths of the starving in the delta, with the American's approval, and delivered it to the military rulers in Lahore. They're expecting a hard time ahead."

"Is this just rumour?" asked the manager.

"May be, but probably not. Our own intelligence is probably better than that of the Yanks. We even have intelligence inside the Yank's intelligence. If I was a betting man, I'd put money on it being accurate."

Satvinder was becoming puzzled by the man's openness with a bunch of relative strangers. "Why're you telling us this? We could use this information in any what way we choose."

"But you won't. My good manager, here, has told us what he knows about you two, the rest we found out ourselves. Doctor Hussain is a Muslim, married to a Hindu, with two young boys who are with their mother, Baka, in Khulna. He tried to change his name when he fell in love with the Hindu girl," he had a chuckle, "but he got it wrong. Despite being a bit of an idiot, he has become a well respected employee of Sensar Pharmaceuticals. They don't want to lose him. His work here has been exemplary and he is a rare commodity."

Akhtar blushed with pride.

"Now you, Satvinder, are a corpse. The walking dead. But that's good. If you weren't the walking dead, you'd be *really* dead. The army, in cooperation with the police, arrested two lecturers a couple of weeks back from the university, but the third on the list was drowned in the floods: that's you. The other two have disappeared into the Dhaka Cantonment, and I must add, also presumed dead. You had a lucky escape. We like your spirit, and your charitable disposition: quite rare around here. I understand from our sources that you learned some of that asset from two adopted children. Where are they now?"

In answer, he looked out of the office window towards the doors. Then, "Are you threatening us?"

"Of course not. We're all in this together. I've a job to do out here, and you three are going to help me pull it off. I know you can do it."

But poor Satvinder's suspicions were still aroused. "You've just dropped me in it with this manager. He's no allegiance to us, he's almost a Bihari. Why shouldn't he do what the other Biharis wanted to do to me in Dhaka?"

"Fair question. There're several reasons. For starters, if he ever spoke to the Pakistanis about our company business, I'd kill him. You don't need to know the other reasons."

An uncomfortable silence fell. The Field Marshall studied the faces of the other three men.

Satvinder suddenly realised how dark it was outside. "I need to check the kids."

He went outside and looked around, but most of the villagers were indoors. Then the kids ran out of a shack beside the clinic: they had been with the nurse. "Dad. What're you doing?" asked James.

"We've a meeting going on at the moment so you can go indoors and wait. We shouldn't be long." He returned to the office.

"Ah, Satvinder, we've been waiting for you. Didn't want you to miss anything."

He sat down beside Akhtar. The Field Marshall heralded an overpowering presence, instantly taking control of the group and leading by exuberance.

"Now, getting down to the nitty-gritty, things are not good for our company's presence in East Pakistan. Our influence will prevent the military from killing you lot for a while, but when the shit hits, control will be lost. And many of you are minorities, and will be as the Jews were to the Germans. I hope I'm not frightening you. Anyway, this pile of grub which you jealously watch over, well it's stuck here. We can't get it out of the country for various reasons, and we don't want the Pakistani Military to have it. What should we do with it?" He scanned the faces. "Akhtar. You first."

He grinned. "Give it to the poor. Eat it before it gets taken."

"Good idea. Satvinder, now you."

"Well, I've built up both fond and frightening memories of the Chars, and now they're starving and diseased. We could deliver the whole lot to the flood stricken areas."

"That's brilliant! It takes in both feeding the poor and helping the stricken. We're getting somewhere." He looked to his manager.

The manager stood up. "We could do what's been suggested, but add some details. The whole world could see how benevolent the company is, by getting your news crews to cover the company's delivery of the aid. The loss of the grain would be compensated by a massive, World-wide publicity campaign. Not international aid, not UNICEF nor Red Cross, but the benevolence of the BanChi World Produce Company."

The Field Marshall was getting exited. "Love it all! *The Americans haven't delivered what they promised, but BanChi have.*' I can see the headlines. Millions of pounds worth of advertising, for the cost of thirty thousand tons of grain. And everybody's happy."

Akhtar reminded, "Apart from the Pakistani Army."

Akhtar and Satvinder were dragging along behind. They felt like they were sitting around the desk at a board meeting, looking down at the World and playing games with the people, like ancient Greek Gods peering over the edge of the clouds at their board-game: who's winning now? The doctor asked, "Is this the end of the village?"

The big man huffed, "It's got leprosy, and it'll have no grain. And you're a minority, living here at the discretion of the Muslims, and you won't, as a village, survive a bloody war. Now, we've had some good brainstorming here tonight, we'll continue tomorrow. I've got some exciting telexes to send."

"One thing," squeaked Satvinder. "You know everything about us, from your sources." He stopped and thought hard. "Am I married?"

The Field Marshall frowned, "You know you are. Why ask?"

"No, am I *still* married? Do I still have a wife and children?"

The big man was struggling to answer, but, "Of course. They live in the Sakharibazar, staying with your uncle, and helping in the shop and the workshop. The girls are back at school. They're all ok." He looked down at a pad and made some notes as the boys left the office. Satvinder had a relieved smile on his face.

The next day came too quickly for the tired children, who had slept on the floor in the living room of the clinic. But James was grown up enough to wake the others. "Come on, Dad. You've got work."

So they all got themselves sorted out, and sat around the small table to eat the lentil soup which the nurse had prepared.

Ablaa asked, "What will we do today? Will we see the orphans in the orphanage?" The pretty girl leaned sideways and kissed her daddy on the cheek. "Will we?"

The men weren't too sure. Although they had gone back to work to cover for the Friday that they had off, it was Sunday, and no clinic, so it was decided to go about sorting some premises out, hoping to have something available before they actually received any of the poor children. But at the back of their minds were the Field Marshall and the words of wisdom which he had put over the night before.

"I had a good night's sleep." Satvinder was happier. "I didn't have the nightmares. I'm so pleased that Kaling and the girls are ok, with Uncle." He pulled his other two children over and they cuddled, Ablaa and James giggling and wriggling. "We'll *all* be together one day."

The children went outside in the sun, and played with a lizard.

Akhtar had listened to the radio before getting out of bed. "A report said that just outside of Sylhat there was a clash between some Muslims and some Hindus. Only four men were killed, but the army Captain, a Bengali, refused to shoot-to-kill at the demonstrators, and he has been removed from his command. And Khan is going to Dhaka to meet with Rahman. It's a bloody mixed message we're getting right now."

They walked over towards the office, past the white Cortina which was still there. The driver was not in his seat.

"Good morning, men!" roared Field Marshall Gnuru. "Off to the temple?"

"No. We don't often go." Akhtar sat down and looked to the manager. "We need some premises for the orphanage. I think we need them urgently."

Gnuru joked, "Got some kids coming?"

"Sort of. One of my patients is on her death bed, and some more will soon follow."

"But our conversation last night: is there a point?"

"You have a lot of respect for us, you claimed last night. So you should know that we won't just give up because of the rumours that you've cast. The children will still be orphans, and there'll be even more if you're right in your predictions. We've just got to carry on with our lives."

The Field Marshall quietened down. "Sorry. Yes, suppose you must get on with it." He looked sympathetically at Akhtar. "You could worry about yourself and your family. Run away. While the going's good, just get out of it all."

That was not the first time running away had cropped up over recent weeks. "Where to? We've touched on this already. Where could we go?"

Satvinder looked on with interest.

"You could go to the Anglia region, near Kolkata. They need a field doctor to work with the slum diseases. You'd be perfect."

"What about the others?"

"Your family could go. I'd arrange your permits if you want to go."

He looked hard at his good friend, and then back at the Field Marshall. "I couldn't leave my friends and work."

"Akhtar." Satvinder punched him on the arm. "You must consider it. It'd get you away from the inevitable. And when the time's right we could meet you there."

The big man boomed, "*All* go! I can get you all work at the Anglia Fort or in the company's factories. I could get you all over there. Get from Khulna to Kolkata, and you're almost there."

They both hesitated, not knowing why. Then Satvinder suggested, "Get Kaling and the girls from Dhaka and I'm up for it. We've got passports."

The booming Field Marshall never flinched.

There was a knock on the door. It was Ablaa. The manager let her in.

"Daddy, the nurse asked if we could get Uncle Akhtar. A girl is in the clinic."

Akhtar and Satvinder made their apologies and followed Ablaa across to the clinic where a girl nervously waited. The little eight-year-old was the oldest daughter of the doctor's mercy-killing patient. "Mummy's dead." She was blunt, and monotoned, and looked so frightened. Ablaa put her arm around her shoulders and sat her down while the doctor went, alone, to check the mother.

Ablaa, looking at James, spoke to the little girl. "We're orphans as well. We'll help you." The girl just stared into space. "You can live at the orphanage." But the girl never responded.

Satvinder suddenly realised the urgency of finding some premises, quickly, but he kept thinking of Kaling, and how they could get away, to India. He was becoming confused about his role in life, a husband or a community worker. But the present job-in-hand was the newly orphaned children. He decided to put the evidence in front of the manager, so he walked with the little orphan girl, James and Ablaa to the manager's office.

"Come in Satvinder, me old mate. Who's this little one?" He pulled a chair out for the girl.

"She's the first of the orphans. Her younger brothers and a sister are on their way, when Akhtar returns. These four children need the orphanage as of now."

The manager looked to the Field Marshall, who just nodded, and so he answered. "Well, there've been a few houses vacated during the course of the disease, and I had planned on dismantling some of them for the materials, to make a larger building to house the children. It would be good to be placed around to the right of here, close to the school. Would that be ok for yourself and the doctor?"

Hope was returning, and Satvinder began to smile. He had even been accepted into the company, discussing business, even without the boss, Akhtar, present.

"Yes, that'd be fantastic. Thank you."

The Field Marshall bellowed, "So I take it you'll not be running away? Not yet?"

He sighed, "Done that. You know what, Satvinder's well dead and gone. I'm sure Kaling and the girls could now safely come here, and make that new life."

Gnuru replied very coolly, "Never lose your dreams, but never lose sight of reality. I've seen many a dead dreamer. Best of luck, young man." He passed one of his business cards to Satvinder, stood up and shook the hands of both men, and then went out to the car, where his driver waited.

Over the next few days the village centre came alive with builders. As some of the unoccupied homes were dismantled by the volunteers, the four new orphans slept on the floor of one of the clinic rooms, where James and Ablaa fussed over them like a couple of old nannies. They were loving their new roles, both being fully qualified to understand the stress and despair that the four children were suffering. Ablaa kept asking different people what would have happened to the children if the orphanage had not been built, but they all just raised their hands in ignorance. She wondered what had happened to the previous orphans, but they also just raised their hands in ignorance. It was a common answer to the many questions that the young teenager put to the locals as she longed to learn about *everything*. And she was turning into the driving force that was needed. Satvinder's and Akhtar's dreams were suddenly creeping into the real World, orchestrated by their thirteen year old charge hand from Monpura. "My mummy made us work at *everything*. She said we will then survive."

The new building, wooden frames tied together with jute, and with a corrugated iron roof, sprung up from nowhere, the chief carpenter acquiring a new assistant, the 'perfectly formed' Ablaa. She got just about everywhere. And after just six days, the new thatched-walled orphanage was complete. Six rooms in a terrace, not a pretty picture, but wind-and-rain-tight, and a home. Each room was big enough to sleep four children.

Akhtar stood with Satvinder, admiring the new home.

"It's gone up very quickly," sighed Akhtar so proudly. "We should get the volunteers together to celebrate."

That evening there was a party in the village square, and many people attended. Food was plentiful, much of it supplied by the company, and much being gifted by the local people in appreciation of the communal effort. It was the first piece of goods news that had been experienced in the village for a long time: they were beginning to help themselves and each other. But as the carpenter and the blacksmith raised a cheer of 'Joy Bangla' many villagers remained silent. They knew that many of their friends were at home in their huts, too ill to attend. And they knew that the army would be calling for more supplies over the coming weeks.

Satvinder remained hopeful. "I think that old soldier, Gnuru, was telling me something about Kaling and my girls." He grinned. "I wonder if they'd come and join me here."

Akhtar never said a word.

# CHAPTER 8 -- SNAKES AREN'T ALL BAD

January, 1971

The four orphaned children settled into their new home, and as they did they began the rest of their lives without their mother. They were more fortunate than many orphans in East Pakistan, and were fed and loved. Satvinder and his two children, along with the doctor, gave them a new life. But the charitable air was spreading. It was contagious and the local people were susceptible to its draw. As five more children became orphaned after the diseased, dying parents mysteriously developed heart failure, the people began leaving food for the children in a meat safe which had strangely appeared outside the orphanage. And Akhtar was advised by his water treatment man that he was running out of filtered water. The people were suddenly believing in their doctor, and even the Muslims were collecting the safe water for their children.

"Doctor," stressed the carpenter, "We need to make more clean water. We should *all* drink the filtered water, not just the children."

And so, at the turn of the year, in January nineteen seventy one, the village took on a new belief in Doctor Akhtar Hussain and his assistant Satvinder. And right up there at the front line, Ablaa and James took it upon themselves to push the dreams even further into the realms of reality and belief. They bullied the manager to source the charcoal and cast-iron turnings which formed part of the filter systems and the water filtration banks were tripled in number. By mid-January they were producing enough safe water to serve the whole community. It was the dawn of a new era.

But things were changing all around in that troubled land.

"Look!" shouted James. "Look what's coming!"

Almost every able-bodied man, woman and child went outside into the mid-day sun to see what James was shouting about. A white Ford Cortina was bumping its way up the dusty lane followed by a Land Rover. They were closely followed by three army trucks.

"Look, Dad! They're coming!" James ran into the clinic to fetch his dad and sister. "Quick, they're coming!"

The children were excited, but the adults not. The army, again. Field Marshall Gnuru's driver parked away from the godowns, in front of the clinic.

Gnuru boomed, "Morning men! Hope everything's well!" He grinned at Akhtar, who nervously smiled back. "Our friends have returned for some more rice. I'll introduce you to the sergeant." He walked over to the three trucks which had been reversed to the front of the godowns. The four men in the Land Rover hurriedly put their tripod and camera together, and began rolling. They were an Australian newsgroup who had recently been filming in Vietnam, and were impatient to get the area, the people and the army personnel onto the newsreels. "Sergeant Haq. This is our very own Doctor Hussain, who has isolated the cause of the leprosy."

The very dark-faced sergeant, sporting a bushy moustache, saluted the doctor. "Sir, my congratulations on your success. We'll not keep you for very long." He was well spoken and a Bengali. "We're from the Jessore Cantonment, the area headquarters of the East Pakistan Rifles. Your people must relax. We are here as friends and protectors."

The manager emerged from one of the godowns as the four soldiers from each truck lined up in front of the sergeant. They were all armed.

Gnuru roared, "My manager will arrange some loaders, and you can then get away. The other lorries will be here soon." He waved his hand at the manager, who responded like a sheepdog. "And while your soldiers keep guard, we'll pop inside."

The villagers were wary of the visitors, but a handful stepped forward to load the lorries. The sooner they were gone, the better.

Inside the office, the Field Marshall relaxed. "This is Akhtar's assistant, Satvinder. He is a charity worker, I think. He also seems to be very suspicious of you."

Straight in there, with both feet. Satvinder raised his eyebrows, wondering how to respond, but the sergeant got him out of a hole.

"Sir, sorry, Satvinder, we're all on the same side. Please relax."

"The same side of what? I'm lost."

"Well, the same side of life. We're here to do some business, on behalf of the people of East Pakistan. We're all Bengalis, as most of the East Pakistan Rifles are, and we're here to do what's right for the people of our proud country. And the Field Marshall assures us that his staff, including yourselves, are reliable, intelligent, and Bengali." He had overlooked the manager's nationality.

A brief moment of silence allowed Satvinder to look into Akhtar's eyes and mind, and he was equally confused. The two friends seemed to have been transported into a different World, full of intrigue and probably danger. He decided to break the ice.

"*What* are you dragging us into?"

"Straight to the point, thank you." The sergeant stood up to make his confession. "We're here to drop off some gear, and to collect some grain for the fight ahead. Did you know that independence is only around the corner? No? Well, the fight will soon be out in the open, and the West knows, as we all know. So, as they prepare to break the back of the Awami League, we prepare to stop them." He looked through the windows, as if to make sure they were alone. "We're placing a lot of equipment here for you. We have stone water bottles, iron turnings and charcoal for the filters, as per your order. They were donated by a group of companies based in Jessore. I'm sure you'll include them in your prayers. The news crew will be welcome to film as we make the humanitarian delivery for these poor leprosy sufferers. And while you, Akhtar, show them the filter systems and keep them occupied, we'll make our other drops in the other godown."

The Field Marshall grinned as he ordered the sergeant to sit down. He turned to Akhtar and Satvinder. "I realise that the sergeant hasn't been straight to the point, so I'll tell you that we're carrying out some work on behalf of Colonel Osmany, the Awami security committee, and the business is that of building an armed force in readiness. We're storing a veritable arsenal of rifles and ammunition in these godowns. I'm telling you this because you're going to be responsible, along with the rest of the company, for the safe keeping of the equipment. Understand?"

The sergeant left the office and went out to the manager to supervise the delivery of the filtration equipment.

"Akhtar, once the delivery is made in here, you can take the news crew to the filter plant, and keep them busy. We'll sort out the guns in *this* warehouse."

The two friends were shell-shocked. They were suddenly in the middle of the civil strife.

The main doors opened, and the three trucks reversed in. The Field Marshall never took his eyes off the manager.

"Why?" asked Akhtar.

"Because you were in the right place at the right time." The Field Marshall grinned. "Maybe the wrong place, but who knows until it all blows up. A para-military force is being built by Colonel Osmany from the Awami's youth section, and from the Ansars who are trained by the police, and from the Mujahibs trained by the army. These guns will be one day used by Osmany's forces, the Mukti Fauj." He frowned deeply. "I fear for all these millions of people, Satvinder. It's still not too late for you to run away."

He responded with a question. "Sir, why're you doing this? Your heart doesn't seem to be in it, at least, not all the way."

The ageing war monger looked down at his fiddling fingers. "Orders. We're all responsible to somebody. I'm responsible to my court." He looked up, and back at the manager. "Akhtar, you need to show the news crew your wonderful filters." He then whispered, "The guns need to come off."

Akhtar and the manager left Satvinder with the Field Marshall.

The booming voice dropped, and he spoke in confidence. "Satvinder. I've been struggling to tell you something." He again looked down at his fingers. "Well, here goes. I have some news from Dhaka. I didn't want to tell you until I knew for certain." An uneasy pause. "Your wife is dead. So are your children." He had tears in his eyes as he fiddled with his suit jacket.

Poor Satvinder just sat motionless and the colour almost drained from his dark face. He caught his breath. "No, Uncle would've let me know."

"Your uncle doesn't know. You mustn't blame him." The officer had told many a family of the loss of their loved ones, and he never found it to get any easier.

"But....." His eyes were filling up. "But how do you know? If Uncle doesn't.... how?"

"I just know. That's all *you* need to know. But they've gone. I'm so sorry, Satvinder."

He looked at the Field Marshall who was trying to make it easier for him. "I don't believe you. Prove it." He was clutching at straws. "How? Uncle would've written." Momentarily the tears abated, and the anger began to boil. "You're lying!"

Gnuru placed his hand on Satvinder's shoulder, but it was banged off. He almost whispered, "Sorry, but you'll have to believe me. They've gone."

"No, prove it! It's all part of this fucking war. You're trying to trap us in your game! You're lying!"

The Field Marshall took a massive breath. "Ok, I'll tell you what I know." He waited for Satvinder to wipe his tears and nose. "Your uncle gave Kaling some money to go to Kolkata, away from the constant threat, and she was to let you and him know when she got there, so you could follow. He hasn't heard anything, and is still waiting. But what he doesn't know, on their way to the terminal, they ran into some street trouble, and the police reported to our agent that Kaling and your daughters accepted a lift from the army group. The police were later called to three bodies which had been found. They were Kaling and the girls."

Reality hit poor Satvinder. He was unable to speak, just cry, as the fatherly figure of the old-timer took him onto his shoulder. He held him there for several minutes, before Satvinder pushed himself away. "I somehow knew. I had dreams, nightmares. They were raped and killed. I saw it in my dreams." He sat upright and wiped his face. "How can I tell James and Ablaa? How? I'll have to work it out. Should I tell them they were raped?"

"You don't know that they were. You just had nightmares."

He just shook his head. "Why else would they take them? For a fucking picnic?" He looked hard into Gnuru's eyes. "Tell me if they *weren't* gang raped and tortured."

The Field Marshall never flinched, and never answered.

Distraught, confused and angry, Satvinder left the office and the godown, and amidst a buzz of curiosity and concern he crossed the village centre, and walked slowly towards the lane.

Field Marshall Gnuru covertly found Ablaa and asked her to keep a special eye on her father so she grabbed James and they set off behind him, stalking him from a distance. He walked very slowly out of the village, kicking stones in rage, and then shaking his head in confusion, but he never looked back. The villagers watched him until he was out of site.

Eventually he found a bank to sit down on, and he watched some workers in the field. But it didn't occupy his mind for very long and he put his head in his hands and cried hysterically, and the field workers, aware that he was there and very stressed, politely carried on with their work.

"Daddy." A whisper came from behind. It was Ablaa, with James. "Can we cuddle you?"

They sat one each side of him, and pulled themselves into his chest and shared his grief, crying with him without even knowing why. Nothing was said for a very long time.

James stirred. The army trucks were coming up the lane. As they approached, the leading truck's door opened, and Sergeant Haq leaned out and saluted the mourners, quietly stating 'Joy Bangla' as they passed.

"Are they bad soldiers, Daddy?" asked James.

Dad wiped his face on his shirt sleeve, and smiled. "I don't think so. They're *our* soldiers."

"Then why're you crying? Did they hurt you?" The little boy pulled himself around into his dad's face. "If they've hurt you, they've hurt us."

Satvinder put his forrid on James's and pulled Ablaa closer. He sadly whispered, "There are different types of soldiers. The *other* type have hurt me." He paused for thought. "The other type have killed Kaling and your sisters. There,

I've said it. Didn't think I'd be able to." The crying started up again, but this time the children knew why.

Their peace was again disturbed when four very large lorries approached them, heading towards the village. They were large enough to carry all the grain from the stores, and the sides were sign-written with 'BanChi Flood Relief'. It was the next stage in Gnuru's plan. And as the lorries passed, they buried their faces under Dad's shirt to avoid the dust.

Once the lorries had gone Ablaa asked, "Are they taking food to Monpura?"

"Yes, some of them must be starving by now."

"Then it's a good job the army didn't take it all. Is that what you mean 'different types'?"

"Not exactly."

James pointed. "Look, Daddy, a snake. That's a poisonous one." They moved along the bank to give it respect. "Snakes aren't all bad, you know. If you leave them alone and don't stand on them, they just get on with their own lives."

"It's a shame that some humans can't behave the same."

Ablaa joined in. "Mummy used to say that people are easy to lead, and easy to manipulate, and even easier to kill." She frowned. "She said, only when nobody else was listening of course, that if you want to kill somebody you just need religion. And it comes in many forms like Islam, Christianity, Hindu and money. She said that with these tools in your tool bag you just need to lead, then manipulate, then get the manipulated to do your killing for you. It's that easy. She was talking about the money-lenders on Monpura. They were evil."

Satvinder grinned at James. "The meaning of life, as handed down by Kolala Nouka." They both chuckled.

Ablaa gently whispered, "I know you're laughing. That's good." The snake had moved away. "The soldiers today are Bengali soldiers. They protect the borders with India. What soldiers are in Dhaka?"

"Hmm, I know what you're getting at. The Dhaka Cantonment has Pakistani soldiers." They all thought for a while. He whispered, "They killed my family. The Pakistani soldiers."

"So, Daddy, they're our enemy. They'll never be brought to justice, so they're our enemy. They killed our family." Another silence fell as they all chewed over the ideas. "We were thrown together by fate, escapees from the storm. And as we've grown to love each other, we must learn to stay that way, even when our enemies are at their most threatening." The thirteen year old adult who had no history of education was extremely educated. She learned from life, not books. "So those guns, which they hid in our godowns, are there to eventually kill our enemy, the West Pakistani army. They killed our family, so we'll kill them."

The mood had strayed from mourning and anger, to one of foreboding. Dad was becoming concerned.

"Should we be talking like this? Especially in front of James."

James chipped, "I'm all right. I don't tell anything to anybody. My dad didn't tell you I'm Christian until he got to know you. And he taught me."

"Ok, we can talk. For starters, who else saw the guns?"

Ablaa was adamant, "Nobody. When that old soldier chap told me about you being sad, I saw them in the store. Nobody else saw them."

"And let's keep it that way."

She thought for a bit and then asked him. "Did the Pak soldiers *shoot* our family?"

His face dropped a little, and frowned, "Yes, they shot them."

"Then one day we'll shoot them back. We'll work with the East Pakistan Rifles to get them out from our land

and we'll be free." She had a puff in her chest which was blowing up like a cobra's neck.

"I think you need to slow down. Let's take one step at a time, and try to stay alive. And maybe we should allow the past to mellow into the past. Try to move forward."

"But Daddy, the past is never dead. In fact it's not even past." She began to giggle. "My mummy taught me lots. *She'll* never be past."

Somehow, the children had gotten right into Satvinder's head, and relieved him of much of the pain from his losses. He suddenly realised, "I've been mourning for a few weeks now. I already knew they were dead. Weird."

The three slowly walked back towards the village.

The village of Chak Sahasa had become, quite involuntarily, part of the fight for cessation from the rule of West Pakistan. They were harbouring arms and munitions for the Mukti Fauj, who was awaiting the call for the rise against the oppressors from the West. They had all become rebels against the state.

But Ablaa just needed to know. "Did they kill them because they're Hindu?"

Poor Satvinder didn't really want to know, so he replied, "Maybe, maybe because they were at the street trouble." He knew deep down that it was likely to be the case, but he was concerned at the young girl's religious beliefs, even though they'd become close. He felt that he needed to know how she felt, so, "If it turned out that it was because they were Hindu, what of it? How would you feel, as you're Muslim?"

She puffed her chest out. "Don't even believe that I would ever go against you or James. I would change my religion if I had to, to keep us together. I might do it anyway. If it was because of their religion, then I'm ashamed of mine. Utterly ashamed."

Satvinder looked forward to the village, which was becoming closer. He was running out of quality time with his children. "Before we get back and have to stop talking about these things, I remember asking you on Monpura what we should do." Despite the overpowering feeling of grief, he grinned. "You gave me a lecture."

The perfectly formed Ablaa looked up at him and grinned with him. "And if you're asking me now, I'd answer the same. You must do the right thing, and God won't help you." She stopped to think. "Throughout the history of East Pakistan the minorities have been persecuted. I wonder what will change when the democracy arrives, if it ever does. I don't think much will change."

"But if you could go a step further, and actually advise me, without God's help, then what would you advise me now?"

A thirteen year old advisor on the subject of life. A clean, un-tainted mind, in-control and brilliant. She spelled it out. "The two wings of Pakistan are an Islamic state. They are, and I believe they always will be, governed by the forces, constraints and intolerance of religion. Now when I was in Khulna I heard a report on the radio from Lahore. The reporter spoke about Bhutto justifying democracy in this Islamic state. He said that *'Islam does not oppose the betterment of the lot of village folk, urban people, peasants and workers.'* He never mentioned the lot of the Hindu, nor the Christian, nor the Jainist." She breathed deeply. "Whatever happens over the past elections, the promises of democracy, or over the fight for independence, you and James will never be part of the victory celebrations. We should all run away, before it's too late."

That profound piece of juvenile advice left Satvinder reeling. But the loss of his beloved wife and children certainly had a silver lining, if one can be so heartless, in that he was free to run away without the guilt of desertion. But where to? Although he had a passport, he could not leave without the two children. Like it or not, he was their pledged father, never

111

to desert them, so where could they all go? There was a lot of dirt and dust floating around his feet and head.

The village centre was still buzzing when they arrived back. The lorries had just about been loaded, every grain being swept up from the floor before the main doors were closed and locked, and the news reels continued to run. The reporters were to accompany the lorries to Khulna where they would be unloaded and dispatched to the distribution centres by boat. One can only guess at how much actually reached the starving farmers and fishermen.

"That's it," boomed the Field Marshall towards Satvinder. "The news men should get plenty to show the World about our humanitarian side, the benevolent BanChi. All good p.r. old chap." He approached him and the children, and shook him by the hand. "You know what, old chap, strength comes from within, but survival often comes from an organised withdrawal. It's not always called running away. Let's keep in touch."

"Are you leaving now? I needed to ask you something."

Gnuru nodded his head, and led the three of them into the office. He closed the door. "What can I do for you?"

"We've been thinking about our future here. We want to get away. This isn't our home."

Gnuru nodded his head and smiled. "You could go back to the southern Chars. Reclaim your patches of land."

"Thank you, but we need to go somewhere where we can live together, without persecution. Is there anywhere?"

"Yes, down near Kolkata, the Anglia region. We've already spoken about it, about the factories and work. You have one of my cards."

"But we don't all have passports. You know our relationships, so how could we get into India?"

The old war-horse thought carefully. "I could possibly get you some work permits, you and Akhtar. But that could take a bit of time, if you can wait."

It was an offer of hope. The men heartily shook hands, and then the lorries, the news crew and the Cortina blew some dust as they trundled down the lane to the Khulna Road.

Colin Hodgson

# CHAPTER 9 -- THE GEOLOGIST FROM JESSORE

As they wiled the evening away Satvinder shared his terrible news with his life-long friend. Strange, but he had kind of conditioned himself in readiness through his dreams, and a macabre sense of relief set about him in that he at last knew what had happened to his family. His mind's natural barriers went up and the visions of the unimaginable terror and pain which they must have suffered were finally put into storage. Akhtar had had no such preparation, and took the news very badly. Like Ablaa he seemed to know that the killings were sectarian, and it added to his concerns for the safety of his Hindu family back in Khulna. And, like Ablaa, it filled him with shame. He told Satvinder, "When you go to India, I want to come with you, with my family. The time's coming for us to run."

Satvinder looked at Ablaa. "Gnuru made a good point. He suggested that an organised withdrawal is the route to survival, rather than running away." They all agreed that panic was not the safest policy.

The week passed much the same as the other weeks had passed, and by the end of it they had fourteen orphans in their care, all under the age of ten. One of the first major headaches was the organising of their days, keeping them occupied and from fighting over their religious roots. Ablaa discovered that, while the school was open two days a week, the five Muslim children had never been. The teacher was Hindu, came in from Dumuria just for the lessons and as she had refused to teach Muslims, the children's parents had also refused them to be taught by a Hindu. The first signs of the

115

gaping cracks in that oh-so tolerant village community had begun to manifest themselves.

By Friday, going-home day for the doctor and his assistants, the problems were tabled. Some decisions had to be made.

But they had other things on their minds for the weekend, such as mourning the loss of Satvinder's family with Akhtar's family back in Khulna. They left the nurse in charge of feeding and watering the children until they could get back to sit around that table and sort out the detailed needs of the mixed bunch of orphans.

They arrived in Khulna quite late that evening due to a demonstration blocking the way as they entered the city limits. The police handled the demonstration well, with only a handful of shots going over the heads of the protestors. The soldiers from the Khulna Cantonment did not need to get involved.

Grief was the order of the day, and the family (without Akhtar but with Ablaa and James) visited the temple to pray. They were Shaivas, and worshiped at their local temple which was dedicated to Shiva the Destroyer. As they faced the shrine, alongside an ornate statue of Nandi the bull, they prayed for their lost friends and relatives. Ablaa and James quietly prayed to their own Gods.

Monday morning came around quickly, and the four were back on the bus chugging towards Dumuria, and Chak Sahasa. The shouts of 'Joy Bangla' each time somebody left the bus were becoming the norm, and anybody not joining in with the chants was soon made to feel outcast, the disapproving stares from the other passengers almost burning into their very minds. Satvinder held his fist in the air and shouted 'Joy Bangla' as he dismounted, and the other travelers fervently repeated his statement of solidarity.

"My friend," whispered Akhtar as they walked along the dusty lane, "are you softening to the idea of patriotism, and cessation?"

A glum reply slithered out of Satvinder's mouth, like a cobra looking for a strike. "They *killed* my family." They said nothing else throughout the walk to the village.

The nurse had done a good job with the children, who were all well fed and beginning to get along more like a family. She reported that another child had arrived, a girl of about six years old. Her widower father had died from chronic renal failure, this time not heart failure. After the little girl's introduction to Satvinder, the clinic was calling.

"Ablaa," the nurse called, "the teacher from Dumuria kindly brought over some children's clothes. They're in number three."

The growing band of orphans spent all morning with Ablaa and James re-clothing themselves, with colourful saris for the girls and kurtas for the boys, and by the end they were a very smart and proud group of children. When the teacher arrived for school that afternoon, they lined up and presented themselves in their new, colourful apparel, including the five Muslim children. Their inbred inhibitions were beginning to fade.

That evening, they sat around the table. Ablaa spoke. "I listened to the radio with Auntie Baka at the weekend and there was a report on President Khan being in Dhaka last week. It's reported that he referred to Sheikh Mujib as 'the future Prime Minister of Pakistan.' That could mean that there won't be a war. That would be really good." She had a sarcastic grin across her face.

Akhtar replied, "Yes, I heard it. It's true. I've been wanting to talk about it with you all in our private rooms. Now me and Baka discussed moving away, but she's concerned about our home. It's all we really have, apart from some money we have hidden." He stretched back and put his hands behind his head. "Now, with the elections looking like they'll lead to proper democracy, we think we should stay here. Where we are, right now."

But the thirteen year old amateur diplomat observed, "Something else which was mentioned on the program, and could cast doubts on the democratic progress, was that earlier in the year, just recently, Sheikh Mujib met with the other East Pakistan representatives and pledged that they would *never* deviate from the six-point idea when framing the constitution for Pakistan."

"So?" asked Akhtar, with Satvinder smiling away in the background. "What about it?"

She giggled. "You two have spent all your lives dreaming about equality and secular governments, and yet you don't know anything about politics." She laughed, and in loving, innocent support, James joined her. "You see, the constitution will be written by the Awami League, and the Awami League alone, based only on their own 'six point' policies, and nobody else's. The seats held by the *other* parties will probably not be represented in the framing of the constitution so it won't be a Pakistan constitution, it'll be an *Awami League* constitution. Now *that's* not democracy! Got that?"

As she stressed her opinion Satvinder burst out laughing. James pushed round and got onto his lap, laughing with him.

She snapped, "What're you laughing at? You taking the piss?"

"No, no. It's just funny." They controlled their fit. "I was just wondering how old you were. You're like a tiny little, perfectly formed Indira Ghandi. How old are you?"

She calmed down, and grinned. "I take that as a compliment. Thank you, Daddy." She was an outstanding mind at only thirteen years old, well, as far as they knew, thirteen.

Satvinder cuddled James as he made his point. "It's good to laugh, but I'm with Ablaa, sorry Akhtar. It isn't going to work, is it? It's beginning to look just like the manager's assessment of the forthcoming government, if it goes through. He called it a democratic dictatorship. There'll only be two possible outcomes: Khan's military rule will carry on, or Sheikh Mujib Rahman's one-party rule will take over, and the only way Khan will hand over power to another dictatorship is if he loses the war. And that's the war that'll be fuelled by those guns hidden and locked in our godowns." He took a very deep breath. "I hope we soon get some news from the Field Marshall about work permits."

Akhtar was thrown back into confusion. "I know you're all making sense, but I'm going to do as I promised Baka, that's keep a careful eye on developments, and be ready to make the decision."

Over the next couple of weeks reports escalated about the persecution and killing of the Biharis and foreign nationals across the country. The Bengali nationalists were turning on all foreign Muslims who were seen to represent the West Pakistan ruling government. Rumours spread that the persecution may have been orchestrated in parts by the para-military Mukti groups, and who, at a very minimum, turned a blind eye. So the persecuted Biharis turned even more to the West Pakistan military for protection, returning the favour with loyalty, information and a ground-floor presence in the communities, as the Pakistani army's ears and eyes. The country continued to divide.

Ablaa and Akhtar maintained their vigilance over the radio reports, keeping the group up to speed on reported developments.

Early February, 1971

Ablaa reports in early February, "The plane has been blown up! Don't know if people were in it." An Indian Airlines plane had been hijacked, and taken to West Pakistan by the hijackers where it was blown up after the passengers were released, and, it seemed in retaliation, the Indians banned all commercial and military flights across Indian airspace accusing Pakistan of "instigation, abetment, and encouragement" of the hijackers. It was reported by some of the radio services that the West Pakistan government was moving many soldiers and machines into the East wing to improve the security as relationships with India strained. Ablaa felt that there may be a more sinister reason for the troop re-enforcement: the annihilation of the Awami league and everything that supports it. But sometimes her young age made it difficult for here to be taken seriously.

"It's an interesting idea but a bit extreme. I do concede, though, that the time is coming for a decision," admitted Akhtar. "I must talk with Baka this weekend, and we must make a decision, and then act on it."

With all the news coming in, nothing seemed to be changing in the villages around Chak Sahasa. Their fifteen little orphans were settling in with their 'foster parents', James and Ablaa, and after some discussion and encouragement from the diplomat Ablaa, the teacher had agreed to take the Muslim children into her classes.

That looked like a result, but was it?

"Satvinder, we need to talk!" stressed the village carpenter. "I've had it in the neck from the blacksmith about the Muslims being taught by a Hindu. It's gonna cause a fight!" The young carpenter, wiry and fit, was the representative of the people to the company. He was a Hindu, but very tolerant and secular in his job as representative. "There's going to be trouble."

The two men, each carrying an umbrella, decided to go for a walk down the lane, and try to work out a compromise. It was overcast, threatening to rain, but still very dusty. They sat down on the bank and looked out across the flat, misty farmland. Well water was being pumped into one of the sections.

The carpenter started the meeting. "We need to keep the village together as a working group, but that doesn't mean we should interfere with individual beliefs. The Muslims must see our community as one which allows all faith to live side-by-side, *without* interfering. I heard across the sundari swamp that *you* are a teacher." He grinned at Satvinder, who did not grin back.

In reply, "I'm a Hindu and so can't be of any help, and besides, I'm a geologist from Jessore." Satvinder's voice was nervous.

The carpenter thought very carefully before continuing. "Ah yes, but have you seen the girls in Jessore, with their wooden guns and their fighting dress? They wear white kurtas and pyjamas with their hair tied back and look just like the army girls, ready and waiting for the fight ahead. Have you seen them marching in the college grounds? They're quite beautiful, but frightening. *Scary*." He looked at Satvinder who was just staring into the ground. "I didn't think you'd seen them. You've never been there, not for years, anyway. Jessore is a stronghold of the East Pakistan Rifles and all the para-military that's building up to fight the Pakistanis when the time comes. We're all just waiting for Sheik Mujib to give the word, and it's war. Are you ready for war?" He cleared his throat. "Well, *teacher*?"

Satvinder finally looked up from his stare. "Who the hell are you? *Just* a carpenter?"

"No such thing as 'just a carpenter'. Your James can tell you that. But I *am* just an emancipated Hindu living in a Muslim world. Just like yourself. Your little girl, the Muslim, she's quite brilliant, and so I'm sure she must have warned you about the amount of military re-enforcement that's coming from Lahore, to put down the Awami threat. Apparently it's for the threat from India, with the hijacking causing just enough tension to justify the West's action. But that's a good smokescreen for the reality of the fight to come."

"I'll ask again, who the *hell* are you?"

"Sorry, Satvinder, that was rude of me. I'm the village representative to the company. I have a role which requires me to communicate closely with the Field Marshall, and he feels it only right that I know who is in the village, especially the trusted ones, like yourself and the doctor. That's who I am. And I need to know who you are."

The geologist from Jessore had learned to be defensive, whilst not forgetting that attack can sometimes be the best defence, so he made his move. "Did you know that the Pak army killed my family? We were in Jessore when they were picked up and taken to the cantonment. Never seen since. The bastards." He found it quite easy to be angry.

The carpenter nodded, "The Field Marshall did tell me that. I'm very sorry."

"So, what else did he tell you? About me."

"He mentioned about your work."

"Which is? Speak! Or shut the fuck up!"

The carpenter suddenly went on the defensive. He took a deep breath and, "Calm down, I'm just interested, as we need to work together. And there are rumours."

"If, just if, you are so close to the Field Marshall, you wouldn't need to ask. He knows who and what I am." He showed an uncharacteristic sneer. "I'll tell you bit of what the Field Marshall knows, and that's it. The rest you can ask him when he returns. I fled Jessore when they were taken, and I believe they're dead. Killed by the Pak soldiers. So now I'm here. That's it!" He was putting over an angry front. "If you've got any problems with me, let's take it up now. And if you don't have any problems with me, shut the fuck up and mind your own business. I'm here because of my geological knowledge, which Akhtar finds useful for his water studies. The *Field Marshall* will tell you the rest!" Well, the carpenter took it all onboard, and believed his story, proving that he had no idea of the truth. Satvinder needed to get off the subject of himself. "Now, *what* about the children?"

The carpenter hung his head. "Sorry. Let's talk about the teaching." There was a silent few moments. "Sorry, I mean the children's teaching *here*. The blacksmith has a relative in the village who has become a widow recently. The doctor will know about her. She's only eighteen, but has a child of about one month, and she needs a home. The blacksmith has suggested that she helps with the children, and gives them some teaching, as she's a Muslin and quite bright. She could help Ablaa as well. If the teacher will work with the widow, they could split the religious teaching. The teacher could do the Hindu teaching, and the widow the Muslim. The teacher can still do the other, non-religious, lessons. It would keep things right."

The heat had gone from Satvinder, but he was very wary of the man. "Yes, that sounds like it could work."

"And Satvinder, I *am* sorry for being intrusive. It's just that I heard a rumour, nothing more. Please don't tell anybody."

They stood up as the rain began, and their umbrellas opened. It did not rain enough to set the dust, but enough to cool the moment. They walked back almost as far as the village in silence, but Satvinder was still curious about the man's intent.

"When does the next crop come in from the villages?"

"March. The godowns will have grain in again soon."

"Good job they're all empty, then." He looked at the carpenter for signs of reaction, but none, and so Satvinder was happy that he knew nothing about the guns. He felt certain that he wasn't *that* close to the Field Marshall. But who was he close to?

The very next day the young mother met with the teacher, and they agreed their times and arrangements. The Hindu teacher was pleased that she would not have to be responsible for the little Muslims' religious upbringing, and their relationship shone from the very beginning. The teenager also struck a relationship with James and Ablaa, and after just a few days had moved into one of the orphanage rooms, taking on much more than just the teaching of the

Islamic faith. She quickly became one of the foster parents, and Tazkia became one of the team.

The next morning, whilst the gang sat around the table, "Daddy, what do you think of Tazkia?" Ablaa grinned as she waited for an answer. Satvinder gaped at the question and looked at Akhtar and James, who had both perked up in anticipation.

"What sort of question is that? She's just a girl."

"Oh no she ain't!" she snapped, grinning from ear-to-ear. "She's about eighteen with a baby. She was married at twelve, so she's old enough."

"Old enough for what?" Poor Satvinder was beginning to feel defensive. "That's not the kind of talk we normally enjoy, is it!"

"It's your mind! I mean old enough for *marriage*, you dirty minded daddy." She began to chuckle. "What'd you think I was on about?"

They all looked at Satvinder and laughed, and then he joined them.

They settled down. "She's very pretty and a widow, good with the children, but she's Muslim. And besides I've got my Kaling….." He stopped dead. The joviality drained from his face as he, for the very first time, actually realised that he was a widower. He did not have his darling Kaling any more. The group sat in silence, a kind of respect, as they all pondered over Satvinder's loss. But the innocence of youth broke the lull.

"Daddy," whispered James, "we're all going out for a walk down the lane today to discover things." He moved around to Satvinder's lap. "We're going to look for inspiration. We're going to start a business for the orphanage."

That returned the mood to normal.

Akhtar said, "That's a great idea. Got any ideas?"

James shook his head, "Naah. But Ablaa and Tazkia have been talking." He huffed, "They left me out, though."

"Ablaa!" Akhtar was surprised, "You've all got to stick together."

"It wasn't like that. We needed to keep quiet about it until we'd spoken to the noodle maker." She leaned over and kissed James on the cheek. "I can tell you now. We're going to make noodles. The old lady is quite ill, as Akhtar probably knows, and people won't buy from her any more because she's diseased. So she said we could do it, as long as we give her some noodles each day. Ain't that good?"

James giggled as he realised that he was back in the fold. He jumped down and went to the door. "We're going walking today. Come on!"

The orphan children had eaten fish and rice and drank the good filtered water from Akhtar's water plant, and Tazkia, with her own baby in her arms, lined them up outside the orphanage. They each held a piece of paper and a pencil. Ablaa, Tazkia and James fell into line as they slowly moved off towards the lane.

"Today," ordered Ablaa, "we're going to find as many wild creatures as possible. And we'll all write down what we find. But don't touch anything without asking us first, or you might get bitten. James is our expert guide."

Satvinder watched the group as they moved towards the lane. The children walked in family groups, hand-in-hand, with James and Ablaa leading and the beautiful Tazkia organising from the rear. His heart was still tearing between the grief of his recent loss and the love for his new-found family. And he warmed as he watched the tiny bottom of Tazkia which flipped from side to side as she walked, her sari shining in the sun and beckoning him to follow her to a distant land of promise. She was a beautiful young lady. But she was a Muslim.

Akhtar stepped out of the clinic. "She's so beautiful, but nobody from the other villages will take her on, as they believe that we're all diseased here. What a waste." He grinned and winked at his mate.

The weather reminded Satvinder of the trip to Monpura, with beautiful deep blue skies, emerald vegetation and a winter sun which warmed the heart. He felt close to God that day, as he had on that memorable trip with Shafia and Mia, but that was just the lull before the storm. On the day of the school nature-walk, there were no such threats of cyclones and the constant talk and reports of war were a million miles away from Chak Sahasa. Things were looking positive, and the poor farming community was beginning to awaken from a period of evil darkness. He looked across the village centre and smiled at the queue of people getting their freshly filtered water from the godown and he noticed people in the queue who he'd never noticed there before, all finding new belief in their doctor and his arsenic theories. The village would one-day swing from being the untouchable band of lepers to a thriving, healthy co-operative, admired by everybody, and maybe Tazkia would then find a suitor from a neighbouring village. He thought to himself, 'to revel happiness, one must first suffer grief. Perhaps my turn is coming.' Something that his old mother had taught him about expectations.

Along the lane, the children were finding a wealth of specimens and every time they did, they had to write down the name of the creature.

James whispered as he pointed to a lizard which was basking on the bank. "I think that's a *short tailed ground agama*. Don't know how to spell it."

Tazkia wrote the name down for the children to copy. Two of the girls could actually write it down without copying which heralded a triumph for the basic teaching they had received from the village school. Ablaa and James copied the name. James then slowly moved on, bending the grasses aside with a stick, until he eventually stopped. He had found something. The young boy quietly and carefully said, "Kalach. Don't get close." He held the grass aside so that the others could gather around. It was a curled up snake, a *common krait*, thirty inches long and dark brown overall, with beige hoops dividing up the body colour. With a slender head, it looked quite harmless. "If we leave it alone, it won't hurt us. But if it *does* bite, it'll kill us." The children all carefully moved back to allow the creature to bask and to learn how to write down its name.

As they moved back onto the lane, a shabby old grey truck approached, driving towards the village and blowing up a dust-storm. The truck stopped and the driver, sporting a bushy, black moustache, asked, "What've you found?"

The children did not answer, wary of the strangers, and one of the six young men in the back of the truck asked, "What is it? We won't hurt you."

James stepped forward. "It's a kalach. That's all."

The driver stepped out holding a rifle, which frightened the children. He was wearing dirty old grey trousers and a short brown kurta, and no shoes. "It's ok. I just want to protect your daddies and mummies." He stepped close to the snake, and shot it. It almost broke in half, writhing and twisting until it became motionless, and was dead. The little children all held their ears as the crack rattled around their heads. "It won't bite anybody, now." He grinned at Tazkia. "This is Chak Sahasa?" She pointed along the lane, and the driver climbed back into the truck, and before they went he ordered, "Stay here until we've come back. Joy Bangla!"

Colin Hodgson

# CHAPTER 10 -- THE DISMISSAL

"What was that?" Satvinder ran out of the clinic followed by Akhtar and some of the patients. Suddenly there were dozens of villagers in the square. They had heard a gunshot. "There!" he shouted.

A dust storm was being blown up from the lane as the old grey truck moved towards the villagers. The mood was intense, and some of the men went into their homes and returned with various farm implements: weapons. The truck entered the village and slowed, and then swung around towards the clinic. It slowed to a halt, facing Satvinder and Akhtar, and as the engine stopped an eerie silence fell. The driver stepped out, and three very young men in similar dress jumped from the buck clutching old rifles, but three others stayed on the truck, and one inside the cab. The villagers were tense and sweating, staring hard at the band of Mukti soldiers.

"This is a glorious day!" shouted the driver, who seemed to be in charge. "We just met some children along the lane. They are clean, pretty children, and you must be very proud of them." He looked behind him at his young troops, and then back at the doctor and Satvinder. "Where's Satvinder, the geologist?"

He stepped forward towards the para-military man, and put his hand up. "Joy Bangla."

The villagers responded with their support and a well timed chant roared up from the crowd. "Joy Bangla! Joy Bangla!" and then silence returned.

The para-military looked around at the villagers, who had surrounded the truck from a distance, and grinned as he returned the statement of solidarity. He then approached Satvinder.

"We have business." He held out his hand and Satvinder meekly shook it. "We have business. Good to meet you."

Satvinder looked at Akhtar and then back, sweat dripping from his forrid. "Are the children hurt? We heard shooting."

"No! We're friends, not animals. I just shot a krait. One less enemy to worry about." He smiled. "You have an office?"

Akhtar suggested, "Use the clinic. Most of the patients have come outside." The rest were gently led by the nurse into the open, and Satvinder and the soldier went inside, alone. Sitting opposite each other at the doctor's desk, they carefully looked each other up and down.

"Will I catch anything from here?" The paramilitary soldier, allegedly afraid of nothing, looked concerned. He pulled at his moustache. "Well?"

"You can get leprosy, and I can get shot. This isn't very relaxing for either of us."

The soldier was very perceptive, and laid his rifle on the ground. "Better?"

Satvinder smiled in thanks. "We're now both unarmed. We've got only common disease here, but no leprosy. I believe that's what you're getting at."

"No leprosy? You have leprosy here. Everybody knows it."

"No leprosy. What looks like leprosy is the result of illness caused by poisoned water. The doctor has isolated the problem, which is arsenic, and it's now being treated. No new patients will suffer the poisoning."

The soldier was beginning to show signs of intelligence and concern. "Is that correct? There are a few other villages who are suffering leprosy and disease. Perhaps the doctor should speak to the other villages."

Satvinder took the opportunity to be the geologist. "We get our water from tube-wells. About seventy yards deep."

The soldier sat quite silently for a while, playing with his facial hair, and then, "They also get their water from wells. That's interesting. The doctor could be on to something. How does he treat it?"

"The water's filtered to remove most of the arsenic. *Nobody* gets the early sickness of arsenic poisoning from drinking the treated water. And then, the long-term damage will not set in."

The soldier said in a morose voice, "Some of my family have been lost to the diseases. Would you arrange a meeting for me with the doctor?" He grinned, "When I'm not a Mukti Fauj I'm a doctor." He stood up and put his hand out towards Satvinder and they shook heartily. "I think we'll get along. Now, would you please show me the filters?"

They left the clinic and, with Akhtar, walked across the village square, the villagers moving aside but remaining alert. The three dismounted soldiers followed, leaving the others still on the truck. The three youngsters stood guard at the godown door. Akhtar proudly presented his filter system to the soldier. He was elated to find a true believer, one who had faced similar patients and who shared the same dreams of clean, safe water for all the villagers in East Pakistan. There was real promise for the future.

The three stood in the large, airy godown. The soldier was just as excited as Akhtar, but "I still have my business to complete. Satvinder, I've been instructed to inform you of your new appointment. The Field Marshall has placed you in charge of this cooperative, and responsible for all of its activities. The secretary has been informed by telex, and she'll help you with all the administration. You'll manage this village with the help of Doctor Hussain, here."

Satvinder stood back. "Why?"

"He trusts you, and Sergeant Haq trusts you. That's all." He walked towards the door. "I now need to speak to Bihari Khan."

Akhtar jested, "There're a million Biharis in East Pakistan and many are called Khan. Take your pick."

The soldier laughed, "But only one in *this* village. The manager."

He put his rifle to his chest, walked out of the godown and moved towards the centre of the open area, and the villagers moved aside. The children were standing in front of the clinic, Ablaa holding a dead snake. The Mukti soldier huffed, "I advised you to stay away until we'd gone!" He pointed to the kids. "Go inside, now! And stay there!" The children all went into the clinic. "Now, Khan! Manager Khan!" he shouted and the manager, wearing a grey suit, moved towards him from the shadows of the middle godown, sweating profusely and with his hands shaking. As he approached the soldier the other soldiers moved from the truck to join the three guards, their rifles at the ready and bayonets fitted.

"What can I do for you, sir?" He was very humble. He shuffled his polished shoes in the dust. "I'm your servant."

The soldier looked around at the villagers before saying anything to him. They were all very afraid of the situation, and Satvinder caught the eye of the carpenter. He was nervous, and soon broke the eye-contact. *'What's that prat been up to?'* he thought to himself.

The soldier stood in front of the manager, with his seven youngsters behind him. "Satvinder is now in charge of the village!" He shouted to ensure they could all hear his words to the manager. "I don't know what you've done but I've been asked to serve you your notice!"

He stood aside, and one of the other soldiers stepped forward. The very young soldier, barely sixteen, stood in front of the manager, shaking nervously. He was ordered to 'commence' and after an electrifying few moments the teenage soldier held his rifle to one side, the newly honed bayonet blazing in the sun. He twisted and swung it, letting out a whimpering squeal. The flashing blade sliced across the manager's stomach, whose face distorted. He fell to the ground, blood began to flow from the deep wound and he writhed, rolling onto his side. He momentarily choked but caught his breath, and began to groan.

"Help him!" shouted one of the women, but the soldiers turned to the crowd, guns pointing and the villagers froze.

The main soldier, the doctor, shouted, "He'll soon be dead! We'll go then!"

But he writhed on the ground, crying, for many minutes before slowing down, and then he began to beg. "Help me. Please. Water. Please." He begged for water, but the guns still pointed at the villagers.

"Nobody help him!" called the soldier, "He hasn't helped you." And so they all stayed away from the dying man, fearing for the worst should they move. "He'll die soon!"

The man lay in his own blood for almost an hour, begging for help and for water, pleading for mercy and crying.

"Doctor," urged Akhtar, "some water wouldn't save him, just calm him."

"I know that. That's why he won't get any water." He grinned. "Bring me and my men some filtered water! Somebody do it!"

One of the women collected some small water bottles from the godown and they were passed around the soldiers, who drank as the manager begged. But he stayed alive for almost two hours, extending his suffering for as long as his poor soul could handle, and quite unwittingly having the final word.

He shuddered as he looked at his executioner and managed to exhume "Jehannam is waiting for you." His body became still, at last. But his final words spooked the young para-militaries, who knew that they were entering a period of eternal uncertainty, when Muslim would be set against Muslim.

The young man who had inflicted the wound took those last dying words very seriously. "Most of these are Hindus! Why we here?" he nervously asked his officer.

His reply was straight down the party line. "They are Bangles. They're our allies and friends and fellow countrymen and you serve for *them*. Never forget what we fight for. Homeland, not religion." He turned to Satvinder. "Satvinder. Doctor Hussain. I must now go, as our business is done here." He was very matter-of-fact about the execution. "We must discuss our other business very soon. I'll be back."

Although they never wanted to, Akhtar and Satvinder shook the soldier's hand, and the old grey truck trundled off down the lane. The whole village was in shock, but as the truck stirred the dust, many of them smiled, relieved that they had gone, but disturbed by the public killing of the manager. Biharis were being killed all over the East wing of Pakistan, often without better cause than that they were Biharis, and sometimes just because they were not East Pakistan nationals. Thousands of foreign workers had begun to leave the country in fear of their lives, irrespective of religion, but the main targets were non-Bengalese Muslims who were seen as the servants of the West Pakistan rulers. That in turn pushed the Biharis even closer to the West's military rulers for protection, dividing communities and breeding suspicion, hatred and the seeds of civil war.

The villagers seemed to accept Satvinder without question as the new manager, but the wretched Satvinder could not. His stomach turned at what he had witnessed.

They sat around the table that evening.

"When I met him, I thought we could be friends," droned Akhtar. "How could a doctor just kill like that? He showed no remorse. And to let him suffer. Why?"

They just sat, unable to answer Akhtar's questions.

Ablaa grabbed hold of James's hand and quietly said, "We all sat in the middle of the clinic room and cuddled each other. None of us dared to look and Tazkia told the children to be perfectly still and silent, so the soldiers would forget we were here. It seemed like days that we stayed there, but they all remained silent, and Tazkia's baby just slept. I hope we don't have to do that again." She pulled James to her and whispered, "We must always stay with each other." They held one another very tightly. She then looked to her daddy. "Do you think the villagers will accept you as manager?"

"Don't know. But I might not accept me. It's not right."

"But Daddy, do you have a choice? I don't think it's an offer."

"No," stressed Akhtar, "no offer there. It was a *command*. And I think the torturous killing of the manager was a warning, to you and everybody else. If you don't do the job, you'll be next." He put his head in his hands. "*Everything* has changed today."

Satvinder sighed. "One thing has changed for certain. Our future." They all sat in silence for a long time before the new manager continued. "We must leave this place while we can. It's February so we still have a couple of dry months, and we should make use of them. We need ideas."

James sat bolt upright. "We could hide in the Sundarbans. Only things to worry about down there would be the tigers and cobras." The Sundarbans are tropical mangrove swamps and forest, covering much of the southern Ganges Delta, and home to the Bengal Tiger and King Cobra. "And the storms, of course. Me and Ablaa know all about the storms."

Satvinder grinned at the little Christian boy. "That's a brilliant idea. But perhaps the Field Marshall could be a safer bet."

Ablaa was way ahead of him. "Safer? I think he had the manager killed. He'd do the same to you if you left your post. *You're* his manager now."

James stressed, "But we could probably get into *India* through the Sundarbans. I bet there's not a fence right down there to stop us." He was beginning to make sense. They sat around the table discussing the idea of moving into India through the Sundarbans, and then cutting up to Kolkata which would only be a couple of hundred miles away. But several things were beginning to get in the way of their loosely laid plans: the fifteen orphans.

Ablaa pulled James to her. "We've discussed the idea of the Sundarbans already. It's a great idea, but if we're to discuss it further, it must be realistic." She paused. "When we lost our families, you made a promise to look after us and love us like your own. And you have. Thank you, Daddy. Now, we've all made a similar promise to our orphans. So, where we go, they go." She almost huffed as she took some deep breaths. The group was silent.

Eventually Satvinder spoke. "As difficult as it may be, with so many children, Ablaa's right." He looked to his old mate. "You have your own family to care for. But I've got to stick with mine. All of them."

At that point the group stood at fifteen orphans, two young carers, a teacher and her child, Satvinder, probably Akhtar's family of four and Akhtar's devoted nurse. Add to that any additional orphans who are almost certain to arrive on their doorstep, and the size of the plan begins to reveal.

James suggested, "We'd need several boats, and lots of clean water."

Akhtar knew that within the next few weeks, he would be orphaning between ten and fifteen more children. There could be more than thirty children to protect.

"Let's sleep on it," suggested Akhtar.

The next morning came around quickly. Satvinder left his mate in his clinic and took up his seat in the office. He sat at the manager's desk for the very first time, and it was a particularly uncomfortable seat.

"I have a telex for you, sir. It's from the Field Marshall."

He thanked his new secretary and settled down to his first ever task in the new role: that of receiving instruction from the 'boss'.

The telex welcomed him into the company in the official role as Cooperative Manager, detailed his remuneration package (which helped to make the situation almost bearable) and scheduled the coming four months of harvest and sowing. The message closed with a promised visit from the Field Marshall within the next couple of weeks.

Satvinder waited for Akhtar's clinic to close, before calling his 'family' together. They sat around their table.

"Things are difficult," began Satvinder. "Although we mustn't stop planning for our move, we need to be sure that we can *safely* leave here. Ablaa reminded us yesterday that the Field Marshall wouldn't take kindly to me running away from my 'duties'. He's coming here within the next couple of weeks. I think we need to speak openly with him about our future. He's a good man."

The group nodded in agreement.

"We must go about our lives as if we're here to stay," urged Ablaa. "The carpenter has been very kind in helping us this morning with building some forms to dry our rice paste on. But he asks a lot of questions. So me and James must almost believe in our own hearts that we're building for our future, right here. If we believe it, we'll make others believe it."

"That's really good," whispered Akhtar. "I've been thinking this morning that we should set a date, and on that date, just disappear, away to our new home."

Ablaa suggested, "Baka and the boys could move here before that date. It would look like you're here to stay, with your family. And the children would need to know nothing until we're all on the move." She frowned. "But we need that date."

"What do you think, James?" asked his daddy.

"If we go into the Sundarbans, we'll need boats. How can we get them?"

Satvinder smiled. "I'm now being paid for my work here. With almost no outgoings I could buy a couple of small skips with my first couple of month's wages. How many would we need?"

"You know the one you came to my home in? We'd get one adult and about six children, maybe seven or eight little ones."

The mood dropped. At least six boats were needed to give the whole group a chance, more if they were to take belongings. The family agreed to keep an open mind until the Field Marshall had paid his visit. In the meantime, life goes on.

# CHAPTER 11 -- THE WAR BEGINS

March 1971

Life goes on, but very precariously. It was the first day of March 1971 when Ablaa listened to the radio address by General Yahya Khan. He announced to the people of Pakistan that the session of General Council, scheduled to be held on the third day of March, had been cancelled. Negotiations between the Awami League leader, Sheikh Mujibur Rahman, and the Pakistani dictator General Yahya Khan, had not been successful. Democracy had been put on hold. In protest Sheikh Rahman called for a Hartal, a kind of national strike, or protest against authority. The village agreed to stay at home the next day and do no work, in support of the national Hartal. They all knew that the only people who cared whether or not they worked that day were themselves, but they felt a sense of national pride and solidarity.

"I don't think Rahman, Bhutto or Khan will ever agree," sighed Ablaa, sitting around the breakfast table. "If the Field Marshall is right, and the West successfully remove Rahman and the Awami League, then I do believe that Bhutto will be next to be annihilated."

They all left the table, heads down, to get on with their lives.

The children's noodle business had got off with a bang. As they spread their rice-paste over the drying-form, Tazkia suggested to Ablaa that they needed another grinding stone, to be able to increase the noodle output and to be able to supply the entire village. The business was ready to grow.

"Will you speak to Satvinder about it, please?" Tazkia asked Ablaa.

She never responded, but thought very deeply, whilst fiddling with her red sari. She watched Tazkia from behind, admiring her cute backside which swung as she spread the thin paste over the dryer. Then, with a smile, she asked, "Do you like my daddy?" She raised her eyebrows, as Tazkia blushed. "I think he likes you."

The two silently carried on with their business for a little while.

"He's a Hindu." The young mother spoke quietly and nervously. "And I'm a Muslim."

"So am I. But me and Daddy still love each other." She bit her lip as she almost let slip about Akhtar's mixed marriage: that had been kept secret from the villagers.

"But you and your daddy are together for a reason. And James. It's different."

Another long silence followed. The two workers carried on with their spreading.

Eventually Ablaa broke the silence. "You go and ask daddy." She giggled. "About the stone, I mean."

The two shared a quiet laughing session, both embarrassed about even touching on the subject of boys in any sort of sensual way.

Then, "Go on. He's in the office. Go and ask him."

With a little more persuasion, Tazkia agreed. "What shall I ask him?"

The giggling Ablaa jested, "Depends what you want to know about him."

"Just the stone!" There was a nervous pause, before the children came out of the school-house and the moment was gone. Tazkia never went into the office.

As Tazkia spread the rice-dough Ablaa covertly studied her face, wondering where her thoughts were leading, maybe towards her daddy and the comfort of love and relationship, or maybe not. She never asked.

"Do you think the carpenter is paying me too much attention?" asked Ablaa. "Lately he'll do anything for me."

Tazkia raised her eyebrows. "He's married. He's a Hindu." Pause. "How old are you? Really?"

A frowning reply, "Thirteen, I think. On Monpura we never worried about age. But I think I'm thirteen." A moment passed as she continued to look at Tazkia's fine body. "You were married at twelve, so why bother about my age?"

"I know, but I married a single person, not somebody else's husband. So you *mustn't* allow him to court you. It's all wrong!"

"I'm not letting him do anything! But he does lots of things for me, like he made all the dryers and the cutting boards."

"That was for *all* of us." Tazkia sighed. "He's just being nice to *all* of us." The eighteen-year-old mother laid her baby down, and pulled Ablaa to her, for a motherly cuddle. "He's a nice man, but you mustn't think of him like that."

That evening, around the table, Ablaa just had to do it.

"Daddy, Tazkia needs to talk to you." She waited for a response. "It's about the business. That's all."

"Wow, that was scary," jested Akhtar. "Your dad thought it might've been about other things."

The widowed man blushed. "*No* I didn't!"

Akhtar smiled, "You did. I saw it on your face. A cross between absolute delight, and absolute fear."

Then James got his two-penneth in. "Daddy, she's really pretty. I like her."

They all grinned as the various thoughts rushed through their minds.

"She *is* beautiful." He began to open up. "I've watched her through this window. And she's so kind." Satvinder played with his fingers for a while as the others watched. "I'm only just now beginning to miss Kaling. And

141

the girls." A hint of a tear formed. "She could never replace my Kaling."

Ablaa moved round to her adopted father, and they hugged tightly. "Daddy, you'll never replace my mummy and daddy. But you're *another* mummy and daddy to me. And to James." A solemn silence hung over the table and Satvinder and Ablaa both wept for their lost families. James pulled himself into the ruck.

They settled back after a while, and Satvinder finally showed a serious interest in love-after-Kaling. He asked Akhtar about his mixed marriage, "How did you get through these years? Does it work?"

The reply was surprising, slow and deliberate. "We've really struggled. It's not all been good." His head dropped. "I lie to most people. This village believes that my wife and children are Muslim, like me. It's best that way. And the boys've had loads of problems at school, especially from the Hindus." He picked his head up. "Be very careful. Very, very careful."

Satvinder placed his hand on his mate's arm, and reminisced. "We both remember those childhood days. The fights we got into because we were so close, but from different worlds. Neighbours, but so far apart." A silence, then, "The Muslim lover. My Hindu school-friends used to taunt me. But it taught me to fight, and to win."

Akhtar screwed his eyes. "Yeah, and I was the arsehole who didn't invite you to my eighteenth birthday party."

"I guessed it was because I'm not a Muslim."

Akhtar nodded. "Some of my family told me that if that Malaun turns up, he'll be in the river. Sorry. I never told you, I was so ashamed."

Ablaa stated, "We're all together now, as one big family. We're all the same."

Akhtar smirked, "Tell that to the rest of the World. *They're* the problem."

She almost whispered. "But there *are* places where we can all live together without intolerance, there *must* be. Not everywhere can be like Bengal. And the Field Marshall said we could go to Anglia." She looked out of the window. "When we go, we *must* go to a tolerant place. Somewhere for all of us." Her stare returned to her dad. "You know what, you could marry Tazkia when we get away from here. If she wants you to, of course. And you'll not get much competition: we're still all a bunch of lepers. The lepers from Chak Sahasa. No-one else'll ever have her."

That ghastly bit of youthful wisdom closed the conversation for the evening.

The Seventh of March 1971

Satvinder made his weekend visit to Khulna alone, with Akhtar looking after a badly injured rice farmer, and the children looking after their other children. He arrived in Khulna, the country's jute trading capital, to find a frightened and disturbed population, following a couple of days of rioting and demonstration. The telephone exchange had been attacked and several employees killed, and small pockets of people had been attacked in their own homes, many killed or injured, and Baka had heard reports of some atrocities involving women and children. Most of the attacks had been against non-Bengali businessmen, and families of the army personnel, and many small businesses had been looted and burned. Baka felt that the attacks were organised, designed to instil fear and panic in those who were fortunate enough to avoid attack. Many guns had found their way onto the streets from the looted gun shops.

On the Sunday the leader of the Awami League, Sheikh Mujibur Rahman, was in Dhaka. From there he made his famous speech at the Ramna Racecourse Maidan amongst a jubilant and aggressive crowd, a speech which, in many observers' eyes, was a declaration of civil war. Satvinder, Baka and her family listened attentively to the radio address and she was able to write her account of what she had heard, which she gave to Satvinder before his return to Chak Sahasa.

Satvinder didn't feel safe whilst at Baka's home and the return to Chak Sahasa was a relief. "I'm glad to be back here, Chak Sahasa feels a lot safer than Khulna. You *must* get Baka and the boys here soon." He was concerned for his mate's family. "I think they should come here this week, and then see what develops in Khulna. You *must* make them come."

Akhtar agreed. He firmly stated that he would go back the very next day, and collect his family. He prayed that the buses would be running, in spite of the Hartal.

The next morning, Monday, they sat around their table in the clinic and Satvinder took a deep breath as he laid Baka's transcript on the table. The Dhaka Racecourse Speech. They looked around at each other as they wondered what Sheikh Rahman had done to his people. Baka and Satvinder had listened to the famous speech on her radio, and she had hurriedly written the transcript, and her memories of the speech were warily read out by Satvinder.

"My dear brothers

"I've come before you today with a heavy heart.

"All of you know how hard we've tried. But it's a matter of sadness that the streets of Dhaka, Chittagong, Khulna, Rangpur and Rajshahi are today being spattered with the blood of my brothers, and the cry we hear from the Bengali people is a cry for freedom, a cry for survival, a cry for our rights.

"You are the ones who brought about an Awami League victory so that you could see a constitutional government restored. The hope was that the elected representatives of the people, sitting in the National Assembly, would formulate a constitution that would assure the people of their economic, political and cultural emancipation. But now, with great sadness in my heart, I look back on the past 23 years of our history and see nothing but a history of the shedding of the blood of the Bengali people. Ours has been a history of continual lamentation, repeated bloodshed and innocent tears.

"We gave blood in 1952: we won a mandate in 1954. But we were still not allowed to take up the reins of this country. In 1958, Ayub Khan clamped Martial Law on our people and enslaved us for the next 10 years. In 1966, during the Six-Point Movement of the masses, so many were the young men and women whose lives were stilled by government bullets. After the downfall of Ayub, General Yahya Khan took over with the promise that he would restore constitutional rule, that he would restore democracy and return power to the people.

"We agreed. But you all know of the events that took place after that.

"I ask you, are we the ones to blame?"

Satvinder took a short breathing break.

"As you know, I've been in contact with President Yahya Khan. As leader of the majority party in the National Assembly, I asked him to set February 15 as the day for its opening session. He didn't give consent to the request I made as leader of the majority party. Instead, he went along with the delay requested by the minority leader Mr. Bhutto and announced that the Assembly would be convened on the 3rd of March. We accepted that, and agreed to join the deliberations. I even went to the extent of saying that we, despite our majority, would still listen to any sound ideas from the minority, even if it were a lone voice. I committed myself to the support of anything to bolster the restoration of a constitutional government.

"When Mr. Bhutto came to Dhaka, we met. We talked. He left, saying that the doors to negotiation were still open. Moulana Noorani and Moulana Mufti were among those West Pakistan parliamentarians who visited Dhaka and talked with me about an agreement on a constitutional framework. I made it clear that we could not agree to any deviation from the Six Points. That right rested with the people. Come, I said, let us sit down and resolve matters.

"But Bhutto's retort was that he would not allow himself to become hostage on two fronts. He predicted that if any West Pakistani members of Parliament were to come to Dhaka, the Assembly would be turned into a slaughterhouse. He added that if anyone was to participate in such a session, a countrywide agitation would be launched from Peshawar to Karachi and that every business would be shut down in protest. I assured him that the Assembly would be convened and despite the dire threats, West Pakistani leaders did come down to Dhaka.

"But suddenly, on March the first, the session was cancelled.

"There was an immediate outcry against this move by the people. I called for a hartal as a peaceful form of protest and the masses readily took to the streets in response.

"And what did we get as a response?

"He turned his guns on my helpless people, a people with no arms to defend themselves. These were the same arms that had been purchased with our own money to protect us from external enemies. But it is our own people who are being fired upon today.

"In the past, too, each time we, the numerically larger segment of Pakistan's population, tried to assert our rights and control our destiny, they conspired against us and pounced upon us.

"I've asked them this before, how can you make your own brothers the target of your bullets?

"Now Yahya Khan says that I'd agreed to a Round Table Conference on the 10th March. Let me point out, that's not true. I had said, Mister Yahya Khan, you're the President of this country. Come to Dhaka, come and see how our poor Bengali people have been mown down by your bullets, how the laps of our mothers and sisters have been robbed and left empty and bereft, how my helpless people have been slaughtered. Come, I said, come and see for yourself and then be the judge and decide. That is what I told him.

"Earlier, I'd told him there would be no Round Table Conference. What Round Table Conference? Whose Round Table Conference? You expect me to sit at a Round Table Conference with the very same people who've emptied the laps of my mothers and my sisters? On the 3rd, at the Paltan, I called for a non-cooperation movement and the shutdown of offices, courts and revenue collection. You gave me full support. Then suddenly, without consulting me or even informing us, he met with one individual for five hours and then made a speech in which he turned all the blame on me, laid all the fault at the door of the Bengali people. The deadlock was created by Bhutto, yet the Bengalis are the ones facing the bullets! We face their guns, yet it's our fault. We're the ones being bit by their bullets, and it's still our fault!

"So, the struggle this time is a struggle for emancipation, the struggle this time is a struggle for independence!

"Brothers, they've now called the Assembly to convene on March 25, with the streets not yet dry of the blood of my brothers. You've called the Assembly, but you must first agree to meet my demands. Martial Law must be withdrawn. The soldiers must return to their barracks. The murderers of my people must be redressed. And, power must be handed over to the elected representatives of the people. Only then will we consider if we can take part in the National Assembly or not!

"Before these demands are met, there can be no question of our participating in this session of the Assembly. That is my right given to me as part of my mandate from the masses.

"As I told them earlier, Mujibur Rahman refuses to walk to the Assembly treading upon the fresh stains of his brothers' blood!

"Do you, my brothers, have complete faith in me?"

Satvinder looked around at his family's faces. He continued with the reading.

"Let me tell you that the Prime Ministership isn't what I seek. What I want is justice, the rights of the people of this land. They tempted me with the Prime Ministership but they failed to buy me over. Nor did they succeed in hanging me on the gallows, for you rescued me with your blood from the so-called conspiracy case. That day, right here at this racecourse, I pledged to you that I would pay for this blood debt with my own blood. Do you remember? I am ready today to fulfill that promise!

"I now declare the closure of all the courts, offices, and educational institutions for an indefinite period of time. No one will report to their offices. That's my instruction to you.

"So that the poor are not inconvenienced rickshaws, trains and other transport will run normally, unless serving any needs of the armed forces. If the army doesn't respect this, I shall not be responsible for the consequences.

"The Secretariat, Supreme Court, High Court, Judge's Courts, and government and semi-government offices shall remain shut. Only banks may open for two hours daily for business transactions. But no money shall be transmitted from East to West Pakistan. The Bengali people must stay calm during these times. Telegraph and telephone communications will be confined within Bangladesh.

"The people of this land are facing elimination, so be on guard. If need be, we will bring everything to a total standstill. Collect your salaries on time. If the salaries are held up, if a single bullet is fired upon us henceforth, if the murder of my people does not cease, I call upon you to turn every home into a fortress against their onslaught. Use whatever you can put your hands on to confront this enemy. Every last road must be blocked. We will deprive them of food. We will deprive them of water. Even if I'm not around to give you the orders, and if my associates are also not to be found, I ask you to continue your movement unabated.

"I say to them again, 'you are my brothers, return now to the barracks where you belong and no one will bear any hostility towards you. Only do not attempt to aim any more bullets at our hearts. It will not do any good! And the seventy million people of this land will not be held down by you or accept suppression any more. The Bengali people have learned how to die for a cause and you will not be able to bring them under your yoke of suppression!'

"To assist the families of the martyred and the injured, the Awami League has set up committees that will do all they can. Please donate whatever you can. Also, employers must give full pay to the workers who participated in the seven days of hartal or were not able to work because of curfews. To all government employees, I say that my directives must be followed. I'd better not see any of you attending your offices. From today, until this land has been freed, no taxes will be paid to the government any more. As of now, they stop! Leave everything to me. I know how to organize movement.

"But be very careful. Keep in mind that the enemy has infiltrated our ranks to engage in the work of provocateurs. Whether Bengali or non-Bengali, Hindu or Muslim, all are our brothers and it is our responsibility to ensure their safety.

"I also ask you to stop listening to radio, television and the press if the media does *not* report news of our movement.

"To all of them, I say this, "You are our brothers. I beseech you to not turn this country into a living hell. Will you not have to show your faces and confront your conscience some day? If we can peaceably settle our differences there is still hope that we can co-exist as brothers. Otherwise there is no hope. If you choose the other path, we may never come face to face with one another again. For now, I have just one thing to ask of you. Give up any thoughts of enslaving this country under military rule again!

"I ask my people to immediately set up committees under the leadership of the Awami League to carry on our struggle in every neighbourhood, village, union and subdivision of this land. You must prepare yourselves now with what little you have for the struggle ahead.

"Since we have given blood, we will give more of it. But, Insha'Allah, we will free the people of this land!

"The struggle this time is for emancipation! The struggle this time is for independence! Be ready. We cannot afford to lose our momentum. Keep the movement and the struggle alive because if we fall back they will come down hard upon us.

"Be disciplined. No nation's movement can be victorious without discipline.

"Joy Bangla!"


Satvinder folded the transcript in half, and walked to the window. The children were up and about, playing like they had not a care in the World. Innocence is bliss.

"That's a war-cry," whispered Ablaa to Akhtar. "You must get your family here."

Akhtar nodded, and then went through to his clinic.

James cuddled up to his daddy, and was joined by Ablaa. The little Christian lad grinned, and then said his piece about the 'famous' racecourse speech which his daddy had so coldly read out. "That was *so boring*! I've never heard anything quite so boring. *Rubbish*."

With a wide grin, his daddy agreed. "Hardly a Churchill, nor a Hitler." He thought for a few seconds and frowned. "Boring but dangerous. If we're not watchful we're all gonna get hurt, so let's be really careful, with everything we do and with everybody we talk to."

Colin Hodgson

# CHAPTER 12 -- THE FIRE-BELLIED CLOUDS

Baka's transcript was handed around the village. The folk listened attentively to the speech as the more educated read it aloud to the others and they all agreed that it was such a boring piece, maybe something being lost during the transcription by Baka, but all knowing just how formidable the message was: 'war is inevitable'. The general mood was reinforced by regular flights of Alouette helicopters and F-86 fighters passing over the villages and with every pass, the children innocently cheered and shouted. The adults scowled.

Akhtar, a cautious man, finally saw his last patient, and made the momentous decision to collect his family from Khulna. But it was too late to travel that day, and so he informed his extended family that he would leave for the bus first thing in the morning. He nervously whispered to Ablaa that should he not return, she should keep the family group together, and continue their loose-laid plan of action.

That night, the very day after the war-cry from the Ramna Racecourse Maidan, the men and women of Chak Sahasa gathered outside, pointing and whispering. They all slowly moved towards the lane, to get away from the light pollution from the small fires around the village square, and they stared. They murmured amongst themselves and gasped as they looked towards the east, in awe of a most beautiful orange glow which lined the underside of the low clouds. The distant world was on fire.

"Khulna?" they all asked each other. "Rayarmahal? Daulatpur?" The more travelled insisted that it was in the direction of Khulna, but none were too sure.

Akhtar stared in fear for his family, and his three friends moved to his side for support. "No. It can't be." Everybody just looked on as the clouds moved, constantly changing the threatening image of hell, and planting nightmares in the minds of the villagers. They could only wonder and imagine.

The women eventually returned to their homes and children, leaving the men to squat around the small fires to hold counsel. About twenty men had gathered, and as Satvinder and his children returned to the clinic, Akhtar joined the discussion group.

"It's started," stated the carpenter. "The fight for freedom has almost certainly begun."

One of the old men sat bolt upright. "It could be just a godown on fire."

"Could be, but I bet it's not." The carpenter was beginning to take command. "We need to find out more about what's happening."

Akhtar played with the dirt, and then nervously spoke. "I'm going to Khulna tomorrow. My wife and children are there." A mumbling went around the group. "I'm bringing them here, to be safe with us. Are we safe?"

The mumbling continued as Akhtar looked around for some response, and he then glanced towards Khulna where the glow continued to line the bellies of the low clouds. After what seemed an eternity the blacksmith spoke.

"We'll have to pray for our fortunes and for our loved ones. But we do have a weapon which could ward the Biharis off: don't know about the Pak army." He smiled at Akhtar, the doctor. "We've all got leprosy. Only the very brave come here."

That seemed to settle the almost non-existent discussion, and so the men rose, spent a little while studying the fire-bellied clouds, and then retired.

Morning came, and it was the ninth of March 1971, the next day after the day after the war-cry from Sheik Mujib.

The radio was still broadcasting and Ablaa reported at the dining table that the East Pakistan Rifles had mutinied in Jessore and much trouble was being reported from Satkira, although it was not made clear quite what the trouble was. Reports of civil unrest, murder, rape and pillage were beginning to find their way through to the country folk.

"I need to go," stressed Akhtar. "I need to see if the bus is running."

"Can I come?" James asked, frowning like a worried old man. "It'd be better if you're not alone."

The doctor looked hard into Satvinder's eyes but permission was not forthcoming. "Sorry, I think it'd be best if you were to look after the other children. Help Ablaa."

"Why? There's nothing Ablaa can't do. Why?" He cocked his little head at the doctor. "I know the way, and I can help carry stuff back here." He moved around the table. "You don't want to go alone."

Akhtar held the boys head to his chest. "Sorry, but it's best you stay here."

As they left the clinic building, into the dank and overcast morning, Akhtar was set back by emotion. About fifty villagers, men and women, had been waiting for his emergence, just to watch as he left to walk down the long lane towards the Khulna road. They feared for their doctor, a man who had turned their despair into hope, and they quietly prayed for his safe return. None of them spoke as he started off along the lane.

James pulled into Satvinder's waist. "Can I walk him to the bus? Please Daddy?"

A moment of madness swept through his daddy's head. Satvinder pulled James around to face him, and kissed his head. "Only if you promise to come back. Safely." With a sad grin, he pushed the boy towards Akhtar, and then grabbed hold of Ablaa. They watched with the villagers as the lad skipped to catch up with Akhtar and grab hold of his hand. For many minutes they all watched the doctor and

James meander along the damp lane, hand-in-hand, heading towards the unknown.

"I couldn't stop him," whispered Satvinder, as if to apologise to Ablaa. "He'll be back. I know he will." But as his best friend and his adopted son disappeared towards Khulna a ray of warm light reached his heart. As he held tightly onto a sombre Ablaa, his hand warmed. Somebody gently took it into hers.

"Don't fret, they'll be back." It was Tazkia. She smiled into his heart, and then slowly released the hand. From a distance her uncle frowned: the blacksmith had noted the contact.

As the doctor had gone off to Khulna, the clinic was closed. Satvinder went to his office, and Ablaa went to her children who yearned to be kept amused: the teacher had not arrived from Dumuria. Apart from the children's needs, the order of the day was the making of rice-dough, the basic material required for the manufacture of noodles.

The 'perfectly formed' Ablaa took a side glance towards Tazkia as they both kneaded the dough. She could see that the young mother was many light-years away in a world of her own, dreaming of something beautiful, fulfilling and exciting. Her hands kneaded the dough, but her face shone with a mysterious desire. Ablaa wondered if it was her daddy's shoulders and neck that she was kneading, softening the stress in readiness for the beautiful act.

"Tazkia?" she quietly asked, "When will you speak to Daddy about the grinding wheel?"

The question surprised and embarrassed her, and she blushed.

"Well?" She looked into Tazkia's eyes. "I saw your eyes when you held Daddy's hand."

Suddenly Tazkia threw herself into her work, bashing the dough about with a vengeance. "*So* did my uncle. *He* saw."

After a while of kneading, Ablaa asked, "What would he do if you were to love my daddy?"

She stopped working, to allow some concentrated thought, before answering. "He once told me, just as my husband died, that he would kill any malaun who touched me." She looked to the ground. "But I think he sees your daddy as different. But then he might not."

"Daddy's spent his life fighting. He's a Hindu in a Muslim country. He might just fight back, so Uncle beware."

Tazkia took a deep breath. "Don't *ever* pit your daddy against my uncle. They neither of them deserve that."

The conversation died and they got on with their work. The other children had given up waiting for the teacher, and so the older ones came to help with the noodles, allowing Tazkia to take a step back, to tend her baby. The children had to take turns at kneading, as there was not enough rice-flour for them all to work.

As she finished cleaning the child, she moved close to Ablaa. "I think I'll go and see the Manager. On business. We need the other grindstone to make enough flour."

Ablaa nodded, but managed not to show her delight, and then, privately, she had a dirty giggle while she watched Tazkia's cute backside flip from side-to-side, walking towards the godowns.

The secretary showed Tazkia into Satvinder's office.

"I'll bring some tea."

Satvinder nervously sat her on the visitor's chair, opposite side of the desk from him.

"This is a lovely surprise." He smiled, "Thanks for that piece of warmth this morning. It helped me to settle."

She did not know what to say, and so just smiled. After a long few seconds she took a breath, carefully considered her words, and began.

"I wanted to...." but the door opened and the secretary entered with the tea tray. The moment had gone, and had been replaced by the silent drinking of tea.

Then, "I was going to say before the tea came, we need another grindstone for the business. Ablaa and I were wondering if the company could finance the cost."

A look of disappointment clouded Satvinder, but he quickly pulled round. "That's a good cause, and would help the further development of the village's self-sufficiency."

"It would allow a surplus. We could sell outside of the village."

"*If* they would buy. We have the *leprosy*."

She held her head proud and calmly continued, "But we don't. Once the World outside knows that, we can be ready with the production, and ready to reap the benefits of that expanded market." The young woman continued with her business proposition. "We have rice. But we're still poor. The income from the bare rice is limited when sold in bulk, and we only have two real options to bring in more wealth: grow more rice; or get more for the rice."

"The Field Marshall has ideas in that area. Grow other crops, to fill in the seasonal gaps. He's keen to take in jute production. And looking further ahead, boiling plant which would increase the value of the crop. And swallow up some of the surrounding villages and farms."

"But that would need more land. Bringing in other farms from around the village would bring in the land, but would also bring in more people to feed and house. The benefits would be lost to the expanded population. We need to work with what we already have. Make more of what we have. That's added value. We have the labour, so that's what we should be converting into additional income. We have the labour to turn the raw material, the rice, into a manufactured good, the noodles. Maybe even package them and retail into the towns. And it wouldn't need the level of investment which the boilers would need."

Satvinder grinned, lay back in his chair and lifted his hands behind his head.

She continued, "So, the grindstone. We can pay for it over a period with the income which it would generate."

He was beginning to lose the flow of the business, becoming dazzled by the beauty and intelligence of the proposer. He was longing to offer up propositions of his own, but he was always the perfect gentleman. He sat forward, arms on the desk and, "So you're not asking for charity? A partnership of some kind?"

"Or a loan, if partnership is not possible."

"Have you discussed this with the other partners? Ablaa and James?" No response. "You must all work together on this."

She became a little fidgety, and began to speak, but stopped. A few seconds later she cleared her throat, and gently whispered, "I *have* discussed propositions with Ablaa. Some about the grindstone, others...." She stopped, a little embarrassed. They looked at each other across the desk. She pursed her lips, and then whispered, "We've discussed *you*."

The teacher had heard what he had hoped to hear, but, like a teenage boy, he was stumped. He felt like he was sinking in the mud as he struggled for some sensible input into the thread, but nothing came. The wooing silver knight simply ogled at the beauty in front of him, wondering blissfully if she was really saying what he was hearing.

"Sorry. I've embarrassed you."

"No." He had broken out from his pit. "Honest, no. Just surprised me." He was coming down to Earth, but still stuttering. "So, what have you discussed with Ablaa? Nothing bad, I hope."

She grinned. "I *have* embarrassed you. And you know what, I'm not sorry. I know I've at least hit a spot." She began giggling. "We discussed you and me." She moved closer to the desk. "We're both widower and widow. Don't you think that they go so well together? Well?"

His hands shook nervously. "But not here. Not when we're so different. Your uncle would kill me if we were to get close. I saw him looking this morning."

Grinning, she whispered, "He'll come round. He doesn't own me, he's just my uncle." She reached her hand across the desk, and held his. "He promised to look after me when my husband died. So I think he'll be pleased for me." A short silence. "Even with a Hindu."

The nervous farm manager was still shaking a little as he asked, "Are you propositioning me?" All he got back was a sensuous smile, which did not help. He wanted to pull her over the desk to him, but he couldn't: he had bottled it. The moment suddenly chilled as he suggested with a business-like air, "Then tell me something about yourself."

As if the business matters had returned, she released his hand and moved back from the desk. "I'm a Muslim, born in this village. My parents have died many years ago, my mother from the leprosy, or poisoning, and my father from being squashed beneath a trailer. My four brothers all moved down south into the chars, and I've not heard from them since." She paused for some deep breaths. "My uncle is an educated man, and taught me to read and write. He says that I can leave this hell one day, and be successful, and he says that I'm too intelligent for this village. He's wrong." Her face frowned. "Just reading and writing doesn't make you intelligent. It does help, though. So when my uncle found this man from Satkira who wanted a bride, he proposed me, and the young man accepted me, against the advice of his family. They didn't want him marrying a leper, but for some reason Mo accepted me. He was eighteen years old, and I was twelve." She paused.

"You don't have to tell me everything. That's not what I meant."

"*I* want to tell you. I need to." She began to smile. "We were married when I was still twelve, and lived here. I was told by my mother, before she died, that I need to have nine children, because we'll need five or six to keep us in our old age and, Insha'Allah, no more than four will die early. So we began making our family." She sniffed. "It hurt me a lot when we made love, but we had to keep trying, and the pain did reduce as I got a bit older, but still no children came for many years." A hint of a tear developed in her dark eyes. "We'd been trying for about four years when Mo became ill with the poisoning. His family disowned him as a leper, and never spoke to him again, but I stuck with him, and about a year later, I became pregnant. It was like a gift from Allah. Mo died before our child was born." She wiped her eyes on her sari. "So my little one is the most important thing in the World to me. He has to make up so much ground, and be as strong as *nine* babies, and be proud and happy." She looked deep into Satvinder's mind. "So I'll not allow prejudice and hatred to rule my little boy's life." She paused, "So, if you can love a Muslim *and* her child without prejudice, love me. Otherwise tell me now and I'll never bother you again."

They looked into each other's eyes for some time. A bond was forming between those two distant shores, and they both dreamed that the ferry crossing could be a smooth and enchanting ride for them both. But the door opened.

"Sorry Tazkia." It was Ablaa. "Little Mo is crying, and I don't know how to calm him."

The moment was broken, but before Tazkia went off to her child, Satvinder stated, "We've successfully negotiated a deal, a loan, which will bring another grinding wheel to the village, if that's agreeable between all three partners." He looked lovingly at the beautiful young mother. He stuttered, "And, yes... I can." He smiled into Tazkia eyes, before she had to leave with Ablaa.

The two girls spent the rest of the day giggling, playing with the other children, and celebrating an unknown achievement: Ablaa wondered if it was the grindstone, or could it be the love? Tazkia never let on that she had received a vague, but direct, answer to another proposition which she had put to him. At every opportunity she whispering to herself, "Yes he can."

That evening, after they had eaten a meal of beans, lentils and 'company' noodles Satvinder and Ablaa settled down. They were very thoughtful, but tried to maintain the normal round-the-table discussions, even though there was only the two of them.

"I listened to the radio earlier," she reported, "A ship called the Swat arrived in Chittagong today, and there has been shooting and killings because the Dockers refused to unload the cargo, which were arms for the Pak army. It could be bad there, I think. It makes me sad that the port where we were so kindly tended, after the storm, has become a land of hatred."

He moved along a bit, and put his arm around his daughter's shoulder. "Just the mention of Chittagong brings back some mixed memories." They cuddled for a while. "I've had such a strange day, with my best friend going off with my son, into an unknown environment, and which could be hell on Earth. I don't know what to think." He kissed Ablaa on the forrid. "And then this most beautiful thing touched my heart which gave me hope."

Ablaa began to giggle, and jigger around. "She never told me anything, honest. I just guessed that something had happened."

"*Nothing* happened. Well, I'm not sure, really." He pulled his daughter tightly to him. "Do you think that Kaling would forgive me if I was to fall for another woman?"

A wide grin came over Ablaa's pretty face as she squeezed her arm around his waist. "I believe she'd *expect* you to. You're here on this Earth, alive, and she's gone, so you must live for both of you. My mummy always said that despite what some holy men might tell you, life is all important, and love doesn't search out a dead man. My mummy taught us everything. Now *you're* teaching me." She pulled round and reached her lips up to his, and they kissed.

She pulled down. "Ain't it funny, that you're falling in love with my mate, and I'm encouraging it. Not sure how I feel about you loving somebody else."

Satvinder suddenly shuddered. He gently moved Ablaa's arm from around his waist and put a little bit of space between them. He had felt something through the kiss. "I'm sorry," he whispered.

"No, it was me." She tried to lay her head on his shoulder, but he carefully rejected it. "You know, Daddy, most girls are married by twelve or thirteen. My real daddy tried to make me marry a boy a couple of years ago, but I didn't want to, and as my mum was not a supporter of arranged marriages or the purdah controls and all that, she said I didn't have to. So my daddy got badly beat up. He stayed away a lot then, and never spoke to me. Never, ever."

"I'm sorry. Must be bad to lose a father in such a way."

"Sort of. But he wasn't a good man. He used to come home and interfere with my sisters. Then once he tried with me because I was getting bigger, and about ten years old. I scratched his face with my nails and he bled, and he ran away. I really don't miss him." She sniffed, "But I miss my mum and sisters. We were a real team." With that Satvinder allowed her back in, and she had a much deserved lay on his chest. After sobbing for several minutes, she whispered, "I'm scared for James and Akhtar. They're my family."

"Me too."

Her sobbing slowed, and she looked up into his face. "Tazkia's beautiful and clever. Is she more than me?" She was stretching up towards his face, but he pulled back. "Daddy?"

"No. You're so perfect. But you're my daughter. My a*dopted* daughter, but still my daughter."

The young teenager quickly snapped a kiss on his lips, and then, seductively, "If you *could* choose, who'd you choose?" She pecked another kiss on his lips. "I'll marry you. I'll do anything for you. *Anything.*" She tried to kiss him again, but he put his head aside. "Would you choose me if you could? Or would it be the other woman?"

Satvinder closed his eyes. He was never the strongest man, the one who should have pushed her aside and maybe sent her to bed with a smack, so he had to answer. "*Yes!*" He was assertive. "*Yes*, if I could. But I can't, *so leave it*. I can't." He calmed down. "I took you and James as my children, brother and sister to my daughters, so that's who you are. My children. And I love you as my children, and that's a real, serious type of love. Probably the very strongest type."

With that, Ablaa stood up and smiled. "I hadn't thought of it like that." She frowned a little. "Then we're a true family. *Nothing* to hide." She turned to face the door to Akhtar's room. "*Uncle* Akhtar said I could use his room while he's away, so I will." She very slowly moved towards the door, and as she did, she dropped her sari over her shoulder, which flirtatiously unwrapped itself to show the 'perfectly formed' body of the thirteen-year-old. She was dark with slight curves, and as the sari settled on the floor, her pert body turned to fully face the astonished Satvinder. It was beautiful, firm, small, shining with health, and totally unmarked, with only the wispy pubic hairs breaking the surface. A vision of heaven. He could not help but to take in the vision of absolute perfection, a temptation which could have challenged the strength of God himself. But Satvinder held firm, and could only think of the moment on Monpura when he looked into the washed-out restaurant, to set eyes on the naked Ablaa, desperately holding onto her dead sister. He was sweating and confused.

She whispered, "Almost forgot," as she walked slowly to him. "I haven't kissed you night-night." She stood in front of his face, her bare breasts almost touching his nose, and she bent down, kissing him seductively with her damp lips. "Night-night, Daddy." She walked to the door, turned, "We must pray for Akhtar and James," and then retired into the room, closing the door on the chapter.

Satvinder just put his head in his hands, and wrestled.

Colin Hodgson

# CHAPTER 13 -- JUST A BUNCH OF FURNITURE

The trip to Khulna.

As Akhtar and James walked slowly along the lane, they held each other's hands so tightly. The villagers eventually went from sight. The little boy kept looking up at Akhtar, as if to check to see if he was crying, or laughing, or whatever, but the doctor kept a perfectly emotionless expression.

"What if the bus doesn't come?" asked the inquisitive child.

Akhtar grinned, "Then we'll have a good, long walk ahead of us. I've done it a few times before. Takes about five hours."

But the bus came, and what a relief. It was almost empty, and the driver reported that many people were not travelling because of the 'trouble', but he was wary of talking about quite what the trouble consisted of.

"My family're in Khulna, and I hope they're ok."

"Where abouts?"

"West side. This side, not far from where you stop."

The driver just shook his head and refused to talk any more. That resulted in making the two travellers even more nervous.

They approached Khulna, and were stopped by a police check-point. The area looked quite normal, and as hard as they looked, could not see anything particularly unusual, apart from the police check-point. The driver got out of the bus and spoke to the four policemen.

"Could you please leave the bus!" called one of the policemen. All six of the passengers dismounted, and lined up along the side of the road. "Why're you travelling today?" asked the policeman.

Akhtar replied cautiously, "I'm coming to collect my wife and children. We have some work which they can help with in my village."

The policeman looked him up and down. "Is he with you?" pointing at James.

"He's my nephew."

The policeman looked to his colleagues who all nodded. "You must be careful and best if you can get back to your village soon. What's your job?"

"I'm a doctor. I have a surgery in Chak Sahasa."

"The leper village." He almost turned his nose up. "Where're your family?"

"Dalgett Road. Close to the west industrial area."

"Then, when you leave the bus, go directly there. There's been trouble in that area, and the Army has lost control of that part. You should be ok, but it's not safe to be in Khulna for Biharis or Paks. Don't get involved with any, just get your family." He raised his eyebrows as if to ask, *'know what I mean?'*

Akhtar nodded his head in appreciation of the policeman's advice, and the policeman returned the acknowledgement.

Once the other four travellers had been questioned, the bus continued into the metropolis. Many shops were closed, and one entire block had been burned out, but most of the scenes looked quite normal. James pointed to a gun shop as they passed, which had been destroyed. They guessed that the contents had been taken onto the street and were being used in anger. But, apart from that, they never saw any trouble.

"This is it," called the driver. "I've been ordered by the police to turn up at the Naskon Police Station for official work. So, sadly I won't be running for a few days."

Akhtar looked at James with a nervous grin, "Five-hour walk it is. Won't be taking much with us."

The streets were much quieter than normal, but relaxed. A few rickshaws were still pedalling around, touting for business, so our two travellers gave one of them the responsibility of getting them to their destination. A little way on, the driver pointed down a side road, where they could see a whole street of burned-out properties. In the distance they could see a tractor and cart, and a team of men loading stuff onto the trailer.

The driver turned to them, "Collecting the bodies. Been doing it all day."

"Why?"

"You live here? Then you know why." The driver looked suspiciously at the doctor. "Where you from?"

Akhtar realised the direction of the question. "I'm from here. I'm a Bengali Muslim. As my nephew is." He frowned at James, willing him to keep quiet.

"Only asking."

But James couldn't keep quiet. He was a child, wanting to know everything. "What sort of bodies? Babies?"

The driver sighed heavily. "Bihari babies and kids, and women, and all their men. All gone, and the police didn't even lift a finger." He forced a grin. "I heard they even got stuck in themselves. At least we know the police are on our side."

The travellers pulled together on the seat of the rickshaw, disturbed by the thought of how the people had died. Akhtar, like most East Pakistan nationals, had grown up with violence, mostly sectarian, but his little companion had not. A tear appeared in the boy's eye, and he whispered, "Did they kill them kindly?"

Akhtar never answered.

They arrived home without seeing any more evidence of mass violence, but right outside their house laid a twisted, bloody body. It was a very young man, or boy, with fair skin. The doctor paid the rickshaw driver before carefully turning the body, and feeling his throat for vital signs. "He's dead," he pronounced to the watching public. His eyes had been gouged out. "Please help me to lay him on the side of the road." Two young men helped him to carefully position the body on the edge of the wet road, but the men would not discuss the likely cause of his killing.

"Baka!" he shouted through the door. "Baka!"

From the back of the house rushed his wife, closely followed by the two boys. They were ecstatic at his arrival home. After a tearful reunion, which masked the reality that he had only been away for two weeks, they settled around the table.

"It's been frightening here," she said, with a hint of depression in her tone. "Are you taking us away?"

The mighty Baka, who had ruled like a fire-breathing dragon, was wizened, humbled by the cruelty of her own kind. She clung onto her boys as if all their lives depended upon it.

"We're going to Chak Sahasa. First thing in the morning."

Akhtar went across the street and collected Baka's uncle. "Are you coming, Uncle?"

"No, this is all I know. I'm too old to start again."

So the travel plans were made. They would borrow Uncle's four-wheeled barrow to carry belongings, and walk to Chak Sahasa. After many, many years of collecting and bartering for their worldly possessions, it took a very short time to fill the barrow and the bags.

"D'you think our stuff'll be ok here, until we return?" she asked.

After a heavy sigh he quietly assured her, "Of course. We'll be back as soon as the trouble calms down. We've packed what we need. Money, jewellery and passports. A few clothes. What else could we possibly need?"

It was a sad night for the family, all knowing that their home could be like the Biharis' homes by the time they returned, but also knowing that when it happens, they'd be better off elsewhere. The mood was positive but sombre and Uncle shed many tears over the course of the evening especially as they told tales which spanned back many happy years. The painful tales of civil and religious unrest which had plagued East Bengal for many decades were never told.

Morning arrived, and they said their goodbyes to Uncle, and to their neighbours. The five all walked silently along the street, pulling a four-wheeled barrow which was loaded up with clothes, bundled inside sheets. They were watched by a hand-full of friends. Before leaving sight of their home, Baka and her two sons stopped for one last look. Once they had left their street, the friends were no longer watching, but many strangers were. They all wondered why they were being watched so closely, until three men approached them.

"Where're you going, and why?" asked one of the men, very bluntly. He pointed to Akhtar, who was taking his turn with the barrow. "You first."

Akhtar took a breath. "We're going to Chak Sahasa. We all have work to do there."

The man nodded, and then pointed to Baka. "You?"
"Same."
"No! Tell me."
She slowly repeated what Akhtar had said.
He then pointed at one of the boys, who replied with the same answer, as did the other two boys.

"You!" He pointed at James. "Tell me where you're from. You're not from here."

Poor James was frightened and his face wet, but he held his calm. Nervously he whispered, "Char Monpura. My daddy was drowned there, and I came here with my new daddy and sister."

The men looked at each other before nodding, and then the original talker spoke. "Thank you. Hope you arrive safely. Joy Bangla!"

They all raised their right hands in the air and chanted, "Joy Bangla!"

The people suddenly got on with their business, leaving the proven 'Bengalis' to continue their journey.

"That was terrible," stressed Baka. "What was the matter with them? I thought they were going to rob us."

As the older son took over the barrow duty, Akhtar spoke quietly. "They were making sure that we're Bengalis." He knew that they would have ended up like the lad in front of their house if they'd spoken anything but fluent Bengali. That thinking was intensified as they walked past the end of the street which led to the Bihari quarter, burned out, and still being searched for bodies, and maybe valuables. The reality was beginning to set in.

"We're almost at the road to Dumuria. It'll take about five hours from there, so we must keep going." They all stopped for a short breather, and a change of barrow pullers. The doctor looked around to make sure that no strangers could hear. "If we're stopped again, we must just tell the truth about where we're going and what for, and speak clearly. Be careful not to bring religion into the talk."

Three Hindus, one Christian and one Muslim. They all knew that the real issues were with West Pakistanis and other non-Bengali Muslims, such as the Bihari, but Akhtar was not going to take any chances, and it was very much a matter of who would be asking. And Baka had spent her entire life as a minority in that Muslim world, but this was different and she felt absolute fear for their future, as she had never felt before. It was to be a very long five hours.

As they left the city they arrived at the same police check-point at which they were stopped the previous day.

"Good morning." One of the policemen recognised the doctor. "Be careful on the road, and if you see any army vehicles, stand well aside. People have been run over by their trucks."

"Will they interfere with us?" asked Akhtar.

"Don't think so, but just keep quiet and out of their way. The army are very stressed, and most of them are confined to their cantonments, but the few that have to come out are sometimes unpredictable. They're frightened." He looked along the road. "You're more likely to see Mukti forces. Keep out of their way. They're also very stressed, but with a feather in their tail."

"Is it true that the East Pakistan Rifles have mutinied in Jessore?"

The policeman smiled, and simply replied, "It'll be trouble for us all. Joy Bangla."

The walk along the Road toward Dumuria and Satkira was hard and slow, with muddy patches almost dragging the barrow to a halt, forcing all four of the males to join forces. It was probably fortunate that few vehicles were encountered, the Hartal had stopped much of the country's business, and so a lot of the poor people were walking to wherever they needed to go. One small family group of men, women and children, stopped to talk to our group. They were on their way to Khulna, to seek refuge from attacks in the towns of Dumuria, and all spoke poor Bengali. They were Muslims from India.

"I don't know what to advise." Akhtar was careful with his words. "We've just left Khulna, and left burned-out properties with the families all dead. Non-Bengalis. You should think carefully about your plans. You may well be walking in the wrong direction."

They left the refugee family wondering, and in utter confusion, but they were not willing to remain in their company for very long. The natural defences were beginning to click in, and by the time they had walked for about four hours, they had learned not to speak to anybody unless forced to. And after about five and a half hours they mustered up some celebratory spirit as they approached the lane to Chak Sahasa.

"We're almost there," chuckled James. "Come on, about half an hour and we're home."

That spurred the team on, and the pace stepped up almost to a finishing-line sprint, with Baka sitting on the cart due to her poor feet. As they neared their destination several workers in the fields cheered the return of their doctor. He'd made it!

Ablaa grabbed hold of Tazkia as soon as they heard the cheer. "It must be them! Come on!"

They ran out of the village towards the group, and met James half-way, Ablaa almost suffocating him with love. Most of the village came out to join the family in the celebration of the return of their beloved doctor. Despite the all-time low, some things were still awe-inspiring, setting a new will in the hearts of Akhtar and his family.

It was beginning to get dark as they bundled their belongings into the clinic, and Baka and the boys were ready to drop. They did not even bother to inspect their new home before taking over Akhtar's room for a night's sleep, leaving the men and Ablaa to take up their usual places around the table. Satvinder rather slyly moved round the table to sit *opposite* Ablaa.

Akhtar noticed the distance between them. "You two been scrapping while I was away?" the doctor joked, but his face took on a more serious slant as he received no response. "Oh no. What's happened?" He raised his eyebrows towards Ablaa.

"Well..." She glanced at her daddy. "Well, no. It's not such as a fight nor an argument." She stopped for thought, and Satvinder studied her pretty face, wondering what she was going to come out with. "No, not a fight. A celebration." She started to giggle.

"Come on, you can tell me. I'm a doctor."

Satvinder looked to the ground.

"Daddy has something to tell you. Tell Uncle Akhtar, Daddy."

Satvinder was lost for words. He'd spent all day sitting in his office contemplating his marital lot, stressing over his love for his daughter, but especially stressing over her love for him. Her behaviour the previous night had managed to set him on top of a peak, with a deathly fall threatening from all sides, and she had sowed enough seeds to make him believe that he had to make a choice between his own daughter and Tazkia. The only difference between the choices was the way in which he would die: death by the blacksmith, or death by the doctor. He sat in silence.

"Ok, Daddy, I'll tell Uncle Akhtar the good news." She stopped while her Daddy sweated. Chuckling, she slowly spelled it out. "Daddy might be getting married."

She put her hand in the air and did a high five with Akhtar.

"Come on, then. Tell me who the lucky lady is."

"Guess! Come on, who do you think is the most suitable young lady for my daddy?" She was getting excited. "Come on, you must know."

Suddenly Akhtar stopped laughing. He could see his best mate suffering, and was beginning to smell a fish, and it was not one of Kolala Nouka's chads. "I think you ought to tell me. It'd be rude for me to guess."

She waved her head around, and rushed round the table to Satvinder, grabbing him around the neck and kissing him on the cheek.

"It's... Ready?" She paused for effect. "It's Tazkia! Who else could it be?"

Satvinder suddenly relaxed, relieved, and pulled his daughter hard into him, kissing her full on the lips. With his face nestling against hers, he whispered, "Thanks. I love you. But... Just wait 'til I get you home."

The three of them laughed and joked for a while.

"Just hang on a minute." Daddy was coming back down to earth. "We haven't arranged anything officially yet, so just keep quiet outside this room. I've still gotta live past the blacksmith!" He again pulled Ablaa to him. "I want an explanation when we're alone. It'd better be good."

Akhtar nodded to his mate. "It's great news, but be careful. You know what I mean." The news of a possible wedding in the family did not seem to pull his spirits any higher. It was as if he had just brushed it aside. "Anyway, d'you want to know about our trip? Yes? Well, it's a mess out there. From what I've seen and what I've heard this independence thing is going mad. If you're unlucky enough to be a non-Bengali, you're in trouble. They're killing a lot of people, not just soldiers, and not just West Pakistanis. And it seems that the East Pakistan Rifles *have* rebelled against the West in Jessore. The policeman didn't want to say much, but if it's anything like Khulna, then they'll be killing the soldiers and their families. And anybody who might smell like they support them. We were checked for our nationality, and I think we'd be dead if we didn't speak with a natural Bengali accent. I actually felt sorry for some Indians who were going to Khulna to get away from Dumuria. I bet they're not even alive now."

That all changed the mood. But Satvinder was not going to be put down into the doldrums. He tried to bring the talk back home. "The kid's business is on a roll. They're getting another grinding stone and gonna be making enough noodles to sell elsewhere. Things are really starting to go for this village." He noticed a lack of response from his friend. "Did you hear me? Things are going forward."

"I heard you. Things are going forward." He put his head down into his hands. "We've just walked away from everything we have. It'll be looted within a couple of days. Don't expect me to be laughing too much."

Ablaa pulled a face of question. "What d'you mean everything you have? Explain yourself. Come on."

Satvinder touched her arm. "Careful. He's been through a lot."

"A lot? *That's* why he needs to explain! Not just to us, to *himself.*" The teenager huffed, and shook her shoulders. "Well, go on, explain what you've left behind." She moved around the table and leaned over, to look him straight in the face. "You've just insulted me, so explain yourself."

"*Just* a minute. Now leave him."

"No! Not 'til he's explained to me what he's left behind!" She swung back to Akhtar and shouted, "*What* have you left behind? *Tell* me!"

The door opened, and Baka rushed out. "What's happening?" James followed.

Their entrance calmed the moment. Ablaa stood up straight and nodded towards James, who then shot round to her side. Akhtar sat up, but kept his eyes closed.

"Please, Ablaa. What is it?" Satvinder mentally urged her to explain.

She played nervously with her sari, and then, "It's us. Sorry." She gently put her hand onto Akhtar's. "Sorry, Uncle Akhtar. It's just us." A short silence hung over the group, then she asked, "Do you want *me* to tell *you* what you've left behind?" They all looked around at each other. "Ok, you've left behind a building and a load of furniture." She looked at Satvinder. "That's all. So don't *ever* get down in front of me over a building and a bunch of furniture."

Baka moved slowly to Akhtar and sat beside him. She never spoke.

"Sorry," whimpered Ablaa. "but *we* never think of the furniture we lost when we lost our families." She left the clinic and moved out into the cool night.

Baka went back to her boys, and Akhtar joined them. Satvinder and James settled down on the floor, and Ablaa disturbed Tazkia, who gave her a blanket and a floor to sleep on.

Colin Hodgson

# CHAPTER 14 -- BHANG LASSY

The next few days were strained. Ablaa's timely outburst had left the whole family reeling, questioning all of their spiritual and material values. Akhtar, the object of her attack, was the only one who felt he needed to thank the young girl. As he sat outside in the evening air, watching another fire as it drenched the undersides of the clouds with orange, he understood. He made his mind up to sort it out.

March 16th 1971

The following morning the entire family where together around the table, after eating, including the 'new' members, Baka and the two sons. More than five days of tension had passed since Akhtar's family had arrived, and little had been discussed around the breakfast table.

"Thank you." Akhtar spoke quietly. "We all owe you a debt." He was looking at Ablaa, who had been very quiet since her outburst. "I've been thinking for many hours about how to say this, and here goes." He fidgeted. "I now know what you meant. I watched the fires from Khulna last night, and I thought about what you said, and no, I didn't leave anything behind. I brought everything that matters with me, out of Khulna. Please forgive me for being so shallow and heartless. Because of our diverse backgrounds, we're not devout religious worshipers and maybe this means we don't get the spiritual guidance from our faith that some others get." He faltered, but continued after clearing his throat. "We all need to help each other with our spirits, honestly and kindly, but with enough venom to matter. I apologise for my unacceptable behaviour the other evening."

For a while nobody spoke, as they looked around at each other. Baka and her two sons were new to the round table, and did not know whether their input would be welcome, but Baka was beginning to return to her bullish ways.

"We thought it was *very* rude. We were tired and stressed. We didn't need to be made to feel sorry about how we felt and what we'd been through." She turned to Akhtar. "And what do *you* have to apologise about? You didn't even say anything."

"Because I insulted the feelings of Ablaa, James and Satvinder. All of them, as well as the memories of the people they've lost. They left much more than just furniture behind, they left *everything*. My everything is still sitting here with me. And I apologise to Satvinder for worrying more about a few bits of furniture than about his beautiful news. He's getting married, and we should celebrate, not moan about a few bits of furniture. *Fuck* the furniture. Let it all burn, as long as we're not there when it happens. As long as we're all here to celebrate good things, then we're lucky. We have a future, and our furniture is not part of it." He dropped his head. "And I humbly mourn that Satvinder lost his wife and children, and James has lost his father and brothers, and that Ablaa has lost her mother and father and her sisters, and that *we* have lost *nothing*."

Ablaa moved towards Akhtar, but Baka pushed her hand out to prevent her.

"I'm sorry if I've annoyed you, Auntie Baka, but I wish to speak to Uncle Akhtar." She began to move around the table, but Baka held her away. She did not push, but moved back and sat by James. "I can speak to him from here." She smiled at Akhtar, and then, "You told me to keep the family together, before you went for Auntie Baka. That's all I'm trying to do, keep us together, and the baggage will all have to stay behind, wherever it is. *We're* what matters."

This time Akhtar stood up and moved to Ablaa, wrapping his arms around her neck, and kissing her on the forrid. He sat back down.

For several minutes they all remained silent. Then, "A truce!" snapped Satvinder. "We're in a sad, dangerous environment, and we need each other. So, let's truce."

They all looked around and nodded, but the silence continued. It was broken by the instigator. She had listened to the radio and she had news to report. "Jessore is in turmoil, with the West Pakistan soldiers and their families being slaughtered by the East Pakistan Rifles and the Mukti Fauj. The radio played it all down, but the carpenter and the blacksmith have both heard from their families in Jessore, and they're killing everybody who's not Bengali. But the radio also reports some good news: Yahya Khan starts negotiations with Sheikh Mujibur today. It could all be sorted soon."

A glimmer of hope spread around the table, which became a little bit contagious.

"I've also got some good news," boasted Satvinder, "I've got a meeting with the blacksmith. Tazkia let it slip that we're sweet on each other, and guess what, he hasn't killed me, yet."

"That's wonderful," whispered Baka. With an apologetic mourn in her voice, "I think Ablaa's right, there are good things for all of us to celebrate and look forward to."

"Thanks. And yesterday the phones worked, and I got a telex from the Field Marshall. He's coming tomorrow."

Akhtar pulled a letter from his trousers. "And I almost forgot. Baka had this waiting for me when I arrived in Khulna. It's in my brother's handwriting." He held the crumpled envelope, wary of opening it. He did not want any more bad news. "Suppose I should open it." He studied the writing. "The envelope's well written, done on a desk or something. Not rushed." He took a large breath, and opened the letter. After a couple of minutes he spoke. "It's good news. It's all good." His face stretched wide with a grin of relief. "He's got a job in London, and wants me to follow him over there. He's already left, and has got rental on a four bedroom house in north London, plenty of room for them and their ten kids, and he's gonna talk to the hospital about a job for me."

The whole family stood up and shook his hand.

"London." He pulled Baka to him and they giggled. "Fancy London? The streets are paved with gold. And diamonds and rubies. And it only rains some of the time." They held each other tightly as the others, all grinning, gave them some space, leaving to get on with their chores.

Once outside, Satvinder called everybody together in a huddle. "Don't mention London to anybody. It may not happen, but also these folk may panic if they think they're to lose the doctor." He looked especially to Akhtar's two sons. "These folk'll quiz you about where you're from and where you're going. Just say that you're here 'til the trouble calms."

The two boys went with Ablaa and James to help them with their noodles business, while Satvinder went off to the office, leaving the Doctor and his wife to open up the clinic. Life had suddenly become normal.

After a couple of hours of fiddling his thumbs and wondering what to do, Satvinder was disturbed by his secretary.

"Sir, the Field Marshall is on the phone."

That was quite a novelty for the farm manager, who had spent most of his life without any telephone contact with anybody. He carefully took the phone, wary that it might bite him.

"Gnuru here, old chap!" He boomed down the phone. "How's things?"

"Err, well. We're getting ready for the next harvest. May have to move the other goods."

"Right. I'll see you tomorrow, but just in case I get shot on the way, be sure to get about a fifth of the rice harvest into the old godowns. You'll want to hang onto it for the village."

The Field Marshall's bluntness knocked a bit of the wind out of his sails, seeding concern that the little bit of good news, Khan and Rahman negotiating, was maybe not so good, but he decided not to tell the others until the Field Marshall had made his visit. He suddenly had an urge to do something nice, and try to break the low spirits so he walked over to the nurse's room.

"Congratulations, Sir." She spoke slowly, like somebody who might not do much talking. "I heard you're getting married to Tazkia. I'm pleased for you both."

He frowned. "Who told you that?"

"Everybody knows. Why?" So much for his secret.

"Oh, nothing. It's about that that I need to talk with you about. Me and Tazkia." He looked around to make sure they were alone. Just nerves! "Could we have a nice meal tomorrow afternoon? The Field Marshall is coming, and also I'd like to invite Tazkia, with her uncle as chaperone. Just do something nice for a change?" He felt a sudden jolt. "I mean different. Your food's always nice but.... You know what I mean."

She agreed that she had enough fish, noodles and sweet potatoes to put something together. The party was set.

That afternoon he sent word to the Blacksmith and to Tazkia, and they both accepted the invite.

March 17th 1971

The usual breakfast gathering got underway. Once the feeding was over, Akhtar asked Ablaa if she had listened to any radio.

"Jessore is under the control of the East Pakistan Rifles and the Mukti rebels. The airport is closed. But there was mention that the negotiations between Rahman and Kahn are not going well and so the National Assembly meeting for the twenty fifth of March is likely to be cancelled. Apart from the reports of many shipments of arms still arriving at Chittagong, they just talk about the breakdown of civil law and the poor people who are being killed and raped."

James sat with his two cousins. "Are they killing and raping children?" he asked.

"I don't know. I shouldn't think so," Ablaa responded, half-heartedly. "I think that we need to get some good local news to keep us motivated. Anybody got any?"

James stuck his hand in the air. "Me!" He stood up on his chair to address his family. "The teacher said that the refugee border control north of Satkira is still open. She knows some people who set off for it just yesterday. We could go there. We don't have to go through the Sundari swamps." He laughed with his youngest cousin. "We could go there soon." He moved to his daddy's side.

"That's a good idea." Satvinder humoured the little adventurer. "But first, I've got some good news. We're having a party this afternoon. The food's laid on and we've got guests coming. The Field Marshall, and guess who else."

"I know!" shouted James.

"I can guess." Ablaa chuckled towards Akhtar and Baka, who both raised their eyebrows. "Who do you think, James?"

"It's the Field Marshall's driver."

Satvinder shook his finger.

"Then it's your girlfriend. It's Tazkia!" James put his hands in the air in triumph and sung, "Daddy's getting married!"

"Shh, you'll tell the whole village. Yes it's Tazkia, but she's got a chaperone. I can't believe it, but the blacksmith has agreed to come with her. And I've got to somehow ask for his niece's hand in marriage. I think he might just kill me."

Akhtar suggested, "I'll make sure I've got a stock of bandages and splints at the ready."

And so the scene was set for the party, and the team dispersed into their daily roles. Satvinder did not have to wait for very long before the children began to shout. A rumble could be heard from along the lane, and it was the Field Marshall's white cortina, but he wasn't alone! Ahead of him was an old Landover, and behind were two old army trucks. They stopped short of the village, and as the villagers looked on, the Landover pulled aside to allow the Cortina to pass. The Field Marshall entered the village alone, and stopped in front of the office. He had no driver with him.

"Satvinder. Always a smile. That's what I like about you."

They went into the office for some privacy. Once the tea had been ordered, Field Marshall Gnuru made his first official approach. "I pray to God that the guns are still safe. I need six sets for those renegades along the lane. They promised me a safe route through once I told them that we have six gun sets hidden away."

"They're safe. All of them. But why have they stopped down the lane."

"Leprosy. It scares them. And I made sure they believed it. It'll ward them away from our village."

"What's happening? Is it bad away from here?"

"In places it's like hell, especially for the non-Bengalis. Hundreds have been killed in Jessore and Satkira, entire families have been cut to bits, some raped first, some blinded, ears cut off. A family of West Pakistanis just outside Jessore were all left with their hands cut off. Three of the children have survived, with no hands. Anyway, that's what I've heard." He frowned. "I've a habit of wiping the smile off your face. I'm sorry."

With his eyes glazed, "But Akhtar was told by a policeman that the army was confined to barracks." He thought carefully. "Makes sense, just ignore that. The poor foreigners are unprotected from the mob. What should I tell the others?"

"Nothing, unless you have to. You could be safe here, with your leprosy. Fingers crossed." The tea arrived. "I'm telling you because you're the boss, the manager, and how you use that information with your staff is for your own conscience." He grinned through his beard, and bellowed, "Well anyway, you're Ablaa's puppet, and you lead the others where she leads you! Ask her what to do."

The two men had a laugh.

Gnuru stood up. "But I need to get rid of those Muktis who wait for the guns. Got some sacks we can use?"

They moved into the other godown, and bagged up six guns and some ammunition. The villagers almost looked away in respect as they carried them out of the village to the waiting soldiers, even though they allegedly never knew what was in the sacks.

The soldiers were a scruffy bunch, with no uniforms, but very polite to the Field Marshall and Satvinder, and clearly saw the Field Marshall as a superior officer, saluting him as he approached. And then they were gone.

"Right, let's sort out the farm business."

They spent the rest of the morning setting the plans for the new crop, which was just about ready for harvest, and the storage arrangements. Gnuru seemed convinced that a long, hard battle was ahead, and so he insisted that a sufficient amount was stored away in the old, derelict godowns, away from the eyes of the warring parties when they turn up to raid the village's stock. "You must all look after yourselves."

The afternoon arrived, and it was time to party. Satvinder was nervous of the blacksmith, and quite rightly so. A Malaun was to ask his permission to wed his niece!

As usual, Ablaa took control, and welcomed everybody as they arrived, seating them in their nominated positions and making sure that Satvinder was the opposite end of the table from Tazkia, with the blacksmith at her side. By Ablaa's instruction, the clinic's waiting-seats were disinfected and set out immediately outside the door, and so the party was joined by the rest of the family, James' and Ablaa's children. The kids, aged from Tazkia's little baby up to about eleven years old, had all dressed in their best saris and kurtas.

The whole thing had grown way beyond Satvinder's intensions. But it had been a (Ablaa) team effort, with enough food to feed them all, and even God himself had promised to keep the rain away. So Satvinder simply floated along with the tide.

The fish (hilsa chad coloured yellow by the turmeric), and the rice, noodles and sweet potato were beautifully garnished with the white flowers of wild lilies, and, with the side dishes of shrimp and shellfish, Char Monpura could be smelled on the prevailing winds in Satvinder's mind. Ablaa giggled as he cast an appreciative smile her way.

James, with Baka's boys, ran the food as the nurse declared it ready and waiting, and without even a single mention of war, the party flourished. Once the children had finished their food, they began to play, but the older ones had made some plans and had nominated one of them to approach the table. A little girl, about ten years old and dressed in her Sunday-best light blue sari, was volunteered to make the approach, while the others watched through the windows and doors. She nervously entered the clinic, carrying a gift, and approached Tazkia. The child stood bolt upright, as Tazkia, one of her adopted mums, turned her chair to sit facing her. The child grinned, showing her missing front teeth, whilst offering up the gift and the orphans looked on with an unusual air of happiness and contentment.

The shocked Tazkia took the small gift, and nervously looked at her uncle. It was a beautiful bouquet of bright pink joba flowers, mounted on a small piece of wood and placed in the centre was an intricately carved figure of a dolphin, and created from a pure white piece of sea-shell. The carving had belonged to the girl's mother, who had been presented with it on her wedding day, and it had been created in the Sakharibazar area in Dhaka. It could have even been made by Satvinder's uncle. But, sadly, the kids had jumped the gun. It was a wedding bouquet! The room fell silent, and stayed that way.

The poor girl stopped smiling as the silence unhinged her nerve, and instead began to cry. The blacksmith, solid, stern and somewhat frightening, stood up and the party awaited the explosion. He stepped around Tazkia, leaned down to the girl and picked her up.

He spoke gently. "Don't cry. You're prettier when you smile." She looked into his eyes, and the smile began to return. "That's better." He looked to the door and spoke up. "Could you children come in here, please?" The kids all filtered in, squeezing in amongst the adults, until the packed room held all the family members. "Now, us adults are too stupid to make some decisions, so I'm hoping you can help me. Your daddy wants to marry my niece, but he hasn't asked yet."

The older children realised that they had messed up, and one apologised to Satvinder.

The blacksmith continued. "No apologies needed. I've been sleepless and agitated about this moment, and you kids can make it easy for me. Now, without the prejudices and intolerance of adults, do you, Satvinder's children, all love your adopted daddy, whether Muslim, Hindu or Christian?"

Ablaa chipped in, "And Jainist."

"And Jainist. Do you all love him equally?"

The children, grinning amongst themselves, began to answer, and all the answers were 'yes'.

The blacksmith waved his head in appreciation. An unexpected smile appeared. "And so, without the prejudices and intolerance of adults, could you, Satvinder's children, all love a new mummy, whether Muslim, Hindu, Christian or Jainist?"

Suddenly a cheer went up from the children, and it was interpreted as a 'yes': they approved!

"Then what can I say, but yes. I also approve."

The party exploded, and the children all received much deserved hugs from the adults, before retiring to their chairs and tables outside. It was a happy day for those orphans.

In good old colonial style Field Marshall Gnuru visited his car and returned with a bottle of whisky and they all made strange faces as they toasted the couple.

"I couldn't get any champagne." He winked at Ablaa.

Evening arrived and the children were put to bed by Tazkia and James, and Baka and her boys all retired in to Akhtar's room. That left the usual evening meeting which had two special guests: the Field Marshall and the blacksmith. But as they settled down around the table Tazkia returned. She moved to her Uncle, the opposite side of the table from her fiancé.

"I hope I'm not disturbing anything. But I'd like to thank my future husband for his faith in our love, which must be strong enough to survive our religious differences. And thank you, Uncle, for your faith in our love for each other." She looked lovingly at Satvinder. "We've not had chance to make arrangements, but we will, and we'll be married. There, I've said yes." She grinned at all the guests, and turned to her Uncle, kissing him on the forrid. "Thank you, Uncle." She retired to the orphanage, joining the ever increasing band of children.

The men were left to their evening, with Ablaa being one of the boys, and it was a friendly, unspoiled atmosphere. The whisky had settled the nerves and inhibitions.

The Field Marshall lumped his heavy hand on Satvinder's shoulder. "I'm very pleased for you and Tazkia. She said it all with her departing speech." The Field Marshall poured himself another whisky.

Satvinder frowned. "I'm sorry, Uncle, that I never asked properly. Events took over. I never got the chance."

The blacksmith tensed and looked hard at him. "For one thing, I'm not your uncle." He moved his tight shoulders around. "But as you're marrying my niece.... Uncle's ok." A big grin transformed his harsh face. "Uncle's ok." Then he held his glass towards the Field Marshall, who topped him up with more whisky. "We don't drink alcohol, us Muslims, but we don't marry Hindus either. Life has become upside down, like a fruit bat forced to survive on pork."

They all sat quietly, expecting him to continue, but he said no more on the subject.

The Field Marshall looked across to Ablaa, maybe wondering when she would take control of the evening, and he did not have to wonder for very long.

"Shall we tell stories? It's a party. We should tell stories about other times and places. Who's first?" She looked around the group. "Come on, Daddy's getting married. Liven up."

"Tell you what," suggested Satvinder, "You start the stories. Set the standards."

She thought for a minute or so, and then, "Yes. I've got one." The storyteller cleared her throat. "It was a couple of years ago. We were in our home on Char Monpura, and our home was also a restaurant, sitting right up, looking over the hard. These two men turned up at the hard in a small skip. They'd been along the shore for something, and one of them was Kala Motabab Hang, the moneylender. Not a nice person. Anyway, they left their boat down near the tide line, and sat outside to have some food, and the other young men who were eating moved aside to be away from them. But Mummy wasn't scared of anyone, and because of that she decided she would be kind to them. After my sister had taken their orders, Mummy went out to them and suggested that they move their boat further up the hard, as there was to be a high tide soon. Hang puffed his chest out and said, 'don't be stupid, and get on with your cooking'. Well, my mummy never took no shit, and we all wondered what she would do. Maybe spit in their food, or even put horseshoe crab bits in? Now my mummy's name was legend on the Char: don't piss with Kolala Nouka. So I bet Hang was worrying by the time they left." She took a break to sip some water. "The next morning me and my little sister, Chumi, had forgotten about Hang. We went out into the damp morning, and Hang was there, scurrying about with his mate, getting annoyed and spitting on the ground. So my little sister, who was very young and was allowed to approach adults, asked them what was the matter. And Hang pointed to their boat, well he didn't, because it wasn't there, gone, and he started shouting. And my little sister put her finger in the air and waved it, and said he was very naughty for swearing, and that he must have upset Allah to have been sent such a high tide." She stopped, and sniffed. "Chumi's gone now. I couldn't save her." After a long sigh, she continued, with a smile. "Well, Hang carried on shouting, and as Chumi tutted at the other man she said to him that our mummy had warned them about the high tide and they should have moved the skip. But Hang still shouted. So Chumi took the other man's hand, and turned him round, saying 'it was a really high tide, look', and she pointed up in the air. There, right at the top of the forty-foot sundari tree, was their skip." Ablaa had a giggle. "The tide had been so high, that it lifted their boat forty feet into the tree, towering above our home. And Hang's friend began to laugh, and he couldn't stop, and he had to sit on the ground with Chumi, and they laughed and laughed. After a while, Hang stopped shouting and began to laugh with his friend and Chumi, and the anger was gone. And I have to say we never knew who'd put the boat in the tree, and til the day she died Chumi believed that it was the tide that had lifted the boat all the way up there."

The group loved it. The Field Marshall had to ask, "So you never knew who put the boat into the tree? Your mother?"

"No, she swore on our lives that she'd done nothing, and that made us love her even more. We guessed it must have been the young men who'd heard the way he spoke to Mummy. But the reason that I thought of the story, and my beloved sister, was Tazkia." She looked to the blacksmith. "Sorry sir, but I don't know you very well and I don't know how strict you are. I told Tazkia that she must be careful coming to this party. That she must make her own mind up if she was to marry Daddy, else not marry him. Sorry Daddy." She moved round the table to give him the accustomed hug. "And I think that it wasn't til she came back and said 'yes' that you were actually getting married."

Satvinder quietly reminded her, "She was always the one making her decision." He looked at the blacksmith, who nodded. "Why would you think otherwise?"

She pushed her way onto his lap. "You might have thought that if you asked, she would *have* to marry you." A pause, and then the story continued. "Hang seemed to forgive everything, you know, with the boat. In the end he actually found it funny. So he came to the restaurant to eat one day, with the same friend, and after they'd finished he called for his little friend Chumi to take his money. He said to her that the food should come out of the money he was handing over, and the rest must be given to our father. She didn't know how much it was, because it was English money. It was a hundred pounds. *So* much money. And me and Chumi thought that they'd found the boat joke so funny, that he was giving us a wonderful gift. We were so happy. Our father exchanged in his old boat and got a better one with the money, and he caught more fish, and we were so pleased. But one day, my mummy and daddy had a fight. It was so bad, that me and my sisters had to go outside. Anyway, Mummy wasn't hurt too much, but next day she called me in. She said that Daddy had accepted a dowry, and I was to marry the nephew of Kala Motabab Hang. That's what the hundred pounds was for. The boy was said to be a nice boy, a few years older than me, but she said that my father should not have accepted the dowry without proper consent." She pulled herself into Satvinder's shoulder. "I was only eleven. And my daddy had sold me." The room was deathly as she continued her tale. "I asked my mummy why they'd sold me to somebody I didn't even know, and she said that that was the way it was. So I asked her if she approved, and she said that she wasn't from the Chars and often wondered why she was even there. And no, she didn't approve. So she asked me if I wanted to be married, and I said no, so she said, 'then you don't have to be'. My daddy was beat up, and I never saw him again. He might have even been killed." After a heavy sigh, and a nose wipe, she carried on. "Chumi never knew what the money was for, or why Daddy disappeared. That's how Tazkia reminded me of the story. She might have said no."

It was not the happiest of stories and the evening needed to move on, so the blacksmith asked, "Who's next? What about you, Field Marshall? Tell us about yourself."

He cleared his throat, wiped his beard and then boomed, "Well, I'm an old soldier, served under British rule, and was in the North West at the time of partition. I don't have any nice stories to tell about my experiences from that time. All bad. I'd prefer to forget them." He leaned back. "But I'll tell you a bit about my family. I'm an orphan, just like those kids out there. I can relate to them, and that's why I love them. My real parents were Jainist, and I was born in East Bengal. After the death of my parents I was taken in by a Hindu family who lived quite close to Calcutta and it turned out that they had a special role in life. They looked after, and still do, an artefact. It's so important that no one person knows the whereabouts of the treasure. It would take the knowledge of many members of the family to piece the jigsaw together. So it's secure, waiting for God to ask for it back." He stopped.

"So, what is it?" asked Satvinder. "Come on, you've wet our curiosity."

"That's the thing. Nobody seems to know. There's some jewellery, you know, like a crown and necklaces, but there's something else which is so important. That's what we've been led to believe over the many years. And the family is constantly pushing the children into careers based on the usefulness to the eventual cause."

"All sounds like fairytale."

"I know. But we've been looking after it since the 1770's. That's just over two hundred years. And it's believed within the family that it's to do with God."

Ablaa was recovering from her own tale. "Which God? Allah?"

"We've always been taught that it's about God, *not* religion."

The blacksmith asked, "But which God?"

"There's only one God and she's not owned by any religion. And it's all about *that* God. That's what *we* are taught." The large frame of the Field Marshall stretched out. "I've seen what our family believes is hell, driven by religion. I've seen it in nineteen forty seven, when many of the Sikhs chose to behead their own daughters when they thought the Muslims were coming. I've seen it in...."

"Gnuru!" Akhtar had finally stirred. "*That's* enough. This is a celebration. Please change the subject."

Gnuru stood up and apologetically nodded his head, then sat down.

The blacksmith held his hand up. "I've a story. It reminds me of our village, and of our very own good doctor." He cleared his throat. "An old storyteller who'd been in the army and been to England told us this story many years ago, but I don't know if it's true. There's a place called Wales, in

England, and the people were split between Methodists and Catholics, and never stopped fighting each other. The community was split down the middle by religion. And very luckily for the people of Wales, in England, they had a mountain of which they were all very proud, and on one side of the mountain lived the Methodists and on the other the Catholics. The mountain kept them apart and so they didn't fight. But one day, during the Great War, a surveyor arrived to measure the landscape throughout England, and he needed to measure the height of the Welsh mountain. A representative group from each of the two communities accompanied the surveyor to the top of the mountain, where he made his measurements." The blacksmith took a deep breath, and then thumped the table. "Disaster! Both the representative groups were furious. They, after thousands of years of fighting each other, actually agreed on something, in that they should hang the surveyor by the neck 'til dead. The bastard had pronounced 'this is not a mountain, it's a hill. That's all. *Just* a hill.' Well, the mountain was ten feet short of being high enough to be a mountain, so, it was only a hill."

He reached his glass over to the Field Marshall for a refill. "For the first time ever, the two communities had to talk to each other without fighting. And they unanimously agreed to hang the surveyor to prevent the bad news ever from going any further. They all agreed. But as they raised the gallows on the peak of the mountain, a little boy asked 'perhaps the surveyor has an idea which would please both parties?' So it was agreed and he was asked. The surveyor said, 'make it twenty feet higher, and it'll be ten feet higher than a hill. I'll then accept that it's a mountain.' But the two communities then declared war. 'We'll raise the mountain.' 'No, *we'll* raise the mountain.' And they could not agree, so the surveyor suggested, 'form into pairs, one member from the Methodists and one member from the Catholics, and work together. One from each community in each pair.' And they grudgingly agreed. Over the next few days the pairs worked and worked to carry soil up the hill, and they worked from dawn til dusk, all working in pairs, one Methodist and one Catholic, until they believed that they had risen the mountain by twenty feet. Everything in the two communities of Wales had ground to a halt with everybody pairing up and giving it their all. They were all so exhausted, but elated by their efforts and success, and as the surveyor was brought back to the peak, they all stood in their pairs awaiting the results. He took his measurements. He looked confused, and then he took his measurements again. He cautiously announced, 'It's a mountain. It's *thirty* feet higher than a hill.' As the crowds began to murmur, the little boy spoke out. 'But it should only be ten feet higher than a hill!' The surveyor bowed his head to the joint committee and confessed, 'my first measurements must've been wrong. It was *always* a mountain.' The committee looked angrily around at the pairs of workers who had worn their fingers to the bone, and all for nothing. They hung the surveyor by the neck until dead, and as the wind blew and the body swung around on the creaking gallows, the pairs all hugged each other and sobbed. The chair of the committee decreed that they should all now go home to their respective communities, but no, the pairs had come to love each other, and did not want to be segregated into two warring sides, and so retired to live all around the mountain, integrated as one, and became the Welsh community, united by an unfortunate error. Maybe an act of God. But the little boy asked, 'why should we live happily ever after and just forget David, the wonderful surveyor who broke down our intolerances?' And so England had a new saint, Saint David, the Patron Saint of Wales."

A small applause went around the table.

Ablaa asked, "Is that how Saint David came about?"

"I think so. The storyteller always said it was a true story, but I'm not sure."

She then asked, "What's the moral of the story? Mine was that 'money can't buy everything'. What's your moral message?"

The blacksmith growled, "It's that 'terrible things can lead to happy endings'. Like the leprosy, leading to this party, tonight."

She raised her eyebrows. "Wasn't it the love between Daddy and Tazkia which led to this party?"

He thumped the table. "D'you think I'd be sitting here drinking alcohol and marrying Hindus if this was a normal World? It's all about the leprosy, and the good Doctor, of course." He smiled. "He might one day be Saint Akhtar, of Chak Sahasa."

Akhtar, "I hope you won't have to hang me, first!"

The blacksmith grinned.

Gnuru carefully suggested, "If you tell the story again, you might want to know that Wales isn't in England. It's in Britain."

"Nit picking! Anyway, they all look the same to me!"

Satvinder chipped in. "Lovely story, Uncle. As you say, just like this place, united by misfortune." He stood up. "But more importantly, my new Uncle didn't come to this party empty handed." The two newly allied men grinned at each other. "I think our esteemed cook has probably sorted it, and so let's party."

Akhtar, grinning from cheek to cheek, went out to the kitchen and returned with a tray of small dishes, each filled with what looked like yogurt.

He cockily announced, "Since this is my clinic, I'm going to make the speech. We've seen the start and almost the end of the spring with only one single celebration: we feasted when the orphanage opened and that was wonderful. But no spring feasts or Holi, just worries. So a bit belated, here we have it, the best Bhang Lassy in the World, compliments of Satvinder's new uncle. Here's to the life-giving spring, and to Satvinder and Tazkia's wonderful future together."

The group all cheered, and went on to get totally stoned.

# CHAPTER 15 -- SOMEBODY I ONCE KNEW

March 18th 1971

The next morning was damp, and it had rained for most of the night. The working area for the noodle business was muddy, even beneath the thatched canopy, and so Tazkia and James did not get started on the grinding work.

"We'll have to get more cover. The proper rains will soon be coming." She sighed heavily. "The children will have to help us to extend the roof that way. She pointed towards the orphanage. As she did, the children came out from eating and joined them.

"Well?" asked James, grinning. "What d'you all think of our new mum? She'll be all our mums. Even Ablaa's."

The group laughed at the thought of Ablaa being demoted to a mere child member, but they soon stopped when she emerged from the clinic.

"What's the joke?" she asked.

James was not scared of his big sister and so, "You're gonna be one of the kids. Tazkia's gonna be your mum."

A little hung-over, she sat down on a dry sack and calmly replied, "It'll be lovely. I think we'll all get on like a tornado."

Tazkia grinned at her mate, and then looked to James. "That pissed on your fire. You'll have to find something else to stir about."

He put his hands in front of his face, like claws. "What, like you being a bossy mum, like a fire-breathing dragon?"

At that Tazkia jumped up and flew towards him, but he was too quick, so she took up the pursuit, and with a throng of giggling and shouting all the children joined in. Just at that point Satvinder emerged from the clinic with the Field Marshall, and they stood back in amazement as a tiny little Benny Hill was chased from pillar to post and around the houses by a screeching bunch of Hill's Angels.

The Field Marshall and Satvinder eventually settled into the office, hung over from the whisky and the cannabis.

"Water. Lots of water." The big man filled two mugs with filtered water. "I've every faith in our doctor. This water's clean, and will get rid of these self-inflicted headaches. It's the de-hydration which causes it." He grinned at Satvinder, who was not used to the excesses of alcohol nor of drug abuse.

They both spent some welcome time in silence, and drank lots of water before worrying about the day's plans, but the silence was soon broken by the secretary.

"We can't get international lines on the phone, but the telex is still working." She handed Gnuru a print from the machine.

He studied the document, sent from their Anglian headquarters, and then explained, "Things are moving forward rather desperately. Our people have news from up north and there's big trouble started to develop in Syedpur and Rangpur. Just about all the Urdu speaking people are under serious threat from the others, particularly from the Hindus. The army are no longer confined to their cantonments, and I would guess that they've probably come out to fight. And they've been reinforced in some areas, particularly around Dhaka. All the cities seem to be in chaotic revolt."

Satvinder raised his eyebrows. "It's good to be in the countryside right now."

"Just how long that lasts is anybody's guess." He pushed back in his chair and pulled at his beard. "There's some even more sinister bad news. The Pak government are expelling all but a handful of selected journalists. That can only mean one thing: they don't want the World to see them when they administer the retribution for the recent inhumanities against the Biharis and Paks."

"Has it really been that bad?" A brief silence and then, "We witnessed some of it, with the manager. Was that you?"

"No. Please believe me. It was nothing to do with the Company, but sadly the Company *did* allow it to happen."

"Could the Company have stopped it? You talk like you're something special."

Gnuru had another fiddle with his beard. "I like you. I love those kids, and Akhtar *is* something special, totally dedicated to his cause. And your little lady, Ablaa, well she's a mind in a million. What a waste if she decides to stay right here. What a waste if *any* of you decide to stay right here. Now, a state of emergency has been adopted by the Company regarding East Pakistan, and I'm telling you this because you're so wrong to say things like 'You talk like you're something special'." He pointed straight into Satvinder's face. "*You're* the Company, as I am and Akhtar is. So please rephrase, to refer to 'us' when you talk of the Company. You're part of the most powerful group of Companies in the World. You're one of us." He stood up. "Because of the state of emergency I've been given leave to act entirely as I feel necessary in all matters regarding the Banchi set-up, so I'm trying to tell you that you're all free to leave this village and to seek refuge in India. I've read between the lines, and listened to a bit of drunken conversation, and I know that you're planning on leaving, but have been afraid to talk to me about it. You think I'll kill you, as you believe I did the other manager. I'm telling you, Satvinder, that you can leave when you want, and when you arrive in Anglia, you'll *still* be part of the Company. I give you my word."

The secretary entered with a tray of tea.

Gnuru continued. "This tea comes from the hill tracts close to Chittagong. Another one of our companies. They've already left."

Satvinder just sat and thought. A great weight had been lifted from his shoulders in knowing that they could leave without the Field Marshall ordering their execution. He was lost for words.

But Gnuru was never lost for words. "The Anglia region is not a pretty place but it's an important place. It's revered beyond any human imagination. It's a place which holds the answers to our future, and it's about God, not religion. You won't find paradise there, but you'll be able to live in peace. It's managed by a sect called the Chi Bantri, and despite what many people think of them, they're all powerful. And something holds the people together as they wait, something bigger than religion, and my family believes much bigger than the Chi Bantri. They all wait for her return." He just stopped, maybe for effect.

"Who's return? You're not making much sense."

"The Mother of God!"

Wow, Satvinder sat back in his chair, and for the first time he saw an old war-monger who had lost his marbles. Barking mad!

"You don't have to believe me. I'm not a preacher trying to convert you, just a friend who wants you to survive. So get to Anglia and wait. Or, you could stay here and be butchered." The old war-monger frowned. "You've all been cocooned here in this veritable paradise of leper-land, while the towns and cities bleed. It's hell for anybody caught up in it. Do you know where hell is? I've seen it over the years, and it's right here. Hell is just a little piece of heaven gone wrong, and hell exists in East Bengal in ever increasing quantity. Get out while you still can."

There was a knock on the door.

Satvinder invited the knocker in. It was Ablaa.

"Sorry to disturb you, Daddy, but Tazkia's uncle has just told her that he's going to Jessore to be with his family, if they'll believe him about the leprosy. He's to stay there if they'll let him."

Gnuru. "Is he still drunk? Jessore's not the place to run to right now."

"He wants to be part of the rebellion there. He's heard just now that it's in the hands of the East Pakistan Rifles and the Mukti. And he wants to stand for his country."

The old soldier sighed. "There'll be many thousands following him. Please wish him my best."

Satvinder held Ablaa's hand. "Can you tell him that I'll look after his niece, and we'll all meet up again soon?"

She grinned at him, and said what he couldn't, "Insha'Allah."

Once she had left, the Field Marshall poured some more water. "Sometimes, when you're dying of thirst, the only thing that matters is water. When you find some water and then get hungry, the only thing that matters is food. When you find some food and you become threatened the only thing that matters is defense. And when you overcome the threat and get thirsty the only thing that matters is water. And so goes life."

Satvinder was beginning to wonder about the sanity of the old man. He had probably seen things which most people would choose never to see, and done things which most people would choose never to do, and the scars were beginning to show. But Satvinder could relate to him. He was making some sense, and so he asked, "When should we go? To this land of mystique where the Chi Bantri rule over a people who just wait. Is there a good time?"

"I know you jest a little. God's too big to comprehend, which is why man has to create religion. It's more black and white. You know what, old chap, if you could learn to see the important things in life in full colour, you'd see what most cannot. Think about it as you struggle through.

And you want a straight answer? Go now." He stood up. "Although I work for the most powerful secret society the World has ever known, I still have to stay alive. I need to get back to Calcutta." He held his hand out and in it were half a dozen business cards. "You should all have one of these. Just in case."

As he turned towards the door he stopped. "Coming?"

Satvinder put his hands on his head. "You know I can't. Unless you can fit about thirty-eight people in the car.

"I'll look out for a bigger car. In the meantime, God be with you."

"I won't even ask which one."

"No. There's only one. Ours."

Field Marshall Gnuru waved to the villagers and to the children as he drove his white Ford Cortina down the lane, through the glorious sunshine of late spring. Satvinder felt an empty hole punch into his heart. "Somebody I once knew."

Over the next few days the family discussed the openness shown by the Field Marshall, and the advice which he had left behind. But it was difficult to run away from something which had not yet happened and may never happen. Baka was adamant that they would not go to Calcutta, but to London, where they could walk the gold-lined pavements in peace. She was a stronger personality that Akhtar, who could do nothing else but to go along with her plans. He was to go to London with his family of a wife and two sons. His other family of thirty four would go to Calcutta.

Some of the issues which were first revealed through the telex were being reported over the radio and had developed into more than just demonstrations. In the industrial area of Jaydevpur, close to the outskirts of Dhaka, militant strikes had begun and many roads blocked causing the shutdown of much production. In addition the foreign-owned industrial premises were attacked and set alight, and so the Pakistan Army responded by opening fire on the demonstrators and arresting many others. Indications from radio reports had over fifty people being shot dead and many others injured, but the family were a little concerned that some reports were politically biased. But at the direction of the thinker, Ablaa, the family did at least assume that the reports were based on truth, although sometimes exaggerated. People had been shot dead in Jaydevpur by the Pakistan military! They at least could believe that.

Further news came on the twenty fourth of March that the northern cities mentioned by the Field Marshall, Syedpur and Rangpur, had come under martial law. In the heavily Urdu-speaking city of Syedpur, East Pakistan's third largest city, demonstrations, some of which were violent and destructive, were squashed by the army forces, who shot dead hundreds of Bengali nationals. It was also reported that several Bengali officers had been arrested or killed as a measure to deter mutiny amongst the ranks. The Pakistan Army moved out of their cantonments with orders to take back control of the towns' law and order.

Similar situations broke out in the country's second largest city of Chittagong, as the reinforcements and supplies continued to roll in from West Pakistan.

But total control seemed a little way off as police and the Rifles regiments continued to support their homeland's demands for independence, and in an effort to maintain control of the air many Bengali members of the Pakistan Air Force were removed from office as mutinies became the order of the day. The Pakistan forces violently removed the enemy within!

All talks between the Awami League and President Khan had ceased. The whole country was in the grip of civil war, with many towns and cities no longer controlled by the military government. Heaven really was going wrong.

The radio was still broadcasting from Chittagong into the evening of the twenty fourth of March 1971.

"We must make some decisions," insisted Ablaa. They all sat around the table and looked at each other. "The radio gives a very black picture of our country, with many towns now in the control of our police forces, and in constant battle against the Pakistani Army and the Bihari sympathisers. And the Mukti forces are having some success against the military, taking control along with the police, and keeping the Pak Army shut up in their cantonments. And we must pray for Tazkia's uncle who's gone to fight for his country in Jessore. He's a brave man."

Akhtar raised his eyebrows. "So you think we should all go off to fight?"

"Sorry, Uncle Akhtar, but that's not what I'm saying. *Don't* put words into my mouth."

Akhtar apologised.

Satvinder suggested, "We need to wait to find out where this may go. The borders near Satkira are in turmoil, and the carpenter has heard that the Indians were not allowing many people to go into India unless they have the correct documents. It could be safer to stay here for the time being. After all, we could come out on top and achieve independence without it getting much worse. During partition people were massacred because of their religious differences, but the Punjabis and most of the East Bengalis are Muslim. It could keep them from outright war."

"Nice idea," chipped Akhtar, "But where does that leave you and Baka, and James. And half this village?" He looked at his wife. "Perhaps you malauns should all go ahead of us. And if it all goes quiet, come back. I think it'll be the Hindus who'll be in real fear of their lives from the Pakistanis."

Satvinder pulled Ablaa and James into him. "I can't." He had an air of guilt in his voice. "We've already done that, gone ahead. Now Kaling and the girls are gone. They were left behind to die."

"Rubbish!" Akhtar thumped the table. "You can't ever blame yourself for what happened."

"I *can*, and I *will.*" The evening discussion was becoming fraught. "Sorry, but I'll *never* do that again. *Never.*"

Ablaa came to his rescue. "Please Daddy, it was the Paks who killed your family, not you. But let's just settle some things about our future. Uncle Akhtar and Auntie Baka, with the boys, will set off to London at some point, and the rest of us, ALL of us, will set off to India at some point. We mustn't split up. All thirty four of us must stick together."

Colin Hodgson

# CHAPTER 16 – OPERATION SEARCHLIGHT

March 25th 1971

The next morning, the twenty fifth of March, was again bright, and the spring spirit still drove the children in their innocent play. They woke the village as they chattered and chuckled, dressing, cleaning, and eating their rice and egg breakfast while their adopted guardian, Tazkia, fussed over them like an old mother hen. And when the war planes flew overhead, they all cheered.

Aside from the noise of the planes the countryside seemed so peaceful that day, and apart from the continued radio reports which painted a hostile and dangerous picture of many East Pakistani cities, everything was calm in Chak Sahasa. There had never been a better time to be an untouchable: *never* had there been a better time to be a leper.

In reality Chak Sahasa was left alone for many other reasons, as were most of the villages at that time. The main emphasis for the rebels and the dictators was on the towns and cities which held such things as the cantonments, the East Pakistan Rifles, the police stations, the seats of power, the commerce, the banks, the foreign embassies, and the mass movements of the people. Since Sheik Mujibur's renewed call for an independent state of Bangladesh, the East Pakistan cities had been in unparalleled rebellion. The East had turned its venom onto its self-appointed master, West Pakistan, and the liberation movement was becoming hungrier by the day, metamorphosing into a monster which devoured all non-Bengali citizens whether military or civilian.

Many of the East Pakistan Rifles had rebelled and driven the West Pakistani military into their cantonments. The police forces had retired into their stations, and thus allowed the masses to control the streets. The freedom of the rebels to openly demonstrate brought about the freedom for retribution, and many a hatred-driven score was settled. Thousands of non-Bengali speaking citizens were attacked and often seriously mutilated or killed. Weapons had become available to the mass as the gun shops were looted, and those who had no guns used whatever they could find: bamboo spears, machetes, and even farm implements. If they had no weapons, it was fists and feet which administered the killings. It was an ugly, cruel rebellion.

As of the twenty fifth of March, 1971, the two wings stopped talking. President Yahya Kahn and his generals had not wasted the previous months, but had martialled a strengthening of the West Pakistani forces in the East wing, and the time had arrived for the East and the West to become reunited. Martial law was the chosen route as the diplomatic roads had all been closed by the inability of the politicians to work together, with Zulfikar Bhuto and Sheik Mujibur at total loggerheads.

Orchestrated by President Yahya Kahn's generals, Operation Searchlight was unleashed. All hope of democratic rule was laid to rest.

The longer-term objectives of the operation were to establish an environment which would allow a settled Islamic state of Pakistan, with the unreliable and unpredictable people of the East being ruled by the West Pakistanis. The East could then be re-educated along proper Islamic lines, termed the Islamisation of the masses, which would stifle any cessationalistic tendencies whilst also embedding strong religious bonds between the East and the West wings. But that was for the future!

In order to reach that future goal of a true Islamic state, the largest in the World, the West Pakistan generals had to confront the present. They had to quell the uprising, and then remove all identifiable objects which stood in their way. They were to install full Martial law into the major cities and towns, arrest Sheik Mujibur Rahman, and annihilate the Awami League and all who stood for it. They were to remove the rebelling East Pakistan Rifles, remove rebelling police forces, execute Bengali officers serving in the Pakistani army and air force, kill the rebellious students and other intellectuals, and frighten the poor slum dwellers into submission. And the Hindus? The West Pakistan junta knew that the ten million Hindus in East Pakistan would never become Islamised.

And so, after most of the foreign journalists had been removed from the country, Operation Searchlight was to begin.

Just before midnight on March the twenty fifth 1971, while our friends in Chak Sahasa slept, the military forces moved out from their cantonments and onto the streets. As the military and Bihari teams sought out and killed Awami party members, the Pakistani military made its assaults on the major problem areas.

Chittagong had come under the control of the troops who had mutinied, and so Pakistani troops were mobilised from Comilla, moving south to face the mutineers and the East Pakistan Rifles.

Jessore, the home town of our blacksmith, had come back into the control of the Pakistani military, and as Operation Searchlight began, they mobilised to move northwards towards Kushtia.

In the northern cities of Rangpur and Syedpur the military enforced martial law and in the eastern city of Sylhet the Punjabi forces battled to win back control.

Our home town of Khulna was in the throws of ferocious combat as the frontier forces of the twenty second continued their war with the rebel East Pakistan Rifles, the police and the Mukti volunteers.

On paper the assault on the East Pakistan rebels was a foregone conclusion, with the might of the tanks, artillery and air force showing no respect for the disorganised rebels who were armed with hand weapons and little else.

The early hours of 26th March 1971, dreams of Dhaka.

Satvinder was restless, and each time he drifted into sleep he was shocked by visions of Kaling, his girls and his uncle in Sakharibazar. His wife and children were smiling with an air of deep sadness, looking down at an old man, pure white. His chest was covered by beautiful mother of pearl which shone with an iridescence, but the man was lifeless. Satvinder's uncle lay in front of Kaling, in peace amongst his sakhari brooches and smiling up at her, but with a tiny tear in his eye.

Satvinder lay back down and closed his eyes. He wanted to see more of the dream and how it had been formed, but it never came back. He lay wondering if his uncle had finally gone to heaven, waiting to be returned as a better being, maybe this time as an almighty tree, even one like Ali's Sundari which saved himself and James from certain death. Maybe anything.

He could not rest. He left the clinic to get some air, and found that he was not alone. Many of the men had left their beds to look and listen: to look at the clouds which again had fire under their bellies, this time from the north-east as well as from Khulna; to listen to the distant sound of artillery fire which wafted for many miles across the light winds; to pray for those who were in personal hell.

"Satvinder. What're you thinking?" It was the wiry young carpenter, almost invisible in the dark.

He looked round towards him. "I'm thinking of my wife and children. And my uncle." He waited, wondering if the young man who had once riled him would offer some much needed spiritual comfort.

"You've a new wife-to-be. Think of her. Your other family's dead."

He appreciated his blunt realism and a huge sigh came from deep inside. He smiled at his young neighbour. "Now that the war's really started, and we're all on the same side, I'll explain where my wife and children are. They're dead. And I'm a lecturer from Dhaka University."

The young man laughed. "We all know that. Always did."

"Is there anything private in this village?"

"No. So relax. We've no secrets."

So Satvinder relaxed. "I spoke to a philosopher once, such a brilliant mind. She spoke of my wife and children and said that 'the past is never dead. In fact it's not even past.' What do you believe?"

The carpenter looked out towards the fires of Khulna. "If I knew what it meant I could comment. Explain to me."

"I've spent a couple of months wondering what she meant. Every time I come up with an answer, I get confused. I fear that one day I'll find out, and not like it."

They watched the distant glow for a while, and the entire village was silent.

Then Satvinder asked the Carpenter, "What d'you know about what's happening in Dhaka? You seem to know a lot, what about Dhaka?"

"I do know a lot, but not everything. But according to the radio broadcasts from Chittagong, all the foreign journalists have been expelled from Dhaka. So they'll move in."

"What'll they do?"

"Kill everybody in their way. And that includes us Hindus. We've more to gain from independence than any other Bengali, so we're the enemy."

"But the EPR are holding them at bay."

"They're in disarray, and are scantily armed. One tank'll probably take out an entire regiment. The East Pak Rifles are just border guards, but the Pak army are an offence army. All we can hope is that they've not enough manpower to come out of the cities. That'll give the Mukti forces time to establish, and we can get arms from friends, then there's a chance. Else we're all dead."

Very soothing words.

Satvinder sat down by the clinic and tried to return to his dream. He was worried about his last surviving family member, his uncle in Sakharibazar. But the dream was gone.

The early hours of 26th March 1971, Dhaka.

The 57 Brigade had rolled into Dhaka at midnight, clearing the road blockages as they went, and removing all opposition, and killing hundreds. The tanks and artillery were not going to be stopped by the small arms of the rebels, nor by the chants of Joy Bangla which were quickly silenced by the army's rifles. They quickly took control of the main streets, indiscriminately destroying many buildings and businesses. As the army killed hundreds of people with their rifles and tank fire, the city panicked, most hiding up in their houses and hoping.

There were many targets, one being the Halls of Residence at the Dhaka University, and the residential flats of the teachers. Many students were killed in just a few hours, and teachers and lecturers were individually sought out for extermination, as part of the eradication of the Awami League movement. The Hindu residential halls were specifically targeted, with hundreds of deaths and violent attacks and many students of all religions were marched out into the university grounds, and shot dead.

Satvinder's uncle could hear the guns and artillery which fired in the distance, but as he sat at his table, head in his hands, he could sense the destruction moving closer to his home in Sakharibazar. His door suddenly rattled, as somebody tried to get in.

A weak voice, whispering, "Please, it's Syed!"

Uncle looked out of his window, before opening the door to his old friend and his wife.

"Thank God you're in. Can we stay here?"

Syed was a good friend of Uncle's, and they had suffered together in the nineteen fifty massacre, both losing their families to the mob, but both remaining to rebuild their lives on their own. Neither of them could explain their will to continue after the horrific torture and murder of their families, but they remained. Syed had since taken another wife, but, like Uncle, the scars never healed.

"Can we stay here with you? We're frightened. And we don't want to stay there." Syed ran a small Hindu temple at the other end of the street. "I don't want to be there when they burn it."

Uncle sat his ageing friends down at his table. "We'll all stay here and wait." He turned the lights off. "It's funny, but I've waited for this moment for many years, and made so many plans of action, like hide here, run there, but here we are, doing nothing. What a cruel life we live in."

Syed put his parched old hand across the table and held Uncle's. "We're too late to do anything. You did it for your boys, got them out. That was your finest achievement." He looked down. "My girls weren't able to go, as you remember."

The sound of shell and small-arm fire moved ever closer. It had reached the Patuatuli police station, just a few hundred yards away, where a desperate battle raged between the Pakistani army and the police officers, and where Kaling's friend Captain Hussain served. He served his country well that night, but never again saw daylight.

The sound of gunfire and screaming was suddenly inside their street. An artillery shell blew up quite close to them, sending everything in the shop into a shake. Several carved ornaments fell from their shelves.

"Leave them," whispered Uncle. "I'll pick them up in the morning."

The noise continued, and the shop rattled to the shock of the shells, but the old folk just sat and stared towards the window. They could then see people outside the shop, and the familiar dappled light from burning buildings appeared on the walls across the road. The street was on fire. Syed stood up and hobbled across to the window.

"The army are at the other end of the street." He spoke quietly, but calmly. "And there are other people ahead of them, who haven't got uniforms. They might be Bihari helpers." He pushed against the glass to get a better look along the street. "They're going into some of the houses." The old man looked away. "We should pray for them," he paused, "and then for us."

The Pakistani soldiers never came further than the end of the street. The tank had stopped, as if to allow the helpers to carry out their orders before any further advance.

"Come away from the window!" urged Uncle.

But it was too late. The window shattered as the back of Syed's head opened up like a volcano, and he fell to the ground. He had been shot in the face, and his blood quickly flooded the surrounding floor as his wife screamed, and Uncle jumped to his old feet. Their time had quickly come. A grenade was tossed through the broken window and they were all gone.

The battle for Sakharibazar was uncontested and fast, with Satvinder's uncle leaving this life in record time. But the area did have one champion to remember: Captain Hussain's men fought throughout the night and the battle was still running into the daylight hours. The Patuatuli police station was one of the few pockets of resistance within Dhaka which actually lasted for more than just a few hours. In the daylight of the twenty sixth locals were drafted in to collect the dead bodies, but as Kaling's spirit looked down on the bloody and broken scene she smiled: the collectors had to leave the Sakharibazar until a later date because the Patuatuli police station continued to stand their ground. They didn't have to wait for very long!

Dhaka was taken back into Pakistani control, Sheik Mujibur Rahman was arrested, and hundreds of supporters and officials of the Awami League were killed. The back of the cessation movement was broken in all but a few cities. Operation Searchlight was a military success.

But before his arrest on the twenty sixth of March 1971 Sheik Mujibur Rahman made his declaration of independence. The People's Republic of Bangladesh was at least declared in principle, but still a very long way from reality.


March 26th 1971, Chak Sahasa


Akhtar had closed the clinic for the day, amidst panic, frustration and general chaos. The people of the village knew that Operation Searchlight had been launched, but the radio reports were sketchy, not really saying which parts of the country had been returned to Pakistani control, and which parts were still battling, but they were quite clear that the operation was swift and, in many areas, very concise. It was reported that Chittagong was still being held by the East Pakistan Rifles and other rebel forces, but that Dhaka had fallen. It was also reported that Sheik Mujibur Rahman had been arrested, and that most of the Awami League officers had been killed.

The carpenter requested the use of the office telephone, in the hope that he could get through to one of his family in Jessore who worked there in the University. He was successful, but his cousin was holed up in their offices, and was unable to report what was happening in the wider scene. He thought, as did his friends, that the rebel forces were being moved out into the safety of the open country. But he wasn't really sure.

"It's certainly begun." Ablaa sat with her family around the table, and stated the obvious. "We must keep our ears to the radio and hope for some direction."

Akhtar looked sadly at his family and friends. "What'll happen now? Rahman's gone, probably dead by now, and the Pak army must be back in control." He held Baka's hand. "I hope we haven't left it too late."

Ablaa cocked her head in thought. "Maybe it's not too late. Once they've put an end to the cessation movements, maybe the country will quickly get back to what we've known as normal. Maybe they've done enough to ensure peace. After all, we've no fighting forces left once the East Pak Rifles are beaten."

The group were not in a talkative mood, so Ablaa continued. "Perhaps if we were to get to the Indian border, we could get work permits, through the Field Marshall."

Satvinder went into the bedroom and returned with some business cards.

"I almost forgot. Gnuru left these for us before he left. I think we should all keep one, and that way, at least one of us will still have one when we need it." He paused. "If we need it."

He handed one to each adult, and the one remaining he kept for Tazkia.

Ablaa continued thoughtfully. "Maybe we won't need them. If law and order is returned, we may be quite safe.

Even the leprosy could still be enough to frighten off the intruders."

They all spent some time doing nothing. None of the men or women had gone to the fields that day, and there seemed to be an unusual amount of people wandering around the village. Everybody was in the dark. The carpenter held counsel around a fire, with about twenty of the more influential members of the village.

"We need to think carefully about the developments, and be ready."

An old farmhand replied. "Ready for what? If the army turn up we can't be ready. If they don't turn up we can't be ready. There's nothing we can do but get on with our lives. If we have a future, we need to protect it by keeping our farms and land, and let's face it, there's nowhere to run to."

The carpenter frowned. "I think it may be different for you Muslims. I heard on the radio that in Dhaka they're shelling and burning the Hindu areas. If you listen very carefully, there's still shell fire in the air. It hasn't ended yet."

"Then *you* worry about what *you're* doing, and let us worry about us!"

They all knew that the Hindus had been big supporters of cessation for many years. And of course the Pakistani ruling government have also known that for many years.

"But we must try to work and live together, as we have for years."

The old man just huffed, and nobody else had anything to say. The village was beginning to break down. Satvinder, who had been listening in, became a little more concerned. He needed to speak with his family.

That evening the radio was still broadcasting from Chittagong. It reported that Chittagong was still in the hands of the East Pakistan Rifles and other rebel forces, but that the Pakistani army had moved south from Comilla in preparation for their assault on the country's second city. And the 107th brigade had secured Jessore and was on the move towards Kushtia, where they expected heavy resistance from the rebels. The reports drew a sketchy picture of the country's state but indications were that most of the strategic towns and cities were back under the control of the Pakistani military. The general exception was the many border control units of the East Pakistan Rifles, in small towns such as Satkira and Kalaroa, just down the road from Chak Sahasa. The Pakistanis had taken the major urban areas, but the rural areas were still East Bengali.

"Although they've taken the towns, they can't take the villages and EPR units. They don't have enough troops." Ablaa was convinced that they would have to stay within the major towns.

"But they have all the guns and tanks. All we have are people, and handguns." Satvinder was not convinced that the Pakistanis would stay where they were. "What's the point in taking control of the towns when all around them is controlled by us? They can't stay like that for long."

The reality was that the West had seventeen battalions and regiments compared to the East's five, but the East had over thirteen thousand East Pakistan Rifles troops. The real problem was the equipment, and the West had under its command all the tanks, all the helicopters, all the artillery, and all the gunboats and destroyers. The foot soldiers of the East with their hand guns were no real match against the heavy artillery and the tanks. The mood was low.

March 27th 1971, Chak Sahasa.

The family arose to a wet and doleful day. They had spent the previous day doing little apart from worry and wonder at what might be going on around them in the towns. They felt quite cut off. Satvinder decided that the day must get back to normal.

"I'm going into the office today. I've work to do. What about the clinic?"

Akhtar sighed. "I must open up. People are still ill. It's been a revelation that no new poisoning cases have come in for about three weeks. Just same old faces, and some new injuries and illnesses. Just as well, as we might not get any new stocks for a while."

Baka. "We're all very proud of what you've done."

The family all agreed.

Satvinder smirked. "You could be the Patron Saint of Chak Sahasa one day. Just like the surveyor."

"What, hung by the neck you mean? Revered by my murderers? That was a strange story." He had a chuckle. "And it was a shame that Gnuru pulled him up about his geography. Almost embarrassed him."

Ablaa cocked her head. "But *I* didn't know that Wales wasn't English."

Satvinder quietly suggested that, "If we get independence, and don't run away, I bet they'll still call us Pakis. What'll you think then?"

Ablaa replied, "I'll not be happy. They killed your family so I'd be quite annoyed."

"But you thought the Welsh were English. How d'you think they'd feel?"

Satvinder was ahead of the race for once, and still believed that they'd be escaping to India one day and that would be when they would have to learn to turn the other cheek when people got their nationality wrong. *They'd* one day be the foreigners.

"It's just a name. Just words."

He went off to the office to try to establish some production plans. As soon as he did, the carpenter was at his door, wanting to know what the farmers should do with their crops.

"Get them in. We've no idea what's going on, so we should carry on as normal until we know not to. What else can we do?"

"You're not the first man to say that."

"I know, I heard the old man at the fire-side. I've had time to think about it, and he's right. All we can do right now is hang on to what we already have. And the crop could be worth a lot more to us than money, as the fighting moves out into the countryside. There'll be a lot of hungry people. The rice'll buy us some time. And besides, we all need to eat."

The carpenter frowned. "They'll need some leadership from their manager. You're the boss, and they want you to tell them what to do." He grinned. "Stand up and speak. Like you used to at the University."

"You're right. They're waiting for my direction. I'll think about what to say to them."

The carpenter clapped twice. "I'll tell them all that you'll address them at teatime. It'll be a bit cooler by then."

And so the boss was to be put on the stand for the first time and he had just a few hours to establish his speech.

# CHAPTER 17 –INDEPENDENCE DAY

March 27th 1971, Chak Sahasa

Satvinder spent a couple of hours pondering over his speech. After years of lecturing to various bands of students, he was finding difficulty in formatting a worthwhile address. He decided to discuss the words with his own 'boss', Ablaa. They sat at the table in their dining room.

"Daddy, darling. They just need to know what to do out on the fields. And maybe a little encouragement so that they all feel part of the community. Just as they've felt for many years." The little teenager shrugged her shoulders. "They need a little bit of leadership, from you, their manager."

"That's what worries me. I just employ them. I don't own them."

"You do more than just employ them. That's silly. You house them, you feed them, and you give them hope in the development of their future. You pay for their medical care, most of it. And if they really needed it, you'd help them through their spiritual turmoil."

"*Never* that. I'm no preacher."

"No, but they respect you to the point where you could if you wished. That's the most important point. They *respect* you."

He put his head down, and scratched his neck. "Why am I the manager? Why? I know nothing about farming."

"But you know about people, who know about farming. You stand up in front of people and lead. That's your job. You're their leader, and they're the farmers. Tell them *what* to do and you'll not need to tell them *how*."

A big grin stretched across his face as he pulled his head up. "I've just had this brilliant idea. *You* be the manager. My assistant, who does all the mouth stuff." He made his lap available as she moved round to him. "You can sit on my knee, at my desk."

She did just that and hugged his head into her breasts. Suddenly she released him and went back to her own seat.

"*Naughty* Daddy." As she flirtatiously tutted at him she waved her finger. "You've got a fiancé, and a secretary. I'm just your mere daughter. Remember?"

Satvinder was instantly hit by embarrassment. "I was only playing. But... it doesn't hurt to have fun, does it?"

The night when Akhtar was away was still hot on Satvinder's mind, but it had to stay right there, on his mind. And so, "What should I say to the men and women?"

"Hmm. First thing, don't even mention religion or differences. Keep it to work, and no play or private lives. Be aware of the tension out there. Every time we hear a radio report we're smacked in the face with 'By the grace of Allah' or 'Insha'Allah'. Keep it non-religious, but end with 'Joy Bangla' for good measure. And just tell them what you want them to do. Maybe a little about what's happened with the Field Marshall?"

Well, poor Satvinder went back to his office with loads more enthusiasm but with little more idea. He spent the day writing a short speech which never once mentioned God nor Allah nor religion.

The evening arrived, and the family ate at the table, while the children ate at the orphanage. Satvinder eventually went out to the village centre at about seven thirty in the evening, and was surprised to find a full house of a couple of hundred farmers. He stood up proudly but nervously in the middle of the yard, with the village folk making a large circle around him. Ablaa, Akhtar and the rest of the family joined the crowd.

"Good evening. Thanks for coming out tonight. Let's hope that the rain holds off for long enough. I don't want to bore you with a long speech, but I do believe that some things need to be brought out into the open, so that we can move forward during these stressful times as a team." He looked around at his employees. "Now things are changing, and we may need to change with them. But as those changes take effect we must all accept that we are a community of farmers and everything that we have comes from farming. We mustn't allow ourselves to lose the little that we have."

The old man who had met with the carpenter stood up. "We have much more than just farming. We have our faith, and now, thanks to the good doctor, we have our health." He sat down.

"Yes, a good point, but I'm just your farm manager. We're all free to follow whichever line of faith we wish, and this meeting's not about faith. It's about farming, eating and staying alive. We must now try to put the political worries aside and get the crops in. We need to feed ourselves, and we need resources to bargain with. Food will be like money, only better, when the war moves out of the cities, and the hungry forces come calling. We may be able to barter our way out of trouble. But it must be in these godowns, not lying rotting in the fields."

The old man stood up again. "So, why did you let the blacksmith go?" He shrugged. "You gave him leave to go: now we ain't got a blacksmith."

Satvinder looked to Ablaa, and she nodded. He suddenly realised that when she interrupted his meeting with the Field Marshall she wasn't just telling him that he was going to Jessore, she was asking his permission for him to leave. For a few seconds he felt used, but quickly snapped out of it.

"Yes, I was pleased to allow him to go to his family. It was his wish, and it was for his country." He was thinking on the run. "Who else would like to leave?" He looked around. "That's not an ultimatum, it's an open question, and will remain open. If any of you wish to leave, just let me know, and it'll be ok. Somehow we'll have to cover for any absentees. I discussed this with the Field Marshall and he felt the same as me: we *must* be allowed to leave when the time is right. None of us know what's in store for us, so this isn't a time for us to be tied down, and I'll not tie you down. But those of you who choose to stay, well, you must get out there and get the grain in. There's no time to waste, so I'll say this only once." He paused for effect. "You've leave to go if you need to be with family, or wish to join the Mukti Fauj, or just want to get out of here, but if you stay, you work. *That's* life!" He waited as the murmuring settled. "Are you with me?"

He was absolutely relieved as the men and women waved their heads in acceptance, but the meeting was suddenly disturbed by the nurse shouting her head off from the clinic door.

"Ablaa! Ablaa! Get in here!"

She shot over to the clinic, as the crowd looked on in bewilderment. After a very long wait of only about five minutes Ablaa emerged out into the evening, to be greeted by a mumbling crowd, all wanting to know. She moved to her daddy and stood beside him, and presented him with a small sheet of paper.

"Looks like we have a message!" He squinted as he deciphered the nurses' hand-writing and then with a yelp, he held the paper in the air. "There's been a radio address. There's news from Chittagong. I'll read what it says." He waited for the mumbling to stop, and then, almost shouting, he read the message.

"It says, 'This is Shadhin Bangla Betar Kendro. I, Major Ziaur Rahman, at the direction of Bangobondhu sheikh Mujibur Rahman, hereby declare that the independent

People's Republic of Bangladesh has been established. At his direction, I have taken command as the temporary Head of the Republic. In the name of Sheikh Mujibur Rahman, I call upon all Bengalis to rise against the attack by the West Pakistani Army. We shall fight to the last to free our Motherland.'" He stopped momentarily. "'By the grace of the people of Bangladesh, victory is ours. Joy Bangla!'"

The crowd erupted into chants of Joy Bangla and the jubilation lasted for many minutes. As the cheering slowed Satvinder raised his arms into the air and like obedient servants they all silenced.

"*Now* we must get on with our lives! Joy Bangla! Tonight we party, tomorrow we work! Tomorrow we work for our future, for our future as the People's Republic of Bangladesh!"

It was like a miracle. Major Ziaur Rahman's brief address had set the village alight with hope, and life for the villagers of Chak Sahasa suddenly looked so lustrous, free from the curse of the arsenic poisoning and free from the chains of their oppressors, West Pakistan. A new mood took control.

Our family sat around the table after the brief party.

"Daddy," ventured Ablaa, "You changed the address. You didn't read what was written."

Akhtar raised his eyebrows and reached out. "Where's that paper? I want to know what you changed." Satvinder pulled the crumpled paper from his pocket and Akhtar read it. He nodded as he read, and then grinned. "I understand." He passed it to Baka to read. She grinned as she explained to James that his daddy had changed the final sentence of the address. He had changed 'By the grace of Allah' to 'By the grace of the people of Bangladesh'.

Ablaa, with abode in her voice, addressed the family, "It frightens me that this's to become a religious uprising. Everything is by the grace of Allah. It's all about Allah." The young girl looked around at the mixed bunch. "It's probably quite easy to declare independence. It's just talk. Now the people will have to die for the cause, while the big noises sit around their tables and discuss, just like we're doing. But I think that, while the big wigs are still sitting around their tables, ours will be broken. We're all gonna have to fight or run."

Little else was said that night, despite independence having been declared. They felt in no mood for celebration.

From the onset of Operation Searchlight the major towns were battlefields, some would say killing-fields. The Pakistani forces, with their utter superiority in arms and equipment, swept most of the opposition aside, but they did a lot more than just restore law and order. The operation was not just about putting down the organised resistance, it was also about ensuring that it would never again return. The intention from the very beginning was about the Islamisation of the people and some of the targets bore that out, such as the slums in and around Chittagong and the eastern parts of Dhaka. Those desperately poor areas reputedly held many of the cessation supporters, like the very poor and the Hindus, and so were raised to the ground along with many of their residents. Within a week of the operation's launch something like half the population of Dhaka had fled or been killed. Some estimates place the deaths in that first week at about thirty thousand in Dhaka alone. Absolute fear and panic resulted.


April 11th 1971, Chak Sahasa


During the next couple of weeks the battles raged across East Pakistan, now Bangladesh, and the deaths mounted, with two notable areas of staunch resistance being Chittagong and Kushtia. The newly formed Republic of Bangladesh had appointed a Prime Minister, Mr Tajuddin

Ahmed, and on April the eleventh Ablaa listened to a broadcast from Shadhin Bangla Betar Kendro. It was the words of the Prime Minister.

"Today a mighty army is being formed around the nucleus of professional soldiers, from the Bengal Regiment and E.P.R. who have rallied to the cause of the liberation struggle. These have been joined by the Police, Ansars and Mujahids and now by thousands of Awami League and other volunteers and are being trained into a fighting force ready to use the captured weapons from the defeated West Pakistani mercenaries, and fresh arms being purchased from funds collected by our Bengali Brothers overseas. In Chittagong and Noakhali we have commissioned Major Ziaur Rahman of the Bengal Regiment to take full command of operations. His heroic defence of Chittagong City against overwhelming odds, which included attacks from the air and sea, will take its place with the defence of Stalingrad in the annals of warfare."

As the family sat around the table they felt just a pinge of nationalistic pride. Although the country was pinned back by the Pakistani forces, it was not to give up. But the price for independence, still a very long way from reality, was high. Blood, lots of blood, and lots more blood, and as the blood was shed the suffering intensified throughout the towns and cities of the People's Republic of Bangladesh.

Akhtar quietly spoke. "The farmers are talking about the thousands of people who make their way along the road towards Dumuria. They've put a sign out at the end of the lane that says 'Leprosy'. That's all it says."

Ablaa. "The poor people're taking notice and they're staying away from us. Just passing straight by. And the carpenter spoke to some young men yesterday. The Pak army are killing all young men and boys who could become freedom fighters. And burning the Hindu settlements. And raping and mutilating the women, and even killing children. They're all getting away while they can, and they told him that he should go with them, and become a fighter. He's thinking about doing it."

Satvinder. "I hope you're ok with this talk, James." The boy nodded, but never smiled. He continued, "Yeah, the carpenter came into my office today. There're nearly twenty young men maybe going. I think they will, especially the Hindus." He took an enormous breath. "He thinks that us Hindus are putting the rest in grave danger. The refugees along the road are saying that the Pakistani army are being helped by many thousands of Biharis. Not all Biharis, some Bengalis, but all sympathisers with the Pakistanis and don't want independence. The carpenter has assessed from the refugees' stories that there're certain targets which the Paks are aiming for. He thinks it's Awami Leaguers, young, fighting-age men, police, Bengali servicemen, and Hindus. They've all got to go." He was silent for a few seconds. "That's what the carpenter thinks."

Ablaa just nodded her head in agreement.

As they sat pondering those disturbing words, similar talk was being bandied around in the World's newspapers and government offices. The atrocities were noted, the genocide was acknowledged, and the blood-letting by the Pakistan forces was criticised. But they all stayed out of the 'internal affairs' of Pakistan.

The Premier of the People's Republic of China, Zhou Enlai, said it all. "Chinese government holds that what is happening in Pakistan at present is purely internal affair of Pakistan, which can only be settled by Pakistan people themselves and which brooks no foreign interference whatsoever." Roughly translated means, "You're on your own, pal."

By the middle of April 1971 the Bangladesh Armed Forces, including the Mukti Fauj, were placed under the command of Colonel M. A. G. Osmani. He was made

Commander-in-Chief, with a brief to organise the many individual liberation groups into a national fighting force.

April 19th 1971, Chak Sahasa

The crops were coming into the godowns at an acceptable rate, despite many of the young men leaving to join the fight. The village had been visited by several individual families who were migrating away from the brutal regimes which lorded their towns, and who had become starved and thirsty. The families were given fresh water and rice, but were also sent away with some horrifying tales of the leprosy. Several of the poor stricken casualties volunteered to sit or lay below a straw canopy outside the clinic, displaying their gnarled and gangrenous limbs to all who dare come along the lane. It seemed to work.

However, that morning, with a little rain falling, the farmers began to arrive back from the fields.

"They're coming!" They shouted. "They're coming! The army!"

Panic almost set in, but there was no time to do anything. A landrover sped along the lane ahead of the rest of the group, and pulled up in the square, facing the lepers. The entire village watched as the driver, wearing a dirty green Rifles uniform and sporting a bushy moustache, dismounted and saluted the leprosy sufferers.

"Satvinder!" he shouted, facing the clinic. "Where's Satvinder?"

From the other side of the square, he emerged, closing the godown service-door behind him. Then, as soon as he realised who was calling him, he relaxed. It was Sergeant Haq, but even more of a relief, it was not the Pakistani army but their own liberation forces.

"Ah, Satvinder. Can we speak in private?"

The sergeant was invited into the godown, and into the office, but before they could close the door the carpenter caught them.

"My apologies, sir, but may I just have an important word with the manager. Only a second." The sergeant nodded, and Satvinder was pulled around the corner. Very quietly the carpenter said, "Nine sets, nine sets. That's what the Field Marshall gave to the Muktis." He then hurried out of the godown.

A little puzzled, Satvinder went into the office with the sergeant. Their previous meeting was relaxed, but overshadowed by the memory of the news which he received from the Field Marshall about the death of his family, and so his memory of the man was blurred. He looked at the dark-skinned, bushy-moustached sergeant with a hint of suspicion. Last time they met he was smart and clean shaven, but this time he was ruffled with a couple of day's growth on his chin.

"You're concerned about something. Do you have something to worry about?"

"No, sir. Just reminding myself about the previous visit. You here for more rice?"

The sergeant smiled. "We could do with some for our men. But I'm here for other reasons. I hope for your sake that the guns are all present and correct. Are they?"

"I presume so. I never counted them." He stood up and paced across the office. "There are some gone. The field Marshall gave them to a Mukti group who escorted him here and back to the border. They're not there."

"How many?"

"I just helped to deliver them to the soldiers." He paused for thought. "There might have been nine that were in the sacks." He began to sweat. The carpenter had dropped a hint that three had gone elsewhere, but his head spun in the fear that he could have misunderstood. "Maybe six, but I seem to remember nine. I'm not sure." He sat down.

"You're a terrible liar. That's not an insult, as I don't like liars but I do like you. So, rather than me having to execute you, for crimes against the Republic of Bangladesh, I'll give you chance to tell the truth." He put his hand onto his revolver. He snapped, "The truth!"

Satvinder put his head into his hands. "Six." His hands shook as he thought about what might happen to the carpenter. "We took six guns to the Mukti. I'm sorry."

Sergeant Haq took his revolver from the holster and banged it on the desk and they then just looked at each other in electrifying silence. Eventually he smiled at Satvinder. "If, just if, only three more guns have gone astray, I'll commend you for a medal." He started grinning. "My men received six guns from the Field Marshall, and they delivered them to us down near Satkira. So there should be one hundred and fourteen left in there. That's a lot of guns. It's the largest stash we have." He began playing with his bushy moustache. "Most of the others have disappeared, and left our liberation forces short, and unarmed. Several people have been executed for their failures. But the Field Marshall has a good eye for reliable people."

The air was still bubbling. Satvinder asked, "What about if there are only one hundred and eleven? Where are we then?"

"Do you a deal. If there are one hundred and eleven, I'll not kill you. But any less... We'll have to worry about that when we get there."

Satvinder nodded in appreciation of not being killed, just yet. Still in a sweat he asked, "The Field Marshall. Did he get back ok?"

"My men took him as far as Satkira, and from there he was on his own. Anybody's guess." He placed his revolver back into the holster. "He's an old pro. If anybody's gonna get there, he will. Now the guns."

The two men walked out into the drizzle and were met by the entire village. Satvinder held his hand in the air and shouted. "These are our own troops. They're our friends and protectors. When the trucks arrive, we need some volunteers to load some sacks of rice. And Tazkia, if there are noodles, please pack some up for our heroes!"

The sergeant bowed his head to the people, and moved to his Landover. He called for three trucks to come into the village.

"Look me in the eye, Satvinder." He did that. "Now, do I need to count the guns?"

He shook his head in answer.

"Then let's chat, while they're loading the guns and rice."

The men left the damp afternoon, and sat in the office.

"It's a good idea. The leprosy sign. But, hey, the lepers at the entrance as we arrived! Very few people want to come here and if I didn't know better, I'd have gone by now."

The farm manager thanked him. "The poor sufferers still have it in them to worry about others. We're so proud that there won't be any new cases."

The men again sat looking at each other for a few minutes.

Sergeant Haq reopened with, "Do you know what's happening in our country? You probably don't. Just what you hear on the radio."

"Will you tell us what's happening? Please?" After the sergeant agreed, he sped through the crowds to collect Ablaa, Akhtar and Tazkia. James stayed with the other children.

They all stood in the office in front of the sergeant as Satvinder introduced them.

"Well, the internal news, in brief, is that the Pak army are still seeking out the Awami League members and killing them off. They're targeting the slum areas, particularly the Hindu ones, in all the towns, and burning them out. They're seeking out and killing or abducting all the men of fighting age, from something like twelve years upwards. They're raping and murdering women and children." He paused for thought. "There are stories of women being gang raped, and then their breasts being cut off and finally killed by pushing a stick into them through their vaginas. They're butchering our people by the thousands."

The family never said a word as they listened to the sergeant's summary.

"Many of the towns have been emptied of all young men and Hindus, either dead or on the run. They're creating mass hysteria, absolute fear for their lives and for the lives of their families. And maybe that's what they always intended. Nobody seems to know. But we're holding onto some areas, and we've captured some worthwhile arms from the Paks, even a helicopter over in Chittagong. That's what we've been told. And now with Colonel Osmani at the helm, our liberation force will one day win through."

He had a drink of water.

"Now what we're hearing from outside is that the whole World is just leaving us to it. It's just an internal affair. But the newspapers are very scathing about how the Paks are handing out the retribution for the bad treatment of both the Biharis and of the Pakistani soldiers over the past few months. They're saying that enough's enough, but won't do anything else to help us. But they're also claiming that the Pak army of about thirty five thousand can't contain seventy five million for very long, and will run out of arms and men very soon. But what they don't take into account is that the yanks for one are still supplying the Pakistanis with arms, and also that not all of the seventy five million Bengalis are cessationalists. Millions of our countrymen are sympathisers. This evens up the numbers, and taking into account the vast superiority of their arms, we're struggling." He hung his head for a few seconds. "But we'll win. One day we'll win." He stood up straight. "They're now forming the sympathisers into organised groups. They're forming Peace Committees. Our own countrymen will be set against us, maybe even armed, but whatever, they'll be supported by professional, organised and well equipped assault forces of the Pakistani Army. The Pakistani Generals must have been planning this assault for months, but the World just sees it as retribution for the atrocities against the Biharis. If we don't win, we'll *never* be equal. And those of you who're Hindu will probably never have a life in this country. Probably not have a life at all."

Silence fell for a while before Ablaa spoke up. "What can we do, sir?"

At last a grin appeared under the moustache. "Fight! There's nothing else *to* do. Fight the enemy at the gate. We need people to use these guns, people who have the commitment to life and to their country. And when we eventually get the help we deserve from the Indians we'll remove the aggressors back to their own country. Insha'Allah." He looked into Satvinder's face. "God willing."

Ablaa mentioned, "About twenty young men have gone off to fight, but've found it hard to be accepted. The leprosy."

"Dumuria. You all come from Dumuria. If nobody knows, nobody cares. Now Satvinder. Who was the young man who thought I couldn't hear him whispering to you?"

He squinted at the sergeant. After a sniff, "Why?"

"I need to speak to him. I want to know what he did with the three guns. Get him in here." He stood up. "No, we'll go out to him."

They all followed the sergeant out to the village centre. As they stood in the drizzle, the entire village went silent. The last time anything like this had happened, the manager was executed.

"Corporal!" He held his hand up, and a uniformed soldier approached the sergeant, accompanied by three non-uniformed men. "Stand with me!" He then raised his voice even louder. "The man who interrupted my meeting earlier! Come here!"

The carpenter, shaking, moved to the sergeant and stood in front of him. He was wet from the drizzle which disguised his profuse, cold sweat.

"I'm a professional soldier. Many of these other soldiers are volunteers, but now they're also soldiers. What I say, they do, blindly and obediently without question. That's what a fighting unit does, blindly obey their superior officers. Understand?" He accepted a vague movement of the head as a 'yes'. "What do you do here?"

"I'm a carpenter and the representative of the workers."

"Not any more."

The village was still in absolute silence, until a small child began to cry.

"Take all the children home. This's no place for young children!"

The mothers took their children to their homes, and Tazkia took the orphans into the clinic. It all felt like déjà-vu.

"Now, carpenter, go and get the guns. Now!"

The carpenter ran off towards the old village.

"Let's hope he comes back with the guns."

The wait was frightening for the villagers. Nobody spoke, until the old man moved towards the sergeant. "He's a good man. He'll be back."

"I know. But I'm a man of philosophy. Until he's here, he ain't here."

The old man retired back to his friends, and some murmuring slowly grew.

Then the carpenter returned. He was carrying a sack which he handed to the sergeant, who then handed it to his corporal, who checked the contents and then who acknowledged the contents to be three guns.

"Right. We have our property back. Now, in your defence, what were you going to do with them? Think before you speak."

The crowd looked around at each other and at the army trucks. Some of them were extremely agitated and nervous.

"I was going to defend our village when the enemy arrived. Now I can't."

"But you can't shoot three guns. Only one. Who else would be shooting the guns?"

The carpenter never flinched.

"I admire your loyalty." He looked to the crowd. "This man's accomplices really ought to step forward before I take to extracting the names from this young man!"

Two of the young farmers stepped forward. Their heads were dropped.

"Right. Now I have all three I can pass judgement for your crimes against the state. You've stolen valuable weapons from the liberation forces. Satvinder. You choose their fate. What should I do with these young men?"

The manager became uneasy and began to pant. But, after a massive breath, he suggested, "Enlist them. Give them the chance to fight the enemy."

The sergeant grinned. "As you probably know, the Mukti doctor who visited a while back would've just shot them. But he's a butcher, and I'm a soldier." He turned to the soldier who held the three guns. "Give these men a gun each. They're with us."

The carpenter looked into Satvinder's eyes. The wiry young man had a tiny tear in each eye, and Satvinder struggled to hold back his own relief, but he did. He just looked to the sergeant and held his hand out. The handshake was limp, but meaningful. "Thank you."

The army left with their rice, guns and new recruits, and saluted their new friends as they drove out of the village. That day 'Joy Bangla' rang out across the flat, damp lands of Bangladesh. That day Satvinder had won the hearts of the people of Chak Sahasa, and had blossomed into more than just their manager: he was now their hero.

He joined Akhtar and Ablaa to check on the children. They had huddled together on the floor of the clinic, and had all been utterly silent for the duration of the army's visit.

Ablaa whispered, "I once said that I hope we never have to do that again. And we've done it again. No more, please."

Colin Hodgson

# CHAPTER 18 – THE ROAD TO DUMURIA

Early May 1971, Chak Sahasa

With the loss of the carpenter and his two accomplices, adding to the twenty or so who had already gone, the village was becoming short of young, healthy men. So the fields were suddenly being worked by many of the younger women of the village, taking their orders from the men, and doing what they could for the community. Some of the fields stretched as far as the Satkira Road, where they were plundered by the migrating refugees and part of the crop ruined. But Satvinder consulted with his men and they decided that, so long as the refugees just stole the crops close to the road, they would do nothing to prevent it happening.

"We all have to eat. It' just a small part of the crop."

It was fortunate that man's fear of leprosy was strong enough to ward off all but the most starving of the fleeing families, but the very desperate ones who did venture into the village were kindly given food and water, and sent on their way without any incidences. However, the women who went into the fields took their children with them, and they faced a different danger, one which took no heed to the leprosy signs: the kalach. On the third of May 1971 a distraught mother lost both her daughters to bites from the snake, causing many of the women to make the decision to stay in the village with the children. The harvesting slowed dramatically, until a meeting of the elders came up with a suggestion that the children all stay in the village and be overseen by Tazkia and the older children from the orphanage. The harvest was back on course.

Very little news of the outside World was getting through to Ablaa, and so she decided to venture along the lane with James to seek information from the travellers. Many told frightening tales of their villages being burned by the Pakistan army, led there by the volunteers, or razakars, the supporters of the Pakistanis. It seemed that many Bengalis and Urdu speaking Muslims sympathised with the Pakistani vision and were being drafted into organised units being termed the peace committees, leading the army to all those suspected of supporting the liberation forces, with cruel and terminal consequences for the men, women and children. It was reported that many young women had been spared the slaughter, to be transferred to the cantonments for the pleasures of the soldiers. Others were gang-raped by the soldiers and by the razakars, to be left as mutilated corpses, with breasts and ears removed. One family of Muslims spoke to Ablaa as they passed. They had fled their village, close to Khulna, after they witnessed the barbaric massacre of several Hindu families, along with a number of Muslims. The razakars had led a platoon of Pakistani soldiers to a village which was suspected of harbouring Mukti fighters. The head of each family was ordered to step out in front of the Sergeant, who then ordered them to show their penes. Those who were not circumcised were sent one way with their families, those who were circumcised were sent the other. The hundred or so villagers who had not been circumcised, those suspected of being without God, were gunned down where they stood. The bodies were then dumped in the village pond. But two of those villagers who had been spared were then accused by the razakars as being liberation supporters. The sergeant stated, "We're not wasting any more time here," so the soldiers were ordered to kill everybody, and then torch the village. The razakars went through the houses for valuables before burning them, and then leading the army to the next killing field.

Others told of stories of kindness from the Pakistani soldiers, but not many. One brave man suggested that they themselves should not have massacred so many Pakistanis and Biharis, and that perhaps God had ordered the retribution. But most just moved on in absolute fear for their lives and their families. Whatever, retribution or the planned Islamisation of the masses, the Bengali people were being sought out and terminated, sometimes by their own. Ablaa and James walked very slowly back up the lane, desperately clutching each other's hands as they cried.

"Our time is coming," she announced at the table. "When God is our only hope, all is lost. Only if the Field Marshall is right can God be worth a toss."

The family all looked around at each other, a little shocked at her cold statement but Akhtar agreed. "It's time. We need to start our preparations for the long walk."

The entire family agreed.


May 17th 1971, Chak Sahasa

"Satvinder! Talk to us."

It was the old, but influential, man who had advised Satvinder previously and another of the elders.

"You're going tomorrow. You prepared?"

He nodded at the two elders. "We've a couple of old barrows, so we can take water-bags and rice and noodles."

"Take plenty, as we've still got *plenty* of rice, and all the water we need."

"Thanks. Akhtar says that the filters've got several months life, and he's left the papers to help you rebuild the filters in the autumn. You should all be ok for clean water. Make sure the children aren't allowed any poisoned water."

The old man waved his head in agreement and took hold of Satvinder' hand. "I don't like Hindus, but over the years, I've got used to you lot. But all emotion aside, I'll be glad to see the back of so many Hindus from the village. When the Paks come, I think we'll be ok. Nearly all of us will be the right kind of Bengalis. No offence meant."

"None taken. We've got to look after ourselves, and then each other." He put his head down. "A mother who's lost her man, joining the Mukti force, has asked us to take her four young children. They may not be the last new recruits, so the band grows, and the job gets harder."

"Well, because of the Doctor's good planning, we can spare four or five stone bottles. That'll keep you in good water for another week or two. Please fill them and take them, for the children." After a timely prompt from his old friend, he continued. "We'd just like to say that our lives have turned around, thanks to the good doctor and his filters. You know, Satvinder, in nineteen fifty nine we lost more than half our children to cholera. Since the wells were drilled we had the leprosy effects but no cholera, but since the doctor's filters, we've had nothing. If he can now sort out the polio and pox, I'll nominate him to join Allah. Please pass on our respects and thanks. He doesn't like talking to us." He looked towards the lane. "We've heard that the Pak army is on the move, in this direction. So make sure you're all gone early in the morning." He beckoned Satvinder to sit down on the floor with him. "Now we've some advice, which we've discussed with some of the other elders and we all agree." He unfolded an old hand-written map. "You must stay away from the main road as much as you can, getting off just after Dumuria and not rejoining until after Chuknagar. The rains are still light, and it's fairly dry, so follow this route through the marshes, keeping south of Chuknagar. The paths'll still be passable for a couple more weeks at least." He showed Satvinder the route on the map. "If we can think of any way to help you get over the streams and rivers without swimming, we'll see you before you go."

"Looks hard, specially with carts and children."

"We think it may be harder through Chuknagar. There's thousands there, lots fleeing because of the rumour of the army coming, and the fucking 'commy' party's been active in the area and stirring things with the Biharis. That could be why the Paks are moving this way and if so, there'll be trouble. So keep to the smaller paths."

Satvinder sat with him and frowned. "All the roads are bad, and getting wetter."

"It's only May. The real rain won't be here for a month or so, and besides, the main road through to Satkira is just a mud lane. So you might as well take the more rural mud lanes, and stay away from that bloody army, the razakars and the communists."

They all pawed the old map. It had been hand-drawn, and showed the lanes and paths between the rural villages, right across to the Indian border. They spent some time planning the route.


May 18th 1971, Chak Sahasa in the early hours.

The family met outside the orphanage at seven o'clock in the dinge and drizzle. It was a depressingly wet day, but spirits were high and the two carts were quickly loaded with water-bags and bottles, and some bags of rice. The children were giggling and excited to be able to put the sacks of noodles onto the cart which they had made with their own fair hands over the previous few days.

"Right, we've a route to follow." Satvinder took Tazkia, with her baby in a sling, by the hand. "We need to make pairs, and support each other as we go, and you three tiny ones can ride on the carts. Me and Tazkia will lead, with Akhtar and his family at the back, then James, Ablaa and our

Nurse can look after the middle of the convoy. We're gonna have an adventure, and it might be dangerous, so whatever happens we stay together and you kids don't talk to anybody unless we permit you. And don't touch anything or eat or drink anything without our permission."

The band of more than forty formed into a line, with one cart at the back managed by Akhtar and his boys, and the other at the front looked after by Satvinder, James and two other of the older boys. They were all set for the off. But before they could get away, the village seemed to wake up. Dozens of folk entered the square to see them off, wish them well and give each child a parcel of dried fish and lentils. Then, as Ablaa stared into the murk, visions of Char Monpura flooded into her mind: a boat, not a naval launch, but a boat. It was being pulled by a lady and three young girls, and they were all crying.

"Please take my girls." She sniffed and looked behind her. "I can donate my husband's boat."

It was a small boat, made of loose wicker and covered by sacking, but then waterproofed with bitumen.

"It's very light and there's some rope inside." She smiled through her grief. "The elders said the children needed it." She hugged her three children, and then pushed them into line, before one of the old ladies gave each of them a food-bag. "Please look after them."

After some discussion, the children were accepted from the doting mother, and the boat placed upside down on top of the water bottles.

It was a black day for the village, losing its manager and doctor, and many of their children, and maybe their future community. As they all watched in silence the band of refugees moved down the lane towards their new lives, nobody knowing quite where or what that was likely to be.

They reached the Satkira Road. It was still early, and the travellers were few, so the first few miles were easy going, with only a couple of problems with the cartwheels sinking.

They managed to reach Dumuria in just four hours. Satvinder and Ablaa discussed the progress and were pleased that the children were keeping up their spirits and their speed, but there was one problem case: Baka. Her rheumatic feet were causing her problems, causing her to struggle to keep up with the children.

"We need to move off this road soon," advised Ablaa. "Just a little way up here."

As they reached the junction which would lead them into the marshlands, Akhtar called the group to a halt. "I'm sorry. We can't go that way." He looked at Baka who was wilting with the pain from her feet. "I'm sorry."

Tazkia released Satvinder's hand, and suggested with a grin, "We'll rest for a while and have a drink, while the four officers establish our plans." They all moved away from the dirt road, to allow the other travellers to pass.

Ablaa, Satvinder, Akhtar and James sat on the low bank. They discussed the options, and eventually asked the nurse to join them.

Akhtar spoke to his nurse. "We've decided the marsh route'll be too much for Baka. We're going through Chuknagar, where the going should be easier, and the rest of you'll go through the marsh paths. As planned. And you can take my bag. You're now the children's doctor."

The ageing nurse smiled. "I'll look after the kids as well as I can."

Akhtar found their destination on the map. "Thanks. And we'll meet you all in India, near Basirhat, here." They confirmed the location. "We'll then celebrate our new lives in India."

It was never a good plan, just a compromise. Satvinder whispered, "Good luck, old mate. I don't like it: we've always said that we'd stay together."

"We will, once in India. But Baka can't do that rough route. We'll be ok, and we'll be back together soon. I promise." He hugged his life-long friend. "And when we're in

India, we can decide which way to go, the slums of Kolkata or the golden footpaths of London."

After a few moments explaining to the children why they had to split up, the two parties departed.

# CHAPTER 19 – PLASSEY THE 'BASTARD'

May 18th to 22nd,1971, The Marshy Route to Satkira

The band of forty left Akhtar and his family on the Satkira Road and went off left, down a lane which was flanked by thatched village dwellings. The local children ran indoors as they passed their homes. It was noticed by Satvinder that the children were dressed raggedly, unlike their orphans, and it made him feel so proud to be their parent.

Our children were becoming tired after more than four hours on the road, but they had to carry on until they felt they had achieved a good day's mileage. The rear, which had been vacated by Akhtar's family, was replaced by the nurse and James, being relieved when needed by Ablaa and the older children. It was easy going for some time, but once they left the village, the path narrowed, and was flanked by wetlands which grew six-foot high jute crops. They felt so cut off from the rest of the world by the dense plantations, and all they could see was the lane ahead and behind, and the dense walls of jute on each side. The unknown route ahead of them was somewhat frightening as they passed through, but Satvinder remembered the words of the elders, 'The rains are still light, and it's fairly dry,' which helped to maintain his confidence in their decision to go around Chuknagar.

Ablaa walked a while with Satvinder. "Daddy, we're getting along well, but the children will soon need to rest. We're doing ok."

So, after about six hours on the road, a virtual lifetime for the young children who were beginning to flag, they found an area which was solid ground and partly sheltered by some mature trees. They set up camp and lit the fire.

"Any casualties?" jested James to the Nurse.

"Only you, if you get cheeky."

The water was carefully eked out, and they all ate some rice and a little of their dried fish for added protein. They were wary of not knowing how long it would be before they could get any more food.

Suddenly the acute hearing of the children recognised danger. Something was coming along the lane, but not yet in sight. There was no time to hide. James ran towards the bend, followed by two ten year old girls.

"Trucks!" James moved a little further around the bend. "Army! The army's here!" They ran back to their team.

Ablaa jumped up and looked towards the dense jute plantation, but there was no time for them to hide. "Don't panic. We can't go anywhere, so just stay calm."

The wait was intense, so much so that the children sensed the danger and all pulled in together between the two carts, as they had been conditioned to do when the army visited their village. This time Tazkia and Ablaa did not join them, but stood in front of the ruck, Tazkia cuddling her little one.

"Just keep quiet," Tazkia whispered. "Not a word."

The truck appeared from around the corner, moving very slowly through the lane which only just accommodated its width. It was grey with a canvas cover on the buck, a Pakistani Army truck. The group froze. The driver waved his hand out of the window as he drove past, but once clear of the group, the jeep which followed blew its horn. The truck and the jeep stopped, and another truck which followed pulled up behind the jeep. The passenger in the jeep stepped out of the vehicle.

"Good afternoon." The soldier spoke Bengali but with an accent. He saluted Satvinder. "A lot of children for one family. What're you doing?" The soldier, a tall, distinguished man with a complexion which was much fairer than the Bengalis, was a Captain. He awaited an answer. "Do you speak Bengali?"

Satvinder summoned up his courage to reply. "Yes, good afternoon, sir. We're going to Satkira."

He walked around Satvinder.

"Why?"

"We're going to India. We've been promised work and homes for the children."

The Captain then walked around the children.

"These all yours?"

Ablaa and James moved to Satvinder's side, and Tazkia grabbed his hand.

"They're all mine, but these're my immediate family." He looked at each of his family members and then moved his gaze to the children, "And these are my adopted orphans. There're thirty four. And this's their nurse."

The Captain stood motionless for a while, looking straight into Satvinder's eyes. Neither of them flinched.

Then, "This isn't the route to Satkira. Why you here?"

"This's one of the routes, avoiding Chuknagar. It's not flooded yet and we have a route planned out in our heads."

The captain was concerned about something so he walked to the truck which was parked behind his jeep and gave an order in Punjabi. A soldier responded, dismounted from the cab and moved in front of Satvinder. He bowed his head in acknowledgement.

The captain nodded his head towards James. "My private will check the boy."

The soldier moved aside from Satvinder and held his hand out to James, who stepped forward.

The Captain ordered, "Show the soldier your circumcised penis."

James looked at his dad who was almost breaking down, then pulled his pyjamas forward and the soldier peered down. The soldier then turned to his Captain, saluted and returned to the truck.

The Captain smiled at Satvinder. "You can relax. I'm not an animal, so relax. Get your children into the back of the truck, and I'll give you a lift some of the way. We're going that way."

As Tazkia herded the children into the back of the truck, Ablaa held her daddy tight by the arm, knowing what he was thinking about: Kaling and his daughters. He closed his eyes, and tears formed, running down his cheeks and onto his shirt. "Come on Daddy. Help us with the barrows."

The two soldiers who were riding in the back were ordered to lift the barrows into the truck, and they were off.

Satvinder sat in shock, with Ablaa on one side and Tazkia on the other, knowing in his heart that he was to follow his beloved wife to another dimension. The children crammed themselves together for comfort and stared at their adopted father, maybe in sympathy, or maybe in total wonderment at what was happening to them. But as instructed from the onset, they spoke to nobody.

"Hello," whispered one of the two soldiers. He was young, maybe only seventeen, and could speak a little Bengali. "Pretty children, well costumed." He was looking at Ablaa, but she kept her head down and avoided any eye contact. He tried again. "All very pretty children. And you."

Tazkia felt that they should acknowledge the compliments. "Thank you. My sister is very shy, but she appreciates your kind words."

The other soldier stopped the young man from saying anything further.

They travelled silently for two or three hours through the lanes, but they could not see out of the truck. Then they stopped and the two soldiers opened the tarpaulin from the back. They were in a farm with two rusty, corrugated-iron godowns, and a river which ran almost beside the yard. They all followed the two soldiers out from the truck and into the rain.

Once outside, the children huddled together, waiting for instructions from the adults, but none came. The adults looked to the fair-skinned soldiers for instruction, but none came. They all just waited for instruction from somewhere, probably from the Captain, but he never came, he went inside one of the godowns. The dozen or so soldiers from the second truck followed the Captain into the godown and thus our group of forty were left to wonder about their future.

The two soldiers, sporting their guns as if to be guarding the group, shrugged their shoulders at each other, and then one of them walked over to the river. He looked across to the opposite bank, fifty to sixty feet away, where the lane continued on from the small ferry terminal, and there laid a small, open ferry. Two civilian men sat on the bank by the ferry, presumably waiting for a fare.

"May I speak?" asked Satvinder, casting his question to the young man who had complimented his children.

"Of course. I only speak a little Bengali. But yes, I would be honoured to speak with you."

"Do you know what they're to do with us?"

The young soldier shook his head. "I don't know, sir. I don't know."

That was the end of that conversation. But the young man couldn't keep his eyes away from Ablaa. She was such a beautiful young lady, so it was understandable, but he seemed obsessed by her beauty. It made her feel uncomfortable, so she kept her head down. She was beginning to realise just how terminal their future might be and, like Satvinder, began believing that they could all be following his family to heaven, or to wherever the Hindus go. But as her depression spiralled downwards towards the fiery gates of perdition another vehicle arrived. It was an old Landover, and six civilian people were on board. It pulled up outside the godown where the Captain could be found. Soon there were several adult men in the yard, all Bengali and dressed in grey jackets, looking like businessmen and staring at the captives, whispering and joking amongst themselves. Then several other Bengali men, these ones dressed in shirts and pyjamas, came out from one of the farm buildings and began discussions with the businessmen, pointing occasionally at the children. They all became agitated before meandering into the godown which the captain had entered.

The rain was beginning to chill the children, and two of the younger ones started to cry, and Tazkia's baby joined them. After a little while there were several crying children, and Ablaa, Tazkia and the nurse chanced their arm by moving towards them.

"Comfort them," ordered the young soldier. "Sorry... please."

The other soldier had become bored with the river, and spoke to his comrade before going into the godown. He returned after a few minutes and spoke to the young soldier.

"We must go inside. The children can rest."

They were led into the godown to the right which stood beside the river. It was almost empty and fairly dark inside, but they found a corner to make their own where the children all ate a little of their lentils and fish, and then tried to settle for a sleep. The day was getting late.

"What's happening, Daddy?" It was James's turn to worry.

"We don't know. It feels like a dream, but I know it isn't."

With that, the young soldier and his comrade entered the godown, and walked hurriedly over to our family. With a strange grin, the young man told Satvinder, "Come with me. And you." He looked at Ablaa. "My friend will stand guard over the others."

Satvinder and Ablaa were led across the yard, and into the other godown. With a gun in his back Satvinder was herded with Ablaa past the men from the Landover, up a flight of stairs and into an office. It had a large window which opened out over the entire yard and standing looking out over his domain was the tall, distinguished Pakistani captain. Beside him was a rifle fixed to a tripod. The rest of the office was sparse, dreary, with just a desk and four chairs and Satvinder could not help but notice the revolver which lay on the desk, totally unattended. He was sorely tempted.

Without turning round the captain ordered, "Take a seat." He waved the young soldier out of the room. Satvinder and Ablaa sat on the chairs facing window, and Ablaa nodded towards the desk, upon which the captain's gun lay. Satvinder nodded in acknowledgement but their chance was lost as the captain turned around. The tall, distinguished Pakistani silhouetted against the light, his shadow casting doubts over the two Bengali's very existence. They shivered in anticipation of their lot.

"Come here!" The captain beckoned them to the window. "This office can control the entire yard and river crossing. It's an important strategic position. And now, with your local knowledge of the paths and lanes, the map, we can control this whole area, south of Chuknagar. What do you think?"

Satvinder looked at Ablaa and thought.

"Speak to me!"

"Yes Sir, you're in control from up here."

"Thank you. But I'm not looking for statements of the blatantly obvious. I want to know what you really think. Speak to me, but honestly."

"I don't know what you mean, sir." Satvinder was lost.

The captain waved his head about, and then pointed at Satvinder. "I'm an intellectual, and so're you, that's crystal clear. Look at those down there." He pointed to the men in jackets as they walked across the yard towards another farm building. "They're intellectuals, but I don't want to talk to them, and that one in front, he's a doctor, the man in charge, but I don't want to talk to *any* of them. I'll talk to them when I have to, and only when I have to. So let *us* talk. Let's talk about us. You first. Tell me about yourself. Like, why you're moving through here with thirty four children. Not your own children. Tell me. I love a good story, and I might choose to write it down one day."

Satvinder lowered his head in confusion, but he felt he had to talk. A little shaky, he informed the captain, "Just as a matter of correctness, for the record, there are thirty four orphans, my wife's baby, and my own two children. That makes thirty seven children and three adults."

The captain waited, then, "I'll make a note. Carry on."

"I've a band of orphans, who rely on me and my family for their survival. That's why we're here, going to India for a new life, away from the war, and the intolerance."

The captain smiled, but said nothing for several minutes. He simply looked at his two captives.

The stress was intolerable: Ablaa finally had to cross the boundaries. She delicately asked, "What're you going to do with us?"

The captain nodded his head. "As human beings, you've a right to know what your fate might be. So, presently, I'm not going to do anything with you, apart from talking. Will you talk to me, honestly? I'm sure you will, as you're my captives." He stood up and walked around the two prisoners. "I'll begin our special friendship by explaining why *we're* here. Now this place is set aside for the Peace Committee. Do you know who they are?" He had no response. "No? Well the Peace Committee are members of your own societies, East Pakistanis, who want us to continue to run the East. They're mostly businessmen who've done well out of the union of the two satellites, and also many who believe that Pakistan should be a true Islamic state, the biggest in the World. They're all good Muslims. They've been formed into organised groups to address the shortfall of our numbers, adding something like a million fighting force to our administration. The World doesn't realise that we're not eighty thousand trying to suppress sixty million, we're over a million trying to suppress fifty million, and the fifty million are made up mainly of women, children and old men. So the Peace Committee are an essential part of our war strategy. Now that we've just about taken back full control in all the major towns, we need to move out into the rural areas, but our numbers are insufficient. Hence the Peace Committee, who'll fill that numbers gap and establish a presence in the countryside. For example, here."

Ablaa was taking it all in, but was confused. "Why're you telling us this?"

"Because I want to talk to you. I've been starved of intelligent conversation for some time. And you two are intelligent. So come on, talk to me. Show me that your reputation isn't misplaced. Give me reason to respect my men's love for you."

Ablaa looked to her daddy for support, but he was equally confused, so she inspired to show that the captain's men's love for them was not misplaced. "What are you talking about? We're intelligent, but that's no reason for your men to love us. They've *no* reason to love us. What are you talking about?"

The captain grinned. "You've been picked up by a Pakistani unit, believed by many to be a bunch of Muslims, but known to us soldiers as a bunch of everything. Do you believe in miracles, or extreme coincidence? Things that drive you through your life for no predetermined reason? Help me, I need some spiritual guidance."

Satvinder replied, "I no longer believe in any of it. Things mainly happen because you make them happen. We're here because we travelled, and wouldn't be here if we'd decided to stay in Chak Sahasa. It was all our own direction. We deliberately came here."

"That's good. So did we." He directed their immediate future to the desk, where they all sat, the Captain opposite side to his captives. "Why has your Christian son been circumcised? Most of my men believe that you're all Muslims, but not all of them. A miraculous choice to check the boy. I could have had *you* checked. I now know what that would've shown my men."

Ablaa asked, "Do you know us?"

The captain took a massive breath. "We know you. The young man in your truck recognised you, and once the children were settled into the godown, he spoke to the other two who recognised you. They're convinced it's you, the one who my young soldier fell madly in love with, and like a miracle we all followed him. I'm talking about Satvinder, Ablaa, and James. I'm talking about how three of my men were sent out with the navy to find survivors from the cyclone, moving up from the bottom of Monpura, moving northwards to your village where you and just a handful of other children survived, and how a Hindu took on a Christian boy and a Muslim girl and became a family. We all watched you for the two weeks while you were in Chittagong, clinging onto each other, supporting each other, loving each other, and we all became believers in your faith. It was a faith which spanned across the divides which we all create, and we call those divides religion. You created a faith way beyond what religion has to offer, belief in each other. *Undoubted* belief in each other. And we watched you believe. And as we openly discussed it in the cantonment, we began to believe. We believed in Satvinder, the equalizer, the bridge between the peaks spanning the grotesque intolerance of religion. We decided that if there really is a God, he'd be something like you. Talk which could easily get us killed in our strict Islamic home land. But it left us with something, and if we survive this war, we'll be believers in God, not man. God is God, religion is man."

He suddenly walked around the room. "Apart from all that, I live for books, they're my passion, and one day I might want to write my own book about Satvinder. 'Satvinder who?' they'll ask. Maybe I'll say 'the Satvinder who went to write his own book about the Chars, but never quite made it' or maybe 'just Satvinder the man who changed our lives'."

He stood up, and after a number of seconds, paced all the way round his guests. "That was nature, or God. Now it's war, and you're still believing in each other. But that's who you are to us: icons. Now let's talk about the war which you're running from. Why do we do it? Every war creates hell. It uses all the tools of warfare including torture, mutilation, rape, murder, absolute fear, mental destruction. They're all there to be used by either side of the fray, and man being man, they all get used. Your people killed my people in the thousands over the past six months. Now my people, and *your* own people, are killing your people by the thousands. Man will be man."

Ablaa huffed, "Blaming our natural instincts doesn't make it right to slaughter defenceless people."

"Then why did *you* do it?" He sighed. "You don't have to answer that. I know that you didn't. But your people did."

"And why did your people kill Daddy's wife and children?"

With a frown across his face, "Sorry. I didn't know that." He paced around the table. "Although we love your spirit and the example you set, we know nothing else about you. Maybe that's for the best. Every war doesn't only produce hell, it produces heroes like your Major Ziaur Rahman, heroic defender of Chittagong where we first met, and it produces legends who inspire and influence, like yourselves. We'll take the name of Satvinder to mean tolerant and just. You never know, your example could be written into history, and even used by the manipulators of man. You never know. What do you think, Ablaa?"

"If we survive, we'll bring these children up in Anglia believing in God, and God alone."

"Anglia? Is that where you're going?" He reacted with sincere interest.

"Yes. We've been offered work and accommodation by Daddy's boss."

"Would that be Field Marshall Gnuru? The man who managed a lot of land around here? And you still don't believe in coincidence?"

She cleared her throat. "How do you know him?"

"Hmm, stranger by the second. I'm Captain Plassey, a member of the Chi Bantri sect which owns a great many companies, including the BanChi Food lot. I've an influential future ahead of me, if I can both impress in this war, and survive it. If you're going to Anglia, I hope to see you there after the war. I have a job waiting for me with the Chi Bantri organisation."

The two captives, or guests, were becoming wary of the situation, one which seemed quite surreal and too good to be true. But Ablaa felt more relaxed, and able to speak openly.

"We're your prisoners. Where does that leave us two legends in your plans?"

"You've never been my prisoners. I gave you a lift."

"But we've been held at gunpoint."

"For your own safety." He thought. "Do you know what this place will be used for? No? Well the site will be used by us as a strategic grouping point, controlling the river crossing, the only one before Chuknagar, but the Peace Committee and its razakars will use it as an extermination camp. They'll exterminate the Hindus and any other undesirables they choose, and they'll be accountable to nobody. It's part of warfare, particularly civil warfare. Their chosen prey will probably all end up in the river."

Suddenly the man who was growing on them wilted back into the professional predator that he was.

"You think badly of me? As I already mentioned I don't wish to talk to these men, these butchers. But I have a job to do for my country, and it's not all pleasant. In fact very little of it is. But if I can help you, then I'll at least have *something* to sleep for. My men are guarding our guests from the men who'll one day be recognised as the butchers of their own people. Doctor by day, butcher by night; accountant by profession, executioner by choice; satisfaction by day, ecstasy by night. I hate them all for what they are, but I have a job to do. And so long as you're here with us, you're safe. Now, when you go across the river, as you need to tomorrow, you'll not have us. Beware of the butchers, they kill their own kind. Or worse." He huffed. "None of us know where this'll all lead."

Satvinder stood up. "In summary, we should all run to India, and then the Indians will have to take the war seriously. Millions of refugees will force Ghandi to do something about it. Then the killing and abuse might stop."

The captain waved his finger in the air. "That's brilliant!" He paused. "Open talk is good, and bad. I'll give you some of the bad. In summary, General Tikka Khan supports the scorched earth policy, in other words he wants the land, but nothing on top of it. His initial assault on the people is an acceptable war strategy designed to save lives. When the World criticises his merciless assault on the people of East Pakistan, they don't understand that it's a strategy which has been used for thousands of years, as it was by one of my wartime heroes, William the Conqueror. Before becoming the Conqueror he was the Bastard, because of his mother's disrepute. But he was also seen as a bastard for other, misunderstood reasons. He was in France, constantly at war. His tactics would be to conquer a town or village, select fifty young men and boys and skin them alive for all the conquered public to see. He'd then send messengers onto the other towns where they would describe what happens if they fight and lose, spreading fear into the enemy, enough for them to decide not to fight, but instead to let them in and be their allies, thus saving thousands of lives. All for the cost of just fifty poor souls. Now, the people of East Pakistan have not given up, so we have to continue the assault. And with a little bit of religious and nationalistic brainwashing, many of the men in our army think on the Bengali as being as low as these low-lying lands, to be exterminated, or in many cases, to be fertilised by the sperm of true Islamic soldiers. They're just animals and their numbers need to be controlled."

Ablaa spat on the ground.

"Please believe me, Ablaa, this isn't my thinking, it's the war machine's thinking. Now getting back to the situation, the Bengalis haven't given up. So what do we do? The Indians are already helping the Mukti with arms. We know that. But coming right round in full circle, to your point about running to India, I suddenly agree with you, Satvinder, and very sadly, with the Peace Committee. We should *not* clear the lands of the malauns by letting them run away, because they'll come straight back with the Indians by their sides. We need to kill them all. You make good sense, Satvinder. I knew I was right to want to speak to you. Thank you. I owe you a great debt."

The young soldier very proudly escorted the shocked couple down the stairs and through the gauntlet of Peace Committee members. They could feel the hatred from their own countrymen, but they were amongst friends, the Pakistani admirers. It was like being best mates with a Bengal tiger, safe under the King's salvation, but just wondering when he'll get hungry.

Knowing that they were guests and not prisoners, they were able to relax and get some sleep, happy in the knowledge that their worshipers overlooked their survival, but Satvinder was becoming increasingly stressed about his input into the conversation.

He whispered to Ablaa, "Have I made him think that he needs to kill all the refugees?"

"No, Daddy. He's a professional soldier, and very intelligent. He doesn't need somebody like you to make him act. He'll do what he does, and no fault of yours. Please believe me."

He had a restless night worrying about it, worrying about his friends who were passing through Chuknagar with the other thousands of refugees. Why didn't he just keep his big mouth shut, and revel in their plain good fortune? Why?

The next morning the soldiers took the family to the riverside, where the ferry was waiting. The local razakars looked on with suspicion and a certain amount of hatred, but dared not make a comment while their 'dictators' were there.

Four soldiers went across first, with the two hand-trucks and several of the children, and then the rest followed.

The Captain crossed with the second wave. He gave a little advice. "You've had a very lucky break, you group of Muslims. Beware that it may not be the same the next time you're stopped." He grinned. "The couple of hours in the truck yesterday made up about forty miles, probably at least three days of walking. So, Insha'Allah, see you in Anglia."

The captain saluted Satvinder, and his soldiers did likewise. But before they parted company, Ablaa finally looked into the eyes of the young soldier. "Thank you, for everything. Maybe one day we'll speak."

Back on the track, they checked the map. They really had made up a lot of time, and they probably only had about a day or day-and-a-half before reaching the main track to Satkira. Their lives were beginning to feel gifted, but it still left a sour taste in Satvinder's mouth when he thought about Akhtar and his family in Chuknagar. As they silently moved along the narrow path he remembered the very first day at Chak Sahasa, when his old mate told him to keep his opinionated mouth shut. One day he'll learn.

They met a number of farm workers on the track. They tried not to talk to them, but were forced.

"Where're you going?" asked one of the farm hands.

"To the Satkira Road."

The worker waved his finger. "We get stopped a lot. The razakars are looking for refugees. Stay out of their way or they'll take you. Or even chop you on the spot." The workers moved on.

Ablaa suggested, "One of us should walk ahead as lookout." So James volunteered. He kept about two hundred yards ahead, but held back if there was a bend so they all kept sight of each other. Eventually he stopped and waved them on. There was a river.

"Right, the boat now comes into its own," chirped Tazkia.

They first took the bottles and rice across river, which was only about thirty feet across, and then the children, and then the adults. The two carts were roped, and pulled across. They just about floated.

"That was easy," sighed James. "I thought we'd be ages. Would've been ages without the boat." The two girls whose mother donated it grinned from ear to ear and the other children chuckled. The family was working like a finely tuned clock.

They had been travelling for about five hours and getting tired, and had moved out of the jute plantations into rice growing land, where they could see well ahead without James being up front. What concerned Satvinder was the openness, and felt very conspicuous. He stood on one of the barrows.

"I can see more jute. We need to get there quickly, and then we can look for somewhere to rest, out of sight."

They soon arrived back into the jute plantations, and so James moved up ahead, looking for somewhere to stop. He found a place which was dry, and off the track. It was almost hidden from the lane.

Satvinder ordered, "No fire. We'll eat noodles and fish, and drink water, but I'm concerned about the razakars. So no fires, and be quiet."

They dished out the food and water, and Satvinder and Tazkia volunteered to go on lookout, taking their food with them. They sat at the bend up ahead. It was a good spot as they could also see right back along the lane behind them for some way, and they had some cover under which to retreat back to the camp if anything came. They felt fairly secure.

They finished eating, and held hands. "Do we need to get married?" Tazkia stared lovingly into his eyes.

"It's probably not necessary under the circumstances. Wouldn't even know how. Would it have to be in a mosque, or a temple?"

She ran her fingers down the side of his face. "No. Wouldn't have to be anywhere, just right here. Nobody would know, apart from our children and God, if we just became married." She snapped her fingers and grinned into his face. "Just like that. Married. Formality all seems an aimless exercise right now, so do you, Satvinder, take me as your beloved wife?"

He grinned, and then gently kissed her lips. "I do. Does that mean we're married? Just like that?"

She pulled him closer to her, making sure she didn't squash little Mo, and nodded. They were married. "We'll tell the others as soon as we get back to the camp. I love you." They shared a long, sensual kiss.

Tazkia suddenly jumped. People were coming from the direction from which they'd come. Six or seven men approached, one with a grey jacket on.

"Shit. They must be following us. What's their problem?"

They hurriedly crept back along the bank to the camp.

"Hide the carts!" They pushed the carts under the cover of the hedge, and all carefully moved into the jute crop. The children huddled together with Tazkia close by, as they had before, and the adults found their own spots. The water was only a few inches deep, so they got right down low, partly submerged and totally invisible from the lane.

They waited and waited. It seemed like a lifetime, but they all kept perfectly silent, each child supporting and cuddling each other. The seven men walked by carrying long jute knives, and the one with the jacket sported a pistol in his belt. They were talking amongst themselves, and not seemingly looking out for anything nor anybody. But then little Mo began to murmur. Then again, but louder. The children looked towards Tazkia willing Mo to be quiet, but another murmur and a grizzle. They would be caught. But Mo stopped. He never made another sound as the men carried on slowly down the lane without any idea of them being in the jute. After some time they felt safe enough to take a look.

"Stay here until I've checked," whispered Satvinder. He crept out, surveyed the immediate lane, and then moved to the bend. The men had moved a long way along the lane, well out of hearing-range. They were safe!

"It's ok. We've made it through." He stood in the camp and waited for the others. Nothing. "It's ok." He stared into the jute for signs of movement.

Ablaa came out with three girls. Her face was becoming tearful, and then the children all began to cry. She grabbed her daddy round the waste, and cried on his shoulder, then kissed him on the lips. Satvinder realised that something terrible had happened, and pushed her away.

"What?"

She pulled his arm to stop him going in. "The nurse is trying to revive him. Don't go in."

But he had to. As he pushed through the jute plants he found the nurse holding Mo, and Tazkia writhing in the shallow water, with James and two other girls struggling to

266

keep her head out of the water. He jumped to their assistance, and pulled his wife from the water, lifting her tiny frame into his arms, and she cried uncontrollably, and hysterically.

She had smothered her little Mo, trying to keep him quiet. He was dead in the nurse's arms.

But the mother wanted her child. She suddenly struggled to get away from her husband's arms and began punching him to let go, so the nurse handed Mo to her, and she relaxed. She looked at the little tot's face which was lifeless, and then pulled him into her breast. As she cradled in Satvinder's arms she cried for her dead son. Her only son.

They slowly moved out into the camp. It had begun to rain, and was soon to be getting dark and it made such a depressing sight, a mother hanging desperately onto her dead baby and watched by nearly forty other children who just stared in disbelief.

The terrible distraction had taken over their World momentarily and they never even noticed, but there they were, watching along with the children. The men. They had returned. Their guard had dropped.

"Good evening." Luckily, it was the farmers who had returned, not the razakars. "Can we help?"

The rural areas of Bengal have long been accustomed to dying children, so the family knew that they needed to get on with life from the offset, and make sure that no other children were lost. They allowed Tazkia to keep her baby until she felt able to bury him, sleeping that night with Mo in her arms, and then setting off in the morning towards their destination, with Mo still in her arms. The farmers returned in the morning and guided them through some alternative lanes, away from the marauding razakars, as far as the Satkira Road, and then bid them farewell and good luck. Tazkia still held tightly onto her baby and Satvinder held tightly onto his new wife.

Colin Hodgson

# CHAPTER 20 – CHUKNAGAR

May 18th to 20th ,1971, The Route Through Chuknagar

As the band of forty went off down the lane to the left, Akhtar, Baka and the two boys went straight ahead. They were taking the direct route to Chuknagar and then onto the Satkira Road, and eventually onto the Indian border. They were hoping that the route along the better roads would be kinder to Baka's bad feet.

The carts had both gone with Satvinder's group and so the only water which they had with them was a water-bag each, hung over their shoulders. However, Akhtar had a cigarette lighter and some extra fuel, so they could boil water if needed. Akhtar was not particularly concerned about the trip.

"We'll be in Chuknagar day after tomorrow. Then we should be in India very soon."

"Then London?" asked one of the boys.

"Yes, then London, after Kolkata. Might take a while, but we'll get there. I promise."

The road was busy, with thousands of travellers making their way towards the border, and the line of runaway families moved slowly, but consistently, stretching for as far as the eye could see. There were people in pyjamas and kurtas, in trousers and shirts, in saris of every colour under the sun, of all ages, some with carts, others with nothing, but they were all the same. They were all afraid, on the run, seeking refuge with the Indian government, and being hunted down by the Pakistanis and their Bengalese mates. Everybody was stone silent, drawn and depressed, and only the children made any sound: they cried.

As night drew in, the column stopped for the night. The weather was warm but damp and so was the ground, so not everybody slept. As Akhtar lay awake, watching the moon pass through a small break in the clouds, he could hear people wining, some children crying, some dogs barking, but no laughter or chat. It was a very long night for the doctor.

Morning came slowly, and Akhtar woke his family as soon as it became light. They needed an early start as Baka could only move at a crawl. He was concerned about her painful feet, and he had given his medicine bag to the nurse.

"When we get into Chuknagar I'll see if I can get some painkillers. I've an old colleague living nearby."

They moved slowly along the road, passing many of the families which had not yet resumed their journey, some of whom were clearly in trouble, particularly the old and the very young. As a doctor he could tell that many were troubled with poor health, and he knew that some would not make it as far as the border. But on that day he was not a doctor, he was a refugee, just like the rest of them.

They eventually arrived at the Bhadra. The river crossing was congested and noisy, with many arguments about the inflated fares being charged to use the ferry. The operators had increased the fares by many times, and a great number of travellers did not have enough money for the crossing, so a large group decided to travel anyway by aggressively boarding the ferry and refusing to pay anything.

"I'll report you to the army, and they'll bash you all!" screamed the ferry operator. "They'll bash you for this!"

But they all still pushed their way onto the ferry, sneering at the Bihari whose ambition it was to shaft the poorest of the poor as they fled for their lives. Akhtar and his family just followed the crowd. They were across the river and still had their little bag of money.

By early evening they were passing through the crowds in Pathkhola, and heading towards Chuknagar Bazar. Akhtar wanted to get onto the west side of Chuknagar before stopping, and then they'd be ready to leave for the Satkira Road in the morning, praying that he could get hold of some painkillers for Baka. They still had a lot of walking to do before they could seek asylum across the border.

The local people were all selling food and drinks to the travellers, but many had no money with which to buy. It was heart wrenching watching the children cry and grizzle for food, but none came their way. Some of the local people gave rice to the children, but most wanted paying.

"Don't drink too much water. We need to go for another three days with what we have." The doctor knew that the conditions were perfect for the spread of cholera, so the local water was not to be trusted. Most of the other travellers had to take their chances and many would pay the price.

The town was packed. Thousands had fled to the area since hearing the rumours of an impending attack by the Pakistani army. Many more had fled there to escape the killing sprees of the razakars and Al Badrs, and the refugees still continued to arrive right until dusk. Sleeping space was at a premium.

During the night a ruckus woke the family. Some thieves had been caught taking valuables from a cart, resulting in an almighty hullabaloo and for some time the Bazar was absolute bedlam. But then it returned to normality. Only the dogs could be heard above the crying of the children.

The morning was damp, again, and Baka's feet were even worse.

"I don't know how far I can walk. I'm sorry."

"I'll go over to see my friend, see if he can give me some painkillers. He's not far away."

And so Akhtar left Baka and the boys by the river while he visited an old doctor friend in the vicinity. The walk was about five to six miles each way, and would keep him away for much of the day, effectively putting off their trek to the border by another day. But without any pain relief Baka would probably never make it.

In the meantime Captain Plassey had despatched fifteen volunteers from their cantonment in Khulna to 'discourage' the people from crossing into India. He had taken Satvinder's words about the refugees sparking a response from India a lot more seriously than he should have, and simply ordered the troops to 'make them think twice before crossing the border'. The troops had their own ideas on how best to do that.

The two army trucks arrived in Pathkhola a couple of hours after Akhtar had left. They were armed with light machine guns and semi-automatic rifles, and as they alighted, they began shooting. In just minutes the sleepy town was a blood bath. The soldiers moved through the town and killed every male they came upon, and any child or female who got in the way, which was most of them. As women smothered their children and men from the bullets, they all died. Then they moved into Chuknagar Bazar, killing and killing, and the only time they let up was to abuse the young girls. They then killed them.

Baka and her sons crouched down by the river with several other refugees, not knowing what to do. Many people jumped into the river to escape, but those who did not drown through panic were shot as they tried to swim to safety. Then the soldiers found Baka crouching with her sons. They pulled the boys away and shot them both, and then violently stripped Baka's sari from her but when they realised how old she was, they cut her breasts off before shooting her through the head.

Eventually the ammunition ran out, but the bayonets did not. They continued their orgy of rape and killing until the afternoon, when they had almost run out of people to kill, but they did not go home empty handed. They took several pretty young ladies back with them to the cantonment for the pleasure of the other soldiers.

Akhtar had heard the shooting while he was at his friend's home and almost ran all the way back to the town. As he stumbled along the dirt road the two army trucks approached him and drew to a halt.

"What are you?" shouted the driver.

Akhtar was not sure of the question.

"What are you? Hindu?"

He panted for a few seconds, before answering. "Muslin."

"Get out of our way then, or I'll run you down." The other soldiers laughed as they tormented the young girl-hostages, before they resumed their journey back to their cantonment.

It was all over by the time Akhtar arrived back in Chuknagar. Death was everywhere: families huddled together, all dead; some women stripped and mutilated; children almost blown in half by the bullets; and many just dead and bloody.

As he looked towards the river bank, his heart broke. He sank to his knees, unable to scream or cry, just pant at the sight of his partly-naked wife and children. They were like all the others, blood-covered and lifeless. He eventually screamed. He jumped to his feet and began running around the town like a madman, searching for a soldier to kill, but they were all long gone. He began shouting at the local people as they began to emerge from their homes but two strong men managed to grab hold of him. They held him on the ground as he continued to scream. Eventually he calmed, and the screaming was replaced by crying. He cried on the shoulder of one of the men.

Neither of the men said anything for some time. They allowed Akhtar to get it out of his system before allowing him to his feet, still sobbing and shocked and shaking like a newborn baby.

Poor Akhtar was not alone. Men, women and children were all around, in deep shock, tending their dead or dying loved ones, and the town was red with their blood. The men took Akhtar and two other men into their home to settle them with hot drinks.

"We'll help you bury you families." The two men were kind, and seemed utterly ashamed of their religion. "It was the Paks. Muslims killing Hindus. We're very sorry, and ashamed."

Akhtar eventually spoke. Very deliberately, "I used to be a Muslim. Until this morning."

No more was said on the subject. The men went out to bury the dead families, carefully stepping around the other dead bodies, but as they approached the river bank Akhtar broke. His head exploded, and he began screaming. Two dogs were fighting over his youngest son, each tearing at the young flesh from his arm and leg.

It was too much for Doctor Akhtar Hussain. He flipped, and as his head was torn apart by the rage, the despair and the confusion, he ran away. He never went back to that riverbank. He just ran and ran.

The massacre at Chuknagar resulted in between eight and ten thousand deaths, the largest single act of genocide in the war, and we'll never know quite who to blame. The soldiers? Captain Plassey? Satvinder? God only knows.

# CHAPTER 21 – THE PYRE

May 22nd,1971, On The Satkira Road

Satvinder's group were safely escorted by the kindly farmers as far as the road to Satkira, west of Chuknagar and into the final leg of the march to the Indian border. The farmers all prayed for the safety of the children and all showed their respects to Tazkia who still held tightly onto her dead son. After thanking the farmers for their unselfish deeds they joined the other refugees.

The travellers were like zombies, walking, but showing very little sign of any other life. One woman, holding the hands of two young girls with blood stains across their saris, took an interest in the group of children from Chak Sahasa.

"Whose children are these?" She stuttered as she asked Ablaa. "Whose children?"

Ablaa looked to Satvinder, but she never answered the woman's question.

"Are they orphans from Chuknagar?" the woman asked.

Ablaa frowned as she finally responded. "No. They're our children. Why?"

The woman held tightly onto the two girls and nodded her head towards one of them. "*These* are orphans from Chuknagar. Their parents were killed with the rest of them, and all they have left of them are the blood stains. Can they join you?"

Ablaa stepped back and held Satvinder's arm. "What do you mean?"

The woman was blunt. "The Paks killed nearly everybody. These girls need looking after." She walked the two girls past Ablaa, Satvinder and the stupefied Tazkia, and offered their hands to the nurse.

The nurse looked to Satvinder for guidance, but received none: he was beginning to break from the sketchy piece of news about Chuknagar. So she took the two girls from the woman and gave them a drink from her water bag.

"The Paks killed all the men, and most of the women. Nobody knows why." She went on to describe the scene, and the thousands of deaths, before just calmly wandering off along the road. She never looked back at the children which she had just relieved herself of.

"Akhtar," whispered Satvinder into Ablaa's ear. He was beginning to break, tears forming in his eyes. "Akhtar."

She pulled herself into her daddy. "We don't know. He'll meet us at the border, just like we arranged. You wait." She kissed him on the cheek.

His face became wet with tears. The conversation with Captain Plassey was ringing around his head and scrambling his conscious thoughts, until Tazkia suddenly came to life. She moved her dead baby aside from him, and gently kissed him on the lips.

She quietly stated, "When we were in the lane, we were married."

Ablaa raised her eyebrows and grinned. "That's wonderful. Congratulations." She sensed that her new stepmother was trying to take Satvinder's mind away from his nightmarish thoughts. "That's wonderful." She reached over and kissed Tazkia on the head.

Then, with an almost angelic tone the young bride promised, "My baby will soon be gone."

She never said any more. The conversation was over.

The children took in their new sisters, and the nurse and James kept them all in line, while Satvinder floated along in a trance with Tazkia on one arm and Ablaa on the other. He desperately tried to forget about Captain Plassey, and his own big, opinionated mouth, but he knew deep in his heart that if his best mate had died, he was at least partly to blame. He quietly prayed.

As the thousands of refugees filed along the road towards the border, they passed lifeless bodies. Some were being tended by their grieving families, whilst others just lay alone, waiting to meet their maker and the solace of death. They were the ones who were to finally leave the hell of Earth, to move onto somewhere else, maybe better, maybe worse, or maybe nowhere. Their faith was all they were certain of. And then it began to rain!

James dropped back to talk to Ablaa.

"Is Daddy all right?"

She looked down at her brother and smiled. "I think so. His war has been a mental one: these others have had much worse than that." She looked around at the bedraggled travellers. "I think we've all been lucky." She took a brief sideways look at Tazkia and her dead child. "Perhaps lucky is the wrong word."

The little Christian lad sighed. "D'you know, when I went to Khulna with Uncle Akhtar we saw a load of burned out buildings, and some dead people? And one street was burned *right* out, all the houses, and they were getting bodies out and throwing them onto a cart. I knew how they came out of the houses, dead, but I wondered how they got into the houses. And I dreamed about it, and they were thrown into the burning houses. As they ran out from the flames, the people picked them up and threw them straight back into them. Even the babies." He took a deep breath. "D'you think my dreams were true?"

Ablaa looked to her daddy and Tazkia for help, but they were both somewhere else, so she pulled the boy to her and shook as she brushed the rain from his face. "I'm only a little girl really, so perhaps I'll give a little girl's answer. Honest... childish, but honest." She took a few moments out to think about the stories that the travellers had told her as they passed by the end of their lane. She then delivering her childish wisdom upon an innocent eight-year old. "The World has turned its back on the East Pakistanis, especially on the Hindus. What you saw in Khulna was the East Pakistani people killing the Biharis, the allies of the West. Now the West is taking revenge, and killing the East, relentlessly, probably ten dead for every Bihari or West soldier killed. Don't know where it'll end, and I don't know who to blame." Pause. "And so people can do whatever they feel they can get away with. There's no law, no religion, and I think no God, to protect any of us. So I think you're right, and I believe that's what happened to those poor Biharis. As they tried to escape the flames, they were thrown straight back in. If not thrown back, just chopped to death. Or perhaps worse. Men, women and children." She again nervously brushed the rain from his face. "We're the children of war. We mustn't allow ourselves to imagine the niceties of war. Just the truth. We should tell the World the truth, and nothing but, and none of it's nice."

Perhaps a little boy of just eight should not be hearing such wisdom, but he took it all in. "How long will the war last?"

With a shake of the head she whispered, "For some, forever. For others, too long. As long as there's opposition, there'll be war. And me and you have been blessed, by God if he really exists, with a high level of intelligence. More than most, so the two of us must grow up with the knowledge of what war is really about. About murdering everybody, until they no longer oppose. Death by whatever means the hangman chooses. Cruel, lingering, pointless." They walked a while without talking. Then she continued. "My mummy told me all about what's called genocide. It's about getting rid of all the people who oppose, or who may oppose. In Europe the

Germans humanely gassed lots of Jews. But people forget that most of them weren't gassed, they were abused and raped, chopped, shot, burned, some mutilated, and often injured too bad to help themselves and just left to die in the freezing cold. That's what happened in Russia, and when the Russians turned the war they took their revenge. Like the West are, taking savage revenge." She looked at James. "Am I scaring you?"

He stared hard into his sister's eyes. "No. Thanks for teaching me. It makes more sense now."

The boy was desperately trying to understand the perdition which was engulfing them. He shook the rain from his hair. "If they're gonna kill all the malauns why didn't that Captain kill us when they picked us up?"

A smile suddenly stretched across Ablaa's face. "Because they knew us. That's all. Pure good fortune." She held James tightly. "Perhaps lucky is the word for us. D'you remember when we were taken from home to Chittagong? And that young soldier tended us so kindly, on the boat and in the refuge, and wanted to know all about us and why we could all become so close with our three different religions? Well, that was him in the truck. He remembered us, and the Captain was intrigued why we were so close. Don't know why, but I guess the Captain's not a deeply religious person himself, and perhaps admired our strength to be able to put aside our own differences. Whatever his real reasons, he helped us because he liked us." She frowned. "But what I don't understand is about the soldier who checked you for circumcision. He confirmed, and the other soldiers all believed we were a group of Muslims."

James began to giggle, and it became contagious. He waived his head about in jest. "That's good. At least I know you haven't seen my willy, else you'd know." He chuckled. "I'll show you one-day, maybe."

"Oh, now that's an offer a girl couldn't refuse. But I'm your sister so behave yourself."

The giggling slowed, and James thoughtfully asked, "Are you really my sister? Like a real sister?"

"Of course, and this is your daddy. He'll never replace your other daddy, but he's your daddy. And guess what," she sniggered, "this is my mummy." She pulled James' head round to look at Tazkia. "When we were in the lane and they looked out together, they got married. So this's *your* mummy as well."

The joviality ended and the two looked sadly at the newlyweds, knowing that they were in deep depression. James gently pulled himself from Ablaa's arms, and moved to Satvinder. They all stopped walking, as James gave his daddy a massive hug around the waist. He then moved to Tazkia and gave her an even tighter hug. She moved her baby aside and looked down into James' face with eyes so sad, and smiled. She then looked straight ahead, and her body language asked James to let go. He did so and moved back to Ablaa.

"I hope you'll always be my sister. Never leaving."

"And I hope you'll always be my brother."

"I know that daddy lost his family in Dhaka, and their baby has died, but he seems suddenly worse."

"He's in terrible shock." She slowed in her walking and they made a bit more space between them and Satvinder. "Can you keep a real secret? A real one, never to be talked about, ever?"

"On my daddy's soul." He crossed his heart.

"Well, I think you need to know, cos you're family." She breathed deeply. "When we were going through the fields and marshes, there was a terrible massacre in Chuknagar. That woman with the girls told us. And we think that Uncle Akhtar and the others were there." There was a disturbing silence. Then, "Daddy thinks it might have been his fault, but he's wrong. It wasn't anything to do with Daddy. It couldn't have been." She brushed the wet from his face and then wiped her own. "Please remember that if Daddy doesn't come round, then we've got to look after him, and understand his grief. But please promise to never ever talk about this to *anybody*."

James nodded. The tears which formed were hidden by the rain, and neither of them was aware that they were *both* crying. But the grief was disturbed as they had to navigate around a family which were trying to revive a young mother.

The rain eventually stopped, and the darkness of night crept in. The skies were full of cloud and no moonlight fell, so they had to rest. They found a space by the road large enough to house them all, and although the rain had let up, everywhere was drenched, so the order of the day was to all squeeze together to conserve their body heat, and also to guard each other against the vagabonds and thieves which had threatened along the way. Their depleting food and water supplies were safely hidden in the middle of the ruck.

The children were exhausted and were asleep within minutes, but not Satvinder. He held tightly onto Tazkia, still nursing her dead baby, and prayed. He had suddenly become afraid to go to sleep, for fear of the nightmares which niggled away at his conscious mind. As soon as he closed his eyes violent visions appeared in which Akhtar, Baka, Kaling and their four children were savagely torn apart by the bullets and bayonets of the Pakistani soldiers, and standing over them laughing was Captain Plassey. Satvinder just stared into the night.

A little way ahead a fire had been lit, and the flames threw sparks into the skies which looked to Satvinder like angels trying to escape back to the normality of heaven. It occupied his mind for a while, until the smell of burning flesh wafted on the light winds to their camp. They were burning the dead bodies, and the smell returned him to his macabre visions. But suddenly he came down to earth. He gently shook Tazkia and she woke.

Looking into her dark face, he whispered, "We could give Mo a proper funeral. There's a pyre up ahead."

She took a few moments to properly wake, and then smiled and nodded. They moved out from the camp without waking any of the others, and walked arm-in-arm around the sleeping refugees, towards the fire. Not a single word was said out loud as they waited their turn to place their baby on the plank of wood, and as the soldiers offered the plank into the fire they both just stared. Something cracked in Satvinder's heart as the plank was turned and the baby disappeared into the roaring fire. He was gone, but as he held his wife so tightly, she at last cried for her son's soul. Maybe she had returned.

Tazkia seemed more relaxed as they arrived back at to the camp. Still in intense mourning she lay with her new husband, amongst the children, and kissed him like she had never done before. She carried on for many minutes, before stroking his forrid, whispering, "Go to sleep. You must sleep, and look after *all* these children. Sleep." As she gently stroked his forrid, she took his left ear into her mouth, breathing deeply, and then whispered, "I love you, Husband. Go to sleep."

As if under hypnosis, he fell into a deep sleep, without a nightmare in sight.

He was woken at daybreak by one of the girls, who shook his shoulder. He rolled over to look up into her face and he smiled, but she never. It was the girl who they first took into the orphanage, after her mother's mercy killing.

"Where's Mummy?" The children had become much closer to Tazkia than Satvinder had ever realised. "Where's Mummy? I'm scared."

He sat up and looked around. She had gone. He got to his feet and looked around, up the road, down the road, but no sign, so he shouted her name many times. A man further up the road helped by also shouting her name many times, but to no avail.

"Ablaa! She's gone." He was beginning to panic. "I've got to look for her."

"No, stop. Just wait and calm down. She's probably just gone for a walk. *Calm down.*"

She held his hand, and all the children pulled around for support, but he didn't calm. "I'll go and look for her."

Ablaa stressed, "No! Let's think about it. We can't split up, else we could all be lost."

James suggested, "I was good company for Uncle Akhtar in Khulna. I could come and look after you."

Grudgingly Ablaa agreed and so the group would stay exactly where they were, while Satvinder went off in search, with James. But which way? He looked at the road ahead, and then behind, and decided to go forward, and look in the area around the funeral pyre. Maybe she was grieving at the bonfire. They both called her name as they moved along the road, and several people asked what she was wearing so they could look out for her, but they came up with nothing. Satvinder was almost white as he realised that she had gone somewhere deliberately, not to be found. His life was imploding.

James led the shocked lecturer back to the group, and Ablaa and the nurse made the decision to move on... they had about thirty other children to take care of! They called Tazkia's name as they went, and as the group passed by the funeral pyre a young Mukti soldier called to Ablaa. She thought he might know her so she approached him, warily, but soon realised that he was a stranger.

"Excuse me, miss. May I have a private word?"

They moved aside from the crowds.

"I wasn't sure what to say, or to whom, but last night a young lady jumped into the fire. We couldn't stop her. We don't know if it's the woman you call for. So sorry."

Poor Ablaa was struck. It was the last thing she was expecting from the young soldier and it left her reeling and confused. She dropped to her knees and her face screwed up as she stressed to bursting point, and then she exploded into an eerie wail. James and two girls rushed over to her. Once she had calmed down a little she stuttered as she looked to Satvinder and spoke.

"I've had some heartbreaking personal news, Daddy. May I speak with James, alone?"

The group decided to slowly move on, leaving James hugging his sister.

"Will you help me? I don't know what to do. I'm only thirteen. I don't know what to do."

They hugged as she had another cry. James looked along the road to make sure he could still see his family. "What's it? We've got to catch up soon."

She sniffed. "That young soldier said that a young woman jumped into the fire last night. He doesn't know if it was Tazkia. What should I do? Please."

"What is childish wisdom? I think it's like we don't know she jumped in, so don't say anything. Might not be her."

"Could I go the rest of my life not telling Daddy?"

"Tell him what? We don't know, so it wouldn't be fair to make him think that she's dead when we don't know."

She thought hard. "Thanks, brother. I love you, as a *real* brother." They set off to catch up with the rest in total silence. In a land of death, it is quite easy to become accustomed to heartache and the many remedies, and so Ablaa wrapped her mind in disbelief. She whispered, "It wasn't her. It wasn't."

James grinned. "I'll do you a deal, sis."

Suddenly she broke out from her stress, almost as if switched off. "Uh, uh. It's no, even before you ask."

"What're you on about?"

She suddenly tickled his ribs. "I know you boys." In a comical voice, "'I'll show you mine if you show me yours.' No way boy." She again tickled his ribs and he screeched.

"I wish I'd thought of that. But I mean, if you don't tell about Tazkia, I won't tell about Chuknagar and Daddy."

A deal was made, and some of the stress of war was lifted from the shoulders of the two little persons.

The next two days consisted of monotonous walking and nothing else, apart from a sharp eye out for the missing Tazkia, and as they passed the dead and dying bodies of all ages, they became immune to the trauma, intent only on their own survival. The children of war were becoming exhausted, but by sharing rides on the carts, they managed to keep going, right until the moment of jubilation – the border!

There it stood. The border, bustling with unhappy, frightened people and soldiers, but the promise of safety and protection.

"We *must* hold on to each other!" ordered Ablaa. If any of us get lost, we may never find each other again, so you children all hold hands. Make four groups, and stay together."

They were accepted through the border control, the Indian soldiers being kind and respectful of the refugees' plight. They had entered into India, which seemed exactly the same as East Pakistan, and stood with many others wondering what would come next. But they were approached by an officer who was overseeing the border operation.

"Good afternoon." He nodded his head. "I'm Sergeant Pica. May I ask why you have so many children?" He looked at Satvinder.

The approach triggered his natural defences, and he finally awoke from his daze. "Most of them are orphans, and we're their guardians. We need to go to Kolkata, in the Anglian region." He waited for a response from the uniformed man, but the man just looked around at the children, and at the nurse. "We don't know what to do now. We've got here, and are now confused."

"Have you walked far?"

"I think it's about fifty miles."

"You've done well. What you need to do now is go onto one of the buses to the camp. But my interest is in you, madam." He looked at the nurse. "You have a doctor's bag. Are you a doctor?"

She bowed her head, and nervously replied, "A nurse. This is Doctor Hussain's bag, but I think we've lost him."

The Sergeant spent a little time explaining the dire medical state in the camps, and after some soul searching the nurse agreed to work with the international aid groups. It was a tearful parting for the nurse and for the children, but before she left the orphans she ordered the sergeant, "Get my children and friends safely to a camp, and ensure that they remain together." The sergeant agreed, and he arranged for them all to travel together in the same bus.

# CHAPTER 22 – THE CAMP

The camp was sparse. It consisted of row after row of tents which had been set up by the Indian government and aid groups, but it at least offered shelter from the rains which had become heavier with the onslaught of the wet season. Thousands of children and women sat around, some almost naked, others well dressed, but all doing nothing. All they had to do was to queue for their rice and water each day. It was a sad, unhealthy environment which bred both disease and discontent, and it advertised the genocide, or gendercide, which had been part of the West Pakistani war policy. It was evident that there were thousands and thousands of women and children, but the few men were nearly all old. Most men of fighting age had been hunted down by the Pak army and their allies and removed from life.

Ablaa and Satvinder sat outside their tent, watching the children doing nothing. "Daddy, can we talk? Like we used to?" Ablaa moved closer to Satvinder. "We've got four tents for all of us. That's ten in each tent. We're *better* than that."

He looked around the camp. There were thousands of refugees in that one camp. "These are all types of people and we're *not* better than them. We're all the same. We're all lost and stuck in the same hole."

She smiled. "You're getting better." She held his hand. "I mean better in that we've had a dream, one which would take us, and the children, to somewhere better, without religious intolerance, and after just two days here I feel the dream is slipping. We're not just running from the war, we're running from our past, and we mustn't stop now. Ever since we ran away from the Char and then from Dhaka, we've dreamed of a place for all of us. This isn't it. Even here I feel threatened when I go out. I'm a Muslim amongst a band of Hindus who've been run out of their homes and country by Muslims. We need to find that place that we've always dreamed of."

He let go of her hand and fiddled with his shirt buttons. "But we're not all here. It's just us."

"You *have* to break out of your mood. *None* of them would expect you to curl up and die. Please Daddy. My mummy told me and my sisters before the storm, 'I'll probably be dead soon. Don't you *dare* die with me!' And now I'm saying it to *you* from Tazkia. She'd *never* expect you to curl up and die."

Satvinder sighed and looked to the sky. "She told me to look after all the children, after we cremated Mo. I know you're right."

He put his hands over his face.

"Don't do that! This place is dirty and diseased! Keep your hands down." She put her head on his shoulder. "Sorry, but we're trying hard to keep the children from catching anything. Don't want you to. You know, there's cholera in the camp up the road. We could lose all the children if it comes here."

Satvinder looked at the children. "I know what you're saying. But we can't just walk away: the army won't let us." He frowned. "But what about Tazkia and Akhtar? They *could* be looking for us. What if they are?"

The thirteen-year old was ahead of him. She had been out with James that morning. "We've thought of that. We went down to the clinic and they've got a big tent with loads of boards. People put notes to their lost ones there, so if they turn up they can read a message."

He was beginning to take a serious interest. "Did you read them?"

"Of course not." She looked away. "We can't read that well. But you can. You're a lecturer."

It worked. Satvinder was suddenly enthused by the idea of reading the notes. "Tazkia could be looking for us. And Akhtar."

They spoke to James and the older children to ensure that they stayed put, and went along to the clinic area. He spent almost an hour reading through the notes which had been pinned to the boards, but nothing of his wife or friends. He was dejected.

"Don't get down. We can leave a note for them. That's the idea. Then we can work out how to get out of here and they can follow." The perfectly formed Ablaa was squeezing her daddy back into his old spirit. She went into the clinic to ask about leaving notes, and they were directed to the aid worker who managed it all. She gave Satvinder a pen and some paper.

"What shall I put? Their names in big letters, but then what?"

Ablaa rather cockily produced a card. It was the Field Marshall's, with a phone number printed on it.

"We can put this phone on the note. They can call that if they can't find us."

So, that was what they did.

Once they had pinned the note up, the aid worker made a suggestion. She spoke quietly. "Is that a number which could help you? If it's official, such as an embassy, the army guard house may allow you to call it. It's worth a try. They're further along the lane, but they only allow official calls for an hour or so in the morning."

Suddenly hope had returned. Before returning to the children, they walked up the lane and found the guard-house. It was open.

Satvinder approached the entrance, but was stopped by a large, bearded Indian soldier.

"Sir, we need to contact my employers in Kolkata."

"Not today. Come back in the morning, and you may be able to call. It depends how busy the lines are."

They thanked the soldier, and returned to their family.

The next morning they discussed their immediate plans. Since it really required the presence of an adult to give them a chance of getting their rice rations, Satvinder had to take the children to the UNICEF food depot, and Ablaa and James would try to make the phone call to the Field Marshall. They were nervous, and not sure if they would allow a young teenager to make the call, but Satvinder going along to get food was just as important, so that plan stuck.

At the guard-house the soldier on the door had been joined by four other armed soldiers, and were aggressively preventing three men from entering. Ablaa and James kept their distance as the tempers flew, and they were expecting a shooting, but the three men left, just swearing and cursing. They ventured to the front of the building.

"Can we help you?" asked the large soldier with the beard.

"Yes, sir. I came yesterday with my father, and asked about phoning his employers."

"I remember." He left the other three to keep guard and went inside. On his return he was smiling. "You can come in."

They entered the brick building which was dark and drab inside, and almost bare except for some wooden chairs and a desk at which sat two soldiers. There was a phone in front of them.

"Sit down!" snapped one of them. "We've a lot of business today, so what can we do for you?"

They sat in front of the desk.

Ablaa spoke. "We were told by the aid worker that we may be able to make an official phone call from here. So we can get our children to Kolkata."

The man to the left was clearly in charge. He had a stripe and asked the questions while the private took notes. "Firstly, what are your names and where are you from?" The private made note. "Now, who would you phone?"

"I have a business card. It's our daddy's employer, the Ban Chi Trading Company."

"We can't allow you to call. It must be the employee. Sorry."

Ablaa's face dropped.

"Why can't your father be here? Is he hiding something?"

"No. He's our only adult. He's collecting rice with the others. We have nearly forty children."

The soldier raised his eyebrows. "That's a lot of children. Why?"

"They're orphans. We've brought them all the way from Chak Sahasa, near Khulna, to safety. Field Marshall Gnuru has places for us in the Anglia region, and our father can continue working for them. If we can get a message to him, we may be saved."

"I don't think we can allow you to phone. It needs to be your father."

Ablaa was close to begging.

"But I don't *want* to phone. I've never used one, so could you phone for me?"

The soldier grinned. "You know what I meant. We have a war situation here." He sighed. "We have rules which we have to abide by. Your father, or nobody. Tomorrow morning, come back with him and he can call the Company. Our phone-line window is about to close, so tomorrow."

They sat motionless, not sure whether or not they had been dismissed.

"You can go now."

Then the soldier taking notes asked, "May I speak to the refugees, Sir?" His superior nodded. "May I take a note of the number and Company name?" He reached over and took the card. "I thought so. It matches a number I rang earlier."

Ablaa grabbed James' arm. "A woman? Named Tazkia?"

The soldier frowned. "Sorry, a man. Akhtar Hussain."

Their jaws dropped.

"Akhtar! It's Akhtar!" They jumped up and hugged each other. "Uncle Akhtar!"

"Stop!" The soldier stood up. "It's good to see happy faces at these dreadful times, but please celebrate outside.

James asked, "Which way did he go, please?"

After consulting his notes the soldier replied, "That way, section H."

They raced out of the guard-house, and danced in the mud before skipping off in the direction of section H. It was turning out to be a wonderful day.

"Now we *have* to find him." Ablaa had sobered up, looking at section H which consisted of a hundred or so tents. "Even if it takes all day, we'll find him. Come on."

They systematically went up one row, looking in all the tents, and back down the next. They asked the refugees if they knew an Akhtar or a doctor, but there were no offers of help. They went along about fifteen rows, and as they turned the corner James froze. He pointed.

"It's him. It is."

They stood looking along the row at a man who was broken. He sat outside a tent with two old women, looking a sorry sight. He was unshaven and drawn, but he was Uncle Akhtar. They had found him, alive.

James suggested, "Let's just run straight up to him, and surprise him."

"No. He doesn't look well. Let's just meander up to him and wait for him to recognise us."

So that was what they did. They casually wandered along the row, desperately trying not to laugh out loud, until their frail Uncle glanced their way, and he almost dropped dead. His face turned grey, but the two children couldn't walk any further, they ran, almost knocking him to the floor as they launched themselves at him. The three of them rolled in the mud, the children laughing and giggling, Akhtar crying. They lay with him as he cried his heart out. He just cried and cried. While they lay, Ablaa looked at his arms, covered with needle scars. He had been injecting himself with something, but she never mentioned it.

"It's you." He had stopped crying by then, and sat up. "Where did you two come from?"

James chuckled. "Chak Sahasa. Same as you."

He playfully grabbed James round the neck, and Ablaa jumped on his back and they all had a wrestle in the dirt. The immaculate reunion.

The whole family group were shocked but elated at Akhtar's return. Not quite the whole gang, but more than they'd expected. Eventually one of the children broke the ice.

"Where's Baka and the boys?"

He stretched his arms out, displaying the needle marks, and smiled. "They won't be coming. We'll have to go to Anglia without them. Tomorrow morning." He clapped his hands and shouted. "Tomorrow morning!" He then just smiled at the kids and they all laughed.

That very next morning they all walked to the guard-house. The soldiers became agitated that more than forty people had descended on their territory, and one took charge.

"You can't stop here! Move on!"

Ablaa stepped forward. "May I speak to the soldiers inside? Please"

The soldier went inside, and then returned with the young soldier who, the previous day, took the notes. He smiled at Ablaa as he saluted the children.

"We found Uncle Akhtar." She glanced over towards her uncle. "Thank you for your kindness. May we wait here for our transport?"

"What transport? You can't leave the camp without proper authorisation." He frowned and looked towards the doctor. "Where do you think you are going, Sir? The phone call never mentioned transport, just to contact you at this camp."

Akhtar grinned. "I asked 'tomorrow morning' and I believe he'll be here this morning. I believe in him. And if he doesn't come today, he'll come tomorrow, or the next day. He'll come."

"But you won't go anywhere without authorisation. You're refugees from another country. Without authorisation you are our *prisoners*. I suggest you get back to your tents before somebody else does."

"Sir," Ablaa chipped in, "could we leave some of us here to wait, and then collect the others when the transport arrives? We'll not be a nuisance."

He spoke to the other soldiers in private, and then approached Ablaa. "We can allow just six to stay here to wait, but wait for what? The message I gave on the phone was very scant, so you could, like most of these people, be waiting in vain. I hope you'll not all be disappointed."

"Thank you, sir. But we've walked a long way, and lost some loved ones on the way. And now we have to carry on believing in our dream. What *else* do we have to do?"

The soldier walked into the building, and returned a few minutes later.

"The corporal has agreed, but no more than six at a time."

As he finished his short statement, he glanced along the lane towards the control-point where an army truck was entering the site. The guards made their checks, and then led the lorry in, parking it aside from the entrance.

"Sorry, but we have work to do. A delivery." More of the refugees were arriving to find out what the movement was all about. Food? Blankets? With little else to do, they flooded into the control-point area. "I suggest you all go and reclaim your tents." He saluted Akhtar and went off to his duties.

Ablaa pulled Satvinder over and suggested to him and Akhtar, "I'll stay for a while with a couple of the kids, and somebody else?"

Akhtar volunteered, so Satvinder took the rest back to their 'homes', if they were still vacant.

"The soldier could be right, Uncle. We could wait here forever for the field marshal."

They found a dry spot to sit, and the two little girls gingerly cuddled up to Akhtar, who welcomed them in.

After a short spell of just watching the soldiers unload the lorry, Ablaa asked, "Are you all right? You know, in your head?" She touched his needle-scarred arm. "Would you like to talk?"

He brushed his hand through one of the girls' black hair. "Yes, I'd like to talk. I'd like to say that we can have a wonderful life, now that I've found my family again. A wonderful life."

"But..." She thought carefully. "But what about the boys?"

He just shook his head and smiled. "They'll be ok. Don't worry about them. They'll be *fine*." He rocked the two girls who began to giggle. "We'll *all* be fine."

Ablaa was spell-bound, unable to respond to his jovial attitude. She still had no idea of what had become of his family and he was not about to tell. He was in total denial.

After a while the lorry was empty, the sacks of rice being put into a small, guarded godown close to the gates, and the young soldier headed back towards the guard-house. As he approached them, his clipboard in his hand, he stopped.

He pointedly looked Akhtar in the eyes. "I need to ask a couple of questions, Sir." He took a pen from his pocket. "What's your name, Sir? And where are you from?"

Akhtar grinned proudly. "I'm D..." He froze for a second, and then smiled. "I'm Mohamed Akhtar Hussain. I'm from Khulna and Chak Sahasa, and am an orphanage worker."

The soldier looked to Ablaa and asked her the same.

"I'm Ablaa Nouka and I come from Char Monpura." She hesitated before smiling at Akhtar. "And I'm also from Chak Sahasa, and an orphanage worker."

The soldier nodded. He was suspicious. "I've heard you called 'Doctor'. Is that right?" He paused, but only for a very short moment. "We're desperately short of medical staff. I've been instructed to put all those with medical or nursing credentials into service here. There're thousands in need of medical attention, and we're expecting cholera to hit, so my orders are to arrest and force those who do not voluntarily put themselves forward. Do you understand?"

Ablaa glanced towards Akhtar before answering on his behalf.

"Sir, we'll all willingly help those who need it. But my uncle's just a Doctor in Philosophy, originally from the Dhaka University. He's been ill himself during the past few days. If the rest of us can be of help, then we will all come forward, and contribute whatever we're able. May I ask, though, that my uncle be allowed a few days to re-align his mental state?"

The young soldier bowed his head and went into the guard-house. He returned with his corporal, who took over.

The corporal saluted Doctor Hussain. "Sir, my private, here, was suspicious that you were from the medical profession." He looked towards Ablaa. "We thank you all for your charitable attitude, but I can't accept you offer. You're *all* under arrest!"

He ordered two of the guards to go to section J4 and bring the children and the adult to the guard-house. "And make sure none of them escape!"

Ablaa raised her eyebrows to the doctor, as if to ask, "What?" but he just shook his head. After several minutes, the two soldiers returned with Satvinder and the children. They were all held at gunpoint by the guards.

The corporal stood in front of them, and puffed his chest out. "You are all under arrest! The papers I have in front of me require that I deliver you into the custody of Private Verde."

The heavily bearded private arrived, as the lorry was turning round and preparing to leave the camp.

"This is Private Verde."

The private saluted the group, and took some paperwork from the corporal. "I've been ordered to deliver you all, secure and unharmed, upon instruction from Colonel Dara who is in office at Fort William. I am to deliver you to Kolkata." He looked around at the group, who all stood gaping and wondering. "The people who I'm to take under guard include the following: Doctor Mohamed Akhtar Hussain, doctor in medicine and specialist in tropical diseases; Baka Hussain, and their two sons; Doctor Satvinder Nair, scholar and teacher; Tazkia Nair and her son Mo; Ablaa Nouka and her brother James; and approximately thirty children from the orphanage of Chak Sahasa. Who can confirm those present?"

The corporal and his private looked daggers at Akhtar.

Ablaa, as always, looked around before responding. She looked at the refugees who had gathered to watch, and then at Satvinder who held the hand of a half-dressed little girl, who held the hand of another half-dressed little girl, who held the hand of a naked little boy. They were skinny, suffering from malnutrition, and were unknown to her. She grinned at Satvinder as she realised that her daddy was waking up, looking out for others, and adopting another three orphans into the family. He was finally back!

"I can speak for the group, sir. I'm Ablaa Nouka, and can sadly confirm that Baka and her two sons will *not* be joining us, *neither* will my step-mother Tazkia and Mo, and that the children from the orphanage now number approximately forty." She nodded her head.

The bearded Private Verde nodded back. "I'm very sorry to hear about the missing members. I'll report that they're no longer with us." An eerie silence fell for a short moment, then the two soldiers who stood behind the children, with rifles across their chests, where ordered to fall out. They moved back to the guard-house.

"We need to move into the lorry, and return to Kolkata. But first, I've been asked to read you a message from the *uncle* of Colonel Dara." He held out a sheet of paper, and scanned the group, coughed, and then stated, "On arrival, the group will attend the local court and, subject to acceptable identification, will be awarded asylum." He paused to allow the group to take it all in. "They will then share a bottle or two of scotch, and as many bottles of lemonade the children can drink, and maybe finish off with a bhang lassy, or two or three." He joined the grinning adults. "Lots of love, Gnuru."

Ablaa stepped forward and fell to her knees, and the soldier began to laugh, and then Satvinder and Akhtar both held their hands in the air, and let out almighty screams. The onlookers were mystified as the children captured the moment and all began giggling and chuckling, not really knowing what at, but following their mums and dads like little clones. The soldier held his hand out for Akhtar to take, and they shook *firmly* and *deliberately*. They were going 'home'.

After an electrifying silence, the soldier ordered, "Now get into the lorry! *That's* an order."

# CHAPTER 23 – THE GREAT LOSS

The lorry left the camp packed with jubilant refugees, heading for the new life where they could all live together, irrespective of their colour or creed: the Anglia slums. But it suddenly became a sad event, much like a funeral. Satvinder looked out from the back of the lorry at the hundreds of women and children who saw them off. The children were sad, depressed, and hungry, some were ill, others were injured, and all were desperate and frightened. Many of the children waved, and many wished.

The mood was damp and lumpy in the truck and the Chak Sahasa children were huddled together at the front, giggling each time the lorry hit a bump in the road. They all watched the three adults chewing the cud and wondering why.

"Don't!" Akhtar touched his best friend on the arm, and then nodded back to the waving children which they had left behind. "I know what you're thinking, we've been here before and you *know* you can't save them all." He smiled, almost as if the recent heartaches had never happened. "You took the children that you could from the Chars, and saved *them*. You took the orphans from Chak Sahasa and saved *them*. Looks like you've got another three from the camp, and you'll save *them*. You're a living saint. But you *can't* save them all."

Satvinder took a deep breath to ward off the tears, and thanked his mate.

Akhtar shook his hand, and then, "But I'd like to say something for my lost family and then I'll *never* talk about East Pakistan again. The past will now be remembered, and will then be dead."

Satvinder pulled Ablaa onto his shoulder and they both thought about her mummy's words of wisdom, 'the past is never dead, in fact it's not even past', but they never said anything.

Akhtar closed his eyes and sat bolt upright. He spoke quietly. "I'd like to say some words to my departed wife and children. My father said these words when he lost my mother. I hope my family are listening to my pledge." He waited for the children to stop whispering, and then dropped his head. "I will take my life into my own hands, and share. I will use my life as I will, and give. I will enjoy my life to the full, and dance. I will do all those things in life, with you right here in my heart. And when the time comes for us to be together again, only *then* will I wonder why. I love you."

The journey to Kolkata in that old army truck was bumpy and noisy and the giggles from the children soon abated as their bottoms became bruised. Thankfully it only lasted about four hours, and suddenly they were there, greeted by the ever booming Field Marshall Gnuru. Over the following few days the group were settled into the slums of the Anglia region, the project orchestrated by the thundering Gnuru and his employers. Satvinder was ordered by the courts to educate the local people, and Akhtar was ordered by the courts to cure the local people. Ablaa, believed to be thirteen years old, was ordered to tend for the children of Chak Sahasa, and of course she took on her right hand man, James, to be constantly by her side. Her real brother.

But the war continued for the other sixty million East Pakistanis and their aggressors from the West.

The massacre at Chuknagar became acknowledged as the biggest single act of genocide during the conflict, accounting for the murder, by the Pakistani soldiers, of an estimated ten thousand men, women and children, and it only took a few hours. It was only a couple of weeks later that the last pockets of resistance where broken. However, Colonel Osmani continued to organise the Mukti forces into a fighting force and, aided by the Indians, the Mukti Bahini began to take the shape of a national fighting unit. Despite having aid from India they were poorly equipped and inferior to the well equipped West, but were a constant thorn in the side as they applied their guerrilla warfare tactics.

The few thousand troops from West Pakistan were reinforced by thousands of Bihari and Bengalese sympathisers, who were organised into Peace Committees, and the West Pakistani generals used them to barbarous effect. Like the West Pakistani troops themselves the Peace Committee members ruled with unaccountable power, and abused that power as they strove to rid the country of the Hindu population. Even the Muslim population were abused, raped and murdered and as the committee took over godowns across the country to house the extermination camps, the Peace Committee slaughtered at will. Some have referred to it as the sheer arrogance of power.

Many city slums and villages were singled out for extermination, believed to be supporters of the Awami League, and on a wet June day in 1971 the Pakistani army, accompanied by many razakars and Peace Committee members, arrived at Chak Sahasa. The village was reported as being Awami League sympathisers, and was sentenced to extermination by fire. The soldiers loosely surrounded the village as the razakars went in with burning torches. The whole village was soon ablaze and as the men, women and children ran from the flames the soldiers shot them. It was like a rabbit shoot at harvest-time. The knowledge that leprosy was present was most likely the reason why they killed everybody and everything that ran from the village, even the pretty young girls who normally would have been taken to the cantonments to be used, abused and raped until they no longer attracted. And along with the life-forms burned Akhtar's clinic and papers, and everything associated with the arsenic poisoning. Chak Sahasa was wiped from the planet, an event which would later prove to be almost as devastating as the war itself.

An estimated ten million refugees flooded into India and strained the Indian resources and foreign aid, almost to breaking point. The internal conflict was spilling out into its neighbour's back yard, but Indira Ghandi, influenced by her Russian allies, was not prepared to intervene, but supported the East Pakistanis with aid and arms. The Bangladesh Air Force began operations in September 1971, followed in November by the Bangladesh Navy. After increasing successes by the Mukti Bahini, and following several incursions across the border by both India and Pakistan, war was declared. India declared war on Pakistan on December 3rd 1971. The 1971 Indo-Pakistan War lasted just thirteen days, but during that time the perdition which had festered in East Pakistan came close to spilling out into the rest of the World as the USA, West Pakistan's allies, sent the carrier USS Enterprise into the Bay of Bengal to intimidate the Indian navy. Two days later a group of Russian warships entered the Bay of Bengal, which successfully countered the American intimidation.

For thirteen days the combined forces of Bangladesh and India, the Nitro Bahini, stormed East Pakistan, liberating town after town, and the West Pakistan army, staring defeat in the face, strove to complete what they had started on March 25th. That original onslaught, codenamed Operation Searchlight, was launched with the intent to kill all the pro-liberation intellectuals, and ensure that the country was bereft of all Bengalese leadership. Nine months after that fateful day they decided to finish the job. With the help of the extreme right-wing Al-Badr militia, they rounded up all those intellectuals who they had missed back in March, and killed them.

The West Pakistan forces surrendered to the Nitro Bahini on December 16th 1971. The war for independence was over for some, but not for others. As with most human conflicts retribution was the next stage. The Biharis and others who had supported the West Pakistan rule were abused, ostracised and murdered as the people of the newly formed Bangladesh reaped their revenge for the inhumanities which had gone before. The surviving Biharis were to be repatriated to West Pakistan, but due to their questionable status as 'refugee or not refugee' and the bureaucratic black holes within the two national administrations, the repatriations to what they believe is their home, West Pakistan, has never happened. Almost forty years later there were still over three hundred thousand Bihari refugees still living in refugee camps within Bangladesh -- three generations of homeless, country less beings, longing for the day when they can call themselves something. For them the past is never dead, it's right now.

Colin Hodgson

# CHAPTER 24 – AFTER THE WAR

Akhtar

Doctor Mohamed Akhtar Hussain was appointed as the Anglia region's tropical disease specialist and was given his own nurse and a well equipped clinic, situated on the edge of the slum. He became a highly respected member of the community, being deeply involved with the many thousands of slum dwellers and their plight against disease. He even looked after *real* lepers, suffering from *real* leprosy.

He never let up on his pledge to Baka nor on his promise to himself. He lived his life according to his final words to his lost family. "I will take my life into my own hands, and share. I will use my life as I will, and give. I will enjoy my life to the full, and dance. I will do all those things in life, with you right here in my heart. And when the time comes for us to be together again, only *then* will I wonder why. I love you."

He was cheerful, optimistic and never down, and lived the rest of his life in denial of East Pakistan. He must have been taking the same drugs as the many East and West Pakistanis who claimed not to have done anything wrong, and who claimed that only a few thousand people died in the conflict. Denial is bliss.

As for his promise to never speak about East Pakistan again, he was absolutely true to himself. He never thought nor spoke about the place, that is, until he contracted one of his tropical diseases. With a festering ulcer on his leg he sat in his clinic preparing himself for his reunion with Baka. He finally spoke about East Pakistan and told his nephew, Syed, what had happened to his auntie and cousins. In 2008 Akhtar finally released the past from its cocoon as he cried on Syed's shoulder, the memories flowing back to him with torturous venom: his shame for his religion; his hatred for the soldiers; his detest for the warmongers who sit behind their desks as the common man's blood spills and their screams sear. It all came screeching back and suddenly the past was no longer dead. But only a few hours later, Akhtar was.

## The Children of War

The children from Chak Sahasa and other places were housed in six adjacent slum dwellings, and mothered by the boss, Ablaa. The conditions were cramped, poor and unhygienic, but they slowly improved their lot by re-establishing their noodles business and earning enough for them to survive. They also continued with their schooling. The teacher was a familiar face, their own foster father, Satvinder. He never forgot what Tazkia's uncle had instilled into her, that education can get you out of the slums, so he threw himself into his duties and into the challenge of trying to teach his own, plus many other, children to read and write: that essential preparation for life.

Most of the children grew up with basic literacy, and some went to work within the old fort, which remains the centre for the area's administration, whilst others managed to find other ways out of the slum. Some took up careers in the Indian army, and three of the girls moved back to Bangladesh as soon as they were old enough. Another four died, and those which were left accepted their positions within the slums, eking out a sparse existence from their noodles business.

Ablaa and James became inseparable. As James grew older, his interests and intellect grew ever closer to Ablaa's.

They were both blessed with outstanding intelligence and so the reading and writing came easy to them, partly because they so wanted to learn. They wanted to become writers so they wanted to know about all things, so that they could tell *everybody* about *everything*. They wanted to tell the World about the liberation war, their war, the cruelty and inhumanity, and the disrespect for human life, but their original idea, that *they* were the children of war, soon melted away into insignificance. They realised that the title belonged to others! After a long time they managed to get the two young girls, whose mother was killed at Chuknagar, to talk about their memories. Those two young girls had had such a different experience to those children from Chak Sahasa, and it also chilled Ablaa and James as they associated a similar end for Baka and the two boys.

The two girls cried as they metered out their story, piece by piece. On that dreadful day in Chuknagar they had watched their mother die. She was stripped, raped three times, and then her breasts were cut off, and a stick forced into her vagina. She died from blood-loss some time later in the arms of her daughters, both about seven or eight years old. The older girl, with little more than a whimper, told of how her mummy just kept saying 'sorry' as her life drained. She looked at Ablaa and frowned. "Why did my Mummy say sorry?" Those two girls struggled for the rest of their lives in everything they ever did. The mental damage was irreparable.

The would-be writers also managed to talk deeply to the three children which Satvinder had recovered from the refugee camp. Two girls and a boy. After a very long time, the children warily admitted that they spoke poor Bengalese because they were Biharis, the enemy.

Ablaa whispered, "There aren't any enemies here. We're all the same. I promise."

They had been living in Khulna with their father, mother and two older sisters when the Biharis were attacked, back in early March. The oldest girl, about ten or eleven, told their story as the three clung desperately onto each other. She said that their house was near the end of the street where most of the Bihari community lived, and they could see out of their window into the street. The Bengalese mob had set light to many of the Bihari properties and the one at the end of the street, right near to their own home, was burning and the children watched the blaze from their window. They watched as the fire forced the Bihari family to run out from the smoke, but were grabbed by the mob and contained, and as the mother, father and son were held, the oldest daughter was stripped and raped. As the girl and her family watched from their window, they shook in fear for the other Biharis who were under siege. They watched as the younger daughter had a rope tied onto each wrist and her hands pulled hard apart as if to stretch her arms. One of the men then set light to her sari and her screams were too much for *our* girls' father and mother, who ran out of their house to help the poor girl. But the mod grabbed our children's mother and father, and just tossed them both into the burning building, before doing the same with the Bihari mother, father and son. The little girl told the story almost without emotion.

Ablaa asked, "Where are your older sisters? Why are you alone?"

"They hid us under the table until the people outside went away. Then we left our home." The three children huddled into each other. "People threw bricks at us when we went down the road, and Nia was hit on her head. She just stood in the street and screamed and screamed and blood went all down her face, and the other people all cheered. And she carried on screaming and they threw more bricks, but the army arrived and shot some people, and we kept walking. We walked forever. When we got to the camp where you were, our sisters went off for rice, and never came back. I think the Hindus killed them."

Ablaa and James had to rethink their classification of 'children of war'. They began to realise that war is so much worse than they had previously thought, leaving damaged people by the millions. Much of that damage is invisible to the naked eye.

Those three children from Khulna lived varying lives after the war. The oldest girl, who told their vexatious story, ended up as a teenage prostitute, and died very early from pneumonia. The younger sister seemed more able to cope with the trauma and as she got older the memories faded. The little boy, Aalap, barely five when the mob struck, coped very well. He had become a regular visitor and friend to Akhtar, and he was heavily influenced by the doctor's new role as a giver and sharer, and so he worked hard right throughout his childhood, saving as much money as he could so that he could one day follow his dream.

Akhtar told him one day, "If you lose your dreams, you lose."

Aalap never forgot his hero's words. He married one of the young girls from Chak Sahasa and they had a beautiful daughter which they called Dilshad, meaning happy, but by the time Dilshad was five, disaster struck. Her mummy was run over and killed by an army Landover. So Aalap decided that it was time to live his dream before he lost it. He gathered his hard-earned savings together and bought an old motor rickshaw. Each day he would count his earnings, feed himself and his daughter, and then go out of his home to feed the other children. Nearly every day he spent everything he had left after feeding himself and Dilshad, and fed the orphan children, the street urchins who had no parents to feed them or anybody to love them. He had been given a life by Satvinder, and his dream was to give as much of it back as he could, to the ones who had nothing and nobody.

## Ablaa and James

Ablaa and James learned very quickly to read and write, and they made industrious use of their abilities. They wrote about the war, about the Anglian slums, about the strange lack of religious commitment in the slums, about the leper colony which was fed by a little witch who stole just to feed the lepers, about the Chars, and anything else which looked interesting. They never attempted to have anything published, so they never knew whether their work was of interest to others, but they did it for themselves. Every time they wrote about a subject, they learned about it and understood it, and that was all they ever yearned for, knowledge.

As we have already mentioned, they became inseparable, and many might suggest that they were more than just brother and sister and often people would suggest that Ablaa had finally seen her brother's circumcised willy, but it was not the case. Ablaa loved her daddy so much, and despite several attempts to lure him into her web, he remained true to his lost loves, Tazkia and Kaling. So she decided to stay on her own and be with James until he meets his true love, accepting that when that was to happen she would spend the rest of her life as a spinster.

Several years had passed when James woke up one morning with an ache in his heart.

"Let's go." He cuddled up to his older sister. "Just to look. But let's go. Daddy'll be ok here for a while."

She grinned. "I'd love to see the village again. The emerald green and blue on a sunny day. The kurpal. The fishing boats. The shrimpers." They decided to visit Char Monpura, and maybe then travel to Chak Sahasa to see how it had fared in the war.

So that was their plan and, Ablaa being Ablaa, nothing was going to stop them. They travelled by the new rail link to Khulna, and then took a ferry to Bhola, completing the final stage as Satvinder had, in a tiny river taxi. They were finally back in Heaven.

Satvinder's story

Once upon a time there was born a future hero. His name was Satvinder and he grew up as a Hindu in a Muslim world, in a poor land of troubles and instability. But he was intelligent and fortunate, his parents being able to give him an education, and so he became a lecturer in English and history at the University of Dhaka in East Pakistan. As one who liked to lecture about equality and freedom he earned himself a name, which was a good thing, and a bad thing: it all depended on which side of the fence you sat, East or West.

In November 1970 he set out on a mission which was sponsored by the university to write about the precarious life on the Chars of the Ganges Delta. There he met God. Nobody knows why, but God's servant, the tropical storm Nora, conjured up an almighty cyclone which hit the Chars so hard that almost half a million people died. From that carnage was born a new family, Satvinder, Ablaa and James.

We all know what followed over the next few months and eventually Satvinder and his new family, along with many orphans, arrived in the Anglian slums in June 1971.

"Where do *you* go?" asked Akhtar, sitting in his clinic.

Satvinder frowned. "According to my religion I've got to hope that I come back *here*. As a tree." He grinned. "I'd like to be a mighty sundari tree which protects a farmer and his family from the storms. But that's not what I now believe. I want to go to Heaven with you, and not Jehannam, I want *Heaven*."

His mate grinned, "Interesting. Becoming a believer?"

"Not in religion, just God."

The two men sat in Akhtar's clinic in silence as they thought about the next step in the conversation. They were both getting old, with the stresses of the war being left several years behind them.

Satvinder put his finger in the air and chirped, "If I'm to come to heaven with you, can you answer me something?"

"Anything, old man."

"In Heaven, is there religion?"

Akhtar pondered the question, and eventually came up with the definitive answer. "There can't be, else there'd be *war* in Heaven. Then we might as well go to hell!"

Both men needed to get back to their duties, so Satvinder left Akhtar to open his clinic, while he wandered off back into the smelly allies of the slums. He had children to teach. Some of those children on that afternoon were his own, the younger ones who had made the pilgrimage from Chak Sahasa to the tolerant slums of Anglia. As we have already reported, the children had fared variously since their arrival, but two of the children that day were the ones who had gone on to 'further' education: young James; and Aalap. They sat with six other teenagers in the school-room, cross legged and attentive. They all wondered where that day's lecture would wander to.

James, by then a young man, asked, "Daddy, do you know about the little witch who steals food for the lepers and Saint Catherine?"

"I do know of her. Why?"

"I met her today and she spoke to me. She was really nice, but giggled a lot." The class was waiting for the punch line. "She told me that Bangladesh is in trouble. She told me why, and then she laughed and ran away."

"Bangladesh will *always* be in trouble. The West killed all those capable of running a secular democratic country."

"That's not what she meant. Worse than that."

Satvinder raised his hand. "Stop! Before we carry on, does anybody know what secular means? No? Well, it means that the situation is not religious and is controlled by the government, not by the religious leaders. Do you think that Bangladesh is secular?"

One of the girls stood up. "My mother says it's been controlled by the Awami League, but now by the military. But I don't know if it's secular."

"Well done. I don't know either, so I'm not going to try to teach, I just want you to think about it. About the wider picture."

James put his hand up. "I remember back in the old days when we used to talk in Chak Sahasa. That man who was killed in the village, you know, the manager. Well you said that he said that when the war is won, if it is, they'll have a democratic dictatorship. What does that mean?"

"It means that when Sheikh Mujibur Rahman returned, and with the passing of time made the laws that *anybody* who stands for the elections must be a member of the Awami League, then *only* the Awami League could win their elections. I believe that was what the manager meant, dictatorship hiding behind a farsical face of democracy."

Aalap put his hand up. "Is it true that the only way they could get rid of Sheik Rahman was to kill him and all of his family?"

"Now we're getting deep. It *is* true that they killed him and all of his family, apart from two who were out of the country, but I don't believe that it was the only way to get rid of him. But, since he was instrumental in eradicating democracy and competition from the elections, he *himself* made it harder to get rid of him in any other way. Bitten on the ass by his own kin."

Aalap responded, "But you don't surely mean that they were right to kill him?"

Satvinder sat back and thought. It had been a long time since the war, but it still hung over him like a thunder storm. Then lightening struck. "No. I don't believe they were right to kill him. But they would have been wrong to allow him to carry on with his personal ambitions, his lust for power. That's *not* what the country gave him and it's *not* what they died for, not unadulterated power."

The students just kept quiet for some time, until Aalap put his hand up to speak. Satvinder nodded his permission. "Sir, Bangladesh is happy to kill when the time comes for reform. Just kill anybody in the way."

One of the girls chirped up. "They killed President Ziaur Rahman. Now they're back under military rule."

James. "And Ziaur Rahman was a national hero. The hero of Chittagong. Ablaa told us all about the radio broadcasts, how he defended Chittagong to the very end."

Satvinder put his hands into the air. "You're right. They'll never stop killing the opposition. I don't believe they know how to conduct democratic process." He turned his back on the students and raised his hands. "No more talk of Bangladesh for today."

James put his hand up. "But Daddy, what about the child witch, My Eyes?"

Satvinder looked at his son. "Did she really talk to you? Properly?"

"Yes, sir. She told me something which you need to tell Uncle Akhtar. She said that many charities, particularly the Save the Children Fund, are investing much money into Bangladesh to save the starvation and disease." He looked at his notes on his lap, but held back, and then he looked at his daddy, testing his interest. Once satisfied with his daddy's attention he continued. "She said that they're going to sink many, many thousands of tube wells. Then the whole country will have clean, fresh water from the underground lakes and aquifers. And then she laughed and ran off into the slum." He frowned. "Why did she tell me that? And why does she think it matters to me?"

Satvinder's face dropped. His memories of the patients who stunk of garlic came rushing into his head, enough to make him retch. "Sorry. You know what that could mean. Arsenic poisoning. I must talk to Akhtar."

The next morning, as soon as Akhtar's clinic quietened, he was there. He had to be careful with his words.

"We've been good friends for most of our lives. We wanted to change the World. We may need to do that right now." He looked into Akhtar's eyes. "Will you talk to me about Bangladesh? Please."

"No!"

They sat opposite each other chewing the cud.

"Please Akhtar. We've been told that thousands and thousands of tube wells are going to be sunk across Bangladesh. Won't they all be poisoned with arsenic?"

"How the hell should I know? I'm a doctor in India. Stuff Bangladesh." He breathed deeply. "My notes are in Chak Sahasa. They can read *them*." He stood up and waved Satvinder out of his clinic, refusing to discuss anything to do with his former country. "But you could speak to Gnuru."

Satvinder met up with the old war-dog in his office close to the Anglian Fort. The Field Marshall boomed out his welcome and fetched a bottle of scotch from his cabinet. "I'm getting old. So drink with me while we still can."

They supped on their large whiskies and made the customary funny faces.

"A bit harsh, this one. Not real scotch. Anyway, what's eating you? You look concerned, and not yet seeing the World in all the colours of the rainbow. You're not seeing the whole spectrum and you're missing something, old boy."

Satvinder grinned at the old man's choice of phrase. "I'm missing my old mate, Akhtar, for one. He won't speak to me about our homeland, and he should."

"Why should he? He lost his family, so did you. So why worry about that cauldron of death?"

"Because they're going to be drilling many thousands of tube wells. They could poison the entire country."

"You don't know that. And who told you about the wells?"

"The witch called My Eyes."

Field Marshall Gnuru roared with laughter. "You're not taking that seriously! She's a child witch, so ignore it. I do." The laughter mellowed to a grin. "Did you ever meet my nephew, the one who kindly had you all arrested at the camp? Well he has something for the witch, and I don't know what. He's an intelligent man, and has become a general, based at Fort William and probably the most senior officer in this region, but he believes in the witch. Weird."

"So you don't think I should concern myself about the arsenic poisoning? You've seen the sufferers. The walking dead, ostracised by their own, just waiting to die from something that they don't understand. That could be millions, not a few hundred. You saw it in Chak Sahasa."

Gnuru reached over and put his hand onto Satvinder's. "But Chak Sahasa won't see it again. It's gone."

"How do you mean?"

"It was burned down during the war. I'm sorry."

Satvinder realised that the papers would have burned. Nobody believed Akhtar when he isolated the problem, so why should anybody believe *him*? And without the doctor's work to back up his wild claims, why should they *not* give the poor children of Bangladesh, one of the poorest countries in the World, good, fresh, clean water, free from disease and immune from the invasion of flood water? And besides, why should he think that all the aquifers below Bangladesh should be poisoned by arsenic? He wondered if he and the witch were the only believers in the doctor's past works. Even Akhtar was denying any interest in the potential disaster.

"What about the test results which he got back from Sensar?"

Gnuru huffed, "Just test results from samples. Nothing about where they came from, or why they were being tested, or anything about how the arsenic was removed.

Just look out of the window at your slum. The World doesn't give a shit about your slum, or about our own *real* lepers who are ostracised, so it's all down to you and me to look after it. Leave Bangladesh alone to their own fate, as they leave you alone to yours."

The old man was probably right, so the concerns wafted into the background as they all carried on with their own daily battle for survival. Life carried on.

A few months later James and Ablaa shook Satvinder to the roots as they announced that they would be going back to Char Monpura.

"It's only for a visit," stressed Ablaa. "We'll be back in a few weeks."

"That's *exactly* what I told Kaling, all those years ago." The loss of his children, albeit for just a while, acted as a catalyst on his darkest thoughts. Suddenly his head was reeling with the memories of his daughters and his two wives, as well as little Mo and of Baka and the two boys. In those few moments of goodbyes the past rose and was suddenly alive and kicking.

*"The past is never dead. In fact it's not even past"* Kolala *Nouka.*

The memories set themselves into his head like a disease. Left totally unchecked the canker spread through his body and into his heart, and despite the cannabis-based medication which Akhtar prescribed, the nightmares about the un-dead returned, taking over his subconscious, tearing his family limb from limb as it tore his heart to shreds. The nightmares came night after night and he found himself one day crying his heart out in front of his older students. Aalap, the Bihari lad, gently took Satvinder by the hand, and led him through the slums to Akhtar's clinic. There, Akhtar faced one of his toughest cases. He *had* to talk to Satvinder about his problems, temporarily laying aside his oath never to talk about their homeland.

"Now that you're calm, we must talk." Akhtar had given Satvinder some herbs which he had been introduced to him by the child witch, My Eyes. It quickly calmed him. "What's causing this? After years of being on firm ground you seem to have fallen into a swamp. Is it Ablaa and James going to the Chars?"

Satvinder played with his shirt sleeve as he thought about it. He tried to speak but nothing came out. Then, "I'm waiting for them to come home. All of them. Only little Mo is dead, the rest are somewhere. I don't know where."

The Doctor almost whispered as he asked, "Who? Who is coming home?"

"Kaling and the girls. I don't know if they're dead. Just the rumours which Gnuru put into my head. They could be out there searching for me."

"Why would Gnuru do that? He had no reason to lie."

"I've thought about that for years, and I think you're right. But how would he know they're killed? Thousands of people were killed at that time, and most went unreported, let alone identified."

"Ok. Makes sense. Is that it?"

"Tazkia. She could come home one day. She could be searching for me. She just walked away from me after we cremated little Mo." He put his head in his hands and sobbed. After a while he stuttered, "Mo, he's dead. I know that. He's dead. But all the others..."

At that point the doctor fidgeted as if to struggle for strength. He stood up and walked around the clinic, then, "Baka and the boys. They won't be looking for any of us. They're waiting for me in heaven. Dead." He sighed. "There, I've told you. I left them dead in Chuknagar." He sat down and composed himself.

Satvinder began to feel selfish. After years of denial and secrecy about his dead family, Akhtar had almost been forced by Satvinder to make the final statement. "I'm sorry.

You must be hurting as much as me. I'll take my burden elsewhere."

"You'll do nothing of the sort! Just sit there, you're my patient!" At that Akhtar began smiling. "I love doing that, being strong and demanding." The two men began to relax a little, maybe due to the herbs which My Eyes had sourced for the doctor, or maybe the old comradeship was beginning to seep back into their lonely lives. "We need to carry on talking, now that we've started. Now, truth is, I believe that Kaling and the girls are dead. Gnuru is basically an honest man. I can't believe that he'd make that up, so why can't you believe him?"

"I don't know. The nightmares. Every night they're torn apart, ripped in two from the crotch upwards. Every night. And Tazkia kneels nearby crying for her baby Mo, who looks across the fence begging to be with her. They're not together, not in my dreams. Mo is dead, the *other* side of the fence. They're not with Mo."

Akhtar put his hand onto his friend's and tutted. "It's just in your head. They're dead, and I've no doubt about it. And you need to make yourself believe it." An enormous sigh seared from his body as he leaned back in his chair. "Maybe this'll help. I received a letter today addressed to you, and I was coming into the slums later to hand it to you. Maybe it's good news." He opened the drawer in his desk and from it handed Satvinder a letter.

The patient carefully inspected the envelope. "It's from James. His writing." He was wary, but excited. "Should I read it? Or should I burn it?"

"It's from your son! You *have* to read it."

He opened the letter and then, without any emotion on his face, read it to himself. He said with an angelic air, "I'm glad I read it. At least I know where Ablaa is. She's with Mo. I hope she looks after him." His breathing quickened as he struggled to hold back the tears.

And Akhtar began to shake as the realisation of Ablaa's death sank in. He studied his mate's face as he read the letter, and as a tear formed in his eye, he asked, "How? Do you want to talk about it?"

Satvinder nodded. In a gentle whisper, "Dear Daddy, I write with inmost shame and despair at what I've allowed. Ablaa has sadly died, and was cremated today. The funeral was attended by some of our old childhood friends from the Char, but most had died in the storm, and so it was a quiet and sad occasion. I now have to wonder what will come of me. I don't know what life will be like without my sister, and so I wonder if it will be worthwhile. She was everything to me, and I know also to you, so I beg for your forgiveness at what I've allowed. We walked from the village towards where my home used to be, and there was a young fox which had become into trouble. She walked through the damp rice field to see if she could help, and I knew what the dangers could be, but I never thought to stop her. As she bent down by the fox, she was bitten by a Kalach. She died the next day. I will never forgive myself, and I will understand if you are unable to forgive. I must now consider my life ahead. All my love, your real son James."

Satvinder held back the tears, and sat bolt upright. He looked up at the ceiling and faintly uttered, "I forgive you. Please come home."

The loss of his daughter had a weird effect on poor Satvinder. He miraculously found himself able to concentrate on his memories of Ablaa and James, pushing the nightmares into the background. It was as if her spirit had moved into his soul, the warmth of her love and devotion spurring him into the future, rapidly leaving the past and all its dark memories behind. As he spoke regularly to Akhtar they fed each other's motivations.

"You know what," chuckled Akhtar, "That old philosopher who you often quote was wrong. The past *is* dead, and we're living in the present and soon in the future. Forget her silly quotes."

Satvinder smiled. "I can't forget her." He saluted the empty space. "Kolala Nouka, philosopher. She gave me her daughter, and I love for that. And she gave me some good advice, through Ablaa. Me, Ablaa and James were talking about our future, way back in Chak Sahasa. She said to me and James that not long before the great storm her mummy scolded her with the words of wisdom, 'I'll be dead one day. *Don't* you *dare* die with me!' She was telling me and James something through her daughter, so don't ever knock her."

"I never would, but must admit, that's a good one. Much the same as my last words to my family. That was something that I'd learned from my dad when he lost my Nan. Life does go on. It has to."

And so Satvinder joined his good friend in denial, a very good place to be. They wafted through their meagre existence, tending the ill and teaching the young, and the slums were good to them. And they both took great comfort as they watched the children of Chak Sahasa slowly disperse into the World beyond, making their own lives and forever thankful of the men and women who had lead them from their perilous youth and into manhood, when they could finally and proudly say, 'This is what I'm going to do'. And they did, some with great success, some with great struggle, but they all did something with their lives. All he really needed to top the cake was to see was his beloved James. But he never came home.

Colin Hodgson

# CHAPTER 25 – THE PROPHECY

Several years had passed, over twenty, when Satvinder received a message requesting him to visit the offices in the Anglia Fort. It was from the Monsignor, the man who headed the company and society which owned much of the slum-lands as well as the local military, Sensar Pharmaceuticals, The Banchi World Food Company, Chak Sahasa, and many other concerns throughout the World. The invite had them all guessing.

Aalap, with mystery in his address, "Apparently the witch-girl told somebody that the Monsignor was a soldier in the war. Nobody knows who, though. They're very secretive."

Aalap, by then the proud owner of an old motorised rickshaw and a pretty daughter named Dilshad, drove Satvinder across the 'no-mans' land as far as the rear entrance to the fort. It was built of red bricks and was originally intended by the British to be the sister to the great Fort William, but had always since been played down as merely a local administration centre. It was by then, however, the headquarters of the massive and very secretive Chi Bantri organisation.

"I feel scared, for some reason."

Aalap put his hand on his shoulder and comforted him. "I'll wait here at the gate until you come out. And if you don't, I'll let the Field Marshall know. He can report it to his nephew, General Dara."

He left his young protector at the gate and was escorted by two armed soldiers across the large drill area, which was flanked by stables and mess halls. He was led into the main building. Inside was a small entrance lobby with some benches, very sparse, and a staircase leading up to the offices. This was the working part of the main building and the whole atmosphere was cool and clinical. A *very* cold atmosphere. He was led around the corridor to the front of the building from where he had an enviable view of the main gates and their guard houses. He never before knew that they were even there. They were impressive, with two magnificent red-brick guard houses, and the enormous gates were lavished with carved elephants. He looked out from the corridor at the magnificent works of art and wondered where he really was. The soldiers eventually delivered him to the suite of the Monsignor.

The secretary welcomed him. "Good morning sir. You must be Satvinder." She led him across the room to another large door and showed him into the Monsignor's office.

His office was roomy, with two fine mahogany and leather desks and leather chairs, and the walls were lined with bookcases. Very little of the structure of the room could be seen behind the thousands of books. It was a fine collection. Behind the desks were large double doors, glazed to display the rooftop gardens and marble patio area and looking out over the gardens was a tall man dressed in a dark grey suite. Beside him was a telescope fixed to a tripod.

Without turning round the Monsignor politely ordered, "Take a seat." He waved the secretary out of the room. Satvinder sat on the chair facing the window, and looked towards the largest desk, upon which the Monsignor's gun lay. After a few seconds of frightening silence the Monsignor very deliberately turned around. The tall, distinguished Pakistani silhouetted against the light, his shadow casting doubts over Satvinder's very existence. He shivered in anticipation of his lot.

"Good morning Satvinder." A massive grin spanned his face as he sat down at the desk which had little on it, except for a writing pad, a pot full of pens, and two unsmoked cigars sitting on a brass ashtray. He was dressed in a dark grey suite, and was quite splendid with his greying hair. "You made it to Anglia."

Satvinder began to feel a dull pain in his stomach as he realised that he was sitting face-to-face with the butcher of Chuknagar, the man who gave with one hand and took with the other, Captain Plassey. The slum-land guest shook a little but said nothing.

"Aren't you pleased to see me? We could be friends. We have a common past."

The pain began to subside, and as he took some deep breaths, Satvinder calmed.

Monsignor Plassey took one of his cigars and lit it. "Do you smoke?"

Satvinder shook his finger.

The Monsignor took a few puffs on his cigar. "I didn't even know you were here until a little bird told me. I understand you've been here ever since the war. And I also believe you're here without the other two legends. Is that right?"

Satvinder looked around at the thousands of books, but still didn't speak. The atmosphere was turning sour.

"Please Satvinder. I remember helping you out. I could still help you out."

Finally the ageing teacher frowned and then snapped, "You *didn't* help Akhtar! Nor the other thousands. You *killed* most of them!" He stood up to leave.

"Stay! I need to speak to you." He put his head into his hands. "Please talk with me. Please."

Satvinder turned back, slowly sat down and looked at the fine man in front of him. The Monsignor, the Captain who had spared their lives with kindness, was begging with his eyes, and sweating.

"Why should I? You've killed thousands and thousands of innocent people. Why?" The anger began to boil. "*Why?*"

"Yes. You're referring to Chuknagar." His voice was getting weak, so he cleared his throat and stood up, as if to maintain advantage.

Satvinder snapped, "*Sit down!* And *stay* sitting down. If you stand up once more and look down on me, I'll walk. And I'll walk straight to General Dara. You're a war criminal, and should be hung. So tell me why I shouldn't."

A little shocked at the outbreak he sat down and looked into Satvinder's eyes. "If I talk, will you listen? Give me serious audience? Before judging me?"

Satvinder waved his head in a figure of eight.

"It was war." The old soldier stretched his shoulders and took in some nicotine. "War. We all get hurt in war."

"Apart from you." He spoke with a scold. "What are you *here*? God? I've heard word on the street of what you are, but now *you* tell me the facts. What are you?"

He cleared his throat. "I'm Monsignor Plassey, head of the Chi Bantri, a trading and industrial group who extend the benevolent hand of charity to many millions of poor people in need. I'm a very powerful man, doing a very caring job." He grinned. "That's the party line. Now my line. I'm the head of an enormous society, or sect, which owns hundreds of companies, and has thousands of influential members. We quietly influence the whole World."

Satvinder huffed, and then stood up. "I'm now looking down on *you*. Are you going to kill me? You look small from up here."

"Please. I don't want to kill you. If I did, you'd probably already be dead. So sit and let's talk." With a pathetic whine, "I'm now begging. Please."

Satvinder looked hard at the middle-aged man. He had fared better than himself... he was very wealthy and didn't live in a slum dwelling. "Ok. Justify what you did. I might not report you to the General. I've spent a lot of years worrying about what you did at Chuknagar, and as an intelligent man, I know that it wasn't just about slaughter. But my best friend's wife and children were killed there. And the mother of two of our adopted children. I've had to live with the private guilt of being part of it. But it was *you* who carried out the murders, maybe with my prompting, but *you* did it." He was sweating. "I never thought I'd meet you like this, so I've not really prepared except that I always promised Ablaa that if I reported your crimes, I would also hand myself in as an accomplice." He looked to his hands. "If Ablaa was alive, she would stop me, but she's not. So justify the death of those thousands of defenceless people."

The Pakistani nodded in agreement and stretched his legs and arms. "What, specifically, are we to consider here? I've not too many things to justify. Where d'you want me to start?"

"Chuknagar! You murdered thousands of women and children. Not killed, *murdered.*"

"Ok. Good place to start. Not many people even know of my involvement in Chuknagar, so I hope we can be friends, and keep it that way. Maybe we can both live out our lives in peace. Maybe not. Anyway, as you know, I have great admiration for William the Bastard's tactics of warfare. Instil absolute fear in their heads and they'll obey. Bit like training a dog, only en masse. So the loose plan was laid to frighten the people out of running to the Indians only to return later with guns and reinforcements, but instead to stay and obey. It went against the ideals of Tikka Khan. He just wanted the lands not the people, so let them run, and make sure they don't come back. But many of the local administration liked the idea of settling the Bengali people back into normal life, producing crops and goods and contributing to the cause of the greatest Islamic state in the World, a united and powerful Pakistan."

He continued. "Some of us felt that if the frightful message from Chuknagar was to get out to the World it would achieve peace in East Pakistan and save tens of thousands of lives. Show them what happens if they *disobey*, and promise kindness and respect if they *obey*." He sucked on his cigar. "Most of the soldiers have been conditioned to hate and look down on the East Pakistanis, even their language was an object of derision. Small people with small minds who breed like rabbits. At Chuknagar they were just culling rabbits."

Monsignor Plassey extinguished his cigar and thought for a while, then, "I think I know why it went wrong. Several reasons. When William strung up the young men and skinned them alive, the messengers took the frightful news to the next town. They had a route and a specific recipient. But the genocide at Chuknagar was not reported. Certainly not to many who actually cared. The message never got out until it was way too late. I do sometimes wonder, though, whether the World would have cared even if it *had* reached their ears."

He stopped talking and closed his eyes.

Satvinder huffed. "There's never good reason to kill people."

"Not even to save others? If the message had got out to the East Pakistanis across the country they may have stayed put and stopped supporting the rebel forces, and life could have got back to some form of normality. That's what I believe. We could have disbanded the idea of the peace committees, or at least controlled their behaviour and made productive use of them. Even try some for the murder of East Pakistanis. We could have re-opened the shops and banks and schools. Get back to normal! Don't you see that?"

He slowly shook his head. "I don't know how you sleep at night."

The Monsignor laughed, "And *you*? Do *you* sleep at night? You don't deserve to, either." He stood up and leaned on his desk towards Satvinder, scowling. "You killed *millions*. Not thousands, but *millions*!" He stepped back and pointed into Satvinder's face. "*You*! You and the good doctor. Just allowed millions to suffer for years, just die in shame and seclusion. The suffering at Chuknagar bears nothing on the suffering of the Bangladeshis over the past twenty years"

Satvinder put his hands to his face as the reality began to bite.

"The witch warned you, but you and the doctor chose to ignore it. Wallowing in your own self pity, you allowed the wells to be drilled with no warnings. You could have changed the whole face of Bangladesh but you chose to wallow in denial, blaming everybody else for everything."

Satvinder jumped up. "The *war* burned Chak Sahasa, and Akhtar's notes. We didn't!"

"But it didn't burn it from your memories. You still knew what could happen when those wells were sunk. Arsenic! And you just left them to it." He paced around the room, never taking his eyes off the sweating Satvinder. "I'm a war criminal, and so are you, and the doctor, and any other of your better-than-thou group. None of you did *anything!*"

Poor Satvinder just hung his head in shame.

"You and I, along with your mates are war criminals. We should *all* hang for our crimes. Think of that when you go running to the General. We should *all* hang. *Especially* you and the doctor!"

The Monsignor's hands were shaking as he sat down. The silence was deafening.

Many minutes had passed before either spoke. The stand-off was interrupted by Satvinder.

"Do you know how it's all gone? You know, the wells and the poisoning?"

The Monsignor nodded. "It's all gone. Just gone, that's how. Over the past twenty years they've sunk thousands of wells, mostly fairly shallow, and tested many for safety and quality. They were all good. *None* were tested for arsenic levels. The WHO estimate something like thirty five million exposed to the risks. That's just in Bangladesh. And the aid agencies are ignoring the warnings, sinking more and more. They should have been warned."

The ageing teacher raised his eyebrows. He at last smiled. "Then why didn't you warn them?"

"Very clever, again turning the blame on others. But the Pak army destroyed Chak Sahasa and the filters, the notes, the people, and, it was believed, the leprosy. Everything is done for a reason. The leprosy." A smirk appeared. "Shall we leave it at that? The past is now dead?"

"The past is never dead. In fact it's not even past."

"A subtle threat, I believe. May I just say, though, that I lost three brothers in the war. We *all* get hurt in war." He stood up and offered his hand to Satvinder. "Can we leave the past and look forward, as friends?"

Satvinder was not convinced, but he took the man's hand. "Maybe acquaintances. But never forget, one day I'll tell my story, all of it. Murder, genocide, arsenic, desertion. *Everything*. And maybe then the past can be laid to rest."

So a delicate truce was called, each man going off into his own World, keeping mum about their past errors of judgement.

Several more years had passed, and the new century welcomed in, when Satvinder bumped into the girl-witch. He was passing through a very tight and smelly alleyway when she confronted him, giggling and jigging about. She was dressed in a dirty, white kurta or top and light blue pyjamas and her black hair shuddered across her shoulders as she chuckled.

"Hello. I'm My Eyes. And you're Satvinder."

He looked down at her. "How did you know that?"

"You're the teacher. Everybody knows. And you're waiting for James."

The mysterious witch raised her eyebrows as if to say, 'well?'

"Yes. But he won't come. Not now."

"I think he will." She grabbed his hand, but Satvinder pulled away. "Scared? Don't be. I'm your mate."

He relaxed and asked, "Why should he?"

She shrugged her shoulders and again grabbed his hand. This time he allowed her to hold it. She thought, and then, "Why shouldn't he? My mummy will, one day. We're all waiting for her, and she'll come. One day, soon."

Satvinder was feeling a real warmth from the tiny hand, and it was beginning to reach his heart. "What do you do to encourage your mummy here?"

"I search for her. And so does Catherine. And Ca'an prays for her. And you should do something to help James know that you want him home. Tell him how much you love him."

She let go of his hand, as the bag of rice in her other hand was getting heavy.

Satvinder dropped his head. "Sorry. That was rude of me. Can I walk with you and carry your bag? It looks heavy."

So he took the bag of rice in one hand and she held his other hand so tight that the warmth almost melted his heart. It had been many years since he had held the hands of his little children, and he only then realised how much his life had emptied.

"I still have lots of children, but they're grown up now. I'm beginning to miss them. I feel like I've got a hole in the heart."

The little girl looked up at him. "Then call James back home. He's missing you so much. And d'you know what, he's worked really hard to convince the aid companies about the arsenic. He's done everything he could."

Suddenly he was feeling full again, warm and snug, as the burden of Plassey's threats of exposure began to melt.

"You're a witch, so will you tell me something?"

She giggled, "Do you believe in witches?"

With a wry smile, "I'm beginning to. But will you tell me what the Monsignor is? Everybody says that you know everything."

"He's just a prat. Don't worry about him. One day he'll find God, and when he does, he'll die. But you'll die with him."

A chilling prophecy.

"I don't think I'll ask any more." They walked on. "Where we going?"

"To the lepers. I stole this rice for them."

"I used to be scared of lepers, but not any more."

"You should be. You're a man, and could easily catch leprosy. This ain't arsenic, it's leprosy."

"And you?"

"Not many girls get leprosy."

He looked down at the witch and wondered if he was seeing Ablaa in her next life. The body of an eight year old, and the wisdom of a saint.

After passing through several tiny streets and bustling alleys she let go of his hand.

"We're almost there. You can go now."

"Go where?"

"To Airport Road, and tell James that you still love him."

Then she was gone.

# CHAPTER 26 – WHEN ALL ELSE FAILS, DEATH LENDS A HAND

His meeting with the witch left Satvinder confused. He needed help from his old pal, Akhtar, and so the next morning they sat in the doctor's sitting room before the clinic opened.

"She's a witch. You shouldn't take any notice."

"You don't believe in witches." He waited as Akhtar admitted that, with his body language. "Which means she can't be a witch, so I *should* take notice. You can't have it both ways."

The doctor grinned. "She's at least woken you up. That's good. And I do have great admiration for her and her dedication to the lepers."

Satvinder looked at the window, as if he was making sure that nobody was listening. "How long have you known her?"

The old man raised his eyebrows. "Hmm. You know what, I don't know. Could be years, could be weeks. I don't know."

Satvinder's confusion was becoming intense. "You can't *not* know. Unless your mind's going."

"It probably is, but honest, I don't. I've known somebody for years, but who? She's eight. The girl I've known is always eight, and I wonder constantly how many there are. That's all I know."

"Ok. Let's just leave it. Anyway, she said I should let James know how much I love him and miss him. Up on Airport Road. What did she mean?"

The two mates sat thinking about her advice for quite some time before the doctor announced, "I need to get ready. We'll sleep on it and meet in the morning."

The elders began their daily routines, each preoccupied by the niggling thought of the witch's advice, and the next morning Satvinder arrived very early at the clinic.

Akhtar opened the storming process. "How did you find *me* at the camp?"

"Well, pure coincidence, that the young soldier told Ablaa about your phone-call."

"Next, why was she talking to the soldier about the phone-calls?"

"The aid worker told us about the phone calls which would sometimes be allowed."

"Next, why did she talk to you?"

"Because she ran the notice board and saw that we had a phone number to call."

"So, *there* you have it. Start at the beginning and put a notice up. And the witch said Airport Road. So, as soon as I close the clinic we'll take a long walk to Airport Road. We haven't walked together for years: it'll be good for both of us." He stood up. "Perhaps you *will* see James again. After thirty-odd years in these slums, something's about to happen. I can feel it in my old bones."

That was their plan. Protected from the rains by two umbrellas they walked slowly but deliberately, all the way through the Anglia slum, past the poorest of the poor and the sickest of the sick, and onto the main road. It took them more than two hours to arrive at a spot which Akhtar thought might be suitable for a notice board. It was in front of an old colonial house which was occupied by the city council, and the officers cautiously agreed to allow a board of about four feet by four feet to be mounted on their front wall. Akhtar's influence was a great help, especially as he was able to get a phone call to the Monsignor's secretary to confirm their identities.

The carpenter at the Fort, a giant of a man, gave them a piece of plywood, cut down to the agreed size, and even went with Satvinder in Aalap's rickshaw to mount it on the wall. With the interest from the carpenter and the rumoured help from the doctor and from the Fort the local people became curious. They all wanted to know what was going on, regarding *everything*.

The biggest question, sparked from the reports that Satvinder was seen walking hand-in-hand with the witch, was 'Is she coming?'. Everybody wanted to know, but the question just left Satvinder baffled.

He had made up a notice to plant in the centre of the board which read 'My Son James, lost to circumstances. Please come home, I have nothing to forgive. My endless love, Daddy.'

Satvinder walked to the board every day to sit by it and wait. But one day an old woman approached him and asked, "Could I put a notice up? I've lost my two sons." Satvinder smiled and waived his head. She sighed, "But I can't write, and my sons can't read."

"Then I'll write it for you and if anybody asks, I'll read it for them. Where did they go?"

"They went off with some soldiers and never returned."

Over the next few months many people asked if they could put up 'lost souls' notes and they were never refused, and the notice board became full. Satvinder would spend many hours reading out the notices to those who could not read, and then one day somebody tugged at his shirt. It was the eight-year-old witch. She quickly held his hand and warmed his heart, giggling all the time.

"Can I put up a notice, please? I'd like you to write it for me."

With an enormous grin Satvinder sat on his stool and the witch sat on his knee. The locals all moved away and watched from the opposite side of the road as the school teacher wrote the note for the witch, nursing her as he went.

'Please come home, Mummy. It's time.'

That simple note sparked a period of mayhem and bedlam in the slums, as they all spoke about the return of the Queen, a rumour which had been kept under wraps for most of the previous thirty years, but hey, it was back. Everybody was preoccupied with the subject, apart from Akhtar.

"She's a witch. You shouldn't take any notice."

"You don't believe in witches." He waited as Akhtar admitted that, with his body language. "Which means she can't be a witch, so I *should* take notice. You can't have it both ways."

"At least she's woken the whole slum up. I've never known them so positive. Does anybody know what they're waiting for?"

"They say the Queen. But nobody seems to know which Queen, or who she is. It's a harrowing phenomenon. I'm beginning to feel like an outsider."

"I know what you mean." Akhtar put his head momentarily into his hands, and then looked up. "There's something else which is scaring me right now. Look." He opened his drawer and took out some photographs. "This one is the first."

The picture showed a black patch on a man's back. It had white spots in the centre.

"It's not leprosy. Nor gangrene. And it looks a bit like some of the early fissures from the arsenic. But it's not growing out, it's eating in."

He showed Satvinder the second picture. "The next day." The area had rotted inwards, and spread. There was a hole in the man's back. "In just one day. Look. This is the *third* day." The wound had moved deep into his body and actually exposed his ribs. "Dead by the fourth day. I've had reports of others, but only one other sufferer has come here. The excitement of the return is being overcast by the threat of a plague. And it's too early for the big ones to take interest. I need to get more samples and isolate the problem. I might get some help, then. Sensar will send somebody over in a couple of weeks once I've gotten some samples and results. This is only a slum, so it's not that important. Another neglected tropical disease."

"I'm sorry. But at least they've got the best man on board."

"Thanks. Do you remember when we left home? I don't want to talk about it, but if I hadn't lost my family, I was going to London, where the streets are paved with diamonds. With my brother, remember?"

"Of course."

"Well, my youngest nephew is here. He wants to help, just for his keep. But I'm not sure if he should come into the slums right now, but he's coming anyway, for better or for worse. It makes me think about Chak Sahasa. I can't help it." The doctor had a tear in the corner of his eye.

"Maybe sometimes you should think about it. It wasn't all bad. Some of it was beautiful."

"I know. You came on board knowing that we had leprosy, but you believed in me. I've never properly thanked you."

Satvinder took the old doctor into his arms and gave him a long overdue hug.

"When I talked you into coming onboard into Chak Sahasa, I knew we didn't have leprosy. You were safe. Now Syed, my nephew, is safe. He's never had polio." He looked down at the ground for an electrifying few seconds. "Neither have you. You're safe."

Satvinder was beginning to understand his old mate. Akhtar had a mild polio attack as a young child, but what did it mean?

"I'm certain that it's some sort of mutation. I'm relating it to previous polio attacks. The very early results show all those with a polio history are at risk. That's what it looks like. But before you say anything, I'm staying put. I'll say this once, and then ask you never to talk about it." He cleared his throat. "I'd rather die here from my work, than be anywhere else. That's the last I'll ever say on the subject of Doctor Hussain and his polio."

Akhtar grinned at his mate.

"And there's more. Syed's coming here to help me, just like you did. And he's got this daft idea that a couple of his English friends can come over and do some fund-raising or something. To help finance my work. And despite having terrible reserves about his friends coming, they're from England and are clear of polio." He began to frown and wave his head. "And besides, a little bird told me that they could be of great help to me in my work." He carried on frowning, "But I can't remember who told me."

Satvinder suddenly had visions of the old Field Marshall when he said goodbye in Chak Sahasa, and his head was not totally in control. Then a thought came to his mind that they should run away. He quietly spoke to himself. "No, we can't. There's nowhere left for us."

Suddenly Akhtar was thinking the very same about his old mate. But that's old age.

"We'll get by, somehow."

Over the next few days the new disease became common knowledge, and the people feared for the worst. It was believed to be leprosy and so all the new victims were sent to the leper colony which was run by an old nun called Catherine. Many called her a saint.

The next morning the doctor stood in front of his clinic and addressed the awaiting patients and soldiers about sending their families to the leper colony. "All you're doing is putting the lepers at risk."

An old man spoke for the crowd, which chilled Akhtar's heart. "Then we're killing two birds with one stone!"

The local administration took the outbreak very seriously. It was decided by the ruling party that they should move the lepers to a new colony on the edge of the slum where they could be in peace and isolated from the general residents. They then strove to ensure that as many of the new sufferers were sent into the old leper colony, so that they could then burn it to the ground. As long as there was no vaccine for the disease, they would eradicate it by fire, just as the Pakistani Army did with Chak Sahasa.

Then it all started. Rumours spread like wildfire through the slums that they'd arrived! Syed's guests had turned up from England, the special ones who everybody had been mysteriously waiting for, for hundreds of years. They would all be saved! The fiery ginger hair of Syed's female friend seemed to turn on the residents as if it was the rutting season. To the lowly slum dwellers she was pure pheromone!

The new visitors, a young lady sporting bright ginger hair and with a bald, middle aged man, went through the slums with the soldiers and medical men to help to re-house the lepers into their new colony building. Nobody knew why they went on the trip, except that it was suggested to Akhtar that they could find the 'trip' very useful. A little bird told him.

Satvinder decided to get away from the hustle and bustle of the slum's new feeling of elation and went to sit it out at his notice board. Whilst translating a notice into Hindi he noticed something odd. The witch's notice had gone. It distracted him to the point where he had to ask the person if she could give him a while before he continued with his translation. He almost panicked at the thought that the witch may have found her mummy, and that maybe her mummy was the ginger-haired woman from England. Ridiculous! He pinched himself very hard, and asked the woman if she could continue with the translation. Once they'd finished, he again looked at the empty space. What if she had found her mummy? It kept coming back into his head that she *could* have done, and if so, then perhaps he could find James. It strangely gave him hope, and he began thinking that he could be as fortunate as the witch.

He could not stop himself from thinking of James, so much so that he had to leave the board for fear of crying in front of his fellow waiters. If the witch's mummy had returned, then there's hope for James. He rushed back towards the slums and joined the furore of the arrival, not even knowing what it was about, but whatever, the slum was for once happy, celebrating instead of mourning.

The very next day the old leper colony was burned to the ground, with all the diseased folk inside, mostly children, and the slum was back to mourning. But what also happened was that Monsignor Plassey decided that the lepers should also be burned out, as they had spent time with the diseased people and could be carriers. Satvinder wondered what his motives were for this most recent massacre. On his way to see Akhtar, he stopped by the open space in front of the Fort gates and looked across at the few people outside the walls. The mood was beginning to steam over the burning of the lepers, especially as it had not stopped the disease from striking down many more that day. He wondered if the Monsignor would explain it away as an act of kindness, just like with Chuknagar. William the Bastard no doubt burned down a leper colony on his march through France, and so that would be the right thing to do!

But more people went down with the disease that day, and catastrophe hit the Anglia slums as never before. Satvinder could not get close to the clinic that evening as the private army left the Fort to enforce an isolation order on the slums, and worse. He managed to find Aalap and his daughter Dilshad, who had been driving the visitors around in their rickshaw since their arrival.

Dilshad sat in the back of the rickshaw with her granddad, Satvinder.

"I'm not sure how to say this, Granddad. It's been a terrible day. Daddy said that it keeps taking him back to

Khulna, when he lost his family." She thought for a while. "They burned the leper colony, and Saint Catherine was burned with it. The people are going to do something. But there's worse." The fourteen year old took her granddad's hand. "They've sealed up the clinic building. Isolated it, and plan to burn it in a few days. Doctor Hussain is in one clinic, and the Doctor's friends are in the other. They're all dying from the disease."

Satvinder shuffled in his seat, and then poked Aalap on the shoulder.

He looked round at Satvinder and simply said, "It's all true, Daddy. Sorry." He carried on driving into the slum. "It's a great loss to you, and to the whole slum. The doctor was a very well respected man. He won't be easily replaced. But the visitors..."

Strange, but Satvinder knew it was coming. Akhtar had already warned him about his polio and its close connection with the new disease, so the shock was minimal. But...

"Aalap, the English haven't had polio. Akhtar was wrong!"

"No! He can rest in peace. The girl, Tracy, spent time in the West Indies as a child and contracted polio while there. Akhtar was *never* wrong." He pulled over and turned round to talk directly to Satvinder. "But the two English people. They were the slum's hope. Everybody thought she was Queen Maya, the Mother of God, returned from her exile of over two hundred and forty years. But she hasn't. She's locked up in the clinic to die, just like any other human being. Just a normal person who they all took for somebody else. Now there'll be trouble, mark my words."

Dilshad, still holding her granddad's hand, looked sideways at him. "There's going to be a war. They're all saying it on the street." She sighed heavily. "Two days ago Robin, the Englishman who they all thought was the Lamma, that's the Queens spiritual protector, gave two hundred rupees to a boy who was in the old colony with the disease. He escaped and came to us to take him to Kolkata city, for a meeting. He gave us the two hundred rupees from Robin, and we took him. Then three of the councillors caught the disease from him. They died today. They say it could be an epidemic throughout Bengal. It was spread to the outside by the actions of the Lamma."

"Why? I mean, why did he send the boy there?"

"To give it to the councillors. Now it's not a neglected slum disease, it's out there. They'll spend much money now to develop a vaccine. And we'll be saved. That's what some of the slum people are saying."

"And do you approve? Killing those councillors?"

"If it gets the results. It could have saved millions of lives."

All the way back to William the Bastard.

Dilshad continued. "The word going around is that the people are going to storm the Fort, and kill the Chi Bantri people if they don't take the plague more seriously. All they're doing is locking us in, and that won't save us, only an antidote can save us. But word has also gone around that the Princess from the Fort will come out and talk to us about midday. She's never been seen away from the Fort. Will you come with us?"

He raised his eyebrows and deep furrows appeared across his forrid. "Poor Akhtar. He'll die alone in that clinic. I think I owe it to him to find out what's happening with the disease." His wrinkled old face grinned. "And very soon, maybe, me and him can discuss it over a bhang lassy, somewhere else."

"Please Granddad, don't talk like that."

"Me and your dad, and Akhtar, have seen it all before. War. We all get hurt in war and we'll all get hurt again here. Let's hope that war doesn't come."

"Then come with us to listen to the Princess. The English people are dying and the people have again been let down, but perhaps the Princess can avert war."

Aalap turned around. "Let's hope so. They'll gun us all down in just minutes if we attack the Fort. She'll avert the war, Insha'Allah."

So Satvinder went with his son and granddaughter to the open area in front of the Fort, to see the Princess. Many thousands had turned up, and they all stood silently waiting for her arrival. Then, across the open area, in front of the Fort gates, could be seen a girl in a white kurta and red pyjamas, wearing a white hood. On her arm was a smaller girl in a white kurta and blue pyjamas, and behind them several soldiers stood to attention. A small group of children sat nearby watching the crowds opposite them. The weather was warm and dry.

"Is that them?" whispered Satvinder. Aalap just raised his hands.

The girl in red pyjamas and her companion walked slowly, arm-in-arm and alone. The bigger girl was hidden by a silk hood which had only one hole in it, for her mouth, and she was being led by the smaller girl. Satvinder suddenly realised that the little girl was his friend, the witch!

As the murmuring got louder and became a roar, a motorcyclist caught the girls up, and they sent him back with a message. The guard on the gate was instantly reinforced.

Satvinder was becoming as excited about the events as the others, a feverish mood spreading. "That's the witch! My friend. Who is she?" He suddenly remembered the boring but oh so destructive speech from the Ramna Racecourse Maidan, and hoped this wasn't to be a repeat.

The girls stopped short of the crowd, and the carpenter moved slowly towards them. He went down on his knees and prayed, and the crowd followed suit.

The two girls stood for a while looking at their minions, the little witch constantly whispering to her bigger Princess, and was her eyes.

"Please remain kneeling, but look to me." Princess Catan spoke very loudly and clearly through her hood. "I've never spoken to my people since the killing of my family. This is an historic day for all of us. I hope not too many are missing due to the disease." She paused for thought. The witch whispered continually. "The plague which has hit us will soon be controlled. The Lamma forced the World to care. The Lamma has now made them deliver the serum." The crowd began to whisper and mumble. "Please give me the respect of silence while I speak to you. Thank you. Tomorrow morning the serum will be delivered to the Fort. You'll be immunised against the disease." She paused and the witch whispered, then, "I understand that you're disappointed by the death of the Europeans. You must never lose your faith." She deliberately stopped and the crowd were visibly begging her to continue. As they began to mumble she stepped in. "I *will* deliver the Queen." The crowd started talking to one another and smiling. "I'll deliver *your* Queen. And I'll deliver the Lamma." The crowd was getting excited, maybe too excited. "But *first* I'll deliver the serum."

They bravely walked towards the crowd who all began praying. As Princess Catan and the witch reached them, they shuffled aside on their knees to allow passage and so they very slowly walked amongst most of the dwellers. It was such a moving occasion that many of them began to cry. An eerie wailing began.

Satvinder could not take his eyes from the witch. Dilshad tugged his shirt. "That's why they call her My Eyes! She sees for the Princess!"

As the girls left the crowd and returned to the open square, the wailing continued. The two revered children turned to walk back to the Fort and the wailing developed into loud shouting and cheering, like a war cry. Satvinder and the crowd followed the girls across the open square toward the Fort gates and the carpenter hurriedly caught them up to defend their backs, but they never looked back. It was as if they had total faith in the poor folk from the slums.

The soldiers at the Fort gate had taken up their defensive positions, guns loaded and ready. Many more had joined the force, but it would never have held the thousands for very long. Maybe, though, the canons which menaced from the turrets would have done!

"Stop!" shouted an officer, but the crowd continued to walk towards them at the same pace as the Princess. The soldiers kneeled and aimed their guns.

The Princess stopped fifty yards from the gate. The crowd stopped behind her.

She demanded, "Put the guns down! That's an order."

The officer replied, "We've instruction from the Monsignor. None of them will pass."

"They don't intend to. They'll wait here in the square for the serum. It'll arrive tomorrow." She turned to the crowd, who immediately went onto their knees. "Believe in me, and believe in your Queen, and believe in God."

They turned, and then walked to the gate and the soldiers allowed the girls to pass. The guns were lowered, but they held their positions. It was going to be long night for all involved.

Colin Hodgson

# CHAPTER 27 – THE CONFUSED

Satvinder stayed there for many hours, with Dilshad and Aalap. He began to wonder what he was doing: was he waging war; was he waiting for the serum; or was he just doing as he was told? He looked around as the night fell, and he was surrounded by thousands of people, many wondering the same.

"What're we doing?" He looked at Dilshad. "What if the serum doesn't arrive?"

"Then this lot will storm the Fort. We'll probably all be killed."

"Why're you so calm about it all?"

"I have this weird gut feeling that the serum will arrive. That's what I'm praying for, anyway."

He could see a lot of Ablaa in the young teenager. Her intelligence was way above average and she was cool, like a miniature Indira Gandhi.

"Why did your dad call you Dilshad? It means 'happy'." He grinned.

"You saying that I'm miserable? That's not nice."

"No disrespect meant, but you're so troubled, particularly right now. Un-happy."

Her head dropped a little. "I'm in mourning. Wasn't just Uncle Akhtar who's been lost. I was very fond of Saint Catherine. She told me that if I really wanted to, I could help her to look after the lepers. We were good friends."

Satvinder pulled her onto his shoulder. "A *lot* like Ablaa."

They cuddled for a while, and despite the furore of the afternoon, they decided to call it a day. Aalap and Dilshad each took one of Satvinder's arms and they walked him home.

The next day the slum was hit by passion and jubilation. The serum arrived, and the entire slum was inoculated. Somehow the Lamma had won the day, maybe from his death bed, and then the word on the street was that the Queen and her Lamma had paid a flying visit, just to look after them when the plague struck. It was quite the opposite from the previous day, when they were just mere human beings with a mistaken identity. The people spoke with pride that they were prepared to wait for another two hundred and forty years for the return of their beloved deities, the ginger-head and her Lamma.

The isolation order had been lifted, and the slum seemed set to return to normal, but after just a few days the people were warned of the pending burning of the clinic, a final 'up yours' to the deadly plague which had been so valiantly defeated by the Lamma. The burning never happened, but, as reported by Aalap and Dilshad who were present as a respect to Akhtar, the Europeans walked out of the clinic damaged but alive. They then disappeared into the distance, and nobody knew where to. They had allegedly lived through the disease and the people celebrated the latest miracle.

The slum went mad as the news quickly spread about the Europeans' survival. The soldiers were dispatched from the Fort to keep law and order as the area was stormed by reporters and news-crews, as well as historians and even holidaymakers looking for something different. Some violence broke out, and the soldiers quelled any act or threat of violence with violence.

"We need to think." Satvinder called a meeting of his family, those who were still local to the Anglia slums. "I suddenly feel like I'm back in Dhaka in nineteen seventy, just before the war. I've this ache inside which scares me."

There were about fifteen of his orphans, including Aalap and Dilshad, but they were no longer children. It was the year two thousand and eight.

"I just wanted to ask the family if we need to run away, again. War is imminent."

Aalap stood up and bowed his head to his dad. "This isn't the same type of war. It's not religious, but cultural. And I don't think there'll be war, maybe just martial law. It seems to be heading that way."

So the family decided to stay put for the time being, and keep a careful eye on developments.

After a few weeks, as Christmas and New Year had passed, the news crews disappeared, bored with the stories of the two missing deities, and the slum nudged its way back to normal, except that the private army from the Fort never went back inside. They remained in the streets, in groups of four, and administered the law in any which way they thought best. Several people were killed by the soldiers, often for very little reason, and Satvinder began to wonder if the Monsignor was getting back to his old methods of policing, those that he had used in East Pakistan. General Dara, the Field Marshall's nephew, must have felt the same, as a presence of the Indian Army was placed close to the slum to police the policing private army. Tensions remained very high.

Whilst sitting at his notice board on a cool winter morning, Satvinder had an unexpected visitor, the little Indian witch. Without knowing why, he was overcome with emotion and cried like a baby as they held hands. The old man wiped his eyes, while the people all around looked away, in respect.

"I'm sorry. When you touched me, it was like one of my children returning."

As usual she giggled. "That's because you have such an enormous heart."

She climbed onto his knee and they both just looked into each other's eyes.

"Should you be here? What about the Fort? The princess?"

She pulled herself closer to him. "My sister's ok. I'll soon get back to her."

"Sister?"

The little eight-year-old in her kurta and pyjamas just smiled, but never answered.

Satvinder broke the quiet. "Your notice went. Did you find her?"

"What would you think if I said yes? If I told you that Mummy has returned, would you think I'm mad?"

His forrid creased. "I've never thought you mad. Pretty, strange, angelic, probably naughty, *very* warm, but never mad."

She chuckled, and then gave him a kiss on the cheek. "I like you. You say nice things and you're a living saint, but best not to tell anybody else." She looked around at the people who had given up on respect, and looked on with great interest. "If I call you, will you come?" She looked at him with a level of begging. "Will you?"

He just nodded.

"And Dilshad? I know her a little, I hope she'll come."

He began to grin. "A little bird told me that when we find God, we find death."

"Is that good, or bad?" She jumped from his knee and ran along the road, and into the slums. She never looked back.

About three weeks later the tension mounted yet further as the news got out to the slums that the Queen and her Lamma had shocked the World by arriving at the Fort for the Festival of Life celebrations, complete with an official invite from the witch's sister, Princess Catan. As some of the soldiers welcomed and supported the Queen's entry into the celebrations they were deemed to have committed a crime against the 'state' at the fort. They were all hanged that very night, and again the seeds of war began to germinate.

"Daddy, are you ok?" It was Aalap. "What is it?" Satvinder had not woken that morning and it was almost mid-day. "What's up?"

He sat up and rubbed his eyes. "Where am I?" He looked at Aalap and suddenly realised that it was his son. "Sorry. I've been lost. My head's spinning."

"I'll get you a drink. I've got something to ask you." He helped his father up and they went for a short walk to clear his head.

"I'm very old and knackered. That's what's wrong with me. Just knackered."

"You forgot the classes last week. Is this the same?"

His dad frowned. "I don't remember that." They walked a bit further. "I'm ok now. What did you want to ask me?"

"You probably haven't noticed, but there's real trouble. Soldiers were hanged last night, and war is threatened, but the Princess in the fort has called a meeting with the fort bosses. They want you to attend, with Dilshad. They want you to represent the slum people, because of your stature here. They all love and respect you."

"Why? Why me and Dilly? It can't just be because of respect. What've we got to offer a diplomatic meeting?" He suddenly started to remember. He whispered, "When I call will you come? And Dilshad?"

Aalap frowned and asked, "What're you on about?"

"She asked me that." They walked quietly for a while as Aalap wondered if his daddy had seriously lost his bearings. Looking into his son's eyes, "We have to go. We've been called." He had a smile on his face, but it dispersed and a worried look developed. "Do you know what comes when you find God?" He looked at his son, then "Sorry, of course you don't. Me and Dilly will be ok."

So in the year two thousand and eight Satvinder and Dilshad were representatives to the people at the Anglian War meeting. It was held in the main court-room at the Anglian Fort.

Dilshad held tightly onto her granddad as the dream-like meeting floated over the top of Satvinder's head, and he became increasingly lost, seeing the other representatives in ever increasing confusion. He was unable to follow the gist, and the meeting ended leaving him totally lost. His age was finally overtaking his body and mind.

# CHAPTER 28 – THE DEATH OF THE PAST

As they left the main building the sun almost burned their eyes. It was like walking from the depths of a cave, so Satvinder waited with Dilshad on the parade-ground, and they both just wondered what had happened while they were closed up in that court-room. Aalap soon arrived in his rickshaw, but was summoned to drive the Queen and her Lamma to their residence, while Dilshad was asked to ride in a splendid stretched Jaguar with some other children. Satvinder was left floating in his own confusion, alone and forgotten on the parade-ground, not knowing what was happening. He suddenly became frightened.

"What's happening?" he asked his old mate, Akhtar. He looked up to the skies. "Am I with you? Can you hear me?" But no answers came back so he just slowly ambled towards the Fort gates, and headed for the slum. The mood was black.

"Hey, Satvinder!" A younger man approached him as he reached the slum. "You're gonna tell your story. They're saying it'll expose the Monsignor."

"Who's saying that?"

"Everybody's saying it. They're saying you know the Monsignor and his past, and you've promised to tell your story soon, and it'll tell the whole World about the Monsignor." The young man held out his hand and they shook. "Take special concern of the soldiers, sir. Everybody's saying that they'll try to stop you telling, it'll expose the Monsignor." He paused. "Would you like me and my mates to walk you home?"

He heeded the young man's words and thanked him, but declined their kind offer. He stood for some time trying to recall any promise about telling the story, but as much as he tried, he couldn't remember anything from the past day or so.

He looked up to the skies, and the heavens turned pure white, embracing all the colours of the rainbow. He asked, "Akhtar, help me. Please help me. I'm lost." But no answer came, and he continued his slow walk home.

He kept to the wider roads and alleys on his way, just in case, but as he approached the blacksmith's yard he saw four soldiers from the Fort's private army. They stood chatting alongside the small stack of pallets and looked to be in a jovial mood. He decided that he was doing no harm and should continue towards them.

"Stop!" One of the soldiers held up his hand. "Stop, old man. I believe you're Satvinder, the storyteller." The soldiers approached him. "You *are* Satvinder. We need to talk to you."

Satvinder walked to them, nervous, but knowing that he had done nothing wrong. The local people all went inside, and the street was deserted, and he began to worry. "What do you need to talk to me about, sir?"

The soldier who had stopped him answered. "Storytelling. You're to tell a tale of warfare and upheaval. Why?"

Satvinder hesitated with his answer, and the soldier thrust his gun forward to encourage him, and looked Satvinder hard in the eyes. "Answer me, old man. Why?"

The gun in front of him brought Satvinder's memories back of the day the manager was executed in Chak Sahasa and he began to fear for his life. "Are you going to kill me?"

"I will if you don't answer my question." He again thrust his rifle sideways into Satvinder's chest. "Do you want to die?"

"No. But I don't want to answer your questions, either. You wouldn't understand."

The soldier hesitated, but he never bit, he simply looked to his three comrades. They all shook their heads, and walked back to the small stack of pallets. One of the other soldiers sneered, "You can run away, again, but I'd kill you before the next ally."

Poor Satvinder was unsure of what they meant, so just stayed where he was.

"Will you tell us why?" The soldier laid his gun on the pallets. "Look, I won't shoot you."

The old man looked around at the empty street. Everything was hazy, out of focus, and his head felt heavy. He looked up for Akhtar but the skies just blinded him momentarily, with all the colours of the spectrum moulding together to form pure white. A flash of the Field Marshall's bearded face seemed to wake him from the dream and he was back in the street, alone and under siege. He squinted and wondered... did he have any friends left to help him? It seemed not. All that surrounded him was fear, and he fully understood that his fate was not their concern, and they should look after their own as he always had. He fleetingly remembered back to the long walk to Satkira, and how they blindly passed by the dying and the injured, and looked after themselves, and maybe he was now the dying: overlooked and lonely. He strangely thought of Aalap and Dilshad, and he prayed that they would not come by, as they would help him, and be killed. He whispered, "Please stay away."

"What was that? Speak up!"

"Sorry sir, I was thinking of my children. I love them."

"We've been patient with you Satvinder as a sign of respect. But we have a job to do, to encourage you not to tell your story. Now answer me. Why tell it? Is it to discredit the Monsignor in some way?"

With his eyebrows raised, "I didn't know I was going to tell it. But why would it bother the Monsignor? What's he to hide?"

The soldier winced. "We've just been ordered to discourage you from telling it."

"To discourage me? That's a familiar tactic with Captain Plassey. Or is he Plassey the Bastard?" He realised that the soldiers did not understand, so he quickly changed his direction. "You want to know why? Trouble is, if I tell you, you'll probably just scoff, and beat me up. So I may as well *not* tell you, and get beaten up."

"Why're you so difficult? We all have family in these slums, and we all know of you and your deeds. Why make us hurt you?"

"Because..." He looked around. Everything was merging into one. He spoke very slowly. "I'm close to the end. Very close, but I need to tell my story."

"Just tell us *why*! The Monsignor needs to know, and we need to tell him. Or else!"

Satvinder suddenly grinned. "If it's for my old friend, the Monsignor, then I can tell you. You just need to tell him that I've been asked to tell it. I've finally met God, and I've been asked to tell my story. I don't know why and I don't know when. *God* has asked for my story, and I can't possibly deny God." He was beginning to feel dizzy. "He'll understand. We're old muckers, both mucked up with our lives. He'll understand. I've found God. Tell him that, and I *know* he'll know what it means, and tell Captain Plassey that I'll see him very soon, somewhere else."

The soldier sighed and picked his gun up. "If we report back that you're going to tell your story, we'll be hung. And besides, you're a Hindu, you don't have a God."

Satvinder's head swayed from side to side as he tried to focus on the soldier. He very quietly stressed, "Before I go I'd like to tell you something: it may help you through life." He paused for a few seconds. "I have God. I used to have religion. Now I've got God. I don't think you can really have both, they conflict."

The ghost-like visions of the soldiers moved towards Satvinder, and he stood up straight. As one of them muttered something, a rifle butt smashed down on his knee, sending absolute agony up through his crumpling body, and he exhaled a weak scream. He was prevented from falling by the soldiers, who grabbed him by the arms and legs, parting the broken knee and searing his entire body with an agony which almost sent him out, but he stayed with them. They dumped him on the pallets, spread eagled him and tied his hands and feet.

The soldiers just looked down on him for a while, as he battled with the pain which extended from his shattered leg right into his head. His eyes hurt so much he could not open them.

"You won't be telling your story. The Monsignor has made that clear."

The pain did not subside, but the body sent itself into shock, fighting the nervous system and producing the natural anaesthetics which made it just possible for him to survive. Satvinder was able to open his eyes.

The soldier looked down with an excited sneer. "Look at us, old man. We're the last people you'll ever see."

One of the soldiers cut Satvinder's clothes away to expose his body and genitals, and began his job as executioner. He cut a semi-circle into his fleshy body, which ran from his left side of his stomach, up and under his chest and back down the right side, the old victim grinding his teeth and writhing from the pain. Then he screamed. The awful screech travelled around the slums, heralding the Kingdom of Hell, and absolute fear pinned the dwellers down. They covered their ears. Satvinder was at breaking point. He was bursting with the pain and praying for death, as he felt his body being pulled and pulled, the pain shielding any knowledge of what was happening to him, and as they peeled the skin from his stomach he again screamed. He hurt so badly for so long that he didn't even know what they were doing or to what, but he could feel every pull and every shove, until he finally begged for death. God answered his call.

"Why?" He looked up at his bloodied executioners.

One last tug left the skin from his stomach hanging over his penis, but all Satvinder could by then feel was the pulling. It almost tickled him and he grinned as the agony soothed and the skies became pure white. He transformed into a feeling of absolute ecstasy. He could see clearly again, smiling up at the soldiers who had tortured him to the point of death and who at that moment cut his genitals off, sealing his destination to the World beyond. But Satvinder was on the edge of the two Worlds, floating between life and death and the soldiers were the black angels from Hell. He stretched his head from the pallet and looked into their faces, grinning with celestial joy, and they ran away.

He had come through it, and the excruciating pain had gone and his head was clearing. He relaxed on the pallets for some time, and then rolled his head from side to side to see if he could see anybody who may be able to untie him. "Hello. Will somebody untie me? I need to go home." Maybe Aalap would turn up and untie him, and take him in his rickshaw. He could only lay there and wonder.

"Wotcha mate." A tiny hand was placed on his forrid. "You alright?"

Satvinder looked up and there was a beautiful blond girl, with piercing green eyes. Dressed in a white English frock, she looked down at him and giggled. "I've come to get your story." She spoke with a cockney or Essex accent, but smiled like a queen. "You ready?"

He smiled back at her. "Who're you."

"I'm Caferine." She grinned. "I'm Caferine, Gayla's sister. You know, the witch."

He tried to look around, but he was unable to lift his head. "Have the soldiers gone?"

The girl, about eight or nine years old, kissed him on the cheek. "They won't be back. So we can go, if you like. We could go for a walk to your notice-board, and you can tell me your story on the way. You promised Gayla when you were in that meeting. You promised you'd tell us your story. All of it."

He smiled and just looked into her face for some time. "It's a long story. What if we don't have time?"

"We've got as much time as we need. We can take a long-cut, to make *sure* we've got time."

He grinned up at her and asked, "Who are you? Catherine? Catherine who?"

She bit her bottom lip. "Yes, I'm Caferine Qeervi and I'm the twin sister of Gayla. You really like my sister, don't you, you know, the witch."

"She's so beautiful. So're you, if you don't mind me saying so." He shivered, his sweat was turning cold. "Will you hold my hand, please. I'm so cold. Never been so cold."

She gently took his right hand and the warmth almost melted his heart.

"I'm to write your story for posterity. That's what I do, write."

"Bet you do a lot more than just write, with a sister like Gayla. Bet you make stories for *others* to write about. But... but you and Gayla, you're so different."

"Me and Gay are exactly the same, but so different. That's why we work so well. But you're s'posed to be telling me *your* story, remember?"

Satvinder was warming to the girl, and wanted to know more. "But who are you? And Gayla? Who are you both? Are you both witches, or is my first guess right?"

"You're tied to a pallet, so I ask the questions. Ve 'ave vays of making you talk." She chuckled and leaned right over his face. "You're in no position to ask the questions. I could just leave you here." She giggled as if it was all just a game.

"But you won't. Not because of the story, but because you won't. I can tell."

She put her cheek to his and Satvinder felt something even warmer than her hand. He felt her heart.

But with his stomach skinned and his genitals cut off, he began to realise that he was in a bit of a pickle, up the stream without a paddle. "You won't leave me, will you? You're too good. Please promise."

She took her cheek away and looked into his eyes. "I'm not here to leave you, just to get your story, and to thank you. Tell you what, old mate, I'll tell you who I am, and you can then tell me your story. Deal? Ok. What I am is *everything*. I'm the twin of Gayla, and we is God."

He began to smile: a little air of disbelief.

"You *will* believe me." She bit her bottom lip. "Whatever, but I don't need to tell you anything else about me. So let's go for a walk to the notice board, and you can tell me everything about *you*." She bit her bottom lip and explored his soul with her big green eyes. "There's something in it for you, a gift. I just happened to be eaves-dropping one day when I heard you talking with Ablaa, and you both believe that the past is never dead, in fact it's not even past." Her eyes shone. "You were both wrong, and right, and that's my gift to you. Once you've told me your story the past *will* be past. That's if you want it to be." She stroked his cheek as she giggled.

The stubborn old man asked, "Before we go, tell me why you've chosen me to tell my story."

She puffed her chest, "Satvinder! You're such a bloody pain! Just get off the bloody pallet and walk! Got that?"

The shock treatment worked and he climbed off the pallet, took the girl by the hand and they set off for the Airport Road. They walked and walked, taking long-cut after long-cut to make sure he could get the whole tale, and nothing but the tale, across to his biographer, passing by the sickest of the sick and the poorest of the poor, who all just carried on with their daily routines as the old Bangladeshi meandered with the tiny little blond girl from Essex. Nobody even noticed them. It was as if they were invisible.

He looked down at the child who warmed his soul. "Am I bad not to have done anything about the arsenic?"

"Silly, worrying about that. That's what life's about, good and bad. Some get it worse than others, but it's all the luck of the draw. And besides, nobody would have listened, not without the doctor's working papers which burned with the people and animals in Chak Sahasa. So fuck Captain Plassey, he's just trying to scare you into silence to hide his own evil past."

They walked past another shack full of child prostitutes and their perverted clients.

"Why don't you do anything about the bad? After all, you and Gayla is God."

"What d'you think God does? Control everything? Naah, not us. Gayla made our children in her own likeness, and the only way for a species to be so strong is to have all the right ingredients, and they include personal greed, ambition and jealousy. And the one that sets you apart from all other intelligent life, control over your own destiny. We'll never try to control mankind, so he'll either make it or break it, and one day believe he is God. That's mankind. If you all just worried about love and happiness, you'd still be grazing the fields with the moo-cows."

He looked down at the child who was leading him through his finest hour. "What're you really like? You can't really be a little English girl, just eight years old, and you don't look anything like your twin."

She pulled at his hand and jigged about. "Well, I like being Caferine. It's fun. And Gayla likes being a little Indian girl. And that's what we really are, whatever we wanna be."

She looked up at Satvinder's smiles, and stuck her tongue out. "So there." With that little bit of enforced naughtiness her mood suddenly dropped. "Whatever we wanna be. That's a fucking laugh. Whatever."

They carried on walking for a long time with nothing else being said. The conversation was stuck on 'Whatever.'

Something needed to break the mood, and eventually it did. She pointed at a little boy who was weeing over a dog, and laughed. "Naughty boy!" She then went quiet for a few yards, and then continued the conversation. "But we weren't always different. You know, Satvinder, perhaps I could tell you *my* story, for posterity. You always wanted to write about the Chars. We could sit and look across the Bay of Bengal from Char Monpura and talk about my past. Fancy that some time?"

"Hmm, don't know. Me, write about God? How long would it take?"

"How much time've you got?"

He shrugged his shoulders.

"Then I'll tell *you*. All the time in the World. Maybe we should think about it and make a date. "

The talk went back onto Satvinder's story, taking long-cut after long-cut until the old man's story had been told, and they finally arrived on the home stretch before the notice board, Airport Road. They still held each other's hands so tightly as the bustling streets carried on with their business. Nobody took any notice of the strange couple. Then Catherine stopped. She looked up and grinned.

"What?" He watched down at her grinning face for a few seconds, and then turned toward the notice board. He stepped back in shock.

"What?" His face turned white, and he shook, totally confounded at what he was looking at. He picked Catherine up and held her tightly as he stared in disbelief at the notice board. There were many people searching the notes, some in colourful saris, others in tidy suits, all smiling and chatting, pointing to the adverts and reading many of them out loud. There was Ablaa and Akhtar standing with Kaling and Baka whilst the children played nearby, and Tazkia's cute bottom popped from side to side every time she moved with little Mo. Even Uncle from Sakharibazar was getting exited over the messages.

He pulled Catherine's face to his, and some tears formed. "What's happening?"

She whispered, "It's your past. It's not dead yet." She squeezed his neck and sighed. "You can join them, if you want. D'you want to?" She pulled her face away to look into his eyes. Her giggling had stopped.

His face dropped as he realised, "You're sad. What's going on?"

She forced a smile. "Can we talk about us? I need to ask you something, something *really* important."

"Of course. But will they go away soon?"

"No, not for a long time. As long as somebody remembers them they'll still be the past. We've got a while yet." She pulled herself back into his neck. "Before we talk about us, I'll tell you a bit more about me. I know you'll understand." The little blond child was close to tears. "I've been watching you for nearly forty years. And the Field Marshall and his family have helped me when I needed it. They're good servants. Anyway, as I've watched I've been so jealous that I've been *ashamed* of myself. I don't have jealousy, but I've felt it. It all started when I had to send Gayla away to the Colony because she was ill, and she had to get her soul reorganised before she destroyed the World. While she was away, in nineteen seventy one, we lost our connection which allowed other strengths to be taken into our souls. She fell madly in love with a little boy called Peter. He died soon after, as he had to, but she still sees him and still loves him. And she's not supposed to feel love. Not like that. And she took in the partnership and strength of one of our very distant cousins. She came back stronger than she'd *ever* been. She's still in love with Peter, and she's got her Daddy back. She's got it all."

She looked towards Satvinder's family and bit her bottom lip. "They'll be here for some time yet. Don't worry." She had a sniff. "Anyway, Gayla came home not just stronger, but *happy*. She's happy, the Creator is so happy, even content, and as I found out more about her love for Peter and her adopted Daddy, and her partnership with Mo's soul, I became jealous of her. We're not supposed to be happy, but she is. So, I heard from a little bird that a man from Monpura had taken on two children who were both different from him, and I checked it out. I watched you care, I watched you suffer your losses, and I watched you take even more children on, those who had nothing and nobody. And again I, the Conscience, felt jealousy. I wanted to be one of those children. I really wanted it." She buried her face in his neck to hide her grief.

They stood in that position for many hours as the night fell, and the next morning rose, whilst she summoned up the guts to do it.

Eventually she whispered, "We is God, the Creator and the Conscience. Will you serve your God?"

He nodded his head.

"Will you..." She stuttered and redrew her breath. "You know, will you do it for me? Will you be my daddy?" She huffed and hid her face. "Please? I ain't never had nobody."

Satvinder didn't know what to say. He wanted to do everything for little Catherine, but what about his family? He just kept quiet.

"You don't have to. But I want you to. I've never had a daddy. In billions of years, I've never had a daddy." She hung tightly into his neck.

With a hint of disbelief he whispered, as his memory began to return, "At the meeting, I thought the Lamma was Gayla's daddy."

She was still morose and looking like a child who had been scolded. "Sort of, but she adopted him. But he doesn't even know me. We were still as one when she took him on and when we split, he was lost. Now he's back, he doesn't even know me, so I'm like the children you took on. I'm so lonely. I've never been allowed to be a daughter, nor a child. I've never been a little girl, not like your children, and I've *never* played children's games." She pulled away and forced a smile. "On Sundays when I don't work, we could sit on the southern point of Monpura and look out over the Bay of Bengal, and wait for Nora to come back. When she does, we could play with the waves and fly with the winds. And we could sing with the kurpals and whine with the foxes, and in between time I could tell you my story and you could write it. And when we're tired of writing, we could make faces at mister cobra, and tease the tigers. It would be like heaven." She kissed him on the end of the nose. "Fancy that? Please? We could make *every* Sunday *our* day. Just me and my Daddy. Please? Absolute Heaven."

He looked to his family. "Won't they be upset if I took you in? You couldn't be one of the kids. Never."

"But *that's* what I *want*, to be a kid. I've never been happy, or a little girl, and I've never had a daddy to play with. I always wondered what it'd be like, to be happy and childish. Or even just happy." She had a massive sigh. "You know what, for six long days me and Gay' have worked, for billions of years. And now we're entering the seventh day. D'you know what's supposed to happen on the seventh day?"

Satvinder grinned. "I think on the seventh day God rested."

"Wrong translation. We'll never rest. But the prophesy suggests that on the seventh day God will find happiness. Gayla's found hers. Please be mine. You did it for all those other children, please make me happy."

She looked to his family. "You don't have to worry about them. You could forget them, then they're not there.

The past'll be dead for you. You won't even remember them existing, just you and me."

"But they'll then be dead, not just the past."

"But they're already dead, honestly, and they're *only* the past. They're just memories, but *real* memories. But you needn't fret: they won't go for a long time yet. Look."

She grinned and pointed along the Airport Road. Walking straight towards them was a middle-aged man, handsome and upright. It was James. He stopped by the notice board and found Satvinder's message. His face lit up, as he realised after so many years that he had always been forgiven, but as he turned to face Ablaa, he didn't even see her. Instead the witch appeared from behind the board and took his hand.

"James," she chuckled, "D'you remember me?"

He laughed. "Of course. Last time we spoke you were just an eight year old child. Now you've grown up into an eight year old child." He laughed, "Time's been kind to you."

Gayla held his hand. "You're just like your dad, how he used to be."

His face dropped.

"Afraid he's died, but he'll never forget you. Sorry. And you're needed to fill his place at the school, and I know you'll be brilliant. Now, can I walk with you home?"

The witch led James along the road, past Satvinder and Catherine, but James never even noticed them. The witch winked at her sister as they passed.

Catherine hugged his neck even harder. "See, James'll remember them all, and so will all the other kids, so they'll not die yet. Not until every memory of them has gone will the past be dead. And you can be with them, if you like. Or..."

He shook his head. "I'd like to be with you, on the Char. But I'll never be able to forget Ablaa and James. They were my life, even more so than the others."

"I've already told you when you were on the pallets, that my gift to you and Ablaa is the death of the past. I can make it so neither of you will ever remember being with each other. You can just worry about what's ahead. The past *can* be dead for you and Ablaa."

He thought for some time, and then nodded his head in agreement. "I'll be your daddy. I *will*. Forever if that's possible." He took one last look at his family by the notice board. "Who're those people at the notice board? They must be looking for relatives."

She pulled herself hard into his neck and grinned. "Suppose they must be, Daddy. Come on, it's Sunday tomorrow! It's *our* day. We're going to Monpura!"

And so, every Sunday for many, many centuries an old man and his tiny blond daughter played at the southern-most tip of Char Monpura, mimicking the kurpals, tormenting the mosquitoes into distraction, swimming with the turtles, and looking into the eyes of mister cobra as he playfully threatened with his fangs and spittle. They shared the warm waters with the Bengal tigers, and lay in the sun with their cubs, waiting every year for the return of Nora. When she did turn up, Satvinder and his daughter stripped to their pants, held hands in the shallow waters willing the tidal wave to approach, then turned and screeched with delight as they raced the wave inland. They never won the race, each time being engulfed and tossed around the island by the power of the waves, but they never let go of each other's hands. They swirled through the sundari trees and shared the torrents with the cobras and the kalach, and giggled and gurgled with every twist. Unlike many of the inhabitants of the Char they always lived to face another storm, with childish delight.

Satvinder and his adopted daughter, God's Conscience, played happily, forever after.

The End

Colin Hodgson